LIZARD AT ARMS

And other Stories from the Lands of Tamalaria

Joshua Calkins-Treworgy

BooksForABuck.com

2010

Joshua Calkins-Treworgy

LIZARD AT ARMS

AND OTHER STORIES FROM THE LANDS OF TAMALARIA

Joshua Calkins-Treworgy

BooksForABuck.com

May 2010

ISBN: 978-1-60215-118-5

Also By Joshua Calkins-Treworgy:

The Tamalarian Tales

Damnation of the Realm: Freedom or the Fire Volume One*

The Dread Knight's Redemption: Freedom or the Fire Volume Two*

A Hunter and His Prey*

Glove of Shadows*

The Amelia City Stories

Roads Through Amelia

Wraiths of Formuth

Spirits Most Savage

The Bob the Zombie Tales

Motor City Shambler*

Forward, Shamble!*

Non-series titles

The Last Days of Freedman High

*Published by BooksForABuck.com

Introduction

Greetings, reader. This is a collection of several short tales that take place throughout several time periods and in many of the various places of Tamalaria. Some of them, which will be duly noted, tie into some of the other major tales of Tamalaria. Several important individuals and beings appear throughout the tales, who have shown up in the major works I have worked on.

Thank you very much for your interest in the realm of Tamalaria, and remember; 'A dream is but a dream, until you act to make it a reality'. Enjoy!

Lizard at Arms

Table of Contents

Tale One: Thwarted

The year was 722 After the Fall of Mecha, in the city of Uragam, in the southwestern region of Tamalaria. Uragam was a town, to be more particular, in that it didn't have all of the conveniences of a city. For instance, it didn't have lunatics baying at the moon in the middle of the night while urinating on a street-torch post. Nor did it have constables ready and willing to drag people off down dark city alleys and thump them around with cudgels before sending them to the jailhouse for an evening. Uragam did, however, have one thing that every city in every region, in every land, in every Reality, has--a young Human man, of about sixteen, who is contemplating suicide.

James Michael Blake sat on the brass-framed bed in his upstairs bedroom wondering how things could have gone so wrong for him. The sixteen-year-old Human glared at his own reflection, taking in the blemishes smattered across his face, the narrowness of his bone structure, and the thick black bruise forming around his left eye. He could still hear the faint echoes of his parents trying to not let him overhear their concern for their only son. He couldn't make out the words themselves, but could feel the overtones in the air itself. 'Poor boy,' those tones said, translating his parents' vocal pitches into actual words. 'How do we help him'?

"By leaving me the Hells alone," he muttered to himself, his own voice cracking slightly as puberty fought for supreme control of his body. It had struck him late, that all-mighty Boxer that tended to uppercut males of all Races at exactly the most awkward and unfair of times in their lives. Or at least, that's what they all thought at the moment they felt the impact in the form of a crackling voice and pimples. Or, in the case of Dwarves, the unsettling and irresistible urge to hack down a tree with an axe-like object, even if no real axes were on hand. Many were the unfortunate pets that had had to make due with being used as such instruments.

James Michael Blake, whose ragged tunics and commoner's boots smelled of dust and old ink, helped his father, Ian, work in the local library on weekends. He took several stacks of returned books and shelved them, often carrying the stacks ten or eleven volumes high. His long, greasy black hair would often obstruct his vision more than the books themselves, and on more than one occasion, he had fallen flat on his ass after tripping over one of the books his clumsy father had dropped behind him. He earned a single gold piece for two days of four hours, shelving books with his dad.

James hopped off his bed, and his thin-soled boots clomped as he landed with all of his weight balanced in his heels. He teetered for a moment in the mostly sparse bedroom, his equilibrium thrown off kilter. Finding himself again, the pimpled boy knelt and reached one long, gangly arm under the brown wool blanket that hung over the side of the bed, grappling for the box he kept under there for safekeeping.

His hand slid over the cold pine floor, his skin rising in gooseflesh as dust skidded and parted on the ridge of his pinky, collecting up uncomfortably beneath his fingernails. Finally, James made contact with his query, and he grinned a small bit to himself.

James drew the rough, time-weathered box from underneath the bed. Only the dust that had been dragged along during its departure from its secret place clung to it--otherwise, the box looked clean and often used. The hinges were, in fact, a little worn, but there was good reason for that.

James opened the box, and revealed to himself, and the spider that had taken up residence in the far corner of the room between the wall and the sloped ceiling, a rather sizable sum of money. One hundred and fifty-six gold pieces, to be precise, which was rather a lot of money during that particular time period. His parents could have used this money to pay off the rest of what they owed on the house, because they only had one hundred and twenty gold pieces left on the thousand gold mortgage.

But with food, taxes, and other expenses to account for, they never seemed to do much more than barely get by on what they had for income.

No matter, James thought. *I'll leave this for them, and their worries will be gone. The mortgage, and me*, he thought with a grim sense of relief. Atop the money, however, was a rather thin, black leather-bound notebook. This was his true treasure. He pulled the book out and put the box back under his bed. He stretched his legs out on his bed as he swung himself into a comfortable posture on his bed, opening the notebook to the first page.

The notebook hadn't always belonged to him, it should be noted. It had, in fact, been owned by many people in its time, all of them dead and gone from the mortal coil. Its prior owner had died only six months before, something that James found altogether comforting in an eerie way.

James's eyes scanned over the sloppily scrawled thoughts that had been panning through the book's original owner's mind as he prepared to do what James was now certain he must also do.

The man's name had been Morten Vansick, an adolescent Elven male. 'Let never the legacy of this book die, though we may ourselves do so,' was the first sentence penned on the paper. 'Let the rules be given as follows. Firstly, if you are in possession of this book, write down first your age, your Race, your gender, and the date. 213, Morten Vansick, Elf, male, 21st of July, 544 A.F.'

James marveled at the dedication that the originator of this document, which he held most sacred, had for its creation. He continued to read on.

'Next, account for the events that have led you to this place you are at, for whomsoever has this book vows that once recorded herein, they are truly and finally committed to taking their own life, in order to end their suffering.'

James had found the Sacred Book among the stack of tomes he had been asked to arrange on the library shelves half a year ago. At first, he had noticed that it was rather small, and, thinking it might be a children's book, decided to look through it for illustrations. But there were simply words, in many different handwritings, and in one instance, in a language other than the Common Tongue. He had never gotten it translated, because the book somehow felt important to him from the moment that he finished reading Morten's submission to the Sacred Book.

After this brief introduction of rules and Morten's woeful times, the Elven youth had recorded exactly the method with which he intended to kill himself.

It was simple and elegant, James had thought as he had read and re-read these passages time and again. The boy had decided to poison himself at the kitchen table, at breakfast, while his mother and father watched. He wouldn't, of course, tell them what he was adding to his drink, so he told his parents months before the final day that he had decided to study Alchemy. He would then drink his fatal tincture, and be whisked away by Death himself into a world free of pain and oppression.

What the Sacred Book did not tell James, however, was what had eventually happened. But he would find that out for himself, soon enough. He would meet with Morten on the 'Other Side,' after he had taken care of himself here in the mortal coil. There, James would ask him how things had gone. He would ask all of the other former owners of the Sacred Book as well, and together, they would be free of their miseries. Or so, he hoped.

James heard the hollow thumping of slow footsteps coming up the steps toward his room, and he rapidly tucked the Book under his pillow and took out his school texts. The usual knock came at his door, so delayed, so afraid. His father, Ian Blake, there could be no doubt.

"Son," came his father's voice, sounding as old and dried out as the books he stacked. "What're you up to, my boy?"

"Door's open, da'." James brushed his hair out of his face.

Ian Blake blew into the room like a will-o-wisp, his own stick-thin form appearing to have little more meat on it than the Grim Reaper. He smiled awkwardly at his only child, revealing a set of teeth that had more in common with coal carts than anyone might be comfortable seeing.

"Wha' tchyou need, da?"

"Well, just wanted to talk, lad," Ian Blake lied, wringing his hat as he always did when he was nervous or concerned.

James hated the way he wrung his only decent article of clothing, because in another month, the old idiot would have to go and purchase a new one at the cost of having food for himself. While James thought of his father as a buffoon, he loved him because he was a kind and caring buffoon. He always made sure James' mother, Rachel, and his son had food to eat at all three meal times. Often, Ian would excuse himself from dinner by saying something like, 'got some overtime to put in, don't worry about my share,' or 'I've got an invite over to Freddy's for supper'. Fred Shaft was the town's librarian, and a sporting Minotaur once one got past all of the muscles and the rather intimidating way he used his horns to balance books as he carried them around the library. Always the books were red, and old, because the way he balanced them was by impaling them. In his library, most of the old books weren't worth much due to decay, so he was willing to spare a few on such transparent scare tactics.

But James knew that there wasn't overtime to be had, and he knew as well that if his father ate at Fred Shaft's for an evening, he'd come home either sick with food poisoning from undercooked meat, or so bloated with food as to make him look sickly. Yet his father always returned about an hour after him and his mother had eaten, and said 'no thanks, I've had some food while I was out'.

If I weren't in the picture, James often thought, *da could get something to eat.*

"Son, how'd you get that black eye," Ian asked, as lacking in tact as ever.

"Boy at school, da," James said, deciding that his last hours with his father should be truthful ones. "Ye see, there's this girl I sort of loik, in that funny way you and mum tried to explain to me was tot'lly natural last year, remember?"

Ian Blake's cheeks flushed, an amazing feat, considering how little blood he probably had to spare such a gesture.

"Well, I've been talking with 'er for months now, and she says she really loiks me, too. Only, when I asked her if'n she wanted to be me girlfriend, this large fellah in me class, Roy Brodart, knocked me so 'ard in the face I think I saw the future," James said, being completely blunt with his father.

Ian put his hand to his mouth and turned his head slowly away, and James felt awful for making his father worry so. After a minute of awkward silence, Ian spoke again to break the atmosphere.

"This girl, what's she like, son?"

"Well, her name is Cindy Rockbeater," James said, his eyes going slightly glassy as he thought of never seeing her again. It would be for the best, he had decided. "She's a half-Orc, but before you go nutter on me da," he ejaculated rather hurriedly, because he knew his parents frowned on Greenskin Races as a rule. "She's very Human-loik, da! Good manners, pretty as a picture, and very kindly, loik mum," he added, because he knew that compliments aimed at his mother always got rid of the stern look his father usually gave him when he asked to go and play with Goblin youths in his younger years. But no such expression came to his father's face right now; instead, in his eyes, there appeared to be a soft sort of understanding, of empathy.

"So this boy, this Roy Brodart, why'd he hit you then, son," Ian asked with a half-smile, overjoyed that after months and months of near-silence, his son was opening up to him again.

"Well, because he's sort of Cindy's boyfriend," James admitted. "And he's an Orc, da. That's why the bruising is so bad off."

Ian put a hand on his son's shoulder reassuringly and gave him a brief clamp of fatherly affection.

"No worries, son. There's plenty of fish in the sea. You think your mother was my first girlfriend?" Ian asked with a coy smile. He laughed aloud and moved away from James. As he was heading out the door, he poked his head back in for just a moment, which James expected--he still had his text books on his lap as his father said, "Now don't be up too late studying, son! You've always got tomorrow!"

Long minutes flittered by on small angel wings before James retrieved the Sacred Book.

"No, I haven't da," he said as he pulled out the box, and wrote a note to his parents, instructing them to use the money he'd saved up to save themselves.

* * * *

Down in the basement, James withdrew a single, oblong tube from a set of glassware that he kept around. He had followed his mentor's instructions precisely, making the scentless poison with the accuracy of a skilled assassin. *Of course, most assassins didn't kill themselves*, he thought smugly. They weren't worthy of the Sacred Book. They went around and killed other people, people who might be happy and want to keep on living, and for what? Money? Damned, they were, he thought as he held the vial to the light spilling in from one of the ground-level windows high on the basement wall. "Bottoms up," he whispered quietly, quaffing the clear liquid with a single effort.

For the first few minutes after consuming the poison, James Michael Blake felt no obvious change in his physical welfare. He sat in one of the old rocking chairs that his father and mother kept stored away in the basement, presumably for when they had company staying for a few days. They didn't have much, but they liked to try to make everyone, with the exception of themselves, comfortable and without complaint.

Then, the sensation of a great huge worm, covered in tentacles and feelers, as well as juices that ate at everything they touched, slithered around in his stomach and lower intestines. "This is it," he whispered reverently as he pitched forward in his seat and began hurling up his meager dinner.

Pain raced through his body, in particular his stomach, the waves synching up with the sloshing whitewash of his stomach's contents as his body rebelled against him. *Uh-oh*, he thought, grimacing as he dropped to his knees, his left hand on his abdomen. *It isn't supposed to hurt like this!*

He wretched back and forth, until finally he was doing little more than dry-heaving, because the inner sea of his stomach had completely dried up.

A strange little thought passed through his head then; the Desperation, the huge desert in the southeastern region of Tamalaria, had once been rumored to be a part of the ocean itself. A lot of stuffy-headed scientists had cited the skeletal frames of some ships as evidence of this, stuck half-up in the sand, but he had never really believed that such a thing was possible, until now. His own ribs felt as though they might poke through the lining of his stomach, shoring up like those great, ancient wrecks in the sands of the Desperation.

Finally, too much pain and too little energy conspired to overtake him. 'Come on,' he could hear the former say to the latter. 'Let's get the little prick'!

James barely managed to crawl on his right hand and knees to a clean and clear spot on the hard stone floor, and slumped over. A feeling of peace washed over him, as liberating as a slave being told he is free. He smiled a wan smile, and welcomed Death with an open heart. He was about to meet him, and he was about to be sorely disappointed.

* * * *

The Death of Tamalaria, or rather the Reality that Tamalaria inhabited, stood out on his front lawn, observing the way the grass swayed despite the absence of any wind. A golden mask-wearing entity stood a few feet to his left, a hand placed under the chin guard in contemplation. "It's the best I can do, Grim," Fate said.

IT SHALL HAVE TO MAKE DUE. I DIDN'T DARE TRIFLE WITH SUCH A THING, Death intoned in his typically flat voice. I HAVEN'T EXACTLY GOT THE KNACK FOR MAKING ANYTHING EVEN APPEAR ALIVE.

"Some day I'm sure you'll get over that," Fate said jovially. He looked at a timepiece of stone that Death kept on the porch of his squat cottage home. "Don't you have an appointment?"

YES. A NEAR ME EXPERIENCE, Death said, guiding his scythe through the air, creating a rift in space-time. I'LL TALK TO YOU AGAIN LATER, FRIEND. FOR NOW, I MUST GO ABOUT MY DUTIES. Death stepped through the rift, and disappeared from his own personal space.

On the other side of the rift, he stepped into a squat, squalid basement with a stone floor, which was here and there caked in thick vomitus. The form of one James Michael Blake lay prone, half smiling, on the floor a few feet away.

Death pulled out his sand timer, gave it a glance, and nodded to himself with satisfaction. Putting the timer away in his robes (where he kept the things in there was his own business), he raised the butt end of his tool, and prodded James Michael Blake in his already sore ribs.

James felt a new pang of pain as something solid and wooden thwacked him squarely in the floating ribs. "Ow, son of a bitch," he grumbled as he got himself into a seated position, holding his side. "I'm fine da, I just took sick," he said, completely unprepared for his mentor's advice to go awry. But when he rubbed his eyes and looked up, his heart skipped a few beats; Death stood before him, the front of his skull vaguely visible through the gloom of his eternal raiment.

"You've come for me," he whispered, awed by the entity before him. He stood to his feet and began jumping up and down elatedly, laughing. "You've come! Oh, I've been so looking forward to meeting..." he trailed off when he looked down for where his body should be.

It wasn't slumped on the floor, though, as he had expected it to be. Then he remembered the pain in his side from being poked with the blunt end of Death's scythe. He looked sidelong at the Grim Reaper, and cocked an eyebrow. "I'm not dead, am I?"

NO, NOT EXACTLY, Death said, moving over to the rocking chair that James Michael Blake had occupied only ten minutes previous. YOU'RE HAVING A NEAR DEATH EXPERIENCE, WHICH ENTITLES YOU TO A SMALL CONFERENCE WITH ME. Death leaned his scythe against the workbench a foot away from the rocking chair, and folded his hands in front of his face, his ancient, skeletal elbows making a soft clacking noise as he set them on the arms of the chair. IS THERE ANYTHING YOU'D LIKE TO SAY FOR YOURSELF? MAYBE ASK ME A FEW QUESTIONS WHILE I'M HERE? I'VE GOT THE TIME TO SPARE. Death's tone went slightly sarcastic.

James's mind reeled, his whole sense of Reality turned in several directions before his rational and philosophical minds, which had recently merged into a single process of thoughts, re-aligned.

"Okay, all right," James began, assembling his questions. "Why didn't it work? The poison, I mean," he said. "I followed every step of the procedure, to the exact measurements. How come I'm not dead?"

Death grinned, mostly because that's all you can naturally do when you haven't any flesh on your face.

A COUPLE OF REASONS, Death said, waving his hands emphatically. FIRST OF ALL, THE GENTLEMAN YOU'RE REFERING TO WAS AN ELF, YES?

James nodded.

ALL RIGHT THEN, YOU'RE A BRIGHT LAD. FIGURE THAT ONE OUT.

James tried to remember the ingredients, but couldn't think of one that stood out among the others. However, after a minute, he realized why that was, exactly.

"Because nothing in that formula is deadly to a Human being," he said, realizing that he should have taken into consideration his mentor's Race. "All right, you said that's one reason. What's the other one?"

SIMPLE REALLY, AND THE MOST IMPORTANT REASON. IT ISN'T YOUR TIME, Death said flatly, rocking the chair slightly.

"I decide when it's my time," James shouted. He then ducked his head and peered over at the door leading out of the basement, but he didn't see any movement.

DON'T WORRY, NOBODY'S GOING TO COME DOWN HERE. NOTHING CAN INTERRUPT US, JAMES, Death said calmly. He reached into his robes and produced from them an ebony cup of steaming tea, which he sipped at.

James watched his robes, but no damp spot appeared. How does he do that, he wondered.

BUT MY TIME HERE IS SHORT. YOU'LL HAVE TO GO BACK TO LIVING SOON.

"So I was thwarted by my own short-sightedness. It won't happen again." James crossed his arms over his chest. "Next time you see me, you'll be there to collect, count on it."

Before he could so much as blink, Death was on his feet and had a single bone fist gnarled in James's shirt, hoisting him into the air. Twin crimson lights flashed in his hood, pure rage boiling through.

ARE YOU GIVING ME AN ORDER, BOY, Death growled as smoke plumed out of his skull. BECAUSE BELIEVE YOU ME, THERE ARE TORMENTS FAR MORE ETERNAL AND UNBEARABLE THAN NOTHINGNESS, AND I CAN GUIDE YOU TO ANY ONE OF THEM! NOW QUIT BEING A LITTLE TWIT AND ACCEPT THAT YOU MUST LIVE! With that, Death tossed the boy to the floor, grabbed his scythe, and tore a rift in the air. WE SHALL MEET AGAIN, he intoned. He left the boy on the basement floor, and stepped through to his home once again. He smiled wickedly to himself as Fate strode over to him, a shining orb in hand.

"That was very good," the astral being said with a chuckle. "You certain you don't want a part in my play? You could take the role of one of the villains quite easily,"

Death just smiled to himself. I'M NO GOOD AT ACTING WITH AN AUDIENCE, he said, taking a look at Fate's all-seeing sphere. I LIKE SMALL ACTS, THE ONES THAT REALLY MOVE PEOPLE.

****

James Michael Blake left the basement, explained to his father that he had taken ill, and went upstairs to lie down. As soon as he hit the bed, he drew the Sacred Book from beneath his pillow and turned to the second entry, scanning briefly through the all too familiar passages. The second owner had been a Gnome woman, who had drawn out a simple plan. She had taken a length of rope and hung herself from a young maple tree near her home in Palen. *Simple, effective, and guaranteed to work*, James thought. He would get on that first thing in the morning.

James slept a dreamless sleep, waking up with the crowing of the roosters down at old Mr. Telwork's poultry ranch. Anthony Telwork was a kindly old Human fellow, and at one time, he'd kept over a hundred chickens and roosters on the property. Now, too old to care for so many and too senile to be trusted to do so, his daughter had moved in and taken over, selling off most of the stock of hens to the local slaughterhouse and keeping the rest to live off of. James had thought the night before, just as he nipped off to sleep, that he would hang himself today. That couldn't be, though, because it was Wednesday, his day to help Mr. Telwork take his bills around town and pay them off. He wanted so badly to kill himself, but he couldn't let Mr. Telwork go by himself, and there wouldn't be time to find a replacement to fill in on time.

But that wasn't until noon, when he would be out of school. As he swung his legs over the edge of his bed, his mother came into his bedroom with a steaming bowl of soup and a cup of tea, setting them on his nightstand.

"Oh no you don't, James," she scolded, her worry-lines creasing her face as they often did when he was ill. She dashed over to him more quickly than usual, and James realized that his mother must have seen his wretch products on the basement floor. She forced him back under his blankets and brought his tray over, setting it on his lap. "I know you aren't feeling well enough to go to school today, so you're staying in. I don't suppose I can keep you from helping Mr. Telwork, but that's five hours off yet. And you aren't to stay for a game of chess like you always does," she added.

James winced slightly. He enjoyed playing chess with the old farmer--it seemed to give the elderly man hope where James had none. He may have wanted to die himself, but he saw no sense in making anyone else suffer because of him.

"All right, mum," he conceded. "But can you send a note ahead? And tell him he'll have to find a replacement soon," James added before his mother left the room.

"Why's that, deary," she asked, concern mirrored in her eyes.

"I've, erm, got plans for next Wednesday," he lied, watching his mother smile wanly.

"Of course dear," she said, ducking out into the hallway.

James looked down at the tray on his lap. His parents loved him dearly, he knew. They would be saddened by his eventual and inevitable loss, but he would be certain to leave them a letter of thanks, and of course, the money he'd been saving. His death would help them live better lives, he reasoned, because he wouldn't be on the long list of their expenses. And he wouldn't have to suffer the humiliation of being beaten up by a half-mad Orc whose girlfriend he'd asked to go out with him.

THEY WON'T BE ABLE TO HANDLE IT, YOU KNOW, a familiar and eerie voice intoned from his bedside, almost causing James to jump and knock his tray to the floor. Death had taken up a seat next to his bed on the right side, opposite the door. THEY CARE TOO MUCH FOR YOU. DO YOU REALLY WANT TO HURT THEM

LIKE THIS?

James went instantly from frightened senseless to furiously indignant in a second's time. "Wha' tchyou know about it, huh," he nearly screamed at the incarnation of Death. "You're Death itself!"

HIMSELF, Death corrected, raising a single bony finger.

"Whatever," James rasped, taking up his spoon and ladling some of the warm broth into his mouth. He nearly choked on it, his throat was so raw from the vomiting the evening previous. But it finally went down, and he felt much better for it. He turned to make a remark to the Grim Reaper, but Death was nowhere to be found. A rift in the air by Death's seat sealed closed behind him.

After finishing his soup and his tea, James's throat and stomach felt much better, soothed and filled. He lay in for a while before getting out of the bed and getting himself ready to go to Mr. Telwork's ranch down the road. His father, Ian, had already gone to work at the library, and his mother fretted over him only briefly, reminding him that he wasn't to stay extra and that she had sent a note to the old farmer stating such.

"He didn't send a return note, of course, but I don't think he minds," his mother said with a smile.

James gave her a quick peck on the cheek, and was out the door and into the dusty streets of Uragam.

James hummed to himself as he made his way down the street towards the weathered poultry ranch, and his heart skipped a few beats as he noticed a long line of people out in front of the old farmer's house.

What is going on here, he wondered.

Francine Telwork, the farmer's daughter, was out on the front steps, tears streaking down her face as a doctor came out of the house and shook his head.

"No," James whispered as he rushed to the line of consoling friends and acquaintances of the old man and his daughter. They were all here, apparently, to mourn the loss of old Mr. Telwork.

James bumped and pushed his way through the crowd, many of whom made comments along the lines of 'hey, show some respect', or 'what are you doing?'

James didn't even try to talk to Francine, who was sobbing so hard that her shoulders shook as the Elven doctor tried to tell her that her father went peacefully. He ignored the doctor as well, and dashed inside the simple farmhouse, making his way to the back of the first floor. The door was slightly ajar, and he kicked it open, revealing to himself old man Telwork's room. On the bed, Mr. Telwork was smiling the smile of the blameless and happy; Death stood near another rift in space-time, and a strange blue light glimmered and sparked jovially behind him.

"You bastard," James yelled at the Grim Reaper, who looked up at him, away from the sparkling light, which he ushered through the rift with a gentle hand. "Why him? Why now? He never hurt anybody, he was a good man! Why d'you have to take him now?"

Death said nothing, but instead took out an old-fashioned sand timer, the bottom of which was filled with sand. Not even a speck remained in the upper bulb.

BECAUSE, IT WAS HIS TIME. HE DID NOT RESIST IN THE SLIGHTEST. HE WAS, IN FACT, RATHER GLAD TO SEE ME.

NOW, IF YOU'LL EXCUSE ME, JAMES, I MUST GUIDE HIM TO EVERNIA, THE HEAVEN OF THE LESSER GOD MOGUN. Death slipped through the rift.

James tried to follow after, but the rift had sealed itself shut behind the Grim Reaper.

Desolated, James sat on the edge of the bed, and held the hand of the late Mr. Telwork. No wonder he hadn't sent a reply note, he thought.

"He couldn't," James whispered to no one in particular. He looked at the old man, squeezed his hand once more, and left the home of the old farmer, feeling cold and dejected.

The old man's daughter moved to take hold of his arm, to speak with him, but James just shrugged her off as he exited the house and then the property.

Tonight, he thought, *I'll do it.* "I just need some rope," he said, moving away from the ranch and off towards the marketplace.

* * * *

"You're certain I'm allowed to do something like this," Fate asked his long-time friend, Death.

Death produced James Michael Blake's sand timer, and Fate nodded. "So, it isn't his time. In that case, I believe the Histories can be made to make a side note of this event." Fate made the slightest of changes to the world below his astral home. A single wave of his hand was all it took--the rest, he would leave up to the Histories, as he usually did.

"Did you ever think about actively interfering?" he asked Death, who was looking down on the mortal coil below. "You know, just to see what would happen."

I'VE THOUGHT ABOUT IT ON SOME OCCASIONS, Death admitted with a sigh. BUT THIS DOESN'T COUNT. HIS TIME HASN'T COME, SO WE HAVE TO PUSH HIM IN THE RIGHT DIRECTION FOR A WHILE. NOTHING WRONG IN THAT, he reasoned, though the words sounded slightly hollow, even to him. The

Histories, he realized, had most likely already mapped all of these events out to the tee. They were frustratingly omniscient like that.

"I suppose you're right. By the way, Truth has been asking after you," Fate said as an afterthought.

OH?

"Yes, she claims that you and she had an appointment, a sort of, well, mortals call it a 'date', I believe." Fate's tone took a teasing note.

IT ISN'T LIKE THAT, AND YOU KNOW IT, Death lied. I DON'T HAVE A GREAT DEAL OF EXPERIENCE WITH EMOTIONS. ONLY SINCE YOU AND I STARTED HAVING THESE LITTLE GET-TOGETHERS. AND DAMN YOU FOR IT, Death grumbled mostly to himself.

"Look, he's at the market," Fate said, peering into his sphere. He didn't have the same range of sight as Death, and for good reason. Death would never confide in Fate what that reason was, but he let Fate know all the time that he hid something from him. Lack of knowledge frustrated the astral being, and Death rather enjoyed watching that golden mask tint slightly red.

Death turned his attention down to James Michael Blake, who was about to commit yet another mistake.

* * * *

"Look, sonny, that's the only length wot I've got," said the exasperated Gnome merchant. "Should be long enough to keep the dog in the yard," he said. James had explained that he had a dog that needed to be kept in the yard until he could find it a new home, and the Gnome, while he was a businessman, and didn't really care what the rope was for, really only had one length of rope. That very morning, he could have sworn he had more. But his tally book, despite his memory, recorded five sales of rope, accounting for the rest of the rope. His cash drawer even added up, much to his relief. *Gotta lay off the sauce*, he thought to himself.

James was frustrated, but he bought the only remaining rope anyway. He had been worried that it wouldn't be long enough, but he would manage. James asked for a dark colored bag in which to carry the rope home, so 'nobody'll nick it,' along the way. After all, he had reasoned with the merchant, if somebody wanted all of the rest of the rope he'd had, chances were someone might try to take the last bit without having to pay, right?

The Gnome gave James a grin and nodded. "That's proper business thinking, son." He stuffed the rope into a black cloth sack. "Ever fink of becoming a merchant?"

"No, thanks. I don't think it's going to matter much what I want to be," James said with a mirrored smile, thinking to himself, *except for a corpse.*

The Gnome had misread this statement, and gave him a low grunt. "One of those there predetermined sort of careers, eh? Family tradition or somefing loik that?"

James said yes, thanked the merchant for the rope and the sack, and headed to the outskirts of the town. The smiling faces of children at play gave him a mild pang of regret as he passed them on his way to the old hickory trees on the hills just west of town. He had been happy like that, once. But with his parents' misery, the beatings he was certain would continue when he returned to school, and the uncertainty of what the future might bring him, he was able to push aside his regrets easily. He would, after all, be better off dead.

Past the businesses in the western district, beyond the fenced in areas holding goats and cattle and other various forms of livestock, James made his way to the low hills just outside of the town. A small copse of hickory trees stood atop the hills, and James smiled softly to himself. He had written a new letter for his parents, and had it kept in his back pants pocket. After all, many children came up to this hill to play their silly little games, and they would surely return to town and ask an adult why the boy swinging from the tree wouldn't come down, and why his neck looked hurt.

He now stood amid the tall, ancient trees. They looked as dead to him as he was hoping he would soon be.

James dropped the black cloth sack, and took out the length of rope. James had, several times throughout the years, dressed up as a hanged man for Terror Day, one of Tamalaria's most widely celebrated holidays. Young children, and sometimes grown men (when they are desperate for attention or sweets), dressed themselves in costumes and went door to door, begging off for free candies. As a result of his experience, James knew exactly how to tie a noose, which he had just finished doing in the time only a professional executioner should take. James turned around, and looked at the hickory.

He hadn't brought anything to stand on, because that would be, frankly, overly suspicious. But the tree he had selected for his purposes had several low hanging branches and multiple foot and handholds, so he would simply climb the tree, tie the opposite end of the rope around a branch, and, with the noose already around his neck, throw himself off. His neck would most likely be broken before he suffocated, he reasoned, but in case it didn't, he would die anyway. It would just take a few extra minutes, he thought, which was no bother when he considered that the end result would be worth the extra wait.

James made his way up the hickory, his long fingernails gathering up bits of bark as he climbed. These trees were old, so he wasn't at all surprised that the bark wouldn't stick. The holds, he was happy to note, however, were plenty sturdy enough to support him.

Halfway up, James was now a good fifteen feet over the ground, and decided it would be sufficient. With the noose around his neck, and the other end in his left hand, James started to crawl out on a relatively thick limb, and reached the midpoint in a minute. He had loved climbing through trees like this as a child, his father always right beneath him, ready to catch him if he fell out. But he never did, despite his mother's warnings and his father's open arms.

James secured the rope's opposite end around the branch, ensuring that it wouldn't be long enough to let his feet reach the ground. Despite the height, he was a tall boy, and he had to make certain that the rope wouldn't dangle too much. Satisfied with his perceptions, James leaned over the side of the branch, and dropped.

In most cases, this would be the part where the tragic suicide of a young teenage boy is stopped by someone nearby. In this case, that wasn't going to be necessary. For a moment, James dropped, eyes closed, towards his final destination. There was the powerful, mysterious sensation of true weightlessness, as though he were afloat in the air as fish were afloat in the sea. But as the weight on the rope dropped, in the form of James's body, a previously unspotted flaw in the rope caused the length to tear, and then immediately after that, snap. James's neck was rubbed raw and pulled a little, but the flaw in the rope was so serious that his full weight hadn't even been transferred through the material before it snapped.

James was deposited hard on the hill below, landing in a gasping, sore-throated heap, gagging and wheezing for air as he rubbed his throat. His eyes were still pressed shut, the sudden rush of blood to his head giving him an acute headache. But his eyes snapped open when he heard something over his head creak; when he looked up, he watched as the hickory branch snapped and fell off of the tree, landing three feet behind him. A familiar aura filled his senses, and he found himself looking at the skeletal feet of Death.

SO, HOW'S THE WHOLE KILLING YOURSELF THING GOING? Death asked as he looked at his fingernails, which, it should be noted, weren't really there.

James took the noose from around his neck and threw the rope at Death as he screamed an animalistic, wordless shout.

"Why are you doing this to me?" he shouted at the top of his lungs.

Death winced a little, and snapped his bony fingers on his free right hand.

The land around James and Death drained of all color, the world shifted into a sort of shades of gray color. One of Death's handy little tricks was pulling himself and any number of people outside of the confines of Time.

I HAVEN'T DONE ANYTHING, Death intoned as he took a seat on the fallen hickory branch. TO TELL THE TRUTH, THAT'S EXACTLY WHAT YOU'RE SO UPSET ABOUT.

James thought about this for a moment as he continued to rub his throat.

"I've been thwarted again," James said sulkily, sitting down next to Death. The astral incarnation of mortality at its end put his right arm around the boy's shoulders and gave him a brief shrug.

MIND TELLING ME WHY YOU'RE TRYING SO HARD IN ANY CASE?

James just shrugged his shoulders and harumphed rather loudly.

"You know that, don't you," he asked, turning to look into the darkness of the Grim Reaper's hood. He could just barely make out the skull therein, and he thought he saw a pair of twinkling lights in the eye sockets.

NO, JAMES, I DON'T, Death said softly, a trace edge of hesitation in his voice. He really didn't know what the boy was thinking, but he had a decent idea. I'M ASSUMING IT HAS SOMETHING TO DO WITH LIFE NOT GOING YOUR WAY.

"Well, there's a lot of reasons, actually." James Michael Blake removed his hand from Death's bony shoulder. It was too friendly a gesture for his liking from a being such as the Grim Reaper. "You see, it started a while back. A couple of years ago, actually. I sort of noticed that my folks didn't have much."

MUCH WHAT?

"You know, personal effects. Belongings, that is," James said, trying to explain a concept that was as foreign to Death as the idea of a world without lycanthropes was to him. "My parents don't make a whole lot of money. My mother works sometimes as a seamstress, and my father works in the library, shelving books."

YES, YOU SOMETIMES HELP HIM, Death said.

"That's right. Well, I noticed that my parents did everything they could for me, but they don't have much of anything to show for it. I sort of figured, you know, maybe they'd be happier without me around."

James regretted the words as soon as they left his tongue, and now, looking into the blaring red lights in Death's face, his heart dropped toward his crotch. *Oh man,* he thought, *maybe he's going to do it now! Do I really want to die? I thought so, but certainly not because of something I said!*

HAPPIER? HAPPIER, Death raged, flinging his skeletal hands toward the skies.

Bright white lightning flashed down all around them, and James Michael Blake skittered back and away from the head Horseman of the Apocalypse.

WHAT IN ALL THE HEAVENS AND ALL THE HELLS MAKES YOU THINK YOUR DEATH WILL MAKE THEM HAPPIER? DO YOU HAVE ANY IDEA HOW TRAUMATIZED THEY WILL BE IF YOU GO THROUGH WITH THIS COURSE OF ACTION? Death reached down, grabbed James by the front of his tunic shirt, and hauled him up off the ground, bringing the boy eye level with him.

Crimson light spilled from Death's eyeless sockets, and he snarled like a beast at the mortal adolescent. THERE ARE MANY THOUSANDS IN THIS LAND LESS FORTUNATE THAN YOURSELF, BOY. SOME ROT AWAY IN DUNGEON CELLS, FORMULATING THEIR ESCAPE, OR MAPPING OUT THEIR LIVES AFTER THEIR EVENTUAL RELEASE. THERE ARE WANDERERS TRAPPED IN DESERTS WHO CONTINUE TO SEARCH FOR WATER. IN SOME REALITIES, BECAUSE THIS ONE ISN'T THE ONLY ONE, HA HA, NOT BY FAR. Death threw his head back for a moment to laugh further. He tossed James back down into the dirt, and let the light in his eyes fade to a calm, loamy green. THERE IS A MAN, A HUMAN MORE THAN A THOUSAND YEARS OLD, WHO SEEKS TO CURE WHAT AILS THE GREAT TOWER THAT IS THE AXIS POINT FOR THOUSANDS OF THESE REALITIES. HE HAS LOST MANY FRIENDS IN HIS LIFE, AND WAS THE KILLER OF HIS OWN MOTHER. YET STILL HE MARCHES ON, CONTINUING WITHOUT REGRET. YOU, JAMES MICHAEL BLAKE, HAVE NO MORE RIGHT TO END YOUR OWN LIFE THAN ANYONE ELSE. IT IS NOT WHAT FATE HAS ORDAINED, Death said, his tone now actually soft, sympathetic. NOW, GO ON ABOUT YOUR BUSINESS, JAMES. AND BY THAT, I MEAN THE BUSINESS OF LIVING.

Death clapped his hands together, and the world around James turned dark, and then pitch black. He had passed out.

****

When James woke up, he found himself in his own bed, looking up at the worried faces of his parents. *Oh boy*, he thought, *here come the questions.*

But the first question out of his father's mouth surprised him, and made him thankful that someone was looking out for him. "Son, didn't anybody ever tell you to make the game loop *after* you tie the rope to the branch?"

Game loop, James thought with wonder. *That's right, if you're setting a rope trap for a rabbit or other small game, you make the loop after tying the end to the branch of choice.*

"Your mother and I appreciate your effort, and it was very nice of you to try to get us dinner fresh," his father said with a sarcastic grin, looking over at James's mother. "But if you're going to try and hunt, ye should learn how to, first."

James sat up slowly, running a hand over his neck, which throbbed painfully at his touch. He looked back and forth from his mother to his father, who both beamed at him with love and pride. *When they leave me alone*, he thought, *I'm getting rid of that book. Once and for all. I don't need it after all.* He looked over at his father, a sudden impulse coming over him.

"I do want to learn how to hunt, dad. I think I'm going to quit school for a while," he said. Neither parent protested his decision, both of them just smiling and nodding amiably. Another thought passed James's mind. "Hey dad, who brought me back home?"

"Oh, I did," his father said, scratching his short beard roughly. "This big, dark drink of water came to the door, told me you'd almost gotten yourself hung trying to set a rabbit trap. Tell the truth, I had a hard time lookin' at him, if you kennit."

James thought he knew exactly what his father was talking about, but left it alone.

His parents told him to get some rest, and as soon as they were out of his room, he dropped to the floor and reached for the book, only to find a single, folded piece of parchment. On it, he read a fine, curly handwriting. He was surprised to find that the letter wasn't written in all capitals. *That voice of his*, he thought, *certainly sounded like it should be.*

'To James:

I have taken the book away from you, and for your own good. Trust me on this, if nothing else; it isn't your time. And don't bother to ask when your time is. Like your elderly friend, whom I so recently took from the world, you will not know until it is done. Remember, James, that the world is not a fair place, and so, life is not fair. That doesn't mean it isn't worth living.

-Grim'

As soon as James ran his finger over the last word, the parchment crumbled into dust.

James smiled to himself, and decided that the next day, he would head to the library, as usual. However, he wouldn't be working. He'd be reading up on how to become a hunter.

The next morning came, and took away some of the rawness of his throat, though not nearly all of it. His mother had made him a large meal, for which he thanked her, and he ate like a wild animal.

"Dad, hold up a minute," he said, topping off his coffee and backing away from the table. "I'm coming with, but I'm not working today."

James Michael Blake explained his purpose in coming to his father, who nodded and seemed to positively beam at his boy. If he proved to be a competent huntsman, the Blake family would never again have to spend money on meat or fruits. James would provide all the food they needed.

Slightly behind them, keeping himself well out of mortal sight, Death floated along through the crowded streets. GOOD, he thought. THE BOY IS HEADING TOWARD HIS DESTINY. STILL, I FEEL A LITTLE GUILTY.

He followed the Blake boys, father and son, into the library, where both men obviously felt at home. James headed directly for the reference section, and his father for the owner of the library, to prepare for another day's work.

James took out a book on game hunting and sat at one of the long tables next to the older metallic bookshelves, which the owner was in the process of replacing with oak ones. Too heavy, the owner had said, and too dangerous if they fell. How right he was... how right he was. A half-Orc, having come in to move the books off of the old shelves and move the old metal units out, accidentally bumped into the opposite side of the unit James was sitting next to.

Death cringed as the unit came toppling down on top of James Michael Blake, crushing the life out of him.

Death moved over toward the shelving unit, and the dead boy beneath. He had hated himself for his deception the day before, but it was necessary. If the Histories got too out of whack, reality would stretch too thin, and the gods, including Fate, couldn't allow that. Nor could

Death, and thus, he had done what needed to be done.

Regardless of his thoughts on the matter, he still felt guilty. He hovered over the boy's body, and swung his scythe down through the ethereal level of his being. The bluish form of the boy's soul floated up and out of his body, and Death could see he was smiling. "So, what was all that stuff you were saying yesterday about, Grim?"

THESE ARE DIFFERENT CIRCUMSTANCES, Death said, feeling a little lame. DON'T WORRY, YOUR PARENTS WILL GRIEVE, BUT THEY'LL GET OVER IT IN A FEW YEARS. YOUR FATHER IS GOING TO FILE A LAWSUIT AGAINST THE OWNER, AND TURN THIS PLACE INTO A BOOKSTORE.

"Does he do well?"

THAT'S PUTTING IT MILDLY, Death said, breathing a sigh of relief. The boy wasn't angry at him, at least. It was almost as if he just accepted things as they were, so long as his parents did well.

HE AND YOUR MOTHER ARE GOING TO BE RATHER PROSPEROUS, YOU HAVE MY WORD ON THAT, which was at least the truth. He'd already checked with Fate that morning, and his gold-faced friend had given him his assurance on the matter. COME NOW, WE'LL DISCUSS MANY THINGS ON OUR WAY DOWN THE PATH, JAMES MICHAEL BLAKE. I'LL ANSWER MOST QUESTIONS YOU MAY HAVE, he said, putting an amiable hand around the boy's shoulders.

"All right, first question," James said, stepping toward the rift in time-space that Death opened with his scythe. "Who wins the soccer match between the Desanadron Destroyers and the Traithrock Crushers?"

AH, THAT, Death said, smiling to himself. WELL, I'M NOT A BETTING MAN, BUT LET'S JUST SAY A LOT OF PEOPLE ARE GOING TO LOSE MONEY ON THAT ONE.

Tale Two: Lizard at Arms

Charamir Kooteck had been a police officer in the city of Ja-Wen since about fifteen years after the War of Vandross. He had enlisted in the military police forces shortly after the death of his tribe's chief, Bael, who had been his leader when he fought alongside the armies of Byron of Sidius, Thaddeus Viper, and Morek Rockmight. But the militant Lizardman chief had suffered a long, painful death at the hands of the Black Rot, which had started to sweep the land. Nobody knew how the disease was contracted, but it only seemed to affect those Races with no regenerative capabilities, and of them, only those who smoked tobacco.

Charamir was now a First Lieutenant in the Ja-Wen military police, and had command of his own precinct. He had only had this position a few months, but already he was starting to develop a permanent headache. Although Ja-Wen sported a population half that of the metropolis of Desanadron, it still supported nearly half a million residents. There were only twenty-four police precincts, and as time went on, the city became more and more overrun by gangs, Guilds, and hoodlums. He simply didn't have enough men on hand to deal with the situation.

As a result, Charamir was now getting into his dress uniform and preparing to head out on foot patrol himself. This was something the Lizardman Soldier hadn't done in years, but he felt it would be good for him. Fifteen years as a patrolman, and then twenty years as a detective had given him a good deal of experience in the field, and he wasn't about to squander that experience by sitting behind a desk all the time. He would leave the precinct in the capable hands of Timothy Hollister, a Sidalis who appeared to be a crossbreed of a Human and a turtle. Timothy had a brother in Desanadron, who apparently worked on the other side of the legal fence, as a fellow says.

The stresses of command were the least of his headache this morning, however, and as he looked in the full-length mirror next to his large oak desk, he rubbed his temples. Unlike most men of his race, Charamir's scales were as hard as those of a Draconus, the dragon-men of the hills and mountains. Those on his head and hands, the only places not covered by his grand uniform, glimmered in the artificial lighting of the ceiling a vibrant, emerald shade of green. As he looked at himself, he thought, *no, command isn't what's on my mind. It's this 'Hookman' that's got me riled.*

During the last month, half of the time he had been in command of the Twenty-First Precinct, a series of bizarre murders had been committed throughout the city of Ja-Wen. Those few witnesses whose statements could be trusted had one common thread, which was that they saw a shady figure with a hook for a left (some witnesses said right) hand leaving the building around the time of the murders. As a result, the Ja-Wen Crier had dubbed the serial killer 'The Hookman'.

"Fucking newsies," Charamir grumbled to himself as he fixed his chain pendant on his upper left breast. It hung down from a button affixed next to the center set to a lower front pocket of the dress coat, and on the end hung his badge of rank.

The royal blue color of the uniform always made him cringe a little when he looked himself over. It contrasted too much with the color of his scales, he thought, but it would do. He didn't mind letting it be known that yes, this was a policeman you're looking at, and don't forget it. But he really would have liked having a personalized uniform. He had gone plainclothes during his time as a detective, but even then he'd worn a uniform of sorts. He hadn't dressed much different from any other detective, with the brown slacks, the white button shirt, and the ties of varying colors. He'd hated the look, but it made him feel professional, and so he went with it without complaint.

"I'll have to remember to put in a request to the boys up top," he murmured to himself, making one final adjustment on his dress coat. He stepped out of his office, and into the main detective division office room. Desks were pushed together with partners facing one another, and all in all, fourteen men were already present and working on multiple cases. Most of the officers in his division were Humans and Elves, with one pair of Minotaurs working together and one pair of Dwarves. A man entered from the stairwell, with a copy of the *Crier* in his hands.

Hollister, Charamir thought, looking at his wrist timepiece. *Nine o'clock, on the button, as always.*

The turtle-man stopped a few paces away from him, and saluted smartly. "Sir!"

Hollister certainly had a way of being formal and by the books, the Lizardman Lieutenant thought, and saluted him back. Nobody saluted unless they were on military status except the Sidalis, whose tie was cornflower blue. Hmm, Charamir thought, that's right. It's Tuesday, cornflower blue day.

"Sir, have you seen this morning's edition of the *Crier*?"

"Do I really need to?" Charamir asked. Despite his cynicism, he took the offered paper and snapped it open to display the front page and its large front picture. It appeared to show an artist's rendition of the Hookman.

"Oh gods in the heavens above," he whispered, reading the headline in bold print: 'Maniacal Serial Killer Eludes Police Yet Again!'

"What the hells is this," he said, turning the paper around and pointing to the headline.

One of the Human detectives, Carl Raffordy, pushed himself from his desk. He walked over, and handed the Lieutenant, or 'Lou' as everyone referred to Charamir, a memo with the precinct's medical examiner's signature on it.

"Oh shit."

"Came in this morning, sir." Raffordy adjusted his tie. It was a nervous habit the Sergeant Detective had picked up over the years, and it bugged the hell out of Charamir, though he never said as much. Despite his annoying habit, Carl was an excellent detective with great instincts, and Charamir didn't want to push him away by picking on his nervous tick. "Second Lieutenant Chambers didn't bring you up to speed this morning, sir?"

"No, she was already gone home when I got here an hour ago," the Lizardman said, reading the medical examiner's report. Gnomes filled most of the scientific positions in the military police, and were only rarely given police duties. This one, Leah Thorp, had done all of the exams for the Hookman's victims. Her report read just the same as the previous seven.

Eight victims, Charamir thought. Fights in the street, honorable combat, weren't considered murder by the codes of the law, and thus never got investigated. But these eight had all been innocent young men and women, none of them any kind of danger to anyone.

I want this bastard, and I want him now, he mentally grumbled. He handed Raffordy the report, which the detective filed in his 'out' basket. "Sir, are you going out this morning? I thought it was tomorrow." Hollister accepted a mug of coffee from one of the lower ranked detectives.

"I'm going out today." Charamir straightened his back and puffed out his sizable chest. "This asshole has killed during all times of the day, and he's just as apt to make a move this morning as any other. Tim, you're in charge while I'm gone." He put a steady hand on the mutant's shoulder. "Make sure that you can get a hold of me if you need to."

Hollister nodded. Grabbing one of the many messenger pigeons from its cage, he set it on the Lou's shoulder for a moment.

After the bird pecked Charamir's shoulder once, Hollister placed it back in its cage, and went to get it fresh water.

Charamir saluted the detectives throughout the room, and headed for the stairwell and the lower floor where the patrolmen maintained their operations. The old oak steps creaked under his weight, and the scent of one of the patrolman's after-shave as he passed him on the steps filled his head with nausea. He tucked his tongue back in his mouth, not wanting to smell any of the morning drunks he was sure to come across when he got into the main lobby.

The main lobby spread out in front of him as he exited the stairwell, with the lockup hall to his immediate right. Ahead of him, perhaps thirty yards away, was the main check-in and booking desk, where patrolman Durin was on duty. Several of his Dwarven kinsmen were being checked in for the drunk tank by a pair of Minotaur officers in their light blue uniforms. A Wererat, ranting and foaming at the mouth, was being bodily dragged by two Werewolf officers back toward the felon lockup, where he would await trial. Charamir couldn't make out a lick of what the criminal was shouting, because he had never taken the time to learn the Wererat language. "They all say the same thing, though," he mused aloud.

He made his way slowly to officer Durin, and the Dwarven patrolman gave him a brief grin and a nod. "Morning, sir," he said. "Wot's on yer moind?"

"That fellow," Charamir said, pointing back toward the Wererat, who was being clubbed by the officers to keep him from going into lycanthrope rage. "What's his story?"

Durin chuckled a little and referred to his log-in book.

"Got caught breaking into Pappy's Diner down on North Bear Street. Officers arrived a few minutes after someone reported hearing shouts from the diner."

"Who was shouting?"

"Apparently, him," Durin said, pointing to the unconscious Wererat. "Pappy's son, David, was getting the kitchen fired up when the rat slipped in."

Pappy was a successful restaurant owner, a Jaft who specialized in mountain folk cuisine. His diner mostly catered to Dwarves, Minotaurs, and Jafts, but people of all races ate the food. His son, David, while not exactly a genius, was a whiz in the kitchen, just like his father. Unlike his father, however, who wasn't much like the other members of the Jaft race, David was highly skilled with the flail whip he brought with him everyplace.

"David do a number on him?"

"Oh yes, Lou," Durin said with another chuckle. "If'n that fellah wasn't a regenerator, he'd a died before we could get 'im 'ere."

Charamir wasn't too surprised, then, that the Wererat was raving. He very well could have been pleading a case of assault, but that wasn't exactly going to go over well. 'Oh yes, your honor, he beat the tar out of me. Why? Well, I think it was because I was breaking and entering'. *Yeah, that'd go over like a torch in an Alchemy shop.*

"Very good, Durin," he said, smiling to himself. "Keep up the good work."

"Aye, sir." The Dwarf turned to hand another patrolman his time card.

Charamir made his way out into the streets of Ja-Wen, and squinted under the glaring sun. Winter had just come to a close in the east, and was making its way across the central region of Tamalaria, moving slowly toward the west. Charamir decided to make a slow, steady beat around the outer perimeter of his precinct's jurisdiction. He would stop and talk to the locals and other patrolmen on duty. That would take him to about an hour and a half to two hours, depending on how brisk he was about his conversations.

Most of the city's residents didn't care much for Lizardmen, a fact he understood and acknowledged. His people had been with Richard Vandross when first the warlock had fallen upon the city, and they had wiped out most of the city of Koreindar north of Ja-Wen. He understood why the local inhabitant's distrusted him, and already he felt some of the residents' eyes upon him.

Be that as it might, he continued down the street, heading north.

Several of the unemployed folks he came across during the first ten minutes of his walk offered him a smoke, but he kindly declined. "The Black Rot runs through my people very quickly," he explained to an elderly Jaft fellow. "We're pretty sure it's to do with those sticks of yours, but I thank you for the offer."

He walked away, his back turned to the middle finger being aimed at his back.

Charamir flicked his tongue out, taking in the early morning scents of the local diners opening up for the day, the twenty-four hour taverns serving their early morning customers, and the sweetly perfumed adolescent ladies on their giggling way to school.

Rumormongers, every last one of them, he thought with disdain as he gave several of them his coldest, most professional smile. *The Human ones are the worst about it, too.* Charamir continued on until the intersection of Forty-Second and Arrow streets. Then, he turned west on Arrow, staying within his jurisdiction.

Perhaps a hundred yards ahead, he saw bright yellow crime scene tape flapping in the morning breeze. It looked very recent, and three of his own patrolmen were standing outside of the four-story apartment building, keeping a close eye on who went in and out. *This must be the place from last night,* he thought, approaching now with an aura of authority.

When he came within twenty yards, he could hear snippets of their conversation, which revolved around the soccer match the previous afternoon between the Port of Arcade Strikers and the Ja-Wen Footmen. He got to within a few yards, utilizing his uncanny grace to remain silent and unobserved, and then he cleared his throat, loudly.

All three officers turned and straightened up, two Humans and one Half-Elf woman, and they smiled nervously at him. "Morning, Lou," the woman said, her voice cracking a little. She threw him a salute, which he returned in kind, keeping a stony cast to his face. He nodded his head toward the entrance of the building.

"There any reason you three aren't inside, keeping the actual scene secure," he asked with mild aggravation. Three pairs of eyes touched base with one another, and then turned back to the Lieutenant.

"Detective Tobia's inside, sir," the woman said.

Charamir looked back and forth at the three of them, and noted with some interest that she was the low man on the totem pole among these three. *Yet,* he mused, *these two cowards are making her their spokesman. They expect me to kill the messenger, not the problem.*

"He was very clear about us staying out here."

Tobia. Charamir shook his head. Vincent Tobia was a Human detective in the department, with a great deal of patrolman experience, and five years of detective work on his resume. He had transferred over from the Seventh Precinct a year ago, and had since cracked four cases on his own merit, working with nobody within the department, and nobody without. A loner by nature, it seemed. The man was of average height, and was slightly heavyset, but damned if he wasn't a good detective. He tended to notice things that got left behind by the crime scene unit boys, but despite his powers of perception, he wasn't very imaginative. He was by the books, and dealt strictly with facts. Mayhap that was why he'd put himself on this Hookman case, to try and get himself to think outside of the box.

Charamir, on the other hand, dealt better with matters of the mind and heart. He didn't precisely use logic or facts in every case, because sometimes those things didn't truly matter. Evidence wasn't always present, but intentions were, and Charamir was very good at connecting those dots. In order to catch the Hookman, he felt pretty certain a mix of the two men's thinking styles was going to be required. He looked down at the patrolwoman, and smiled his toothy smile. "Thank you, patrolman. What's your name?"

"Woodgrove, sir," she said, snapping off another smart salute.

"Patrolman Woodgrove. Good. You're in charge out here for the time being, understood?"

She positively beamed at the Lieutenant, while the two men behind her fell back a step. "Keep everyone who doesn't live here or wear a uniform out. No newsies, and if one of the little fuckers tries to slip you money for a peek inside, you three take him in for attempted bribery of a peace officer. Got it?"

All three saluted and nodded, and Charamir ducked under the police tape and headed inside.

The Lizardman Lieutenant followed the scent of Tobia's after shave faultlessly, going up several sets of ramshackle stairs to the third floor, and down to the taped off doorway leading into the scene of the Hookman's latest caper. His tail swished behind him of its own accord, and he stilled it with an effort. *One of these days*, he thought, *I'll have to have an Alchemist remove the damned thing.*

To the taped doorway he stalked, looking inside before entering.

Sure enough, standing a few feet away and pulling on his short salt and pepper beard was Vincent Tobia, Vinchenzo to his friends.

The detective pulled on his tie, another nervous tick that Charamir noted but said nothing about.

The Lizardman cleared his throat meaningfully, and Tobia looked up at him, a vicious little smile quirking across his lips. "Hey there, Lou," the Human said.

"Detective Tobia," Charamir said with a nod. "How goes it? Find anything the crime scene boys might have left out?"

Tobia approached the taped off doorway, and ducked out under it, forcing Charamir to move aside.

Tobia ran the slow but certain slope toward middle age, and his stomach, rather prodigious, showed out over his belt in a deceptive display. Large as the man was, Charamir knew he was no pudgy pushover, and gods help the criminal who thought he was. The Lieutenant had seen Vince Tobia take more than a few men down, and hard.

"Not much, Lou," Tobia said, insisting on using Charamir's nickname of rank. Tobia looked back into the apartment and pointed toward a south-facing window. "Except maybe that. There's a little bit of a scratch in the wood of the sill, and there's a fire escape outside the window. I think maybe that's the way our Hookman left. Might be something in the alley worth checking out."

"Then let's check." Charamir turned and moving back to the stairs.

Tobia followed immediately behind, apparently eager to work with his superior, which most members of the department weren't. Down the flights of stairs they fairly flew, each man eager to have a new piece to the puzzle of their current case, and neither wanting the other man to find it first.

Once they were outside, Charamir came up short, and was almost plowed to the dirt by Tobia, who had just enough time to stop his forward progress.

Charamir looked with growing disdain at Fredrick Sholt, one of the reporters for the *Daily Ja-Wen Times.* The reporter, a sniveling Kobold with a shrewd eye for details, was presently trying to plead his case for going inside with Officer Woodgrove, who was resolutely denying him access.

As soon as Charamir started to turn toward the alley, he heard the little newsie's voice calling to him. "Lieutenant Charamir! Sir, if I could ask you a few questions!"

Aw, great, Charamir thought. *Now I have to deal with him.* He turned and smiled amiably enough at the Kobold, who was already tearing ass around Woodgrove toward him.

Vince Tobia, thankfully, had already dealt with this newsie on previous occasions, and stepped forward to deal with him on the Lou's behalf. Standing next to Charamir this way, the two of them looked a little like a pair of politicians. And when it came right down to it, Charamir thought, wasn't that basically his job now? A commanding politician in charge of his precinct? He didn't like to think so, but that was what it boiled down to, nine times out of ten.

"Ah, detective Tobia," the Kobold sneered, looking up past the belly toward the Human's face. "So good to see you're also on this Hookman case."

"Who says this has anything to do with that, Freddie," Tobia asked condescendingly. "Who you been talking to you little snake?"

Before Charamir or Sholt could move to stop him, Vince Tobia, a man known for his quick temper, reached down and plucked the Kobold up by the front of his green tunic shirt.

Tobia wasn't that big for a Human, but Sholt was only two and a half feet tall, short for even a Kobold. His legs twitched and kicked this way and that as he struggled to free himself from Tobia's iron grip.

"Who you got up your sleeve, Fred?" Tobia shook the Kobold roughly, making the little reporter's teeth clack together violently.

"Vince," Charamir said, low and warning. "Not too rough with our little reporter friend."

To the Lizardman's relief, Tobia set Frederick Sholt down on the ground.

The Kobold shifted his shirt, smoothing out the wrinkles, and cracked his neck.

"I should have you reported to the Council," the Kobold cried out, pointing an accusing finger at Tobia. "You can't abuse me like that! The press has a right to ask questions, you, you troglodyte! Who I talk to is my business!"

Ah, Charamir thought, *now I can ask a few questions.*

"And it's ours now, as well." The Lizardman smiled wickedly.

Fred Sholt looked up at the Lou and cringed at the sight of those teeth, all angular and seemingly ready to bite through anything.

"You know, Fred, if your contact has information that's relevant to our investigation, we need to talk to him. Keeping mum about anything that could help us would be obstruction of justice, and I think you know all too well what that could mean," Charamir said in his most friendly tone of voice.

Sholt looked aside, his cheeks flushing bright red.

"Yeah, I know, I know," he said, waving off the Lieutenant's underlying threat. "You're a real prick, you know that?"

Charamir shrugged his shoulders at this, having been called much worse things in his native tongue.

The Kobold heaved a sigh, and shook his head. He pulled out a small yellow steno pad, and wrote down a single name, tore off the sheet and handed it to Charamir, who passed it on to Tobia without even glancing at it.

"I'm supposed to meet up with him tonight, around seven of the clock. Draffords Park," the Kobold reporter said. "If you want to talk to him, come along. Remember, seven this evening."

Sholt started away without further comment.

Tobia was reading the name, and then he tucked the paper away in a back pocket. He tapped Charamir on the shoulder, and nodded his head in the direction of the alley.

"You coming, boss?" he asked.

"No, you go ahead," Charamir said. "I'm just out on patrol for now, but meet me back at the house at around one this afternoon. We'll discuss anything you find then."

Tobia gave a half-assed salute, which Charamir returned in kind before heading down the street. He knew that Tobia would find something, and he wanted to give the detective time to analyze whatever he found on his own. Charamir's style of analysis and thought would only muddle Tobia's detection methods, and for now, he didn't want to do that. He'd put his own head to Tobia's in a while, but for now, he wanted to get going on his around town observations.

Down the block he padded, stopping into Shlep's Coffee Shop for a cuppa before moving on. Coffee did wonders to clear his head, but cuppa was even better. Down through the gathering crowds of the street market he went, giving greetings here and there, and taking reports from the occasional patrolman he passed by. It seemed that nobody had much to report this morning, other than their own thoughts on the Hookman case, but one patrolman did tell him of a rather interesting street fight he'd had to break up a few hours before. Both combatants had been hauled off to the precinct house, and Charamir could talk to them if he wanted when he got back. He resolved to do so, and thanked the patrolman for his report.

Now he turned down another dusty street in order to stay within the confines of his jurisdiction, and found himself passing in front of a group of homeless Humans, each with a cardboard sign saying 'Need money for food'. He dropped them a few tinnies for their troubles, enough to buy the group of hobos food or drink (he suspected the tin pieces would go toward the latter rather than the former) and passed them by.

In front of one of the district's libraries, he stopped and looked up at the open doors. A sign out front advertised a book signing by a local author, Dale Forth, and he decided to stop in and peruse the shelves, maybe even meet the local boy done good.

When he walked up the short steps and into the main lobby of the library/bookstore, he saw that the author in question was away from the signing table at the moment, but a long line stood waiting patiently for his return. Charamir looked at the books on the table, entitled *From the West It Came,* and decided that perhaps he wouldn't give the author his time after all.

Charamir walked slowly over the hardwood floor toward the non-fiction section of the library division of the building. He already had seven reference books out on loan, but he figured a nice rounded figure might be best when he returned them all. He scanned the shelves without much interest, until finally his reptilian eyes fell upon one new book that made him take a sudden, sharp breath. It was a reference book--that much he knew because of the section it was in--but he hoped against hope that it was mislaid. *In Search of a Serial Killer, by Harrison Jones.*

Charamir pulled the book off of the shelf, and as soon as he opened it to its table of contents, he knew it was a true crime compilation.

The book was divided into sections by city, and then further by criminal. The first section was devoted to the city of Desanadron, and had a list of eleven psychopaths listed. Charamir was familiar with most of the names listed, except one of the more recent ones, a Telvor Winston. The second section was for the Port of Arcade, and had four listings. The third section was for Ja-Wen, and thankfully, didn't include the latest menace on the list, the Hookman. However, he was put out of sorts with the sixth and final listing, which didn't have a proper name. "The Sharpshooter," he read aloud, and remembered immediately that particular case.

Two years ago, up in the northern precincts, the police had chased a man who had been named the Sharpshooter for the method of execution he used--a high-powered rifle smuggled out of one of the ruined cities of the Age of Mecha. The killer had targeted and killed several members of the governing Council of Ja-Wen, sniping each member from one of the high rooftops of the buildings around their homes. The man had finally made a mistake, however, for after six members of the Council had been slain, the police had been able to piece together his pattern. They had arrested the man, a disgruntled and mad as a hatter Gnome by the name of Jim Twink, and booked him on six counts of murder. He had gone through a very short trial, after which he had been executed by firing squad. Very ironic, Charamir thought with a smile.

He scanned the section concerning the Sharpshooter, and was pleased to find that by the time this book had been published, the case had not yet been solved. How long would it take, he wondered, for some other author, or this very same one, Harrison Jones, to write out a book about the Hookman? Probably not long, he decided, putting the book back on the shelf and leaving the library/bookstore.

Out on the street, he realized how long he had been inside, and headed back off down the street. He finished his cuppa, throwing the empty cup into a waste bin, and turned once again at the corner of Fifth and Shore Street.

On Shore Street, Charamir started thinking over the Hookman case again. He wanted to keep a clear head during his patrol in case a situation arose nearby that required his attention, but this early in the day, not much happened in his precinct. He thought of how the mysterious killer operated, breaking into people's homes, then striking them with a heavy, blunt object. Each victim showed signs of head trauma, but only enough to knock them out. Next, the Hookman would bind them to a piece of furniture, and gag the victim with one of their own articles of clothing. In most cases, this turned out to be a shirt, but once it had been a balled up pair of socks. How disturbing would that be, Charamir thought, to have the last taste of your life be your own dirty socks? He shuddered at the idea, and moved on.

He tried to think of any connection between the four men and four women that had been slain. In each case, they had been bound, gagged, and then slowly, laboriously dissected, apparently with some sort of hook, from what the medical examiner had told the police. The work had been messy, and in two instances, the intestines of the victim had been pulled out and thrown about their living rooms, almost as if cast off in frustration. Had this killer been looking for something inside the bodies of his victims? Had some mad impulse taken him over and told him to rummage inside their guts?

Mayhap that was the case, but for now, he couldn't think about that. He needed facts right now, not hypothesis. *Which is exactly why you're going to let Tobia handle things for now,* he thought bitterly. *Let him get you the facts, then work with him on the motives.*

Without having quite realized it, Charamir found himself standing before his own precinct house again. He sighed, and headed inside, checking his timepiece. He had burned two hours of the day, for which he was glad. He had accomplished this bit of daily chores, and was not to be found wanting.

He walked inside the main lobby, and found Durin's check-in desk clear of officers or miscreants. He approached the Dwarven officer, and cleared his throat again. It was, he had found, the best way for him to get someone's attention without seeming rude. Durin looked up from his paper, and smiled at the Lou. "What's on yer mind, sir?"

"Patrolman Frisk told me we had a couple of street fighters in this morning. They still in lockup?"

Durin nodded, and pointed toward the General Holding corridor.

"Thank you, Durin."

The Dwarf picked up his paper again, and Charamir winced when he saw it was the morning edition of the *Ja-Wen Times*. He would probably be included in Sholt's next article, most likely under the heading 'Police Brutality! When Will You Be a Victim?' He didn't care much for the idea, but he would let it go, for now.

Charamir swept himself quickly down the General Holding corridor, his tail swishing across the cement floor, and he soon found himself being spat at by the various individuals in the lockup cells.

Where the hell's the watchman on duty for these scumbags, he thought, looking for a moment at the empty desk down at the end of the row of cells.

He walked slowly down the hall, looking for the two men that had been described to him, a Simpa and a Khan. The were-lions and tiger men had been fighting since time out of mind. They usually kept themselves civil when not out in the wilds and their precious Allenian Hills region, but occasionally racial tensions exploded in civilized areas and towns. Apparently such an incident had occurred here, in his jurisdiction, and he was loath to take two men to court for something that could be handled with a simple set of threats and promises.

In the last two cells standing opposite one another before the watchman's desk, he found the Khan on his left and the Simpa on his right.

The Khan, a sleek and angular fellow dressed in the simple tribesman's pants of his people, paced back and forth while he wrung his hands before his bare chest, growling in the tongue of his people. The Simpa, on the other hand, appeared to be doing nothing more than thinking, seated cross-legged on his rather small cot. He was wearing a set of bib overalls over a yellow shirt, and had his hands clasped together in his lap. Charamir cared not a whit for the look of lax concentration the man was giving his hands. In his experience, a man who looked so deep in thought was usually thinking over future violence.

"All right, you two, front and center," he said aloud.

The Khan darted to the bars of his cell, snarling and growling at the Lizardman in his dress uniform, which by now was covered with spit. The Simpa took a moment longer getting to his own cell bars, shaking his head to clear himself of his momentary reverie.

Charamir saw, with some amusement, that the Simpa couldn't grip his cell bars because the man's hands were too large to fit between them. The Khan, he noticed, still had a few bruises that hadn't healed up. The Simpa, on the other hand, looked completely undamaged.

"All right, gents, let's hear it. I want to know both sides of this story that you can provide." Charamir pulled the steel folding chair out from behind the watchman's desk, setting in the middle of the two opposing cells. He took a seat on it, and crossed his left leg over his right. "I'll hear from you first." He indicated the Khan.

"Soku colauwikai," the Khan said, bowing slightly. "Ishim vook tanabek," he began, but was silenced by Charamir's upheld left hand.

"In the Common tongue, please," the Lizardman said with a sarcastic grin.

The Khan warrior harrumphed at this, but nodded his great tiger head.

"Very well, green one," the Khan said. "I am Desik, of the clan Mortis. I have traveled here to the city of Ja-Wen to locate and bring back my wayward son, Tesik, who has abandoned our people out of foolishness. He is to be a warrior, as his father is and his father's father before him," he said, thumping his chest with a balled fist. "But he left us, for he claimed to have no want for our war against those savages," he said, pointing an accusatory finger at the Simpa. "And when I found my boy, who should he be walking with, but this *vokodu*." The Khan once more stabbed a furry finger at the Simpa, who simply stood in his cell, smiling a lopsided, almost absentminded smile.

Charamir didn't know a lick of the Khan language, but he was pretty sure he had an idea of what *vokodu* meant, and it wasn't kind.

"That man has poisoned my son's mind, and his heart, against my people and against the calling of a warrior! I want his throat in my teeth!"

Charamir once more stilled the Khan warrior with an upraised hand, and turned his oblong, blunt snout toward the Simpa. "All right, now you, big fellah. What's your side of the story?"

The Simpa gave Charamir a low bow and a charming smile to replace the odd one, and stood up tall and stiff, his hands behind his back.

"I am Talon, of the clan Vahn, member of the class known as Bishop," the rumbling were-lion said. "We are holy men blessed with magic, and charged with the spreading of the word of our god Liso and our goddess Lison. The boy in question heard our god's calling, and came to the city seeking aid and fellowship. He was pointed in my direction, and I happily took him into my home, to give him answers to his many questions. He told me of his father's wishes for his life, and told me as well that he wanted no part of the ancient war over the Allenian Hills region. When this barbarian came upon us, I had just purchased breakfast for my pupil and me, and he attacked me without warrant."

"A bold faced LIE," the Khan cried, thrashing against his cell door. "'Twas you who came at me, Bishop! What sort of peaceful god commands his chosen children to set themselves upon the questing fathers of wayward sons?"

"Gentlemen, please," Charamir held up both hands now. "Let's take a step back and put things in perspective. Desik, do you know where your son is now?"

"Probably at this preacher's house," the Khan said, spitting on the floor. "I want my son back, officer, and out of this zealot's grasp! I want to have this preacher arrested for kidnapping!"

"I kidnapped no one, brute!" Now there was a flush of anger in the large Simpa's face, and Charamir could see the desire for murder in those cavernous green eyes. "You were the one trying to hold him against his will! Against the will of the gods Liso and Lison! You, blasphemer! You!"

Charamir stomped one heavy foot on the floor, and brought silence to the hallway.

"All right. We're going to get the third side of this story right now, the truth," Charamir said. "Every story has three sides to it. Side one, side two, and the truth. The boy will offer the third side, I should think.

"You," he shouted, addressing the officer who had just come out of the locker room. "Write down this man's address." The Lou pointed to the Simpa Bishop. "Send a couple of officers to pick up a Khan youth there. Have the boy brought here, to me, and we'll straighten this whole mess out."

The watchman took the address and darted past the Lou and up toward the front desk.

Charamir frowned. "Gentlemen, settle in and be silent. We're going to be absolutely silent until the boy gets here."

* * * *

Thirty minutes later, after both the Khan and the Simpa had been waiting patiently on their bunks for 'the boy' to arrive, two patrolmen came down the General Holding hallway with a Khan youth between them, each officer holding an arm just under the elbow. They deposited the boy in front of Charamir, who took in the family resemblance between his prisoner and the youth. "Hello there, son," Charamir said with a soft smile. "You're Tesik, correct?"

"Yes, Tesik, son of Desik, of the clan Mortis. Your men claim that my father is here?"

Charamir stood aside, revealing the boy's father to him. "I see. Ah, I see you have my teacher here as well," the youth said. "What do you intend to do with them, officer?"

"Well," Charamir said slowly, drawing out the 'l' for a moment. "That partially depends on what you have to tell me. Now, the two of you are going to be absolutely silent for this, or I'll have you both charged with public assault." Charamir addressed both men but kept his eyes on the boy. "Now, tell me what happened this morning, to the tee. And no lies, Tesik, unless you want both of these men to go to jail, and yourself with them."

Tesik nodded, and his father sat gloomily on the floor of his cell. The Bishop, Charamir noted from the corner of his eye, simply sat cross-legged on the floor, no trace of emotion on his face.

"Well, I should begin when I left the Hills, officer. My father wanted me to take the test of the warrior, which I had no wish to do. I had told my father many times that I heard a voice telling me to abandon the Allenians and the way of the warrior. I sought teaching where I knew I could find it--here, in Ja-Wen. When I first arrived, though, I was lost. I didn't know where to go, or what to do. That was when Father Talon found me, only a few hours after my arrival. He told me the god Liso had told him of my coming, and that he was to be my instructor.

"This morning marked the tenth day of my instruction and the first day of many tests that I am to go through. First, the Father bolstered my stamina with a good meal, after which we were to head to the fields due west of the city for my first test. That was when my father fell upon us, screaming bloody murder and threatening Father Talon."

"He told you no lies, boy," Desik raged, on his feet once more.

Charamir whipped his tail toward the cell, banging the bars of the cell with a loud clang.

"Sit down, Desik, and let the boy finish his side of things! Now, please continue, son." He smiled once more at the Khan youth.

"Thank you. I tell no lies, officer, for that is what occurred. My father threatened violence, and when he did so, Father Talon wrapped me in a defensive barrier spell of the Bishop school of magic. No sooner had he done so then my father tackled him to the ground, seeking to bludgeon him with his bare fists. However, Father Talon was able to deflect most of the blows, and returned only one in kind to my father's face. When they were both back on their feet, Father Talon merely parried and tossed my father about on the ground. Once my father took a hard fall on his chest, but still he came at my teacher. That was when the other policemen came. I fled the scene, and headed back to my teacher's home, as I had been instructed to do if there was ever trouble. That's the truth, officer. That's all of it."

Charamir nodded, and crossed his arms over his chest as he mulled the situation over. If Desik had only chosen his words better, there would have been no arrest made. If he had demanded the Simpa give up his son, the two men could have fought almost to the death without any interference from law enforcement. However, the Khan had simply threatened death on the Bishop and attacked him. No challenge offered, none accepted, and according to the city's laws, that meant the Khan warrior had to be charged with public assault. But did he? Did he really have to be dragged through the muck? *No,* Charamir decided, shaking his head. *Best to spare the taxpayers the expense of a trial.*

The Lizardman Lieutenant stood up and squared himself with Desik. "You have heard your son's testimony, and now we know the simple truth of things. In accordance to city law, I should have you sent to the trial cells, but I don't think it needs to go that far. Your son has expressed his wish to follow the Bishop path, and the good Father Talon wishes to teach him. Your son will be well cared for, I'm sure. Won't he, Father?"

"Indeed he shall, you speak true," the Simpa Bishop said, his hands still folded in his lap.

"And Tesik, is it still your wish indeed to follow the Bishop way?" Charamir asked, raising a scaled eyebrow at the boy.

"Indeed, it is," the boy said, giving the same bow that the Simpa had.

"Then this last question is for you, Desik of the clan Mortis. Will you let your boy live his life as he wishes?"

The Khan warrior dropped his chin to his chest, knuckles standing white on his hands as he gripped the bars of his cell. He growled deep in his throat, and let his hands drop from the cell bars. Desik sauntered to the back of his cell and kicked the brick wall roughly, sending a small tremor through the wall and floor that Charamir could feel in his feet and wandering tail. Desik came back to the bars, and hung his head. He raised his upturned palms in defeat.

"Yes, I relinquish my claim on him, though he is still but a boy. You, however," he said, pointing across to the Simpa. "You will send me routine messages of his progress and well-being. If I find I have reason at any time to come back for him, you had better steer clear of me. Understood?"

The Bishop smiled, nodded amiably, and got to his feet.

"Good," Charamir said. "This business is settled then. Father Talon, I'm going to let you out first. You take the boy back to your home for now. Let the testing go until tomorrow. An hour after you're gone, I'll release you," he said, turning now to Desik. "Please don't give my officers any reason to arrest you again, because next time you will go to trial."

He turned to the watchman and motioned for him to unlock the Bishop.

Father Talon stepped out, and was embraced immediately by the boy. The two of them left, speaking in hushed tones to one another, not a word of their conversation understood by anyone they passed.

"Watchman, one hour and you let him go," the Lou said, pointing to the Khan warrior. "I'll be up in my office if I'm needed again. If I'm needed," he said, pointing to the watchman on duty meaningfully. "Be sure you're at the desk, not in the back."

* * * *

When Charamir finally got settled in behind his desk to read the morning's reports, what he read wasn't entirely reassuring. Over a dozen so-called 'eye witness reports' concerning the Hookman lay before him, skimmed over and dutifully forgotten. Several arrest reports regarding small time thieves being caught in the act caught his attention more than they should have, but he needed a break from the Hookman case at the moment, and he poured every bit of his focus into these.

"Hmm, no surprise," he mused, looking at the race of each of these criminals: Wererats, every one of them. Their kind just seemed naturally attracted to criminal and illegal activity.

These too he set aside eventually, looking at the timepiece on his wall. Almost one in the afternoon, and he hadn't gotten lunch.

Charamir walked around his desk to his office door, and called out for Hollister. The turtle man dutifully appeared a moment later, saluting. "Sir?"

"Tim, could you send someone down to the Happy Burger? I'm sort of missing lunch right now."

"Sure thing sir," Hollister replied. He pulled a small notebook and a pen from somewhere in the mysterious depths of his shell. "What do you want sir?"

Charamir rattled off a short order, a handful of Happy Burger Supremes, a large carton of fries, and an extra order of chicken strips for good measure. He was pretty sure he wasn't going to be going off duty for a while yet, and might very well let dinner slip his mind as well.

Hollister hustled downstairs, where Charamir was certain some poor patrolman just coming on duty was going to be stuck with the actual errand. *Oh well*, he thought, returning to his desk, *I had to pull my fair share of gopher duties when I was a street beater.*

Charamir returned to the eye witness reports, picking one out at random from the pile, and read it over thoroughly. A middle-aged Jaft by the name of Ho'kra Mandoom had apparently seen a man rushing out of the alley next to the crime scene last night, a man with a hook in his left hand. The wording, Charamir realized, was different in this report from all of the others, one vital way. "*In* his left hand," Charamir whispered to himself, musing. "Not *for* a left hand," he said, again in a hushed voice. He looked from this report to another witness statement, which said only that the individual being questioned heard a bit of ruckus from the apartment above her own.

When Charamir's food was brought in, he tore into it with a vengeance, shooing away the uniform who brought it to him.

After three of the five burgers slid down his gullet, he stomped to his door, and called out, "Tobia, in here, now! If he's not here, somebody go get him in the next ten minutes or you're all pulling overtime! Unpaid!"

At the invoking of the term 'unpaid', the detective level of the police precinct turned into a flurry of movement, men running this way and that, calling to each other their proposed routes of inquiry in search of detective Vincent Tobia.

Fifteen minutes later, the heavyset detective was standing in the Lou's doorway, smiling his sarcastic grin. A toothpick waggled at the corner of his mouth, and he picked it out and stuffed it away in a coat pocket. "You wanted to see me?"

Charamir simply nodded, indicating the seat across the desk from him. He wiped his lips with a napkin, and let out a thundering belch as Tobia closed the door behind him. "Nice one, Lou, very nice. Seven out of ten."

"Thanks, Vince," Charamir said, pushing the Jaft's statement across to him along with one other. He had taken the time to underline the most important, at least in his mind, set of words on both statements. "Now, read the one on your right first," Charamir said. Tobia picked up the right hand document and scanned it briefly. "Anything stand out to you?"

"No, not really. Same crap, different paperwork. Am I supposed to notice something here, Lou?" Charamir smiled derisively, and took the reports back, underlining the selected sections that caught his eye. He handed them back to the detective, and as Tobia adjusted his tie, his eyes widened. He brushed sweat off of his forehead with one considerably large forearm, and tapped the witness report that stood out. "This guy says the perp was carrying a hook. Everybody else told us the guy had a hook for a hand!"

"Precisely." Charamir dug into one of his remaining burgers. He let it slop down onto its wrapper, and set the half-eaten load of greasy-meat-and-rabbit-food-on-a-bun down. He wiped his hands on a napkin, and folded them together with the napkin between. "Vince, where in the city of Ja-Wen would we find somebody who uses a hook in his or her chosen vocation?"

Tobia appeared to consider this a moment as he set the reports down on his side of the large desk, clearing his throat. "And for the gods' sakes, you can take that tie right off, man."

Tobia nodded, ripped the tie off, and stuffed it in one of his pockets.

"I'm thinking either a butcher shop, or one of those moving outfits," the heavyset detective said. "The movers use big hooks to move wooden packing crates if they can't get a good hold with their hands. I know, Jeanie and me used a few of those crates when we moved from 82nd over to 14th last year."

"The hooks," Charamir said slowly, thinking things through, trying to use his imagination. *This is it,* he thought, *the two men in this office right now are the only ones who really have any idea how to carry out this case. Vince will handle all of the facts, and I'll have to get inside this psycho's head. Strange, but it's going to work*. "Did they look like they could be used as weapons?"

"Hell yeah," Vince said, scrunching up his face and rubbing his throat. "One of those stupid lunks nearly caught me in the neck when I came out of the house to grab my fishing gear! He came back with the hook like so," he said, rearing his right arm back to demonstrate. "I was only a couple of feet away. If Jeanie hadn't called out to me to ask me ta bring in the china box too, that asshole would've either slit my throat or left me uglier than I already am!"

"Hard task to accomplish, I imagine." Charamir stood with a smile, standing up and offering the last burger to Vince, who declined with a wave of his hand.

"You're not exactly prepared to win any beauty contests there, scale-face," Tobia retorted amiably. "I'm gonna head on over to the Manlifters office and start asking some questions of the supervisors. May as well start somewhere, right?"

Charamir nodded, and off Vince Tobia went, out of the office and then the precinct.

Charamir headed over to his window that faced out into the streets of the city, and pulled two of the slats apart, taking a hard look into the faces of the myriad people who flowed here and there. Most of them would awaken tomorrow morning with simple thoughts in their heads, many concerned with nothing more than the business of working their job, feeding their families, and taking care of the rent and other bills.

Would another citizen of his precinct, of his city, be killed on the end of a hook before dawn?

* * * *

Around eleven-thirty at night, Charamir decided it was time to call it a day. He gave up his office to the night commander happily, and changed out of his dress uniform into a pair of blue slacks and a white button shirt with short sleeves. He reached into the beaten armoire in the corner of his office and took out his tan trench coat, slinging it over his left arm, and resituated his weapons on his belts and back strap.

Out in the city, the street lamps had been lighted by members of the night watch, the torch light flickering and illuminating the streets with a downy light. A thin, moist fog roiled through the streets of Ja-Wen, giving the city around Charamir a sort of ethereal glow and atmosphere.

"'Here for but a blink of the eye', my friend," he whispered to himself, his forked tongue darting in and out of his mouth to get a good whiff of the night air.

Something smelled awful, and a few minutes later, heading toward his usual watering hole, he was approached by a pair of beggars, who he instantly identified as the source of the funk in the air. He gave them a few gold pieces, warned them not to waste it on booze, and headed off again for his own liquid enjoyment.

His tavern of choice was a dingy little tavern on Tankard Street, the busiest drinking area in the whole of the city. The tavern's title was The Scaled Gullet, and catered mostly to his people and Draconus.

Like almost every other bar in the whole of Tamalaria, however, it was owned and bartended at all times by a Dwarf. As he pushed open the full-sized door, the cerulean tinted air of the bar's interior blew past his body to mingle with the fog, and the door creaked shut behind him.

The inside of The Scaled Gullet was decked out in a humble fashion, with plain hardwood plank flooring, simple oak tables in the shape of sewing spindles, and large stones for seats. Lizardmen and Draconus preferred this arrangement because they were natural rock dwellers. It was the reptile in them, they mostly assumed. The bar itself was a long, low affair, kept at about the average Lizardman's waist height so that Horace, the owner and present bartender on duty, could more easily tend his patrons. Low, seat-shaped stones on spinning bases stood rooted to the floor in front of the bar, only two of these having occupants tonight as Charamir approached.

Cigarette smoke chuffed from the corner of Horace's mouth, and could easily be blamed for three-quarters of the tavern's air coloration. The stocky Dwarf consumed about three packs a day, and had a slowly developing case of the Black Rot, which would probably kill him in about fifteen more years. Whenever he started to hack and wheeze and people asked him if he was all right, he would reply by simply chuffing away a huge cloud of smoke into their face.

He looked up from the mug he presently held in one hand, wiping it out with a cloth in the other, and smiled broadly at the sight of one of his best paying customers.

"Oy, 'ow you doin' boss," he asked as Charamir settled himself into a chair a few seats down from the Lizardman and Lizardwoman at the left end of the bar. "The usual?"

"Yes, the usual Horace." Charamir draped his coat over the back of his seat, letting most of it spill on the wooden floor, and took the glass tumbler full of gin from Horace. The Dwarf brought him a mug full of house ale and set it next to the small tumbler, and smiled as Charamir pushed seven tin pieces across the counter to him. Silver was no longer used as currency in Ja-Wen--too many lycanthropes.

Charamir downed the gin in one go, and grimaced as it burned its way down to his stomach, where it splashed and mixed with the remaining burger he'd eaten from his lunch before leaving the department house.

"This Hookman case really has you bent, don't it," Horace asked the Lou as he set to wiping down the bar with an oiled rag.

Charamir smiled easily at the barkeep, who had an ear to lend to anyone willing to talk, and who never repeated what was said to him, not even for money. Horace stood only three feet tall, but his integrity, Charamir thought, stood miles above his head.

"Yes, Horace, yes it does. How can you tell?" He tipped back his mug of ale and drained half of its contents.

Horace merely pointed to the empty shot tumbler and the half-emptied mug still in the Lizardman Lieutenant's hand.

"Oh, yes. I don't usually move so quickly, do I?"

"Nope. Not unless, that is, a case has you bent. 'S a little thing, but I have two good eyes in me head, and you've been comin' 'ere for years, bucko," Horace said.

"Ever consider becoming a cop?" Charamir asked, finishing off his ale and wiping his scale-hardened lips.

Horace belly laughed and shook his head, spraying a little cleaning solvent on the bar and wiping it off with a fresh rag, leaving the dark wood of the bar gleaming.

"Can't say as I have since I left the force back in Traithrock, friend," Horace said. "That was a crazy toim, too. The War of Vandross, you know. Last great war this continent has seen for a while, thankfully." His eyes glazed over slightly as he lost himself in memory.

"You serve in the battlefronts?"

"Who, me? No, no, I was just a constable, you understands," Horace said, shaking his head slightly to clear it of memory. "No, we was never loik this city's system. Coppers and milit'ry men was always separate entities, ye ken it. I never saw action in that war."

The Dwarven barkeep paused for a moment before continuing. "Say, have you considered bringin' in outside help on this case? Maybe a Bounty Hunter?"

"No," Charamir said, thumping his empty mug down on the counter, hard. He flushed with hot pride and frustration. "I'll not resort to that. Myself and one of my detectives are working hard on this, and I'm not going to hand things off to some freelance braggart! Not a chance, Horace," he said more levelly.

"Sorry, mate. It's just, you know, I happen to know there's a really good one in town." Horace let the statement hang in the air.

"Portenda?" Charamir raised a reptilian eyebrow. He shook his head and laughed rather sarcastically. "I think not, Horace. Word is he just left town for Desanadron, in the west. He owns an apartment building there, too. Seems to me he owns property just about everywhere these days."

"Oy, I think that's what he wants to do full-toim when he retires from the whole Bounty Hunting gig." Horace returned to the duty of cleaning mugs, which barkeeps the multi-verse over seem to be constantly catching up with.

Charamir thanked Horace for the drinks, and got up, grabbing his coat and heading out of the smoke-stained air into the foggy streets of the city.

The fine white street-clouds had thickened and started to swirl about in strange little whippoorwills as Charamir started off for his abode.

Somewhere in the streets of his precinct, a young bard played the last notes he'd ever strum out of his guitar, as a large metal hook came around from behind him and speared into his throat.

* * * *

"What a fuckin' mess," Vince Tobia said in the pre-dawn hours of the following morning. He had just returned to the latest crime scene with Charamir in tow, the Lizardman dressed in a simple pair of khaki pants and a blue button shirt with a yellow tie. Little pictograms of lizards and snakes basking on heated rocks dotted the tie here and there, a gift from his ever-loving sister a few years back.

Charamir thought it was a cute little tie, but damned if the thing didn't choke him. He loosened it as he looked down at the shocked visage of the slain drifter, a hole punched in his neck, blood pooled around his head.

The mess Tobia referred to was the long, deep crush of civilians and reporters trying to push past the dozens of uniformed officers that responded to secure the area. Someone in the crowd screamed, "Why isn't anything being done about this? When are we going to be safe from this maniac?"

Humans, Charamir thought. *Too many of them in this city, and most of them too young to remember the terror Richard Vandross brought down on the city.* Compared to that war, the Hookman was a teddy bear.

But with more and more newspapers cropping up all over the continent, and the Gnomes setting up these 'radio transmission towers' for broadcast of world events from one place to another in a manner of mere hours, the police and militaries of the realm were coming under more and more pressure to 'hop to it'. Civilians started forming protest groups to force their local governments out of power. Citizen watch-groups sprung up in the smaller hamlets and townships. Science, technology, and the modern media conspired to bring about an age of information-sharing, and Charamir thought the whole continent would be better off the way it had been for centuries.

"Sir, sir, Kent Fishman with the *North Ja-Wen Babbler*! Can I have a minute to ask you a few questions," some huckster cried out from the press of bodies before the guarding officers.

Charamir looked up from the body at the reporter, a Human fellow who looked like he'd just been informed of the late-breaking news on his way to the bathroom for his morning piss.

"Vince, could you take care of that man," Charamir asked softly, turning back to the body. He heard some muffled grunting from the reporter's direction, and then heard a high-pitched shriek of pain. Someone hollered 'police brutality,' another of the new media's favorite terms, and Charamir hunkered down next to the medical examiner, who was jotting her final notes on the subject as the cadaver wagon pulled up with its two-horse team in the lead.

"Final conclusion, doc?" He looked into the face of the female Gnome as she stood to her full height of two and a half feet.

She stared bleakly up at him, her eyes still full of sleep and a touch of sorrow.

"Killed sometime around midnight last night." She glanced at her notes. "Single puncture wound to the throat with a hook. Probably bled out before the lack of oxygen had a chance to make him really suffer." She sighed heavily. "I gave him two gold coins a few days ago."

Charamir nodded and looked down at the medical examiner for a long moment. He knew she lived over in the 9th district, which would place this man in the Fourteenth Precinct just a few days before. A bard, a drifter, but one who apparently hadn't been doing too well over that way.

"Anything else, Leah?"

"Well." She scrunched up her thinly bearded face. "This fellow just came into town not too long ago. And from what I've gathered about all of the other victims, none of them had been in town for more than a few months."

Charamir thought it over, recalling his conversation with Tobia the day before. *Movers,* he thought. *Every one of the victims has been relatively fresh in town.*

That's it! I have to talk to Vince, he thought, scanning the area for the pudgy detective.

"Sir?"

"Where's Tobia? Did you see where he went after he took care of the reporter?"

"No sir," Leah said.

Charamir tried to look over the heads of the assembled officers and citizens, but his view was obstructed by two large Minotaurs in uniform.

The Lizardman dashed into the crowd, parting them with thickly muscled arms, and found Vince Tobia near the back end, trying to push his own way back through.

"Vince! Follow me!"

Tobia asked no questions, and soon the two officers were a good two hundred yards away from the mob. "Vince, I think I've worked out the Hookman's motive, or at least his pattern of victims!"

"What? There is no pattern, sir." The Human detective pulled his superior out of the main road before he could be run down by the cadaver wagon.

Leah waved to the two of them as she bumped along on the back of the open wagon, and they nodded to acknowledge that they'd seen her as well.

"Sir, they vary in age, gender, race," Vince Tobia started.

Charamir waved his hand back and forth, catching Vince's attention and silencing him.

"Vince, Leah was actually the one to give me the idea, and you too." Charamir's heart was beating rapidly now. "None of the victims have been long-time residents. They're all from out of town. They're outsiders, Vince! Which means our man is either a mover, or someone who at least has a thing against newcomers into the city. Maybe a little bit of both. Did you find out anything interesting yesterday from that moving company you went to check out?"

"Um, hold on a minute." Vince reached into his inner breast pocket. He drew out a green memo pad, and flipped it open. He slipped past a few pages and came to his latest entries. "Here we go, sir. One of the part-timers, Ton'tara Mekshu, just quit to go join the Pro Relocation Company. They've got a warehouse and all of their moving wagon trains over on Hailstorm Road, in the thirtieth district. That's Fifth Precinct territory, sir," Vince said, eyeballing his boss worriedly.

"Something wrong with the Fifth that I should know about, Vince?" Charamir crossed his sizable arms over his chest, and waited for the detective to answer, because the man wasn't normally the sort to look worried or hesitate like he was doing at that moment.

"Well, sir, it's nothing big, really," Vince Tobia lied. "Just a simple misunderstanding between professionals."

Charamir took a moment to consider Vince's reputation, his mannerisms, and his past record. The man had a fairly clean slate, though several of his former partners throughout the system had complained about his often brutal interrogation tactics. He'd even made a full-grown Khan man cry once by consistently mashing the poor slob's balls with his size ten loafers. Charamir hadn't cared much about that, though; the suspect in question was a rapist, already convicted and sent through corrections once. Without his tool of the trade, maybe he'd learn something different.

"And how simple was this misunderstanding, Vinny? Was it politics? Was it a fistfight? Did you fuck his sister or something?"

"Um, well, sir, his sister's my wife, actually," Vince Tobia confessed. "Jeanie has a brother who's a sergeant over in the Fifth, and they never got along too well. I was at the Spotted Goose a few months back, and he happened to walk in and start talking trash about her to me. I, sort of broke a chair over his head, sir," Vince said awkwardly.

Somehow, Charamir wasn't entirely surprised. He'd seen Vince defend his wife's honor on a few occasions, because apparently she'd been a bit of a tramp in her youth. Vince didn't truck with anybody who claimed to be an ex-boyfriend or, more infuriating to the man, an 'ex-customer' of hers.

Charamir patted Vince on the shoulder and started to lead him around the corner onto Elven Ear Avenue.

"No worries, detective." He gave the man a companionable shake. "I'll do all of the talking. Just leave things to me, Vince, and we'll get all the cooperation we need."

* * * *

"I'm very sorry, Lieutenant, and I sympathize, but we simply won't cooperate with this savage you call a detective," Captain Violet Arrowhead said as she seated herself behind her desk.

"I beg your pardon." Charamir was stunned almost to the point he couldn't speak. Here was a fellow police officer, a pleasantly husky Storm Tribe Werewolf woman in her full bestial state and wearing a power suit with knee-length pant sleeves, smiling at him as she refused to offer assistance. "Violet, we've got a serial killer on our hands and we may be able to get closer to him! You've got to let us work the area!"

"I don't *have* to let you do anything, Lieutenant," she replied, using the rank with emphasis. Her gray fur was slicked to her skin with sweat on this hot, muggy day, and for just a moment, Charamir found himself wondering what she looked like in her humanoid form. He brushed the thought aside, and glared angrily at her. "And you will address me as Captain, Lieutenant Kooteck. At least so long as my office door is open."

Vince Tobia huffed aloud, stood up, and went to the door, exiting the office and pulling the door shut behind him.

"There, that's settled," Charamir said, moving over to the door and office windows, shutting the blinds. He whirled toward the Captain, who had crossed one hairy leg over the other and leaned back in her comfy swivel chair. She undid the top two buttons of her blouse and started fanning herself with a manila folder on her desk. "Now let's get something straight between you and I, Violet. I like you, as a person and as an officer of the law. But you're being highly unprofessional here."

"I don't think so, Charamir." She stood and slid open one of her windows that overlooked the city. Her office, unlike his, was four stories up instead of only two, because the Fifth Precinct housed the city's Anti-Gang Unit on the second and third story. She turned to face him, and sat down easily on the windowsill, shifting her form into her humanoid state.

Hot damn, Charamir thought. *She's gorgeous!* He shook his head, cleared the thought from within, and tried to pry his eyes away from her ample breasts and set them on her face. It took a few tries, and she laughed openly at him, noticing the effort it took. "I'm being very professional. I'm taking over this part of the investigation."

"Bullshit, Violet," he snarled, sitting down heavily in one of the visitors' chairs. He put his feet up on her desk, which apparently didn't blow over too well with her, because her body involuntarily shifted right back to her bestial state. "You're turning this into a pissing contest, and all because my detective happened to break a chair over one of your grunts' head."

"That could have been brought to the attention of the Commissioner, Char, and I did you and that fat son of a bitch a huge favor not doing just that," the Captain countered right away. She flew around the desk and pushed his legs off of it.

He could smell her thick musk odor on the tip of his reptilian tongue, saw the swelling and retreating of her chest as she panted in the heat and anger. *Oh, couldn't you do that in your humanoid state? It'd look soooo much better,* he thought, giving in once again to his more carnal instincts and thoughts.

"I know, Violet, and I can't begin to tell you how much we thank you for that. But we caught this thing first, and I want to nab this fucker myself." Charamir got slowly to his feet.

In her bestial state, Violet stood a full inch and a half taller than Charamir, though in her humanoid state she was a foot shorter than he. The smell of her sweat, the swell of her chest, and the slenderness of her body even in this form, all conspired to turn this meeting into one big come-on for him, and he fought against it with all of his willpower. "Please, just, let us do our job."

She grinned widely at him then, showing rows of dagger-like teeth only inches from his face. She took one step closer to him, and to his own horror, he could feel a part of himself rubbing against her thigh.

Well, that's embarrassing, he thought. "Is that the *only* reason you're here, Char," she cooed, leaning her lupine snout in close to the side of his reptilian head. "Because you know, what you're thinking of besides your job is pretty taboo stuff." She whispered those last words directly into his ear slit.

Charamir, remembering the real reason he was here, took several flustered steps back and watched her throw her head back and laugh as she took on her humanoid form. She shook her head gently, and smiled invitingly at him. "All right, I'll give you clearance. But only because I like you, Char." She returned to her seat behind her desk. "When you've wrapped this Hookman case up, why don't you and I have a little, well, less professional chat." She eyeballed the bulge at the front of his pants that refused to go away.

He cleared his throat loudly, and made the 'eyes up here' gesture with his right hand.

"I think I'd like that," he said with an awkward smile. "And Violet," he said, opening the office door.

She looked up from her paperwork and raised an eyebrow.

"Thanks." He pulled the door shut behind him, and found Vince Tobia standing off a few feet to one side of the door, sipping coffee out of a Styrofoam cup.

"Everything go okay in there?" Vince asked, sipping his coffee.

"Just fine," Charamir said, sighing heavily. He looked down at his groin, and was pleased to see that it had finally calmed itself down for the sake of his integrity. "We've got the go-ahead. Let's get the hell out of here."

"Not too friendly, was she," Vince asked with a half-assed grin. "Still sore about me clobbering my brother-in-law?"

"A little bit, Vince, just a little bit," Charamir lied. He'd done an awful lot of that lately, he thought.

* * * *

Ton'tara Mekshu, it turned out according to his supervisor, had just headed out that morning to service a move paid for the week before. "Guy's a real blessing," the Elf supervisor said as he offered the officers a cup of coffee while they walked with him through the warehouse. "Any time someone asks for the day off, he's willing to come in and work the shift for them. He gets a lot of hours, all times of the day, too." The supervisor stopped in front of a set of shelves to log in new inventory. "He tells me he was born and raised here in the city."

"Mr. Waters," Charamir said, pulling out a notepad of his own. "What's Ton'tara's race?"

"Oh, he's a Human," the supervisor, Waters, said. He didn't take his eyes from the shelves or his clipboard.

"And, does he mention anything about his political views or opinions, Mr. Waters?" Vince looked over at his superior with a skeptical look, but was pleasantly surprised by the supervisor's response.

"Well, he does seem like a bit of an isolationist." Waters turned to face the officers as he marked the final box on his sheet. He tucked the clipboard under his arm, and directed Charamir and Vince to a square card table that many of the employees used to eat their lunch at or play poker. "He doesn't mind moving folks from one part of the city to another, but he really grumbles when some out-of-towner decides to go from temporary digs at one of the hotels to a permanent residence. Of course, a lot of the guys do," Waters said.

Charamir and Vince exchanged a quick, grinning nod, and turned their attention back to the supervisor again. "Has he made any abnormal requests, Mr. Waters? Anything out of the ordinary?"

The supervisor appeared puzzled, and crossed his arms defensively. *Oh boy,* Charamir thought. *This is where he asks...*

"What's this all about anyway, gentlemen," Waters asked. "If you suspect or know something about one of my employees, I want to know about it right now." The Elf took off his baseball cap and set it down on the table.

Vince brought the conversation to a close before Charamir could think of how to respond, thankfully. He stood up, sighed, and stretched.

"Thank you for your time, Mr. Waters. We'll be getting back to you."

As the two detectives started down the street, Vince paused to pop a cigarette into his mouth, and struck a match on the seat of his pants, lighting and puffing on his smoke. "What *was* that last question about, chief," he asked Charamir.

The Lizardman liked and respected Vince Tobia, as well as Leah the medical examiner, but something that her reports revealed to him that it hadn't to her or the pudgy Human detective leapt to his mind.

"Vince, do you remember the Seventh District Slasher," Lieutenant Kooteck asked, guiding his associate around the corner.

The Fifth Precinct's territory was home to a dense population of criminal hangouts, pawnshops and street-side food vendors, and Charamir unerringly veered for a hotdog huckster. "Two dogs, mine with ketchup and relish. Vince?"

"Mustard and sauerkraut," the detective said without so much as a glance at the Half-Jaft vendor. "Yeah, I remember that hump. Went around the Seventh District hacking up hookers. Seven victims all totaled, hey thanks Mack." He tossed his half-smoked cigarette to the cobblestone street to smolder itself out. "And when they finally caught him, they found a bunch of the girls' parts in his ice box. He'd been nibblin' on 'em for weeks." Vince bit into his weighted hotdog.

Charamir raised an eyebrow at the vendor, who had turned from his natural light blue shade to a sickly green in the face.

"Vince, let's take this conversation elsewhere." The Lizardman moved away from the squeamish vendor.

As soon as he felt they were safely out of earshot of the half-breed, he continued for the detective, who was still chewing his food. "Yes, we found him because someone mentioned that the good doctor seemed to be keeping the strangest night hours. A uniform officer made a note of it, and brought it to the attention of Major Suren over at the Eleventh."

"The bodies had been cut apart with surgical precision," Tobia supplied as Charamir tore into his own early lunch. "Body parts removed. I think the M.E. on that one was Coburn." Vince Tobia chuckled. "I remember for a while we were running around all of the examiners' offices, checking them out just to make sure, ha ha!"

Charamir didn't join in his laughter, because Leah, who worked almost exclusively with their department, had taken a large amount of offense to having her own lab rummaged through as if she were a common criminal. Charamir had still been a detective at the time, but he'd already developed a mutual respect with the Gnome woman. That case and the inquisition brought down on the heads of the city's examiners had nearly destroyed the good working relationship that he prized so much.

"Chief, what's your point in bringin' that old news up?" Vince tossed his empty wrapper into a refuse bin.

"My point is, HEY YOU TWO," the Lizardman suddenly roared, pointing to a pair of young Wererats who were handing something in a small white baggy to a teenage Human. The entire trio looked up at the officers as Vince drew out his badge and his baton. Thunder magic crackled around the wood of his weapon, and Charamir smiled wickedly at the little criminals.

Before he and the detective could so much as take a step forward, the three youths screamed and darted in three different directions, dropping their baggies and money to the street. Charamir had only been addressing the drug dealers, but since all three had left without their things, he felt even better.

Vince headed across the street and picked up the baggy, looking at it critically. He opened it, took a whiff, and his eyes watered, widening as Charamir approached.

"What was it?" the Lieutenant asked.

Vince Tobia walked a few feet, and started dumping the contents down an open gutter vent.

"Slipstream," the detective said, shaking the baggy out and then dropping it, too, down the drain. "Nasty shit, sir. Works on Humans, Elves, Gnomes and Lizardmen mostly. Dangerous."

"Narcotics on it?"

"Oh yeah, and don't worry sir, I've got a few drinkin' buddies over at the Second where they're based out of," the heavyset Human said, standing up. "I'll have them come around the area and scope it out. Now, what you was saying before. About the Slasher and the Hookman, because I hope you're going to tie this together for me."

Indeed I shall, Charamir thought. He pitied Vince his lack of imagination, but damned if the man wasn't valuable. He remembered every case that Charamir referred to, even if he hadn't worked it himself. Charamir attributed Vince Tobia's encyclopedic knowledge of the city's legal history to his love of law enforcement. If ever a post of command were offered to him, Vince would probably refuse, preferring the footwork of a detective. *I think I do too, come to that,* the Lieutenant thought.

"Indeed, I am. We took the connection between the medical examiners' reports on the victims, and coupled it with the offhand comment of a citizen that a foot patrolman had been smart enough to write down, address and all. When all of the factors were added up..." he let the statement hang in the air for Tobia to finish.

"We tracked down the good doctor and found the Slasher," the Human detective said, snapping his fingers. "That's right! Turned out the guy had been a combat medic for years, and his wife started hooking on the side because she didn't think he was giving her enough of an allowance. He turned his rage out on other pros ta get back at her! Okay, so, you're looking for unusual requests made by movers because, why?" Vince lit another cigarette.

Charamir and the detective walked around another corner of the sidewalk toward a coffee shop. The Human wouldn't need the caffeine, but Charamir had only consumed two cups since getting in that morning, and he was sore for another dose.

"Because, Vincent, Leah's reports all state that the wounds were made with a hook. *A* hook, never *the same* hook. Hello, medium coffee, dash of creamer, load of sugar," he said to the pretty young Lizardwoman tending the counter.

Charamir took a moment as the woman turned around to admire the pattern of her scales on the back of her head, as well as the fin-like spines atop her shoulders.

Vince gave him a friendly nudge, and cocked his head toward the serving girl.

Charamir smiled and nodded at his companion, and the two of them looked up when she handed him the coffee and said good-bye. They exited the coffee shop, and Vince laughed out loud.

"Aw man, the look on your face there was precious." He gave the Lieutenant an amiable punch on the shoulder. "You know she was way too young for you, man," he added, to which Charamir raised a hairless eyebrow. Vince planted the cigarette in his mouth, inhaled, and led the ranking officer back down the street, back toward their own Precinct house. "I know how to tell a Lizardman or Lizardwoman's age, sir."

"Oh, so you know about the, ah,"

"Yeah, the size and stiffness of the scales," Vince said. "The smaller the individual scales and the softer, the younger they are. How old are you, sir," he asked with a sardonic grin.

"Oh shut up, Vincent. Look, back to what I was saying." Charamir blew on his coffee and took a sip. He grimaced. "Too much creamer. Anyway, back during the Slasher murders, the medical examiners all agreed that the same weapon had been used to kill the girls, even if several tools were used to dissect them. The reports stated very clearly that the implement of death was the *same* knife. Ergo, my friend," Charamir began.

"If we find a mover who's been requesting new hooks," Vincent Tobia said, his eyes glowing with revelation.

"We find our Hookman."

* * * *

In the early evening, an Elven man dressed in khaki pants and a beige button shirt came upstairs to the detective division of Charamir's

Precinct house. He had in his outstretched hands a large plastic crate, a blue, open-topped affair filled with folders.

Timothy Hollister got up from his desk, one of the few still occupied at this late hour by a daytime officer, and asked the Elf what he could do for him.

"Boss said to send these over." The Elf handed the unwieldy crate to the Sidalis.

Hollister set the crate easily down on his own desk, only requiring one arm.

"What are they," the mutant asked politely, smiling at the Elf as the man handed him a clipboard and a pen.

"Don't know, don't care buddy. Just sign the bottom line." The man tapped his foot impatiently.

Hollister signed the clipboard, and bade the man adieu.

Charamir and Vince Tobia came out of the files office behind Hollister, both of them having spent the last few hours combing through the old notes they kept on the Slasher case to confirm their suspicions from earlier in the day. They had thus far read through five of the seven victim reports, unable to locate the last two, but they indeed did find that every examiner had agreed--the same weapon had been used.

"What's with the crate, Tim?" Charamir asked, rolling down his shirtsleeves.

Hollister had been looking at the copy sheet he had been handed after signing the clipboard. Now he looked up at his superior.

"Well, I don't understand why, Lieutenant, sir, but a man just dropped these off from a moving company." The Sidalis held the sheet out to the Lizardman, who snatched it free, glanced at it, and handed it on to Vince, who had removed his tie hours ago.

Charamir dipped his hands into the crate, took a third of the folders, and headed for his office.

"Vince, you take a section, and you too Tim," he called over his shoulder.

"What am I looking for, sir?" Hollister asked.

Charamir's office door closed with a loud bang, and Vince Tobia fished in for his third of the pile. "Detective Tobia?"

"Employee requests for hooks," Vince grunted as he dropped his heavy load on top of his own desk across the aisle from Hollister.

Tim needed no more explanation than that; he knew this case had been eating away at his Lieutenant. Every commanding officer's first major case ate at them until it lay closed in the file room. Most did not have the good fortune to ever solve their first major case, and they were usually written off as 'unsolvable' because the man or woman in charge simply hadn't seen enough major cases to deal with the situation.

Perhaps, Timothy Hollister thought happily, *Charamir Kooteck will break that mold.*

* * * *

At fifteen minutes past midnight, Vince Tobia finally found what he was looking for. In truth, he had found what he was *not* looking for almost immediately. Their primary suspect hadn't requested a single new hook since working for the new moving company. He had, in fact, requested several days off to get married to a woman he'd met from out of town, and according to the afternoon supervisor's notes, he had changed his opinion of out-of-towners rather quickly.

However, the day shift supervisor, the man they had spoken to earlier in the day, had ordered a crate of mover's hooks from Solomon Strafford's Smithy Shop a week before the first of the Hookman murders. One employee's request for a new hook had been immediately denied by the day shift supervisor. As a week went by, several more requests were put in, each one denied by the Elven man that Vince and Charamir had spoken with that very same day.

"And as you can see here, Vince, the afternoon supervisor just approved a request addressed to him yesterday. He took it from the day shift super's crate in the man's office."

"We have to find him," Vincent Tobia said in a rush.

Charamir shot up from his chair and tore his trench coat from its hook on the wall. "I think the Hookman's next victim is going to be the afternoon supervisor."

"Right," Charamir said with a wicked grin as he strapped his service sword on his hip. "Because the Hookman certainly wouldn't truck with someone else handing out his tools.

"Timothy," Charamir shouted as he ducked out of the office.

The overnight Lieutenant was sitting at an empty desk, waiting for the Lizardman to leave for the night. Both she and the Sidalis shot up from their seats as Charamir called to Hollister.

"Sir," he said, saluting stiffly.

"Hollister, get your mace, you're with us. Chambers!"

The woman stood stiff and erect, suddenly as militant as the Sidalis. "You take care of this house while we're gone! If anything comes in, any news at all, you send me that pigeon." Charamir pointed to the messenger bird that Hollister had appointed to him a few days before.

Chambers nodded, and headed into the commanding officers' office.

Hollister headed off to the equipment room, returning a minute later with his spiked mace on his left hip. "And Chambers!"

The woman returned to the doorway, standing to attention once again.

Charamir smiled benevolently at her, and said, "And if any newsies come snooping around, break their ever-scribbling fingers."

She smiled back finally, and gave him a comical salute.

Charamir's blood was up. He felt the thrill, once again, of the hunt.

****

When the three officers showed up at the Pro Relocation Company's warehouse, they were not at all surprised to find the night watchman inside the small security office, gutted like a fish.

That makes an even ten, Charamir thought bleakly, unsheathing his sword silently from its leather scabbard.

Vince Tobia left his crackling weapon in its loop for the time being, to avoid throwing off light and noise, and Hollister kept the head of his mace low to the floor as the three of them moved stealthily, one by one, through the second door and into the darkened warehouse.

The large interior of the warehouse smelled faintly of dust and grime, and machine oil long since dried into the concrete floor. The moving company used autocarts, useful little mecha devices designed and patented by a Gnome fellow in Desanadron about a year back, and the oil most likely was for them. In the dim gloom of the central chamber, with only moonlight spilling in from the skylights above, Charamir could faintly make out several of the contraptions ahead and to his left. They glinted in the thin moonlight, strange, arachnid-looking devices that ran on an energy source he could not begin to fathom.

Though Charamir and Vince's movements remained still and quiet in the dead air of the warehouse, Hollister was having difficulty. His large, heavy feet clomped whenever he took a normal sized step, and he wound up taking up the rear of their line as they moved along the outer walls of the main warehouse interior.

Makes sense in a way, Charamir thought rather uncharitably. *He's the one with the huge fucking shell armoring his back.* But he didn't think they would be ambushed from behind by the Hookman. He assumed for the time being that their serial killer was up in the supervisors' office, which was set at the top of a set of steps against the wall they were trying to approach by way of sliding along another two. A single torch burned dimly in the sheet metal wall's bracket next to the office door, which Charamir could see was open a crack.

As they slid along the last wall, perpendicular to the one they wanted, Charamir cocked his head to the side and brought up one of his scaled hands. He thought, for a moment, that he'd heard movement out in the center of the warehouse space, somewhere among all of the shelving units and machinery.

He put a finger on his free left hand to his ear slit, and both Tobia and Hollister nodded. *Shit, so he's not in the office. But it's so dark in here, he could be hiding anywhere, waiting for us.*

After all was said and done, Charamir would look back on that night and think that Hollister's devotion to duty and his mutant body had saved the three of them. One of the autocarts' engines blared to life, and a set of blinding light flashed them all in the face as they turned to look at it. Hollister, reacting out of pure instinct, stepped in the way of the autocart as it darted toward them at top speed, smashing aside crates and knocking over shelving units. He turned around and crouched down, pulling his head and arms into his shell, waiting for the impact.

Charamir threw Vince aside and leaped away from Hollister as a maniacal laughter tore through the air.

There erupted a sudden crunching sound, and Charamir thought for just an instant that Hollister's shell had caved in, crushing him under it and the autocart.

He lay sprawled on the floor for a moment, and rolled over onto his back just in time to kick a shadowy silhouette that was standing over him in the crotch.

Thinking he'd just saved himself from the Hookman, Charamir sprang to his feet, and felt Vince's familiar, chubby fingers gouge into his shoulder. "It's me, you fucking dolt," the Human detective growled as he clutched his aching balls.

Charamir, stunned at having struck his own subordinate, looked up then at the crashed autocart. It had crumpled on impact with Hollister, the entire front end crunched up around his shell and leaking thick gobbets of oil from the shattered motor casing. However, there was no driver in the bucket seat, and he scanned the surrounding area with his slowly adjusting eyes, spotting movement a short way off.

The Elven supervisor they'd interviewed earlier was crawling away from the accident, a bloodied hook in his left hand.

Proper procedure would have been to send Vince around one side of the shelving units and take the other, boxing the suspect in and forcing him to surrender. Charamir wasn't feeling quite so generous at the time, however, and he motioned for Vince to help him push on the unit that towered over them. Tobia smiled, and together, the Lizardman and the Human thrust their arms into the shelving unit, slowly toppling it into the next one, which started a domino reaction.

The Hookman looked up for a moment and screamed as thousands of pounds of crates packed to the rim with people's temporarily housed belongings crashed down on top of him.

There was a loud squelch, and a pool of blood started to form from underneath the pile.

Charamir smiled savagely, picked up his discarded sword, and sheathed it. Vince looked at him, hands on hips, panting. "Let's go check on Tim," the Lieutenant said, and together, the three officers exited the warehouse. Their work here was finished.

Out on the streets, a cigarette in his mouth, well-earned as far as he was concerned, Charamir spared one last thought to the Hookman; *Good old-fashioned justice.*

****

Excerpt from the *Ja-Wen Crier*:

Today, officers Charamir Kooteck, Vincent Tobia, and Timothy Hollister were awarded medals of honor from the city's Police Commissioner for finally solving and closing the Hookman murder case.

Through use of standard investigation measures, Lieutenant Kooteck and Vincent Tobia, along with the assistance of a medical examiner, discovered a critical component of the case. When conjoined with information gleaned from interviews with several individuals, officers Kooteck and Tobia discovered the Hookman's motives for killing his victims.

With the assistance of Timothy Hollister, who accepted his medal after being released from a local healer's, the officers cornered and attempted to apprehend the Hookman in Pro Relocation Company's warehouse in the Fifth Precinct's territory. Captain Violet Arrowhead stated that she was aware of the officers' operation, and had given them clearance to proceed on their own initiative and instincts. During the apprehension attempt, detective Hollister was run down by an autocart, and detective Tobia was physically attacked as well. Thankfully, neither officer was seriously injured.

Due to a tremendous amount of resistance, officers Kooteck, Tobia, and Hollister were forced to use lethal force to stop the suspect. However, the city Commissioner had this to say of the trio's actions: 'I have no doubt in my mind that the officers involved exercised every option available to them, resorting to lethal force only as a final and extreme necessity.'

This marks the closure of Lieutenant Charamir Kooteck's first major case since taking command of his Precinct.

Tale Three: The Big Fight

"Are you really sure about this," Lee Toren asked the huge, lumbering Simpa with the tiger stripes on his arms and upper torso. Portenda the Quiet enjoyed a reasonable income as a landlord, a much better one from his Bounty Hunting contracts, and didn't really want for much in terms of material possessions. He consistently found himself somewhat bored, however. He loved to roam the lands of Tamalaria, taking months at a time to simply explore the plains, the forests, the swamps, the hills, and even the dessert known as The Desperation in the southeast.

His big problem lay in the fact that he seldom met a real challenge in combat. He possessed a complete arsenal of both mecha and traditional weapons, from his first .38 revolver to the jagged, beaten spear he still carried on his broad back. He had trained in several forms of unarmed combat, though none for very long, and had a few very peculiar powers at his disposal. Those powers stemmed from one very important fact.

He was a freak of nature.

Portenda was the offspring of a Simpa, or Werelion, father, and a Khan, or tiger-man, mother. The two species had never produced a live birth in all of Tamalaria's history, and never should have. The Gods themselves forbade it. Portenda had received outside interference that allowed him to come into being. Fate and Death had conspired to let him be born into the world, much to his own father's chagrin.

Many months ago, he had aided a Human Alchemist by the name of Jonah Staples in finding and rescuing his sister from the clutches of a mad Alchemist, Genma. Genma had turned out to be Allen Staples, the boy's uncle, and the madman was bent on turning his niece into a clone of his late wife through the use of science. With the aid of Jonah and his girlfriend (who was now his wife), Portenda had tracked down Genma and his tower, and the three of them, with the additional help of a Kobold mage named Kobuchi, destroyed Genma and his tower of Alchemical beasts and monstrosities.

The experience had been a challenge, a welcome one at that, but Portenda still hadn't felt pushed to his limits. However, a contact of his in Desanadron had recently sent him a letter, telling him that if he was really looking for a match, he should track down and challenge a Red Tribe Werewolf by the name of Ignatious Stockholm who lived in the sewers. It was said by Portenda's contact that nobody in the whole of the city was a match for the burly Red Tribesman, and the man offered Portenda ten thousand gold pieces to instigate a fight with this

Stockholm character. Portenda, never one to frown in the face of a hefty paycheck, and learning that Stockholm was a leader in the local thieves' guild, accepted the task immediately.

After nearly a month of traveling in his bestial state across the land from Ja-Wen to Desanadron, Portenda sat in a worn down old tavern, telling Lee Toren, another of his contacts, his plans.

"I only ask because, well, ol' Stocky isn't exactly someone to screw around wif, mate," the Gnome Pickpocket said, quaffing his ale.

Portenda made no reply, simply downing his own drink with measured gulps. "Nobody has any idear how old 'e is, or just what exactly he's capable of. You may want to reconsider this agreement of yours."

"I already sent word to my business friend."

Portenda's low, gravely voice grated against the nerves in Lee's ears. He hated the Simpa Bounty Hunter's voice because it almost never held any sort of inflection aside from anger or violence. Aside from the voice, the man's eyes bothered him the most, so gray, so dead-looking. *Not too much different from Akimaru's,* the Gnome Pickpocket thought. "I told him to expect a show."

"Aw, hell's bells," Lee grumbled. "Well, what're you doing hangin' around here, then? Shouldn't you be out lookin' fer 'im?"

"Nope. And you know why."

Portenda's voice again made Lee wince. Yes, he did indeed know exactly why Portenda had come to this tavern. He'd come here because this was Stockholm's favorite watering hole when he came up to the surface of the city, which was less and less often since the whole Glove of Shadows escapade. The Simpa Bounty Hunter had asked around, made inquiries, and found out from the locals just where and when to expect his opponent. That habit set him apart from other Bounty Hunters. He didn't snoop around and make himself suspicious. He came right out and asked people, often quite politely, about his targets' whereabouts and routines. Often, he got the information he needed with some simple prodding. Nobody could remain hidden from him for long.

Lee Toren almost screamed when the saloon doors pushed inward on the palm of a furry, red arm.

Ignatious Stockholm, standing tall at around seven foot two, his arms and legs like tree trunks, his chest easily a good half a foot broader than Portenda's, sauntered into the tavern with a stiff look on his face. He wore his sleeveless chain shirt over a pair of blue trousers, a loose fitting garment to allow him a full range of motion. He only had two weapons on him, his broad, double-headed war axe on his back, and a rapier sheathed in a simple loop belt on his waist.

Unbeknownst to either Portenda or Lee Toren, Stockholm had his own contacts throughout the city of Desanadron, and he knew full well that someone had been asking after him for the last day and a half. According to most of his contacts, the guy was 'big as an ox and twice as nasty-lookin.' One woman had described him as having 'the deadest eyes I've ever seen.' Stockholm had not only seen the big man sitting with Lee Toren through a tavern window they were seated near, he could smell the bastard a mile off. It was a scent he recognized, because the two men had met once, briefly, in Ja-Wen, during the quest for the Glove of Shadows.

Portenda smelled like death.

Stockholm had an immediate advantage over Portenda, in that Portenda had grown to sort of a public figure throughout Tamalaria. Few people knew who Stockholm was, or how important a man he was to the land.

He also had a disadvantage. He knew he wasn't going to kill his opponent. He didn't think Portenda intended to kill him, but he couldn't be certain.

The Red Tribesman ordered a honey ale from the barkeep, who eyeballed him, then Portenda. He gave Stockholm his large stein of ale, and hustled into the back room, suddenly loaded with important work in the kitchen...where it might be safe.

The other patrons present also found various reasons to excuse themselves, asking their friends' forgiveness, and the friends didn't mind at all, they had someplace to be as well, *and hey, say hello to the wife and kids for me, oh right, you don't have a wife or kids, well, that doesn't matter.*

Lee Toren watched with silent wonder as the tavern cleared of all other life. Despite the free space at the bar and the various assorted empty tables, Stockholm came directly from the bar to the table at which Lee and Portenda sat. "This seat taken," he asked politely, pulling the chair back that Portenda had been resting his feet on.

"No. Please, have a seat, friend," the Simpa Bounty Hunter said levelly, his tone neither raising nor lowering one iota.

"Um, you gents moind if I just, ah," Lee began sputtering.

"Get out of here, Lee," Stockholm said curtly. He saw a flicker of surprise in Portenda's eyes, but the Simpa-Khan hybrid made no other sign of discomfort. Though the Bounty Hunter's powers of perception were supernaturally acute, Ignatious Stockholm's nose was naturally keen as well, and he could smell the traces of both races in this big man's blood. He hadn't noticed that when first the two men had met.

Armed to the teeth, Stockholm thought as he scanned the Bounty Hunter. *Spear on back, sword on hip, small caliber revolver on other side, two frag grenades under the table, and he's keeping his posture relaxed. Oh, he's good.*

From the other side of the table, as Stockholm lifted his stein to take a drink and Lee Toren bolted from the tavern through the window behind him, similar thoughts ran through Portenda's mind. *Gods, he's big. Axe on back, double edged, rapier on hip, though why he'd bother with a pig sticker I don't think I understand. Red Tribe, so his claws probably reach a full eight inches when he extracts them fully, big teeth. His shoulders are slightly slumped, probably expects me to make the first move. Muscles are relaxed, so he's gotta be pretty good at controlling himself. This may be fun after all.*

Portenda prided himself on being ready for anything, anything at all, when it came to a combat situation. Most of his contracted targets didn't guess at his purpose until he struck out at them, but Ignatious Stockholm surprised him after finishing his ale.

The werewolf set his stein down on the table, and leaned back in his chair. "You're here for me, aren't you?" He smiled wickedly.

Not only did the question take the Bounty Hunter off guard, but the half-mad smile at the potential confrontation to soon begin sent a chill up his spine. *Why does this guy bother me so much,* he wondered? *He's just another Werewolf. I've taken plenty of them down. Of course, they're not all the same.*

"And if I am?" Portenda finished the last of his own drink, easing the mug to the table. "What then?" The Simpa Bounty Hunter tensed his legs, ready to spring to either side should the Red Tribe Werewolf choose to launch the first assault.

Stockholm's smile lessened a little, and his eyes closed slightly, taking away the sense of madness in his visage.

"Well, then we'll have ourselves a little problem. You see, I believe violence has a time and a place, where it is appropriate. Perhaps even, essential." Stockholm pushed himself slowly from his seat, taking his stein around the flip-top part of the bar counter, and pouring himself another drink.

He's being awfully casual about this, Portenda thought.

When the Red Tribesman returned to the table, he took Portenda's glass, and headed back, pouring him a drink from the same keg. He returned once more, set the glass down in front of Portenda, and started to take a drink from his own stein. "It's honey ale. Try it. I think you'll like it," Stockholm said.

Ever suspicious, Portenda took a good hard whiff of his drink, and found that he could make out the underlying ingredients. Hops, barley, honey, a little cane sugar, and several other standard ingredients. The Werewolf hadn't tried any dirty shit with his drink, which spoke rather loud volumes to Portenda about the depth of his opponent's character.

He might be a criminal, a leader in the thieves' guild, but an honorable man sat across from him, a member of one of the longest-living tribes of Werewolves in Tamalaria. Red Tribesmen were said to be capable of wielding great magic, but none of the people Portenda had interviewed on his way to Desanadron, or within the city itself, thought they'd ever seen this particular werewolf use a spell of any kind.

What a few folks *had* told him mostly pertained to Ignatious Stockholm's viciousness. Brutal, competent, and efficient, much like himself. A few Monks had even informed Portenda that Stockholm routinely attended large-scale martial arts tournaments. Whenever he entered, he took home the gold. This factor alone kept Portenda from leaving his weapons behind for this challenge; he was a solid unarmed fighter, but he couldn't imagine standing toe-to-toe with the big crimson warrior for long that way.

Portenda tipped his glass back and drank off a healthy portion of his ale. As he brought his head and the glass back down, he paused, genuinely perplexed by the Red Tribesman's activity.

Stockholm held a peppershaker in his left hand, and was shaking the black stuff onto his palm, then dispersing it slowly into his own stein.

Stockholm smiled at the Simpa Bounty Hunter, and returned to his task. "Gives it an extra little kick, I find. Would you like to try?"

This, Stockholm thought as he poured some of the pepper into his hand, *is probably not very fair, but who said a fight had to be fair?*

Portenda pushed his glass forward a little. When he did, his upper body shifted just a few inches toward the werewolf.

Stockholm drew his hand toward the glass, and just before he opened his hand, stuck his snout close to his hand, blowing hard on the pile of pepper in his paw.

The powder flew into Portenda's eyes, and the Bounty Hunter howled with sudden pain and surprise at this underhanded but effective tactic.

Stockholm upended the table, knocking it clear to the other side of the tavern with a crash.

Portenda's vision had blurred into a watery nonsense the moment the first particles of pepper struck his eyes. *Dirty bastard,* he thought, mentally smiling as he howled in rage and shock. *Oh, he's good! He's very good!* Before he could fully clear his vision, he felt the table pull away from his thrashing legs and heard it crash far away on the other side of the tavern.

Stockholm reached down and plucked Portenda up off of the floor with one huge, thickly muscled arm, his thin red fur barely concealing the size of his flexing joints and musculature. His hand on the Simpa's throat, he thrust his hips into Portenda's and hurled him aside, sending the Bounty Hunter crashing through the glass window that Lee Toren had used for escape a few minutes before.

Portenda felt the raw physical power in the Werewolf's body when Stockholm grabbed his throat. By then his vision had improved by a couple of degrees, but he was still essentially blind.

He didn't need his eyes working properly to hear the low rumble of the Werewolf's growl as Stockholm hauled him into the air and hip-tossed him out of the building.

Glass exploded outward, thin shards of it getting through Portenda's thick yellow vest and golden fur.

With his ears tuned up, the impact of his back on the glass rang in his head like a grenade at close range, but he kept enough equilibrium to land in a sliding three-point crouch outside in the street.

Dozens, perhaps scores of people scattered from the surrounding area, none of them wanting anything to do with whatever was going on here.

As Stockholm stepped outside of the tavern through the main door, he looked left and spotted the Simpa, fully stopped in a three-point crouch.

Can't let these people get hurt over this nonsense, Stockholm thought. "Everybody clear out," he shouted, sending a few of the stragglers into a frenzy of movement and confusion.

Portenda, not usually the sort to resort to dirty tricks himself, let the coldness of his professional persona wash over him. The Red Tribesman bellowed a warning for the few remaining people to get out of the way, and when he did, Portenda rose to full height and plucked an unfortunate young merchant off of the sidewalk. With a twist of the man's arm he sent the merchant sprawling toward Stockholm, whose natural instinct was to crouch down and leap forward to catch the man.

As soon as he did, Stockholm pushed the man to his feet and sent him running along, just as Portenda leveled a tremendous punch into his lupine snout.

Blood sprayed and a few of his fangs flew out of his mouth, but Stockholm otherwise took the blow pretty well, only staggering back a few feet. Before he could completely clear his head, however, Portenda drew his .38 revolver, and took careful aim.

"Aw, shit," Stockholm growled. He screamed as three bullets slammed into his left leg, his right forearm, and his stomach. This last impact sent him flying to his back, bleeding onto the dusty street.

Portenda watched each bullet fly its individual course, satisfied that he could now gain a little speed and initiative on the big man. He holstered the revolver, and sniffed deep, drinking in the metallic odor of Stockholm's blood. *So pure,* he thought, tasting the odor a little bit on his tongue. *And so, well, old.*

He drew his spear from behind his back, and prepared to leap up and land with the point down through the Werewolf's chest. He was pretty sure it wouldn't kill him, but it certainly would put a quick end to the fight.

Before he could even crouch for the initial leap, however, Portenda felt the cruel, wooden crack of some piece of outdoor furniture breaking over the back of his legs.

The blunt force of the blow wasn't much, but he now had a sliver under his skin, and the suddenness of the blow made him wonder if perhaps the Werewolf had some sort of telekinetic ability.

When the Simpa Bounty Hunter turned his head, however, he spied the merchant he'd tossed at Stockholm coming at him now with a second porch chair. This one broke over his face, because the man had already been in mid-swing when he looked into the enveloping, terrifying eyes of Portenda the Quiet.

BLAM-CRACK! The chair broke apart across his leonine face, breaking his nose and staggering him. The sound of pounding feet quickly approaching alerted him to Stockholm's approach, but when he instinctively thrust the spear in that direction, it bit nothing but clean air.

Stockholm, watching the merchant attack with a second piece of outdoor furniture, took advantage of his opponent's temporary confusion. He started running in Portenda's direction, and just as the Simpa got his second hand on his spear again, he thrust himself up onto the outer wall of a nearby sundry goods store, running along the front of it like a spider. When the spear lanced out, Stockholm kicked off of the building with uncanny acrobatic grace, and whipped a roundhouse kick into the side of Portenda's head that could kill smaller men.

The moment his spear bit clean air, Portenda saw the incoming blow out of the corner of his eye. *By all the Gods this guy's still too fast!*

KER-runch! Portenda had shifted his weight a little, which helped...some.

Stockholm's kick connected, sending Portenda flying down the road, a limp heap of weapons, light armor and experienced muscle and bones.

As he flew, suspended in the air by the force of his most recent blow, he had just enough time to wonder if, perhaps, he'd made a big mistake in coming here without more thorough information on his target. *Stockholm defied gravity,* he thought as he landed heavily several dozen yards away, sending shocked and fearful citizens in all directions. *How the hell did he do that? And where's my spear?*

Stockholm took a moment to force his regenerative factor to push out the lead slugs that had buried themselves in his body. The came out one by one, painfully squeezing back past torn muscle and blood vessels. The one in his stomach made him howl like a dying animal as it popped back out of his stomach sack, spilling corrosive digestive fluids amid his other organs. He wiped the fur on his forehead back over his sloped, wolfish head, feeling it plaster itself down with slick, briny sweat.

Portenda, up on his dazed feet again, mentally kicked himself in the ass for coming into this whole fight so half-assed and unprepared. He had managed only one decent bit of damage, and that was by shooting the big red prick, but he only had three more bullets chambered, and he didn't truly wish to risk innocent bystanders with a missed shot. "The sword it is, then," he muttered to himself, drawing the big broadsword from his hip.

He stood at the ready as the Red Tribe Werewolf charged down the road at him.

Somewhere else in the city, a rather well-to-do fellow laughed as he watched the play-by-play on a Mage's Eye orb.

* * * *

"My goodness, did you see that," Vernon LeBlanc cried gleefully. His high, reedy voice echoed throughout his posh and lavish study, with its bearskin rug and highly oiled hardwood floor. Shelves of old and expensive books sat, dusty and unread, along the walls, hundreds of tomes of invaluable knowledge, wisdom and fiction. Every one of these books remained untouched.

The only other person in the room was a serious looking gentleman in a black suit with a white tie. Over his left eye was a monocle, and his pointy nose, needle-like in appearance, never seemed to point down from the ceiling. Such was the countenance of Reginald, Lord LeBlanc's personal attendant. Reginald, like most other butlers of the Human variety, took his duties very seriously and with great pride in his service to the family. Reg's father had served the LeBlancs, as had his grandfather, and his great-grandfather. He was the fourth generation of humble attendants, and sometimes, he wondered if perhaps he should be the last of that 'noble' line.

Vernon LeBlanc, Reginald had noticed as time passed by, was a completely selfish, crude, and egomaniacal little prick. Not that he'd ever say so out loud--heavens no, that wouldn't be proper manners. Yet here his lordship sat, watching a Mage's Eye that Reg had himself cast for his lordship, as two rather large fellows pummeled one another back and forth.

He worried that the current Lord LeBlanc had spent too much money on this entertainment.

* * * *

Stockholm usually kept a very short list of things to bear in mind when facing a man with a broadsword. The list went like this: First, check his stance. Second, check for signs that he's fatigued. Third, use a projectile weapon if one is available. As Stockholm brought himself to a skidding halt ten yards from Portenda, he went through this list. The stance Portenda took up had first been used, Stockholm thought, in the Third Age, and was called the Samurai Boshen. His hands both gripped the hilt of the sword, and he stood leaned back with the blade up next to his head, edge upward, point toward his opponent, Stockholm.

Secondly, although Stockholm had landed a nice solid kick, and had started this all by blinding the Simpa and tossing him out of a glass window, Portenda showed little sign now of fatigue or injury. Lastly, as for projectile weaponry, well, he didn't have any, and his opponent did. And as he'd already demonstrated, Portenda had one hell of a quick draw.

Well, this guy's not such a pushover after all, he thought, drawing out his rapier with a practiced flair.

"Do you really think you're going to hurt me with that little pig-sticker," Portenda asked.

Stockholm gave him another of his mad grins, and took up a fencer's stance.

Apparently, he does. Portenda dashed ahead, lunging with a stab to the chest that Stockholm nimbly sidestepped.

As the Werewolf jabbed with his rapier, Portenda dropped and rolled, bringing the broadsword across Stockholm's unarmored lower legs in a shallow cut across both shins.

More of Stockholm's blood spilled to the street, and the Red Tribe Werewolf decided that enough of his own blood had been spilled without payback in kind.

Portenda finished his roll, springing to his feet next to an office supplies store. He'd used the stab as a feint, only trying to score a good enough blow to slow the Werewolf down. As he gathered himself and started to retake his stance, flaring pain lanced through his right shoulder as Stockholm brought his left hand around in a hammer blow to the clavicle. With his right hand he stabbed his rapier through to the capped hilt in Portenda's side, the narrow tip coming out the other side of the

Simpa's yellow vest. The two combatants were now literally touching foreheads, each growling with a measure of both pain and blind rage.

Portenda thrust his large, leonine forehead forward, mashing Stockholm's lips back against his teeth, sending a fresh gout of blood from his mouth, and the Bounty Hunter took his sword and slashed upward, cutting a thick diagonal gash across the Red Tribesman's chest.

Got to put some distance between us, Portenda thought. He took one full-legged leap away from Stockholm, landing some twenty-five yards away. In mid-flight, however, he managed to twist his body enough to toss a grenade down at Stockholm, who was focusing on regenerating the cut in his torso.

When Stockholm had the wound almost completely shut, he heard something small and metallic clatter to the street a few yards away from him. Groggy from the effort of healing himself, Stockholm opened his eyes slowly, trying to blink away the double vision affecting his view. He could smell his own blood on the road, could still feel the sting of the iron ripping through his abdominal muscles and pectorals. Before he could react, the frag grenade let out a concussion blast before the fiery explosion of the incendiary device scorched his side and tossed him through the air over Desanadron.

Stockholm crashed back down through the wooden roof of some poor man's two-story cottage, his momentum carrying through the citizen's closet floor and into his kitchen, where he stopped with a meaty thud.

The citizen in question, a Lizardman who had just purchased the cottage, remained in his chair as the dust settled around him, and his kitchen table creaked, finally giving beneath Stockholm's weight. The man didn't even flinch; he'd seen stranger stuff in his time living in Palen, the city of magic.

The reptilian fellow took a look down at the Red Tribe Werewolf as he bled all over the tiled floor, coffee cup still in hand, and he leaned down to get a closer look and speak to him. "Um, you still alive, mister? If so, you might want to get a few bandages."

Stockholm vaguely heard the man, but he concentrated at the moment on the exquisite pain in his right ribs and leg. His ribs had been bruised by the concussion blast, two of them broken jaggedly, and his right leg bled profusely from shards of shrapnel and a wire hangar from the Lizardman's closet. A blue, tropical-theme button shirt was still hung from the thin piece of metal. He congealed loudly, and started to move a little, reaching down to remove the pieces of metal from his leg.

Portenda, meantime, looked down at his hip, and realized to his satisfaction that he'd grabbed the Number Four grenade to hurl at Stockholm. Thankfully, no other innocents had been in the area, already evacuated from the streets near their confrontation. Portenda wondered if the police would be showing up to try and minimize the risk to civilians not engaged in this honorable combat. If the two combatants are kept to each other, and the battle is honorable, the police usually wouldn't get involved. However, he had just used an incendiary device, and the deafening blast might attract attention.

The Simpa Bounty Hunter breathed in deeply, and followed the scent of booze toward a tavern on the next street over. Passing through the alley, he took a moment to wonder if the fight was over. When he reached the end of the alley and took a heavy double-punch to the face and stomach, he knew it was not.

* * * *

Stockholm yanked all of the metal out, and hauled himself to his wobbly feet. The Red Tribe Werewolf focused all of his energy on regeneration, and healed himself completely in only a few minutes' time. When he completed this, he thanked the Lizardman for removing the hangar ("Not a problem, it is my shirt after all") and headed outside.

He spotted the Simpa slowly sauntering into an alley far down the road, totally unaware of him. Stockholm sprinted as fast as he could down another alley, onto Shield Street, and headed to the end of the alley that Portenda would be exiting. He listened closely to the approach of the Bounty Hunter, and when he judged the time right, he came around the mouth of the alley and blasted Portenda with a double-punch.

Portenda's nose and part of his faceplate cracked under the Werewolf's fist, and his stomach muscles bunched painfully from the lower blow.

"This could go on for days, you know," Portenda mused as he scrambled back on all fours, trying to get to his feet in a hurry. He wanted his sword in his hand again, and finally realized that Stockholm's rapier was still all the way through his body from left to right. He got to his feet and pulled the rapier out, hurling it like a throwing knife at Stockholm, who twitched his head aside and caught the handle of the rapier. Here in the alley, Portenda knew he couldn't use his broadsword or his spear (which he'd retrieved) effectively. He could, however, stave the Werewolf off with lunges of the spear if he was smart about it. *Or the gun,* he thought, drawing the revolver and squeezing the trigger quickly.

As his hand dipped for the mecha weapon, Stockholm rolled forward, avoiding the first bullet. As he came out of the tuck roll, he extracted his claws and slashed upward, sinking them deep into

Portenda's stomach and tearing through muscles and organs as he ripped upward.

Blood splashed and sprayed them both, covering their muzzles and clothes, muddling their sight and nostrils.

Portenda delivered a crushing uppercut to the Werewolf's lower jaw, breaking the bones and staggering him back down toward Shield Street.

Before the brawl could spill out onto a main street again, Stockholm let Portenda come at him with another punch, the revolver holstered for the time being. The Red Tribesman brought his hands up in an outward block, whipping his hands across Portenda's face, punching his wounded stomach and using his free hand to block any incoming blows. He then finished the technique by hammer-fisting Portenda's shoulder for the second time during their melee.

Portenda screamed as he dropped to his knees, bringing Stockholm's dropped rapier up and stabbing it into his thigh. "You should've sheathed it when you caught it, big guy," Portenda chided in a level tone of voice as he was grabbed by the back of the head and kneed with crushing force in the face. He lost consciousness for a minute, and when he awoke again, Stockholm was sitting down in the alley next to him, sheathing his rapier.

Stockholm surprised the Bounty Hunter once again by handing a flask over to him without turning his head.

"I thought we could both use an intermission," Stockholm said bluntly.

Portenda took the flask and drained a good half of the harsh, biting whiskey within. He made a face and handed it back, feeling the right side of his jaw for the break he was sure would be there. Happily, it wasn't. "We're being watched, you know."

"I am aware," Portenda replied curtly. "The person watching us paid me quite handsomely to stage this fight."

"I hope he's getting some good chuckles out of it," Stockholm grumbled after taking down the rest of his whiskey. "And it really *is* a good thing you got your money in advance. We've done an awful lot of property damage, and someone's going to have to pay for it all."

Portenda sat up and thought that over for a minute.

"By the way, that really small grenade on your belt, what's it do?"

"You know about grenades, do you," Portenda asked, facing Stockholm with an upraised eyebrow.

"Oh yes, most certainly," Stockholm replied. "I may not look it, but I've been around a while, my fine golden friend. Since the Age of Mecha, in fact."

Portenda wondered if the man lied to him, but he recalled then just how old the blood in the streets had smelled when he shot the Werewolf. If Stockholm claimed to be over a thousand years old, he supposed it was possible. "So, what's it do?"

"It's a Number Three." Portenda unclipped it, and held the tiny grenade in the palm of his hand. "It's a freezing grenade. Small blast radius. No blast radius, actually."

Portenda looked at the aged piece of technology. "It hits its target, I use a separate remote to detonate it, and instant frozen target. Here, where's that," he started, and realized that Stockholm had moved about twelve feet down the alley. "Oh, shit."

Stockholm pressed the green button on the remote he'd lifted from the unconscious Simpa and watched as the tiny grenade exploded, coating Portenda in a thick block of ice from the neck down.

At the last moment, the Bounty Hunter had hugged it to his stomach to keep his head clear, so he wouldn't potentially suffocate inside a block of his own weapon's freezing chill. He turned his head what little he could, and cursed in his native tongue at Stockholm.

"The same to you, pal," Stockholm replied, tossing the remote down by the Bounty Hunter's encased feet.

* * * *

"Oh, I wish I could hear what they're saying." Vernon LeBlanc watched the shimmering square of light before him. Presently, an overhead-diagonal view of the Red Tribe Werewolf and the Simpa Bounty Hunter showed them sitting next to one another, panting and talking in an alley. While Portenda had been unconscious, LeBlanc watched the Red Tribesman pluck a tiny object from his back pocket as he lay sprawled on the alley floor. Now, as Stockholm inched away, he pulled that very same item out and pressed a button on it, encasing Portenda in a block of freezing ice.

Reginald, being the only servant present that Sunday afternoon, heard the doorbell ring downstairs and excused himself to see to whomever might be calling. He descended to the first floor, carrying himself with his usual measure of pride and pompousness, and when he opened the left door, he felt something short and sharp being pressed against his lower stomach.

He looked down, and found a Gnome in simple tan leathers standing there with a huge grin plastered to his face. The sharp object appeared to be a dagger, and as far as Reginald was concerned, it stood as the sharpest, most pointed dagger he'd ever seen. Of course, every other dagger he'd seen was a part of Lord LeBlanc's personal collection of highly valued weapons, all kept under enchanted glass.

"May I help you, mister, ah..." Reginald offered.

"Toren." The Gnome's scraggly white beard bounced as he spoke. "Lee Toren, me foin butlah chum," Lee had tracked down Portenda's business associate as soon as he left the fight, and found the man bound to his own bed with thick white ropes. The contact informed Lee that Vernon LeBlanc, a wealthy estate owner in eastern Desanadron, had sent armed men to force him to contact Portenda, and arrange a fight with Ignatious Stockholm.

LeBlanc had apparently tried to gain influence with the Hoods, but Stockholm had refused the man's money and request to be allowed to run a portion of the Guild for his own purposes.

Enraged, Lord LeBlanc had sought a means to take revenge on the Red Tribesman, but nothing lethal. "His goons told me he knew I had been in touch with the big guy," the captive said as Lee undid his ropes. "Lord LeBlanc was certain that Portenda would be able to trounce the Werewolf. Any idea how that's going?"

"Not a clue," Lee had told the man, cutting him free at last. The contact thanked Lee for his kindness, and gave him directions to LeBlanc's manor, telling Lee to be cautious.

"The current Lord LeBlanc is a little, well, out there," the contact warned. "And I guess he's got a lot of guards hanging around the estate. Just be careful, Lee."

The Gnome Pickpocket had found few troubles sneaking around the estate, avoiding the few guards on foot patrol, and now he stood with a dagger against the butler's stomach.

"Please, come in," Reginald said. He was nobody's fool, and though he was a relatively talented Q Mage, he wasn't about to waste his energy by trying to stop the thief. "Take whatever you'd like," Reginald said quietly as he backed into the main meeting chamber.

Lee cocked his head to one side, confused, and Reginald let out a weary sigh. "I tire of the lordship's whims and fancies, Mr. Toren. I have no more desire to serve him as a personal attendant."

"Are you serious," Lee said, watching in dumb wonder as the butler opened a bureau drawer and drew out an expensive-looking cigar, popping it into his own mouth and striking it alight with his bare fingertip. "And you're a magic user? Why don't you just blast me from there?"

Reginald had swiftly removed himself from the tip of the dagger once inside.

The former butler shrugged his shoulders, and removed the accursed monocle from his left eye. For the first time in years, he could completely make out the room around him.

"Because, Mr. Toren, as I have made clear, I have no more desire to serve. I think I'm done with this particular vocation. Now," Reginald said, rummaging around in a nearby closet. "If you'll excuse me, I'm off to take a few things that rightfully belong to me. After all, I've cared more for some of the objects of art around here than Lord LeBlanc has bragged about owning them. Good day, sir." Reginald pointed to a staircase before heading off in an opposite direction.

Lee started up the stairs, searching for this mister Vernon LeBlanc.

* * * *

Stockholm had only finished half of his purchased meal at The Golden Goose when his sensitive nostrils flared at the scent of Portenda the Quiet. He sighed heavily, and looked around at the diner.

Not many customers, but he was going to have to interrupt their meal. He stood, hopped up on the table, and put his hands around his snout to amplify his voice. "Everybody get out! This place is not safe." He bellowed, growled and roared, snapping his teeth at a family of Elves in the far corner to get his point across.

As soon as he turned to look at the main doors on the lower level, he spotted Portenda. Rather, he spotted Portenda's spear, and was thrown in a graceful arc as it ran him through and pinned itself and the Red Tribesman to the floor a few scant yards away from the panicked Elven customers.

"Perhaps I didn't make myself plain," Stockholm said to them with a snarl twisting his lips.

When Portenda broke free of the quickly melting ice block, his rage had blown through the barrier of professional calm. His senses tingled, and as he got back to the mouth of the alley that had been his prison for the last hour, he could hear the heartbeat of every civilian walking up and down the street, smell the sweet, briny odor of different tinted sweats, and could see every action taken around him. He watched an Illeck woman discreetly tear part of a shirt hanging from a street vendor's hangars, then immediately ask if she could get a discount on the damaged clothing. The vendor, perplexed at the damage, shrugged his shoulders and agreed to take half the price off for the shirt.

Two and a half miles away, up the road and over a hill, his nasal passages could just faintly make out the target, surrounded by mouth-watering aromas.

"Diner." Portenda said nothing more as he prepared his spear. He took it in his right hand and dropped his rucksack to the street, pulling out a length of rope. He tied the rope to a loop on the end of the spear, and fixed the other end to his left hand. The Bounty Hunter hitched his pack up onto his back again, and headed down to face his foe.

His highly tuned ears heard Stockholm warning the customers, and as the first few flowed out of the diner past Portenda, he took quick aim and launched the spear at Stockholm, who foolishly stood atop his table on the upper level. Portenda barked a harsh laugh of satisfaction as the weapon impaled and tossed the Red Tribesman back. Portenda faintly made out some smartass remark from the Red Tribe, and he started to haul on the rope tied to his left hand.

Stockholm mentally gauged the damage done to him by the spear, and thanked the Gods and Goddesses that he hadn't been gravely injured.

As he sat up, though, the spear came back and pierced him once again with the two back-facing points, sinking in around his spine and jerking him.

Stockholm looked down and saw that a rope was tied to the end of the weapon. "This is going to suck," he managed before being hauled crashing through the wooden banister of the second dining level.

Screaming, he flew through the air, and crumpled to the floor as Portenda leveled a solid punch to the right side of his face.

Twisting on the floor, Stockholm used his claws to cut the rope free, and landed with a splintering crash through another dining table when Portenda side-kicked him.

Portenda wasted no time, taking full advantage of his enemy's wounded state to pounce on top of him, pressing the air out of Stockholm as he landed heavily on his torso.

Stockholm had only just managed to remove the spear and toss it aside, and blood sprayed from his open wound when the Simpa landed on him, sitting on his barrel-like chest. The Bounty Hunter pummeled him twice in the face and jumped off to the side, searching for his spear.

Crawling toward the Bounty Hunter, who had taken home this second round of combat in a hurry, Stockholm spotted the spear, just tucked under a table that had been knocked over. It was too far away to reach, but the Simpa's ankles weren't. Rather foolishly, Portenda had written Stockholm off for the time being. When he looked down at Stockholm, he lifted his right foot to stomp down on the Werewolf's back. As he thrust his foot down, Stockholm rolled to the side, and used his extracted claws to hack apart the tendons in the back of his attacker's ankle.

Portenda screamed in pain, and lost his footing quickly, tipping over onto his side and rolling away from Stockholm.

Just when I thought I finally had him good, the Bounty Hunter thought. *I took it to him for a minute there, but he keeps finding openings in my defenses! How? I've never been taken down so many times in one fight, so handily! There's got to be an advantage I can press. Something must be available to me other than the gun.*

With any other target, Portenda would have used the revolver without prejudice. With this foe, however, he knew it wouldn't do much, and could be construed as slightly dishonorable. He'd already made one dirty move with the merchant in the street, and he'd paid for that in spades. The distraction hadn't hurt, but the roundhouse kick to the head certainly had.

Stockholm, still dazed from the shock of the attack, continued to crawl toward the diner's exit. He looked over his shoulder, and saw that Portenda was giving chase, hopping along on his good left leg.

The Simpa reached into a pouch and pulled on a leather glove, snapping it in place. From another pouch, he took out a silver coin, and he leaped with his left leg on top of Stockholm, blowing the air out of his lungs yet again.

Portenda kept the silver coins around for a reason, and here his opportunity to use one faced him. He landed heavily on Stockholm, and pressed the coin into the top of the werewolf's skull. Stockholm's flesh smoldered and smoked, and crimson fur disintegrated at the touch of silver, but much slower than Portenda assumed it would.

Stockholm moved beneath him, but it wasn't painful thrashing, as the Bounty Hunter had hoped for. Stockholm rolled fully beneath him, and smiled as he grabbed Portenda's wrist and snapped it, bringing his elbow across and pulling against the blow.

"Silver doesn't work so well on me, friend." Stockholm grabbed the coin as it dropped toward his chest. He tossed it out to the street, and brought his hips up and toward his head.

The Red Tribe Werewolf wrapped his feet around Portenda's head, and hauled off, tossing him several dozen yards to the back of the first level dining area.

Portenda landed hard against the wall next to the swinging door that led back to the kitchen, the entire building shaking as he struck. A Jaft cook with a paper hat came out next to him, a big, heavy cleaver in his left hand, and looked down at Portenda.

"What the hell's going on out here?"

Portenda said nothing. Using his unbroken left hand to snatch the cleaver, he hurled it unerringly at Stockholm's chest.

It whooshed through the air, end over end, and Stockholm slid to the side, dodging the weapon and grabbing it out of the air as he had his rapier. He spun in a circle, keeping the motion and kinetic force going, releasing it back at the Bounty Hunter, who managed to slide all the way to the floor just before the cleaver could take the top of his head off.

"I don't get paid enough for this shit," the Jaft cook said, running back into the kitchen and out a back door to safety.

The Red Tribe Werewolf and the Simpa Bounty Hunter both took a moment to regenerate their wounds, Stockholm recovering almost completely, Portenda only managing to heal his ankle and his wrist to a degree that would leave it functional. They panted in the darkened diner, staring across the distance at one another, both of them on wobbly legs. "You can't keep this up," Stockholm said, his breathing leveling out much quicker than Portenda's. "You know that, don't you?"

"I know no such thing." Portenda kept his stance neutral and passive. "I was foolish enough to land my attacks and stay close. That's all." Portenda heaved in air in huge gulps.

"True enough," Stockholm conceded. "From a distance, you're quite the foe. But you can't beat me in close, Portenda. And you can't stay at range forever. You're too aggressive for that, too used to having your way with your opponents." Stockholm stood up straight and pulling something from a back pouch.

Portenda readied himself for an attack, but watched silently as Stockholm placed a cigarette in his mashed and bloody snout, lighting it with a discarded lighter on a nearby table. Though he often chided Flint for the habit, the werewolf did occasionally indulge himself. He chuffed out a cloud of sky blue smoke, and then sent a ring through the cloud, smiling slightly. "You're good, though, I'll give you that."

"Good enough to take you down, Mr. Stockholm," Portenda said, thinking through what the Red Tribesman had said. *What, does he think he's some kind of teacher? I've taken out things twice his size, and with ease. But he's not some monster,* his more reasonable, rational mind spoke to him. *He's many, many times older than you for starters. Secondly, he's stronger in a physical sense. And he takes everything you do to him and uses it to his own gain. He said as much that you are good at range. Use that to your advantage, find a way to* keep *him at range.*

"A few times, yes." Stockholm tapped ash into an empty tray on the diner's bar counter. "And in case you're wondering, yes, I'm stalling," Stockholm said, grinning that mad grin again.

"What? Why?" Portenda eased himself over to a stool at the bar counter. Stockholm hopped over the bar, and grabbed a mug, pouring Portenda an ale from a bottle. He slid it down the bar counter to

Portenda, who caught it with ease. "These little intermissions are nice, by the way."

"Yes, I think so too. Gives us both some time to heal, and gives me a chance to try and figure out how much we'll owe the city by the time we're done." The huge Red Tribesman slowly approached the Bounty Hunter from the other side of the counter. He brought the ashtray with him, and tapped again into it.

"What are we up to now?"

"Oh, I'd put it around two thousand gold pieces." Stockholm leaned over the counter with his arms next to Portenda's.

If one were to walk into the front doors of the diner, they would assume that perhaps there'd been a brawl, but few would suspect it had been between these two warriors. They looked like bosom buddies next to one another this way. "As for why I'm stalling, I believe you may have been deceived about your contract."

"What makes you say that?" Portenda took a slow sip of his ale, feeling its alcoholic warmth wash into his stomach. Stockholm finished his smoke, and stamped it out in the ashtray.

"Think about it. Have you ever been offered a contract to just pick a fight? A non-lethal one? And don't try to bullshit me about this being a fight to the death, because if it were, you'd have taken the opportunity to come after me when that grenade blasted me into some poor slob's cottage."

"Or you would have torn me apart on several occasions," Portenda countered. He was tired, and his regenerating process was slowing. Stockholm spoke the truth--he couldn't keep this up. He had taken a severe beating today, and unlike the hundreds, perhaps thousands, of people and creatures he'd fought in his comparatively short life, Ignatious Stockholm could take him down at any time he chose. It had taken all of this recent pain over the course of perhaps the last two or three hours to appreciate the fact that he was not, in fact, the top authority on combat in the land.

"If this had been a hunt and capture mission, I would have disabled you with stealth. If it had been a state-sponsored hit, and you were deserving of death by my standards, I would have brought my sniper rifle."

"I knew a pretty good sniper once upon a time," Stockholm said, smiling as he lit another smoke and poured himself a brandy.

"Oh yeah," Portenda asked, easing back on his stool. "Who was he?"

"A Cuyotai, a fellow police officer in a city that no longer stands," Stockholm said quietly, his smile fading a little. *Uh-oh, I may have opened a wound,* Portenda thought, looking into the big man's hazy, misty eyes. Stockholm wiped his eyes clean, and continued. "It was in the time before the Fall of Mecha. He and I worked together a lot on street patrol, mostly dealing with gangs and whatnot. He and I were close. Very close."

"Friends can be like family I suppose," Portenda said, thinking briefly of Jonah Staples and his parents.

"Oh, we weren't family. He was my boyfriend," Stockholm said bluntly.

Portenda lost his focus and calm, and sprayed ale out of his mouth in sheer surprise.

"Oh, don't be like that, Portenda. It's not exactly a big deal," Stockholm growled, grabbing the brandy bottle from under the counter and pouring himself a fresh shot.

"I'm sorry," the Bounty Hunter said, barely holding in a gut laugh. "It's just that, well, nobody told me that you were, well, you know," he said, clearing his throat as politely as he could. "Not that it has any bearing on this business."

"Exactly," Stockholm said, downing his fresh shot. "Now, back to the matter at hand. Your contact wouldn't hire you to just beat on someone, right?"

"Right," Portenda said, bringing his focus back to business. "It does seem a bit odd."

"But the money was up front, delivered, so you didn't ask any questions," Stockholm said with a slightly scolding tone.

"I made sure you were a criminal. Other than that, right again, Ignatious." Portenda sighed heavily, and accepted another mug of ale. "So, what's your point?"

"My point is, I have a few enemies around here, Portenda." Stockholm stubbed out his second cigarette. "But much like these cigarettes, they don't bother me often. So, whoever hired you to hurt me is someone of influence and deep pockets, and only a few people in this city can afford ten thousand gold pieces on having me attacked."

"Stockholm?"

"Yeah?"

"That Mage's Eye is sort of twitching above us right now," Portenda said, not actually being foolish enough to point up. "We have to keep going until it fades out or is dispelled. Otherwise, I assume there's going to be trouble."

Stockholm smiled broadly, and flipped the Mage's Eye the bird.

"Then let there be trouble. I'm done beating the shit out of you." The Red Tribesman laughed garishly as the Mage's Eye twitched. "I suppose we could give it one final show."

"I agree." Portenda took the brandy bottle and smashed it against the side of Stockholm's head.

Bloodied and soaked with shards of glass and brandy, Stockholm continued to laugh as the Mage's Eye blinked, and disappeared.

* * * *

"How dare he," Vernon LeBlanc fumed as the Red Tribesman who denied him his share of the Hoods flipped off the Mage's Eye. "Reginald, get in here and recast this spell," he shouted, eyes still locked on the fading vision.

He heard his butler's approaching footfalls and gasped as a dagger pressed against his cheek.

LeBlanc only turned his eyes, and he saw a Gnome gentleman he knew very well from the town crier and other publications, as well as from descriptions of the fellow. "Lee Toren," he breathed.

"In the flesh, me bucko." Lee tossed a pair of handcuffs onto Vernon's lap. "Do yeself a favor an' put those on. We're goin' fer a walk, you an' me."

* * * *

The Mage's Eye vanished, and still blood poured out of the side of Stockholm's face as he laughed. "Ah, the element of surprise. And to think, I was going to wait until you went to take a drink and smash your mug into *your* face!"

"Sorry about that," Portenda said with a chuckle. "I just decided to take the initiative, that's all. How's your face?"

Stockholm stood, pulling pieces of glass from his snout and his ear.

"Pretty good," Stockholm said. "How's yours?"

"What?" Portenda lost his vision for a moment as the Red Tribe Werewolf hit him in the face with a wicked backhand blow.

Portenda fell off of his stool to the floor, and wondered if perhaps the fight was going to pick up again despite the lack of need or inspiration.

As he shook his head, Stockholm launched himself over the counter and landed on his feet, his body loose and relaxed.

Portenda scooted away a few feet and stood up, blocking effectively when Stockholm came at him with a pair of hook kicks. He counterattacked after the second block, bringing his right elbow up toward Stockholm's face.

The Werewolf ducked the elbow and jabbed Portenda several times under the arm, striking the nerves and control points much as Portenda liked to do to his opponents. Ninjitsu finger strikes dotted his right side as Stockholm lashed out, and the Werewolf stiff-palmed Portenda in the center of his chest, knocking him flat to the floor.

Portenda put up his left hand to stop him, his right arm limp from a nerve strike. "Okay, okay, I concede! I concede." He rolled back and drew his revolver, firing once into Stockholm's chest, just above the previous bullet wound.

Stockholm twitched back, and Portenda would have fired again, but there was a silhouetted figure in the doorway behind Stockholm. A pair of figures.

Stockholm laughed, pried the bullet out with his claws, and turned around as Portenda holstered his revolver and approached. Standing side by side, the huge bruisers found themselves looking down at Lee Toren, and a man that Stockholm recognized from recent dealings.

"Vernon LeBlanc," the Red Tribesman growled as he gave the Human a bloody smile. "Lee Toren. Thanks for the delivery, Lee."

Portenda smiled up at his new friend, and cracked his knuckles. He turned back to LeBlanc, who remained cuffed as Lee Toren took his leave to stand watch outside.

The Gnome Pickpocket struck up a cigarette, and smiled hugely as he heard two rather intimidating voices speak in unison from behind him. "We have to have a little chat," the voices said.

When the constabulary found Vernon LeBlanc, he had been covered in cooking grease, had feathers stuck to his otherwise naked flesh, and had been hanged from a grammar school flagpole by his underpants. Hands cuffed behind his back, a leather coin pouch had been shoved in his mouth as a gag. Inside of the pouch was a single silver coin.

LeBlanc moved out of Desanadron the following afternoon.

Tale Four: The Realms of Tamalaria- A Guide

The following is a guide to the topographical, political and economical division of the continent of Tamalaria. It was written in the year 865 A.F. by Vandabar Swellskin, a Gnome Scholar who resided in the city of Palen. It begins with a brief explanation of the lands' timeline in reference to the present date of publication in 865 A.F.

Greetings. My name is Vandabar Swellskin, and this is my brief guide to the realms of Tamalaria. At the time I am working on this for you, the citizen of this great and spanning continent, it is the year 863 A.F. I suspect the finished volume shall not be massively reproduced for a few years, but I shall attempt to make all entries relevant.

Firstly, allow me to explain a few historical notes to you, reader. You may or may not be aware of this fact, but the suffix A.F. stands for After the Fall of Mecha, which ended Tamalaria's Fourth Age, the Age of Mecha. The Ages I shall be referring to now are the recorded and accepted timelines for the entirety of the realm and all of its historians and scholars. Members of all Races and Classes have agreed to these recordings.

The First Age of Tamalaria lasted for approximately 2300 years, and had no sub-title. Records and tomes seem to indicate that there were a surprisingly small number of Races and Classes known to the civilizations of those times. However, records indicate that the ancient Elven Kingdom was established in the middle of the Age, in the southwestern forests known also as The Great Forests. It is the only known monarchy to have lasted since the First Age.

The Second Age of Tamalaria lasted approximately 2200 years, and was known as the Age of Magic and Discovery. During this era, many of the schools of today's magic were first established or discovered and studied. The lycanthrope Races, who had not appeared in any records available from the First Age outside of myths and legends, seemed to emerge during this time. The first of them were very tribal in organization and nature. Also during this age, the other races discovered that the lycanthropes had total control over their physical state and mind. Though savage, they weren't the slaughtering, slavering beasts that the old legends made them out to be.

The Third Age of Tamalaria lasted approximately 1400 years, and was later dubbed the Age of War. Many more Races made themselves known, coming out of their sanctuaries to join the larger societies. Classes and ways of life were invented in the last 400 years of the Second Age, and this trend continued into the early Third Age. However, in the Third Age, many of the famous Racial wars were waged. Political wars sparked off in the middle of the age, finally deteriorating into small skirmishes with small, armed militias. The best known of these wars was the beginning of the seemingly eternal War of the Allenians (which struggles on to this day), and the First Elven-Dwarven War.

Another problem from the late Second Age, the undead, seemed to creep up and take control of the realm during the Third Age. They appeared in swarms, along with the legendary Vampires. Together they formed a great and oppressive Vampire Nation, centered in the middle of the continent. The head clan, Clan Allenian, named the vast, hilly region, after themselves. After the Vampire Nation's defeat in 422 Third Age, the Khan and Simpa, who were the primary Races defending the lands against these creatures, turned on one another, claiming full ownership and rights to the Allenian Hills. If you're a current resident of Tamalaria, you know full well that at the time of this guide's publication, that war is still being fought.

The Fourth Age lasted approximately 600 years. It was known as the Age of Mecha. Science and technology thrived during this period, to the point that much of the civilized world nearly destroyed itself.

At the end of this age was the Fall, during which technology mysteriously malfunctioned or simply destroyed itself. Many artifacts from that time period still exist, as do the scientific arts developed during the Age of Mecha. However, the scientifically minded of this, the Fifth Age, or After the Fall of Mecha, question the sciences and theories handed down to them. Why? Well, because something clearly went wrong.

Enough of that. On to the major and distinctive regions of Tamalaria.

The Elven Kingdom

This territory shall be mentioned first since, as I've already mentioned, this is the oldest established society still standing. In the southwestern part of the continent, covering about 1/10 of the land's total mass, is a great forest, which is inhabited largely by and ruled completely by the Elves. Now, Elves can be found anywhere in Tamalaria, but nowhere else in such high concentration as this forest. The capital is the city of Whitewood, which houses the royal palace, and boasts a population of approximately 45,000. There are five other major cities in the kingdom--Varvex, Blackwood, Farsik, Lugonden, and Fletcherville. Each of these cities supports roughly 25,000 citizens each, and there are nearly a dozen other small townships that support hundreds of citizens each. There are also the military outposts, but these are largely uninhabited except in times of war.

The Elven kingdom began as and has remained a successful monarchy. The rule of authority goes as follows: The King, his first-born son the First Prince, second-born son the Second Prince, the Queen, first-born daughter the First Princess, second-born daughter the Second Princess. Allow me to further explain; first, there is the King. If he has a son, the Prince is regarded as having the second most authority in the land. Then the second Prince. Then the Queen. Then the King's daughters. As you can see, the kingdom is very much a patriarchal society. I personally find this strange, because among the Elves, females tend to have cooler heads and the most magic potential. Sons of the royal family, the Princes, always have greater standing than even their mother the Queen, regardless of the number of sons born to the royal family.

In the first two Ages, the monarch was the supreme ruler, and relied on the royal family and its Dukes and Duchesses to enforce its rule. In the early Third Age, King Michinendi the II dissolved the use of Dukes, Duchesses, and Earls and such in favor of a secondary form of government. These individuals would be elected into their position by the people, and would hold the position until either death, or a high crime was discovered to be committed by the person voted in. This was the Council of Elders. These men and women, usually 10 in number, listen to the voice of the people, and advise the King or Queen or Prince, or whoever is in power in the royal family, what they should do.

An interesting note: Ever since the War of Vandross a scant 20 years ago, the Elven Kingdom has been without a King or a Prince. It is governed by a Queen, who has not yet decided on any suitors, for she does not relish the idea of relinquishing her rule, which has been fair and just.

The Elven Kingdom is bordered on the north and east by plains, and there is a stretch of land about four miles long south of the forest to the shore of the ocean. The western fringe of the forest in bordered similarly. The primary inhabitants of the Kingdom are Elves, Half-Elves, and Cuyotai (Werecoyotes).

Desanadron

In the western-central plains of Tamalaria, there stands a great metropolis known as Desanadron. The word 'Desanadron' is taken from two words from two separate languages; 'Desan', which is Dwarven for 'Mighty', and 'Adron', which is from the oldest Human speech, meaning

'Fortress'. While Desanadron is not a militaristic city, it is enormous, with buildings reaching upwards of thirty stories. The city has a mixed population of nearly one million civilians and troopers today. If you have never seen a particular Race or Class, visit this city once--it's guaranteed you'll check every one of them off of your list.

Desanadron is a city-state that stretches for approximately 50 miles in all directions from its center. It is the mother city for several smaller villages and townships further to the west and to the east, and one township to the south, Vershak. The city was first erected in 974 Third Age as a monument to the hope many held that the wars of the Races were over forever. No Race or Class of civilian or trooper was or ever has been denied admittance without very good reason (i.e. criminal status). That is the city's finest selling point, in fact; diversity.

Desanadron is governed by a High Council of twenty-five publicly elected Councilors. A Councilor's term of service is ten years, at which time they must campaign to be re-elected for their seat. However, unlike in some other city-states, if the majority of the city's citizenry petitions for the removal of a Councilor from office, the rest of the High Council has no choice but to remove that person from their ranks. This is not a written law; it is simply the traditionally understood custom. If the people will it, the High Council must abide it. The only exception for this is in matters of war.

Desanadron is situated with its southern outskirts a grand 940 miles north of the Great Forest/Elven Kingdom. Vershak is 660 miles from that same border. There is no majority Race or Class in Desanadron proper, but most of the citizens of Vershak, the largest protectorate, are Human, Lizardman, Jaft or Half-Elf.

The Northwestern Territories

The Northwestern Territories, aptly named, primarily consist of foothills in the south and large mountain ranges and valleys throughout. These Territories stretch from the western ocean shore to about the middle of the continent. The southern border clips in closer and closer as one goes from west to east, as the mountains shore up, giving way to plains and grasslands.

Situated in the middle of the northwestern-most ranges is the Dwarven city of Traithrock, capital of the Dwarven Territories, which exist within the Northwestern Territories. Traithrock is a stout Dwarven city, exposed to the frost, snow and wintry winds of the mountainous northlands. It boasts a population of nearly 67,000 Dwarves, and a handful of Minotaurs and Jafts, as well as Gnomes, the Dwarves' less physical, more scientific cousin Race.

Surrounding Traithrock are many different valley hamlets, underground townships, and northern coastline villages. Minotaurs, tribal in nature, camp in family units throughout the craggy heights, while Jafts usually stay close to the ocean. They have a natural love of sailing and fishing, though they are largely averse to submersion in anything but salt water. As a result, their villages are usually no more than a mile away from the northern ocean. A few Draconus and Lizardman settlements can be found throughout the foothills of the region, though these few and far between. There are also several Monk training monasteries hidden throughout the mountain regions.

The primary Races of the region are Dwarves, Jafts, and Minotaurs. The primary Classes are Soldier, Knight, Gaiamancer, Boxer and Monk.

The Allenian Hills

As I mentioned earlier, the Allenian Hills is a large, hilly region in the center of the continent, named after the primary Vampire clan in the Third Age. These hilly lands are gorgeous, or would be, if it weren't for the constant warring between the residents, the Simpa and Khan. These two lycanthrope Races, Werelions and Weretigers, kill each other in the region at every available chance. The Simpa, while typically a very noble and honorable people, often resort to their more savage roots while engaged in this eternal war. Outsiders, meaning anyone who is not a Simpa or a Khan, are targeted for raids or forced enlistment in either side's cause. In the case of the cunning and cruel Khan, women of the Human, Elven or Half-Elven Races unfortunate enough to wander too close are taken and raped, then slaughtered for food.

There are, however, two roads and one township in the Allenians that are, by a signed and agreed-upon treaty, neutral territory, and are not subject to claim or raid. The two roads, Roamer's Way and Sanctuary Road, are used little, and mostly by traders. The town, which is accessible from either road, is called Trapperstown, and has a permanent population of only about three to five hundred citizens. The Allenians are roughly double the area of the city-state of Desanadron.

The primary Races of the region are Simpa and Khan. The primary Classes are Soldier, Knight, Berserker, Pyromancer, Aeromancer, and Bishop.

The Lucara Marshes (a.k.a. the Red Marsh)

A small marshland in the south-central plains, just east of a large fiefdom to be mentioned later. It is filled with poisonous bogs, monstrosities, and is considered a sacred training ground for Necromancers. The topography of the Lucara Marshes is something of a mystery; the bog trees shift and change position with the passing seasons. It is oft rumored that they have gained a malevolent sentience of their own over the eons. The trees are of a strange wood, called Ghostwood, which cannot be easily cut or burned.

The Lucara Marshes are much too volatile for any permanent townships or hamlets to arise within. Certain Lizardman tribes of an evil bent are often found camping within for short periods of time. However, there is one single point of light and hope within these swamplands, the Temple of Unaki. Unaki is said to be a forgotten God, one who was once worshipped by the early Necromancers, who practiced their art for the purpose of society's betterment. In the Second Age, Necromancers were few and highly skilled, and they raised the dead in order to perform labors too deadly or dangerous for the living. These early Necromancers were scholars more than sorcerers or witches, and made use of magics lost to them now to communicate with the souls of the dead for bereaved family members and friends of the dead.

The Temple of Unaki still stands in the center of these swamps, and on occasion, a Necromancer with benign intentions will still go and provide an offering of magic to the Temple. There is a legend that states that the Temple is partially sentient, or that it houses the flagging spirit of Unaki, who holds down a great and terrible spirit or monster buried deep beneath the bogs.

The Fiefdom of Lemago

A large empire in the south-central plains, the Fiefdom of Lemago is home to many of the Monks, Dragoons and Samurai within the lands of Tamalaria. Rare scripts and scrolls dated from the Second Age tell of a mysterious warrior who rode into Tamalaria from another world, another reality it would seem, and taught the first warriors of the empire the arts of the Samurai, and the way of Bushido. Since that time, the small fiefdom grew into the vast empire that now stands there.

The Fiefdom of Lemago briefly hosted the armies of Byron of Sidius, the Elven Kingdom and Lord Viper of the Port of Arcade during their march on Mount Toane during the last stages of the War of Vandross. They were given supplies and shelter for a few days before passing through on their way to end the warlock's siege on the lands. The Fiefdom is governed by an Emperor, who is chosen in a rather unique method.

The Fiefdom of Lemago has always, throughout its long history, been ruled by an Emperor. When the old Emperor passes away, his family is reduced to the status of Kishimura, which in their unique language stands for 'royal advisors'. The new Emperor is chosen by an ancient Gold Dragon who lives in a cave along the southern shoreline by the name of Suthara Mintokowka. This great dragon only emerges from his cave to select a new Emperor, and his choice is never questioned. He is worshipped by many of the empire's citizens as a dragon-God. A tad foolish if you ask me.

The Fiefdom's economy is strong, though it operates in a rather strange way. Instead of using metal coins for currency in most cases, it uses an overall barter system. People are paid with lands, goods, and services instead of money. As a sort of sarcastic twist, many who live outside of the empire call it the "Golden Lands", for almost no gold is used for currency. Their laws are few, but very strictly enforced by the Samurai who are mostly employed as lawmen. The act of grand theft is usually punishable by death. As a result, thieves tend to stay away from the empire.

The Empire's capital is Sunome. There are only two other major cities, Houten and Fong. Many rural villages make up the majority of the citizenry, along with one military training ground where Samurai are trained. Many Monk monasteries dot the landscape within the empire.

The primary Races of this territory are Humans, Elves, Half-Elves, Draconus and Sidalis (mutants). The primary Classes are Monk, Soldier, Samurai, Dragoon, and Q Mage.

The City of Ja-Wen

Many refer to the city of Ja-Wen as the 'sister city' of Desanadron. Ja-Wen is situated on the exact opposite side of the continent from Desanadron, far in the east. It is a sprawling city, supporting roughly 230,000 residents of all Races and Classes. Like Desanadron, it has a greatly mixed population. It is governed by a High Council like Desanadron, but the Council answers ultimately to the Governor, who is elected once every five years by popular election.

Ja-Wen is also home to a unique group, known as the Unified Bounty Hunters' League. Ja-Wen is host to the land's primary Bounty Office, where official and unofficial contracts are posted, reported, and signed on for if the contract is only for private Bounty Hunters. Most bounty offers are open to whomever can accomplish the task first, but some ask for discretion and the use of only one agent; such contracts are usually posted in this central office.

Ja-Wen is arranged by Districts, and then further divided by areas populated primarily by one Race or Class of individual. They are numbered, but most have nicknames, like the 'Kobold Quarter', or 'Stench Town', a slang term given to the primarily Jaft-inhabited neighborhood.

Where Desanadron enjoys a great deal of outside trade, Ja-Wen primarily survives on internal business. Residence in Desanadron shifts often, as people come and go--often many times in a matter of only ten or twelve years. In Ja-Wen, people find solidity and permanence. Its population swells with each passing decade.

During the War of Vandross, half of the city was leveled, and much of it was damaged beyond repair. However, when people returned, they made large efforts to rebuild and replace what had to be done such with. Ja-Wen is closely linked with Fort Stone, which is situated two days' travel north of its northern gates.

Unlike Desanadron, Ja-Wen is bordered on *all* sides by a massive stone wall, upon which guards are routinely posted.

Also unlike Desanadron, Ja-Wen has no separate body of police and militia. During times of continental peace, the army acts as guards and lawmen. During times of war, they act as guards, lawmen, and troopers. All recruits are put through rigorous training in the military fort situated to the east, along the coast, for just that purpose of training.

There are no primary Races or Classes in Ja-Wen, though it should be noted that there is a higher concentration of magic users in the city than in Desanadron.

Palen, the Capital of Magic

The city of Palen lies a week's travel on horseback to the north and slightly west of Ja-Wen. It is a city perhaps one quarter of the size of Ja-Wen, which is half the size of Desanadron in the far west. Palen is known as the Capital of Magic, because 98% of the residents who dwell there are magic users or scientists of some type. All forms of magic can be found in Palen, including Void Mages, who learn magic spells and abilities by being struck with them. All forms of science can also be found within the city's protective barrier.

Situated within the exact center of the city is a tall tower named the Spire. Inside of the Spire, mystical lodestones create a magical barrier around the city that wards off many creatures and individuals with malicious intentions. The barrier also serves another purpose--to solidify and manifest into being any and all spiritual creatures that pass through it. This includes Ghosts, Ghasts, Geists, Ghouls and Wraiths. Yes, even Wraiths are allowed within the city's limits, so long as they do no ill within the city. Priests of all of the major religions also have large churches within the city, and exorcists patrol the city full-time to ward against evil spirit creatures.

Palen is home to the largest library in all the land. It is a magnificent, six-story tall building with every conceivable reference tome and novel within its shelves. Many of the books I read in order to learn about Tamalaria's long and rich history I borrowed from there.

Palen has an economy that is based in currency, like most cities and towns, but curiously, they do not allow silver coins of any kind within the city limits. This is largely due to the powerful lycanthrope mages who study within. Silver armor must be turned over to the officers of the Watch, and silver weapons must remain sheathed unless one is attacked by a spirit creature that is weak to the metal.

Palen is also home to a very unique creature, one who has existed for a very, very long time--one of the Great Sages. The Great Sages, is it said, are the direct creations of the earliest Gods, and house the greatest and most ancient spells and arcane arts. The Great Sage is named Gulhen, and remains isolated in his manor on the eastern edge of town. Only a few are allowed to see him, and only by invitation. Attempting to walk up to his home often triggers magical traps that can kill, maim, or cause a man to run mad.

The city of Palen, curiously, has no central government. The laws of the city are formed by the Watch. If a leader needs to be named, it would have to be the Commander of the Watch. At this time, the post is held by a highly skilled mage by the name of Loren Drumac. She is an Elf, and studies all four of the elemental schools of magic.

Palen's primary Races are Human, Gnome, Elves, Half-Elves, Cuyotai, and Ursas (Werebears). Most of the city's Priests are Ursas, due to their gentle, passive nature.

The Port of Arcade

Situated on a peninsula north and slightly east of Palen, the Port of Arcade was once a large township dominated by thieves, murderers and criminals of all walks of the underworld life. Under the leadership of Lord Viper, it was turned into a fairly honest city, with a form of government, laws, and a semblance of a Watch. Now, however, that Lord Viper is dead, it is degenerating back into a lawless town where only the brave, criminally minded, or suicidal dare enter.

The Port of Arcade is also a major staging point for seafaring individuals, most of whom pay rather large bribes to the local crime bosses for safe passage and use of its docks out into the northern ocean.

The only people who pass through with impunity are members of large and well-known thieves' Guilds, or the Jaft and Minotaur sailors who permanently keep ships docked. These two Races often show up in vast numbers with entire crews, equipped and ready to sail. No matter how good a thief you are, you'd be a fool to try and steal unnoticed from these large, brutal, war-like peoples.

Perhaps two days' walk to the west of Arcade is a large, permanent Jaft village known as Skuren, or 'Sea House' as the word is literally translated from the Jaft tongue. During the Third Age, this township swelled to the size of a small city when a short-lived war was waged between the savage Jafts and the Minotaurs for ownership of the region.

The more tactically-minded Jafts won that war, and a grudging respect has been long since established between the two mountain- and sea loving Races.

The primary Races of Arcade itself are Wererats, Gnomes, and Humans. The primary Classes are Pickpocket, Rogue, Son of Night, and Ninja.

Well, that about wraps it up for the major locales of Tamalaria. There's the Desperation, the large desert in the southeast, but strangely, that region shrinks with each passing century. One final area of mystery remains, and I'll go over it only briefly, for it is not spoken of except in whispers and rumor and myths throughout the land's history, and the region often changes location, appearing for brief periods of ten or twenty years, and then it disappears completely.

Nowhere

Nowhere is a vile place of concentrated evil and malign purpose. It is dominated and populated by demons of all sorts, and monstrosities that cannot even be described. I myself have heard a few first-hand accounts of the place, but the individuals I interviewed about it all seemed a little short of a full deck, if you know what I mean. Only two men that I spoke with seemed to have come away unscathed, but they shuddered to think about the place, and were reluctant to speak to me about it. They were Ramone Svilak, an Elven Paladin, and Ramrock Headbutter, a Jaft Soldier.

Nowhere appears once every two or three decades, and completely swallows a small area of the land that is largely uninhabited for about ten to twenty years. Anyone in the area becomes magically displaced, thrown to the far points of the compass by some mysterious force. Most survive the process, but few are left completely intact. Most suffer dire diseases with no known cure, or are driven completely mad, like those unfortunate enough to stumble within Nowhere's borders.

On the outside, the region appears simply to be a sunless, barren wasteland inhabited by nothing for endless miles. However, a sort of shimmering wall of force marks its boundaries, and anyone who wanders within finds themselves in a blackened, scorched territory full of crags, hills, and desolate lands full of tough, black grasses. The interior of Nowhere is somehow magically expanded, and one can travel for weeks without reaching the other side. At least, so I am told.

One can expect to find vile creatures of murderous bent, undead, and demons everywhere. Only a few sanctuaries dot the bleak landscape, and volcanic rifts and rivers split the lands of Nowhere. Only the brave or stupid enter willingly and on purpose. The Order of Oun sends dozens of Knights, Paladins, and Priests inside every time it appears; almost none of them return.

Ramone Svilak told me a tale of a certain old Kobold who has a shack in a swampland forest within Nowhere. The Kobold claims to be the father of their Race, and has in his possession certain scrolls that convinced Ramone that his claims were truth. He is trapped in Nowhere, and cannot leave the sanctuary of his shack except to go into the basement, which magically replenishes itself with supplies of food and drink. The Kobold simply calls himself Neermack, which is Kobold for 'Race-sire'.

Ramrock spoke to me of a black lake, which he called Arako Suluhan, which is Jaft for 'Birthplace of Evil'. He claimed to see demons being spawned from the black water, and he admitted, rather embarrassed by the fact, that he fled from that place as swiftly as he could.

Further questioning revealed to me that every single person who is a member of the cult known as the Blessed Children of Maragshet, the Mad God, has at some time been to or near Nowhere. I believe further research may bring a reason for this pilgrimage to light. Is Nowhere the home of the Mad God on earth? I can only assume so, for most who return from Nowhere immediately join the cult.

Tale Five: And Then There Were Three

The year was 742, A.F., and Gwen Surefire, Half-Elf Aeromancer, wasn't entirely sure she would live to see her next birthday as the ship she traveled on came under arrow attack by a roving band of Lizardman raiders.

She had been traveling along the Martak River from just east of Desanadron for five days, hoping to make good time away from the big city on her way to Palen, where she anticipated receiving instruction from the elusive Great Sage who dwelled there. Her mastery of wind magic was complete, and she hoped that he would invite her to an audience where she would ask to be taught the last spells of Aeromancy, the lost, ancient spells that had remained hidden from all mages throughout the land.

She had left Desanadron to the north and east, through a large shipping port along the river, where she paid a handsome sum of gold to a Jaft shipping captain to bring her on board for the long trip east. The blue-skinned humanoid had warned her that they often encountered raiders along the way, especially when the ship passed on the river through the Allenian Hills region, where Khan routinely tried to smuggle aboard and steal from them. A few of the more honorable Simpa often asked them to stop and sell them any spare supplies they might have, but the more savage Werelion tribes raided them outright, just like the brutal Weretigers.

"I'll help deal with them," Gwen had promised. Now, however, as she cowered in the pilot box on deck, she wasn't so sure she could be much help. Gwen wore light leather armor, and had been skimmed by an arrow loosed by one of the Lizardman raiders. The arrowhead tore through her flimsy armor like parchment, and she didn't want to be riddled with more of the weapons.

The captain, steering the ship with a lack of concern, looked back and down at where she sat, crouched with her hands over her head.

"Some fucking help you are, Elf," he spat with clear disdain. "Sorry, *half*-Elf. Can you steer at least?"

"No," she yelled over the sound of the first raiders screaming as they leaped on board the deck and started clashing with the other Jaft crewmen, who all attacked the intruders with spears and war hammers.

The Lizardmen, who were of one of the less civilized tribes of their Race, fell swiftly to the skilled and efficient tactics of the blue-fleshed warriors, whose natural stench had taken Gwen a full two days' time to become accustomed to.

"I have no experience with sailing!" she admitted.

The captain sighed heavily, and veered the boat toward the southern shore of the river.

"Hold on then! I'm going to beach the ship temporarily!"

"I didn't pay for you to do that," Gwen shouted, her pride insulted by his clear lack of appreciation for her magical prowess. *Then again*, she thought, *I'm not exactly demonstrating any of that power.*

"You didn't pay me to allow you command of the ship, either, bitch," he growled back at her over his shoulder. "Now either get out there and start wielding your magic, or prepare to beach!"

Flustered, Gwen stood to her full five feet of height, glared at the grimacing captain, and ducked out onto the deck. She saw with a small measure of relief that the crew had mostly repelled the raiders, but several Lizardmen were sneaking on board from the other side of the deck. *They must have used small boats to get to the other side. Well, let's see what they do about me!*

Gwen strode confidently forward, whispering words of power and drawing on her magic.

"Suvien shwartz," she cried, thrusting her spread fingers toward five of the raiders who had drawn weapons.

They had a moment to face her before a tunnel of white wind blasted into them, tossing them screaming overboard to crash into the river.

The Jafts turned to face the unseen assailants, and several of them gave her an appreciative thumb's up for her effort.

Gwen smiled and nodded at them, seeing the stunned looks on their faces a few moments before she was sent sprawling by a Lizardman who struck her upside her head with a heavily mailed fist.

White light exploded behind her eyes as the reptilian warrior struck her, and as she landed in a limp heap near the opposing railing, the Half-Elf Aeromancer felt a twinge of emotion she wasn't very familiar with--fury. In all of her years of study of magic, she had rarely been tried by such warriors. Gwen was young for a Half-Elf, only thirty-six years old, but she had trained vigorously in Desanadron to become a master of her chosen art. To be brushed aside like a fly by such a, such a *brute,* she thought, was not only unacceptable, it was insulting!

Leaping to her feet, her head still throbbing, she heard only the harsh, guttural laughter of the Lizardman who had struck her. He held a wicked scimitar of a blue-tinted steel, and was handily cutting down the Jaft crewmen who came between him and Gwen.

Blood splashed and the crew members fell as the apparent leader of these raiders approached with ease and an unsettling grace.

"Everybody get out of the way," she screamed, her usually light and lilting voice carrying all of the authority of a regal princess or queen.

The Jafts all seemed to hear her, and probably discerned her intentions from the sudden rush of magic she brought to bear.

The Lizardman raider smiled blithely at her, and brought his scimitar up, licking Jaft blood off of the edge with his forked tongue.

Gwen felt a quiver of illness in her stomach, but bit back the urge to vomit at such a sight. She wove her hands in the air, drawing symbols of arcane power at her sides. Magical power thrummed through her body, and the reptilian warrior paused for a moment, concern and curiosity mixing in his expression. Before he could move to defend himself, Gwen unleashed one of her most powerful spells.

"Singen Jukuhow!" Gwen drew her hands together in a forward clap, bringing the symbols crashing into one another in the air.

From her joined hands came a tremendous thunderclap that rocked the entire boat. A set of three rings of force wavered toward the Lizardman.

The reptilian warrior brought his hands up feebly to ward off the magic, but to no effect. As each wave of power struck, it shredded first his clothes and armor, then his scaled flesh, and finally his muscle tissue, leaving a pile of bones and organs teetering grossly on its feet. The corpse staggered a few feet, and then dropped with a splash of blood and guts to the deck.

A triumphant roar arose from the crewmen, and the rest of the Lizardman raiders, their attention focused solely on their handily slain leader, were tossed overboard by strong Jafts who lifted their quarries by the throats and hauled them over with ease.

Gwen, spent from the amount of mana used in her spell, sat her rear end heavily on the deck.

A large shadow loomed over her after a moment, and she looked up into the face of the captain, who cocked a bald eyebrow at her. "That, was impressive," he said to her just before Gwen passed out.

* * * *

When the Half-Elf Aeromancer awoke, she found herself swathed in soft, velvet sheets upon a lavish bed she knew was not the one in her assigned quarters. She tried to sit up, but a wave of vertigo halted her efforts.

She closed her eyes, and heard the heavy breathing of someone seated near the head of the bed. She opened her eyes, and saw the captain sitting in a rustic rocking chair, his arms crossed over his huge, bare chest.

"Where am I," she asked, surprised at the weak quality of her voice.

"You're in my wife's quarters, though she is not pleased about it," said the captain. "I never properly introduced myself when you paid for your passage on board. I am Gronen Mattock. I know you are called Gwen, and I apologize for my harsh words to you up on deck."

Gwen waved his apology off, finally managing to sit up with help from the captain, Gronen.

"I didn't know you were married, captain," she said with a smile as he handed her a mug filled with steaming tea.

Gronen's face remained in its semi-permanent scowl, and he nodded.

"She is the ship's cook, if you must know. Her name is Thelma Mattock. You ripped that chieftain apart, by the way," Gronen said, taking a sip from his own mug, which Gwen could smell was filled with coffee instead of tea. "Where did you learn such powerful magic?"

"I trained with a Guild in Desanadron," Gwen informed him. She looked down into her mug, and drank half of the contents within. It was sweet, flavored with a drop of honey. The tea warmed her stomach, which she was reminded now was pretty much empty. She hadn't eaten all day, and would have to request food be brought to her. "I have been studying Aeromancy for quite some time now. I am on my way to Palen to hopefully learn the most ancient of Aeromancy spells from a Great Sage."

Gronen made a somewhat rude noise from his throat, and spat on the hardwood floor.

"Something wrong," she asked.

Gronen got to his feet and stalked a few yards away from the bed. "I've met this Great Sage you speak of on one occasion," the Jaft said in his harsh tone of voice, his back to Gwen. His black brigandine pants seemed rather small on him, Gwen noticed, as though the leather and iron-banded trousers could barely contain the musculature of the man wearing them. "He sent a messenger pigeon to our vessel, requesting we ship something for him from Desanadron to Palen. We prefer not to take shipments across land, but he requested that we personally deliver the item in question. When we disembarked, me and a quarter of my crew traveled by arranged horses to Palen, north and east of our port. When we arrived with his package, which was in a large wooden crate, he did not even come out of his manor or to his front gates.

"Four of my men tried to take the crate to his front door, and were torn apart by strange, black magic before they covered a quarter of the distance," Gronen growled. He half turned toward Gwen, who finished her tea and set the mug on a nightstand near the other side of the bed from the rocker. "The bastard only came out after they were slain, and laughed at us like a lunatic! And do you know what he pulled out of the top of that crate?"

"You didn't know what it was," Gwen asked, surprised that the captain of the shipping vessel wouldn't have inquired.

"We were paid handsomely not to make any inquiries, or open the crate itself," Gronen muttered. "We gave our word to his servant, and we are Jafts. We are honor-bound to keep our word, Gwen of the Half-Elves." He reached over to a coat rack and pulled on a chain shirt over his bare upper torso. "He pulled out a scepter of some sort, and swept it with a flourish over the corpses of my men. They arose from the ground, and at first, I was gladdened. However, when they turned to face me, their eyes were empty, soulless orbs lacking any true sight. They followed him into his manor, and I never saw or heard from them again."

Gronen left the cabin then, slamming the oak door shut behind him.

Gwen used the uncomfortable silence to think over what she had just learned about the man she intended to go learn from.

* * * *

An hour after Gronen left her, Gwen got up from the bed. She was about to head out of the chamber and return to her own assigned quarters, when Thelma Mattock entered the cabin.

Thelma, like the other females of her Race, did not stink like the men of the crew, and her head was graced with a full pate of luxurious hair. Her stark, raven-black eyes pierced into Gwen's own, and the Half-Elf felt a tad diminished by the naked glare she was being given.

"Are you finished with mine and my husband's bed," Thelma growled with clear anger.

"Yes, and I am most thankful for the use of it," Gwen stammered, her heart racing. She had barely recovered enough of her mana through rest to defend herself, should the need arise. Thelma seemed highly offended by her very presence, and Gwen skirted past her and out of the cabin, into the hallway below the uppermost deck.

Her own quarters were one more level below, in the bottom deck, where only she and one other crew member had quarters. The cargo hold dominated the bottom deck, and her quarters were pressed in tight all around as a result.

Once she was in the hallway, Gwen wanted to get topside and find out how close to the Allenian Hills they were. She knew she would be needed to defend the vessel again once they were within that region, and she needed to know how much time she had to rest, eat, and recover her mana reserves. Checking herself quickly for her few worn possessions, she headed up to the top deck, into the clean, crisp air of early evening.

Only a dozen or so crewmen were up on deck, most of them adjusting ropes and mounting weapons on the side railings. Two of the men busily and happily swabbed the deck, cleaning it of the blood that had dried to the boards. A group of four rather gloomy-looking chaps were slowly, reverently preparing the bodies of the few Jafts who had suffered wounds too serious to regenerate in the earlier scrap with the Lizardmen raiders.

Deep, searing guilt bore down on Gwen's conscience. *Could that have been prevented, if I had simply helped out earlier on in the battle?*

The Aeromancer shook her head to clear it of such thoughts, knowing full well that it would do her little good to dwell on the matter. These Jafts knew the risks of being sailors on the rivers and seas--it came with the job.

Gwen looked to her left, to the pilot box, but didn't find the captain there. The first mate, a man named Shtur Bonebreaker was at the helm, piloting the ship with a practiced ease as he chuffed away on a pipe. The Aeromancer realized with a start that in the five days she had been on board, the only person she'd really spoken with at any length was Gronen. She had made no other acquaintances on board, and none of the crewmen exactly went out of their way to speak with her.

Suddenly feeling very alone, Gwen headed to the south-facing edge of the ship and leaned on the railing, looking out at the flat grasslands there.

When a crewman came near, checking the surrounding area for signs of any more raiders, she asked him how close they were to the Allenian Hills.

"Still another full day, day and a half, miss," he replied, and left her to her thoughts and private council.

A few minutes later, Gwen heard the heavy footfalls of another crewmember, and when she turned her head to see, she was surprised to find that it was not a Jaft, but a Human.

The man wore a simple yellow tunic over faded black jeans, and he wore a rapier on his left hip, as well as carrying several vials and pouches on his right side.

Why haven't I seen this man before, she wondered.

The stranger smiled at her, and his thin, black mustache curled as he did so. She could see that his eyes were a wonderfully deep shade of green, like her own, and his face was otherwise untouched by scars or signs of age.

Gwen blushed slightly as he gave her his charming smile. She was herself rather unattractive, she thought. She had a young girl's face, with no blemishes at least, but with none of the graceful curves or lines of her mother's own Elven visage. She had just time enough before the man spoke to also remind herself that unlike her mother, her chest was also just about as flat as her back. She was rather unremarkable, she thought, and so she was puzzled by this stranger's sudden approach. By and large, by her own observations, Human men only approached women they knew as friends, family, or potential lays. She didn't know the man, wasn't related to him in any way she knew of, and so she immediately thought he might be approaching for the latter reason; to get some cheap thrills.

"Greetings, mistress," he said, his voice husky and pleasant, as he gave her a slight bow.

She turned and pressed her back to the railing then, and flushed completely.

"I am Aaron Horn, a Human as you can plainly see, and a practitioner of Aquamancy," he said.

Ah, so there's the tie-in, she thought as he rose to look her in the eyes. *A fellow magic-user.*

"I saw your earlier spellcasting against the Lizardman raiders, and was thoroughly impressed and intrigued. I would have helped, but as you know, the Jafts have a natural fear of water and ice magic." His smile revealed a row of perfectly aligned teeth to Gwen, and she found in it a rather disturbing natural attraction.

Behave yourself, girl, she chided herself. *You're on this vessel for business, not pleasure!*

"I am Gwen Surefire," she said, and curtsied politely. "Half-Elf and Aeromancer, Mr. Horn. And I'm sure that captain Gronen would have willingly put aside his discomfort if aid could have been given against the raiders."

"Oh, I'm sure he'll allow me to help if we are set upon by Khan or Simpa in the Allenians." The Human Aquamancer stepped closer.

Gwen tried to press herself further into the woodwork of the railing but found that it had no give, as she should have expected. Butterflies fluttered around in her stomach, and she felt more blood rush into her cheeks as he neared her. He smelled wonderful to her nostrils, like jasmine and musk blended subtly together. After several solid days of being around the natural rot and body odor of the blue-skinned, bald warriors on board, she supposed any scent was welcome.

"I'm sure he will," she replied. "Tell me, what business brings you on board?"

Aaron Horn strode up next to her, and leaned forward on the railing, and for a brief moment, Gwen saw the captain out of the corner of her eye, grinning bemusedly at the two of them. *Oh, he's going to have something to say about this, I know it.*

"I am heading east, to Palen," he said.

Gwen's heart skipped a few beats, and he continued, with Gwen hanging to his every word. "My brother Steven lives there, and has recently lost his wife to a tragic accident." His voice now dropped a note with regret. "She was an Alchemist, and was experimenting with various poisons, as they often do. While mixing two of these, she formed a gaseous mix, which she inhaled and which then killed her."

"Oh, my," Gwen said softly. She put a hand on Aaron's shoulder. "I am so sorry for your loss."

Aaron Horn smiled at her, and patted her hand on his shoulder. His touch was icy and frozen, his magical power seemingly contained only by the barest of thresholds.

"I thank you for your kind words," he said. "But the loss is my brother's not mine. I go to console him as best I may. What of you, Gwen Surefire? What business brings you on this vessel?"

Gwen withdrew her hand, and leaned over the railing in the same fashion as the man next to her.

"I too head to Palen," she said. "I go to seek the Great Sage who lives there, to learn the last few ancient spells of Aeromancy not already in my arsenal."

"The Great Sage," he asked, giving her a perplexed look. "But I thought that was just a rumor that he lived in Palen!"

Gwen smiled broadly at him and shook her head. "No, it is true, he resides therein, on the eastern border of the City of Magic." She looked out over the plains once again. She spotted a far off caravan, several covered wagons heading east and slightly south. The failing light of the evening made it impossible for her to see exactly how many people were in the caravan, or of what Race they might be. *Probably heading for the trading town in the Allenians,* she thought. *I hope they'll be okay. I hope we'll be okay.* "I only pray he will invite me to his manor to learn from him. He only invites a few mages each year to train with him and I am not a resident of the city. I can only hope that he will read a request from me if I send it."

She heaved a sigh and listened to the sounds of the ship passing through the deep water of the river, feeling a cool, comforting wind pass over her forehead from the south. Aaron remained beside her for a few minutes, and then he excused himself. "A man has to eat," he said with a grin. "I hope perhaps we'll have the opportunity to speak again during our trip." He gave her a grand, sweeping bow, then took his leave and headed below decks, leaving Gwen alone and wistful.

She saw the captain approaching as soon as Aaron Horn was out of sight, and she didn't care much for the lopsided grin on his blue face.

"Something I can help you with, Captain Gronen?" she asked haughtily, turning once more to the railing. "Or can a girl enjoy the view in peace?"

Gronen laughed at this, and shook his big, hairless head.

"No, no, I just wanted to give you fair warning. This isn't a cruise ship, Ms. Surefire." He gestured over his shoulder. "The other passenger, Mr. Horn, may tickle your fancy, but you should be cautious about flings at sea."

"We're on a river, captain, not at sea," she pointed out with a note of scorn. "And as for any 'fling' you may infer, I'll have you know it's a girl's prerogative to make herself happy. Given my isolation aboard your ship, I think a spot of Mr. Horn's company will suit me nicely." She turned to face the muscular sailor with her hands on her hips. "Or is that sort of behavior not allowed on board?"

Gronen laughed again, a hoarse, gravely sound, throwing his head back and waving his hands defensively.

"Do not misunderstand me, Ms. Surefire." He wiped a laugh-induced tear from his right eye. "I'd just hate to see you get hurt because of any misunderstandings. That's all."

Gwen harrumphed loudly and left the deck, heading down for her private, cramped quarters. She could hear the captain's laughter in her mind as she lay down on her small, uncomfortable cot.

* * * *

Gronen had taken a nap earlier, so that he could pilot the ship that night as they passed closer to the Allenian Hills.

His wife, Thelma, entered the pilot box at around midnight, smiling gently at her husband and offering him another mug of coffee.

He thanked her, and kissed her lovingly on the cheek.

"I'm sorry about getting mad at you about the Half-Elf girl," Thelma offered, taking one of the two spots on the bench behind the spoke-riddled wheel.

"It's understandable, dear." He took a quick sip of the hot, strong liquid. He set it down on the small, square elm wood table next to the helm, and stared out at the deck.

His navigator signaled down and back to him from the crow's nest, and the captain turned the wheel accordingly. "I'm worried about her, though."

"Was she injured worse than we thought?" Thelma asked, genuinely concerned.

Her husband, whom she loved more than the ship and the open seas, looked back at her over his broad shoulder, and she could see the scowl on his face.

"No," he said, returning his gaze forward and taking another pull of his coffee from its purple ceramic mug. "It's the other passenger, the Human. I believe she is infatuated with him, and I don't trust that son of a bitch one bit."

Thelma laughed aloud, and stood up, putting her arms around her husband's well sculpted stomach.

"You just don't like him because he's handsome, and he's an Aquamancer," she chided amiably. She kissed the back of his neck, feeling the tremor that ripped down his body.

"It's more than that, and please, dear, I'm trying to pilot the ship." He chuckled lightly. "If you keep that up, I'm going to have to call the first mate up and take you down to our cabin." He cleared his throat, and attempted to clear his head. Partial success was attained there, which was enough to let him continue. "He's shifty, Thelma, and what's more, one of the men caught him snooping around in the cargo hold yesterday. We're not carrying anything that's contraband where we're heading, but I don't like having anyone but the men in there. You know that."

He sighed as she gripped him in a fierce, brief embrace from behind.

She released him, took a sip of his coffee, and sat back down on the bench.

"I know dear. What do you want me to do about it?"

"Keep an eye on him." Gronen once again adjusted the ship's course by the navigator's gestures. "And post a guard inside the cargo hold. If he sneaks in again, I want him clapped in irons and locked in his chamber. I'll have words with him personally after that."

Thelma got up, gave him a kiss on the cheek, and moved out of the pilot box to carry out his request.

He was left alone then with his thoughts, and he wondered, not for the first time, which he loved more--sailing, or being alone with his wife in their cabin. As always, he chose the latter over the former with a wide smile.

* * * *

Gwen was awakened by a rough shaking on her shoulder. When she opened her eyes with a flutter, she found the first mate looming over her, his face covered with a cold sweat. "Come topside, quickly! The captain wants to have a word with you, and there may be trouble for us all!"

"What's wrong?" she murmured, hurriedly tossing aside her bed sheets and grabbing her only weapon, a smooth-headed mace that she kept for when her mana reserves dried up. She had only minimal training with the weapon, but its weight on her hip gave her reassurance against her worries, and she followed the first mate up to the top deck of the ship.

He didn't give her any further explanation, and when she came out of the stairwell to the top deck of the ship, she saw why the captain had sent for her.

The ship's sails were unfurled, but there was no wind to press the ship onward. Captain Gronen, looking more than a little tired, stood silhouetted against the early morning sunlight that pressed down on the lands surrounding the river. He hastily approached her, and gave her a curt bow of his head. "We normally have the river's current to carry us along, Mr. Surefire, but our cargo for this trip is too heavy, and we are weighted down too much to continue at more than a turtle's crawl. We are hoping you can provide us with enough wind current to get us going at full speed again."

Gwen smiled at the request, confident in her ability to give the captain more than a little boost of speed. "I can give your vessel all the speed it can manage," she said, heading over to the pilot box's left side, and climbing a ladder affixed to the side for scouts who would watch for pursuit on the open seas.

Once atop the pilot box, Gwen summoned up her magical power, and sent a powerful gale into the sails, speeding the ship along at twice her normal cruising speed.

Captain Gronen laughed and called up to her. "Slow it down a little, Gwen Surefire! My first mate is a competent pilot, but not so good at such high speeds! You don't want us to crash, do you?"

She pulled back a little on the magic, a spell simple enough for her to maintain for a number of hours.

"Very good! When you feel a natural wind current again, let go of your power! I'll be below, getting some rest!"

Gwen gave him her okay, and continued with her task with pleasure. She continued to provide power for three hours, until the natural breezes began to carry them again, and then she released her flow from the sails. The ship continued on at the same pace, and she descended the ladder to find Aaron Horn waiting for her at the bottom.

"Very useful, aren't we?" he asked with a grin.

Once again Gwen felt her face flush with a quick burst of blood. Her dreams had been full of images of the man, and in these dreams, she was engaged with him in acts she had only heard and read about. She felt a strange rush of energy in her loins, and she found she could not speak.

"I was wondering if you'd like to have an early lunch with me in my quarters," he asked suddenly.

She nodded mutely.

He took her hand, and guided her below decks.

His own quarters, she noted, were much like the captain's, and Gwen privately wondered how much he had paid the captain for such accommodations. A meal had already been laid out for them at a lavish elm wood table, and they sat across from one another before the plates and bowls.

They enjoyed the well-prepared meal in comfortable silence, and when they finished, Aaron asked her to tell him more about herself.

"Well, I was born and raised in Desanadron. I'm a Half-Elf, as you are aware, and I'm thirty-six."

"Pretty young, even for a half-breed," he commented, taking a swig of mead from his glass mug.

She didn't care for the term he used, but coming from him, she guessed she didn't mind so much. He had struck her as handsome during the evening before, and found him even more attractive by the daylight coming in through the portside window of his chambers. *I wonder if he'll ask to bed me*, she thought, her heart and stomach aflutter.

"Yes, well, every bird has to leave the nest eventually," she said, looking away as she blushed. "I joined one of the mage Guilds in the city, the Compass Points Guild. They study, teach and practice the four elemental schools of magic."

"Compass Points," he asked. Then his face lit with realization. "Ah, I get it! Four points of the compass, four elemental schools of magic! Very clever." He took another chug of his ale. "How long did you study with them?"

"Ten years." She flipped her long hair aside with her left hand. Its chestnut hue glimmered in the light coming into the room, and she wondered for a brief moment if perhaps he found it as pretty as her father had always said it was. "I studied under a Sorcerer Supreme, Ranatome Vukshak, a Gnome Aeromancer. He's one of the most skilled in all the land of Tamalaria. He knows two of the ancient Aeromancy spells, but he refused to teach them to me. He claimed he did not have the right, and that I, like he, would have to discover them on my own," she said with a small growl. "I hated that."

"I can imagine." He stood with a flourish, heading past her to an oak armoire. " "Would you like some wine? I brought some of my own for the trip," He stood with his back to her, opening one door and pulling out a fat bottle of red fluid.

"Um, sure," she stammered. *When did I last have alcohol,* she asked herself. *It must be months since my last glass of wine. Mom and dad were never keen on me drinking the stuff.*

Gwen had lived in the Guildhall for the last two years, but she still obeyed a lot of the rules laid down by her parents during her upbringing, especially those rules set by her father. He never resorted to corporal punishment, but he used the classical guilt trip like no one else she knew, and of all of the emotions in life, she despised feeling guilty the most.

Aaron Horn poured her a glass of wine, and handed it to her. She took a sniff of it as she swished it around in its glass, and her nostrils flared at the wonderful aroma of mixed fruits and berries.

He took his seat once more, and smiled broadly at her. "It's a fine wine, I assure you." He finished off his own ale.

She took a sip, and marveled at the light taste of it in her mouth. She could detect no trace of alcohol in it, which pleased her further.

"You can hardly taste the alcohol, can you?"

"Can't taste it at all," she said, quaffing the whole glass in another large gulp.

He laughed aloud, and poured her another glass. They continued to talk about their own respective pasts, all the while spied upon by a keen set of eyes and ears.

Thelma watched through the spy hole in the wall between his chamber and one of the crewmen's rooms, and listened to the two of them prattle on for a while. When the girl was bobbing her head and trilling drunkenly, Thelma moved out of the room. She was going to let her husband, as captain of the ship, decide what to do next.

Because as far as Thelma was concerned, the girl was on the verge of being taken advantage of, and Thelma preferred to watch Gronen hurt people instead of doing it herself.

* * * *

Gronen had been sleeping fitfully, and was already quick to anger when his wife roused him. "What the hell is it?" he asked her gruffly as he swung his legs over the edge of their bed.

"I just thought you'd like to know that Mr. Horn has gotten the girl quite drunk in his private quarters."

The immediate grimace of fury and concern on her husband's face caused her to inch away from him.

"I would like to remind you, dear, that you agreed to give him access to the room when he paid, and promised him privacy while on board," she said, a tad more cautiously.

"To the hells with that," he groused, standing up and moving swiftly over to where he kept his war hammer hung on the wall. Instead of grabbing the heavy stone weapon, he pulled on his chain shirt and a pair of heavily plated metal gloves. "I promised the girl we'd take care of her as best we could, and I'll not have her taken advantage of on *my* ship. Not on my watch." He headed out of the cabin with Thelma on his heels.

"Gronen, what are you planning to do," Thelma asked, worried that perhaps she had judged wrongly in coming to her husband with the knowledge of what she'd spied. Her husband was prone to unspeakable violence when it came to defending women, a fact that she enjoyed when certain fools at port insulted her honor. She'd watch with glee as Gronen beat said fools into bloody masses of quivering meat, and he didn't limit his physical punishment to any one kind of man. He'd slugged it out with skilled Werewolf fighters a few times, and for the most part, came out on top. Only twice had he been bested when someone insulted his wife or offended her otherwise, and in each instance it had been by Minotaurs who had lots of experience with Boxing arts.

But Gronen was also a very clever man, and he gave Thelma a sly grin over his shoulder. "Why, nothing much. I'm going to ask him to come up on deck to prepare for defense against Khan and Simpa raiders. It's a half truth, so it'll blow over pretty well," he said.

Thelma marveled at her husband's ingenuity, and followed dutifully as he knocked on the Human's chamber door.

* * * *

Gwen had gotten herself into a state of mind that she often referred to as 'pleasantly fuzzy', which essentially meant that she was drunk enough to laugh at anything. Aaron Horn turned out to be somewhat of a comedian, and had her nearly in stitches when there was a knock at his door.

Aaron smiled at her and stood up, heading over to the door as she drained her seventh glass of wine.

Aaron Horn opened the door. There stood captain Gronen with his wife, Thelma, looking somewhat stern next to him.

"Mr. Horn, I apologize for the intrusion. I was hoping, however, that you might be able to come topside and prepare to aid us with any raiders, Khan or Simpa, who might come at us within the next few hours. We are almost into the Allenians, but we have been attacked before this close to the region by members of both Races," Gronen lied, his own face inscrutable.

"Oh," Aaron said, clearly taken aback. He turned partially and looked at Gwen, who smiled and waved with drunken friendliness at the captain and his wife. "Well, um, I was just talking with Gwen, and we were having a good laugh," he said, trying quite clearly to cry off of Gronen's request.

"I understand, and as I said, I apologize for the intrusion. But you did offer to help us defend against raiders, Mr. Horn, and I need to hold you now to that offer," Gronen said with a small, terse smile.

Aaron Horn slumped his shoulders, and hung his head with a brief sigh. When he looked up, he beamed at the married Jaft couple with his disarming smile, and he nodded.

"Very well. Um, I don't think Ms. Surefire can help much right now. She's had a bit of wine, and she's, well, she's rather drunk, I'm afraid," he said bashfully. "Perhaps she should just lie down on my bed, if I'm going to be on deck."

"I'll help her back to her own quarters." Thelma slipped past Aaron Horn and gathered the Half-Elf girl in a fireman's carry.

Gwen laughed explosively at her, and pounded on her back.

"You two go on ahead. I'll join you shortly," Thelma said.

Gronen put a huge arm over Aaron's shoulders, and led him upstairs as Thelma rushed Gwen down to her quarters.

Once inside, Thelma set her on her bed, laughing and twitching, and produced a yellow pill from one of her pouches. She handed the pill to Gwen, who stared at it with bleary eyes.

"Take it now, Gwen dear," Thelma said with a soft smile. The Half-Elf Aeromancer swallowed the pill, and a few minutes later, gripped the sides of her head before Thelma handed her a slop bucket to vomit into. "That's to be expected, dear," she offered, rubbing Gwen's back softly.

"Oh, my head." Gwen felt a deep, throbbing pulse in her temples. She could remember nothing after her second glass of wine, and it troubled her that she had blacked out while remaining completely conscious. She'd seen such a thing happen once with her father, after he'd come home from a tavern rather drunk. He had cooked something awful in the kitchen, devoured it, and passed out in the dining room. Gwen's mother had left him there to sleep, claiming it would be a 'learning experience' for him. *And oh, he learned all right,* Gwen thought as she clutched the bucket and hurled again into it. *He learned that he should never mix certain foods ever again.* "What happened," she asked softly, her voice scratchy from the explosive fit of vomiting.

Thelma continued to rub her back soothingly. "Well, I think you came very close to being taken to bed, dear."

Gwen gave her a shocked glance before returning her attention once more to the bucket. The last of her lunch escaped her stomach in one final, tidal rush, and she felt very deeply tired afterward.

"Without your knowledge or consent," Thelma continued.

"Aaron wouldn't have done that," Gwen offered weakly, unsure herself of what may have happened. She liked Aaron Horn, was attracted to him physically and because he was a fellow magic-user. Her own mother had a thing for Human men, and apparently, she had passed this liking on to her only daughter. "He's not like that."

"Do you want to take a chance on that?" Thelma asked quite seriously. "Relax for now, and get some rest. The pill clears the body of all toxins, and you may need to recover your strength. We will indeed be in the Allenians in a few hours. I'll send someone down for you then, but until that time, rest." Thelma eased Gwen back onto her bed and covering her with a blanket. "Perhaps later, without the influence of alcohol on you, you can decide what you want to do with Mr. Horn. But give it some thought, first."

"Why are you being so nice to me?" Gwen asked, suddenly a little wary of the woman's intentions. "When I was in your quarters, you were staring daggers at me."

Thelma laughed aloud at this, and slapped her own knee with mirth.

"That's only because I was tired and wanted to rest, dear! Kind of hard to do when there's a little Half-Elf girl in my bed, isn't it? Think no more on it, and get to rest, right now," she admonished with a smile.

Just like mom, Gwen thought as she let sleep claim her. The last words she heard before passing out were, "You'll need the sleep if we need you."

* * * *

When the two men got up on deck, Aaron Horn looked around at the surroundings of the vessel, and harrumphed. "I don't see any raiders." He turned to face Gronen, who was giving orders to some of his men in their native tongue. "Captain, do you really think we'll be attacked before entering the Allenian Hills?"

"We might be, Mr. Horn, and I'd rather not risk it," Gronen said. He felt a little guilty about deceiving the man, but until he knew more about his strength or weakness of character, he wasn't going to take any risks. "We are naturally wary of your breed of magic, but it could prove very useful. Now, do me a favor, and go up there to my first mate," he said, pointing to the man he mentioned. "He's setting up the spear launchers, and I'd like you to lock some spells on the spears themselves before they're loaded."

Aaron smiled up at the big man then, and chuckled softly to himself.

"You know about locking spells? Are you a magic wielder yourself, Captain Gronen?"

"No," the Jaft admitted. "But I've had years of experience dealing with them. I may not fully trust Aquamancers, but you seem capable, competent. No please, carry out this request, and make ready in case there are raiders." Gronen watched with a guilty pleasure as the man sauntered off toward the first mate.

Gronen continued shouting orders until Thelma came up from below. "How is she," he whispered to her.

"Marga avenso ni cutock men-wha," she whispered back. 'The girl was ill, but now is resting'.

"Sapira nu guan do amikana sutocku," he said aloud. 'For what reason do you address me in our native tongue'?

"Munoki sumono, tu turmondo si tu siva pleadas." 'Because dear one, the Human may have good ears'.

Gronen nodded, understanding his wife's wariness. He took her by the arm, and headed to the pilot box, relieving the temporary pilot for a few minutes so that they could speak plainly out of the Human's earshot.

"When we pass the traders' town in the Allenians, we'll stop off and ask for a lawman or local magistrate," he said bluntly, reacting smoothly to the navigator's signals.

"Why?"

"I want to see if they have any information on this Aaron Horn. He told me that he'd been through the area, and anyone who comes to that town has to register with the local law offices. He claimed to have come through only a couple of years ago, so he'll still be on file."

"You're really quite suspicious of this man, aren't you?"

"Well, think about it dear. He paid me seven hundred gold pieces for the trip and the use of our finest guest cabin, a fee far beyond what I would have asked for."

"That's more than we're getting for the cargo," Thelma almost shouted.

He stayed her with one open palm held toward her. "Sorry dear."

"That's okay," Gronen said, staring hard out toward the Human, who was busily locking spells on spearheads being loaded into the launchers. "Yes, I understand your surprise, but I didn't want to mention how much he paid me until I had reason to suspect the payment. But honestly, who carries around that much gold outside of the safety of a local market? Two kinds of men, dear. There's your common thieves, or the rare but dangerous sort."

"You think he might be a wanted criminal or something?" Thelma now wished that she had tossed the man overboard when she came on deck. Somehow, she suspected that he was going to cause trouble not just for the Half-Elf girl, but for everyone aboard the ship.

"It's possible, I suppose." Gronen took his hands off of the helm just long enough to crack his gnarled knuckles beneath their armored gloves. "For now, that's secondary business," he grumbled, placing his hands on the helm once more. "We're entering the Allenians."

Thelma instinctively tensed. She hated this part of their longer trips, because the Allenian Hills were hostile lands, and the river narrowed considerably, though it retained its depth. Their small trading vessel could withstand a lot, but the crew was small in number, and many of them were new recruits, freshly taken on after the last major trip. How would they fare against Khan or Simpa in direct combat, she wondered?

Pretty soon, she would find out.

* * * *

Gwen Surefire awoke on her own at around four in the afternoon, her head clear and her mind sharp. She recalled the majority of her early lunch with Aaron Horn now, and remembered drinking an awful lot of wine. She chided herself silently for being so foolish. She swung out of her small bed, got her mace into its leather loop, and headed topside.

Up on deck, she gasped as she realized that the ship now sailed through the narrow section of river that wound through the Allenian Hills region. The ship might come under heavy attack at any time, but she felt panicked for another reason entirely. She looked at the armed and ready crew aboard the ship's deck, and knew instinctively that some of the younger men had never seen combat with anything more threatening than a handful of unskilled Humans. *If a pack of Khan or Simpa come on board, most of these men will be slain in short order,* she thought.

Aaron Horn stood amid the blue-skinned warriors, looking confident with his casual stance, his charming grin constantly in place.

She approached him with her hands behind her back, shy like a schoolgirl. "Greetings, Aaron Horn," she said as she got within five yards of the Human Aquamancer.

He turned and gasped at the sight of her, and for just a second, his smile seemed to falter.

"Oh, Gwen." He sounded a tad out of breath.

She felt his magic all around her, much of it coming from the mounted spear launchers on the right-hand railing.

"I didn't expect you up so soon! You were so drunk, I had to ask the captain to have you taken back to your quarters."

At the sound of his lie, Gwen shivered a little inside. *Why does he lie to me so? To protect my feelings? Or to protect something of his own?* Suspicious though she felt, she forced herself to smile winningly at him and stand on her toes for a second. It was one of her nervous gestures, and she could see from the way he reacted to it by grinning once more that this time *she* he disarmed *him.*

"I'm really sorry about that, Aaron," she said, twirling a bit of her chestnut hair around a finger playfully. "I should have warned you that I can't hold my liquor. It's been so long, though, that I didn't want to stop, because I though that might offend you or something."

Aaron Horn laughed harshly at this, and waved a hand in dismissal at her.

"I wouldn't have been at all offended, dear," he said. "Ah, I believe the captain wants a word with you." He pointed toward the pilot box.

Gwen turned and saw Gronen motioning for her to approach him.

"Something you wanted, captain," she asked, looking from Gronen at the helm to Thelma, on the bench behind him.

"I need to know that you're well enough to help us defend the ship," he said flatly. "And don't guess at it; the Khan certainly won't if they show up first. The Simpa are generally more reasonable, and honorable, but the tiger men always present a problem when they get near the ship. They'll set the ship aflame if they have to."

Gwen considered the question a moment, and tapped into her reserves of mana. She found an ample stock of magical energy at hand.

"I'm able and willing, captain," she said confidently. "It won't be like last time if something happens, I promise. I won't hesitate."

He looked away from the helm for a moment and gave her a fierce smile.

"Good, because the last time was just practice, miss. I assure you, Lizardmen attacking when we're still in the wide parts of the river are nothing compared to the Khan that may set upon us. And if we're unfortunate enough to run into the savage Simpa tribes, expect no mercy. They're powerful and ruthless." He faced out of the pilot box again. "Take up a position, and make sure you and Mr. Horn don't get in each other's way. You don't want to create a crossfire situation."

Gwen nodded, gave him a shallow bow, and headed out on deck, her magic brewing inside.

As the sun set in the distance at around eight in the evening, the navigator spotted the first raiders of the region and called down to the crew to prepare for an attack. "Khan warriors, a pack of ten or eleven stro--" He was struck in the head by a long javelin thrown from the shore.

The navigator fell from his perch to the deck below, his brains and blood spraying across the wood as he struck with the weapon still in his skull.

Three fully-grown Khan in thick chain armor leaped on board, and the first of this trio was brutally smashed in the chest with a stone war hammer by the ship's first mate. The Jaft warrior reared back his weapon for a second blow, and when the dazed Khan finished shaking off the impact of the first strike, the first mate crushed his skull flat with his hammer. Blood sprayed across onto each of the Khan's companions, who dashed past on either side of the Jaft, raking his sides with their long, curved claws.

The Khan on Gwen's right tore straight for a pair of the new recruits, the Jafts raising their weapons fearlessly like all members of their Race.

When the Khan stood a few yards away, the Jaft men roared mightily and charged forward.

The Khan warrior leaped up past them, and tore their throats out with the talons on his bare feet.

Both crewmen fell dead to the deck.

Gwen stood paralyzed with shock and fear; *so fast, so powerful,* she thought as she started to back away from the Khan, who identified her as easy prey. The Weretiger snarled and snapped his jagged jaws at her, and when he lunged, instinct alone saved the Half-Elf.

"Vera Dopna," she whispered, pointing one finger at him and releasing a disk of concentrated wind.

It flew at the Khan and cleaved his head in half, leaving everything from the flaring nostrils down to shuffle forward one step, then two, and finally drop limply to the side.

Thick, coppery-scented blood spurted from the gaping hole that had been its head as Gwen shook violently with fearful tremors. Unlike with the Lizardmen, however, she kept her wits about her, and stayed alert for more assailants.

Gwen looked over toward the opposite railing and found Aaron Horn forming a barrier of ice around a Khan and then kicking him overboard, to either break his neck on land, or drown in the river. He moved around the deck with a natural ease as the melee flowed around him. Even the new recruits moved with a little discomfort, so how did *he* move with such unerring footfalls? She'd have to ask him about it later, if they had the chance to get together again.

The third Khan, she saw as she looked away from Aaron, had fallen under Gronen's brutal, unarmed assault. The large Jaft captain punched the unfortunate Khan over and over in the face and chest, finally landing a solid blow to the tiger man's stomach. As the lycanthrope doubled over, clutching his gut, Gronen doubled his fists together and drove them down against the Khan's spine.

There issued from the body a horrible crunch, followed by the dropping of the Khan to the deck as it screamed bloody murder and started to drool. The Khan's eyes rolled around in its head, and its body thrashed about the deck violently, the legs and arms going this way and that as they were wracked by involuntary death spasms. Finally it lay still, blood and saliva dripping out of its upturned face, which seemed to stare in death at Gwen.

Unsettled by this image though she was, the Half-Elf Aeromancer had the presence of mind to duck when one of the crewmen called out to her, pointing over her shoulder.

A long sword's blade whooshed over her head, and she spun on her crouched heels and sent a gust of wind into the new Khan assailant's body, tossing him overboard. She sprinted for the railing, and saw three more Khan getting close enough to make the leap onboard.

Gwen Surefire summoned forth another of her more devastating spells, and brought a small tornado down onto the group of Khan.

They screamed soundlessly in the torrential spin of the tornado's cone, deprived of oxygen, clutching at their throats as they suffocated and were slammed into one another and the nearby hillside mercilessly.

Gwen felt a surge of dark glee as they died by her hands, and she turned back toward Gronen, who gave her a silent thumb's up from across the deck.

With the remainder of the raiders blocked by her tornado, the ship sailed onward, down the river, toward the central stretch of the Allenian Hills. The crew's first encounter with raiders had only garnered them two fatalities, a total that Gronen still found unacceptable.

* * * *

Gronen and Thelma warned the two magic-using passengers they might be called on again shortly, then watched them head below deck.

Gwen seemed to shy away from another encounter while Aaron Horn seemed thrilled at the prospect.

His crewmen complained about being terrified of his magic, but Gronen assured them that it was a calculated and necessary risk. "His magic is on all of the spears in the launchers. However, if we're boarded again, we'll need him a second time."

"She released a tornado from above," Thelma said as she took his place once more at the helm, while Gronen sat on the bench behind her. "She's quite powerful for one so young."

"So was Androna Melika, and it didn't get him very far, now did it," the Jaft captain said. Androna had been one of the two Jaft recruits slain during the attack, and though he was indeed a powerful magic user with healing spells, he didn't have a single offensive spell in his arsenal. He had stupidly charged into the Khan attack, and now the crew was out of a healer for the rest of the trip. Gronen thumped the bench hard with a mailed fist. "These trips through the Allenians cost us more lives every time, Thelma! What are we to do?"

"Well, we could try bypassing them by taking the southern rivers, Gronen," she offered, to which he waved his hand impatiently. "Of course, that would take us weeks out of our way, and we're paid to be swift. Perhaps it's time we seriously considered a bigger ship and a larger crew. You know, sail the oceans like we've talked about."

Gronen muttered darkly to himself and crossed his arms over his chest, sulking.

"This is my fault," the Jaft captain said to himself. "If I had just refused the job and taken some time off, we wouldn't have lost those men."

"And then our new recruits would have quit, or asked you for money for their own time off," she pointed out, steering deftly in tune with the backup navigator's directions. "And Gronen? We lost three men, not two. Sostho didn't recover from his head wound."

"Hellfire," Gronen swore. "Piss and blood, we are cursed with this route! Thelma." He came to a decision. "You are correct. After this trip, we take the men to Ja-Wen, and we leave the boat behind. Perhaps we'll find someone looking to buy it off of us at port." He felt unhopeful about their chances of finding a buyer so directly.

The ship sailed on.

* * * *

Gwen lay naked and shivering in the large bed next to Aaron Horn, who had already fallen asleep. She'd wanted to speak with him after their lovemaking, but he had closed his eyes and passed out, snoring, almost immediately. They'd barely spoken a word to one another on the way to his quarters, their bodies still thrumming with adrenaline from the combat above. It was her first time, and though she didn't know what the hell she was doing, Aaron made it quite clear that he knew his way around a young woman's body. At first there had been pleasure, then a bit of pain as the act got underway proper, and then pleasure resurfaced once more. Her nerves still tingled, and now she felt a strange compulsion to express her emotions properly with him.

But he was asleep. When she brought her arm over his torso, he rolled his back toward her.

Gwen felt a twinge of pain at this, but thought twice about her discomfort. *He's tired from the use of magic, and the sex, that's all,* she reasoned. She slipped quietly from the bed, used his shower stall in his bathroom, and dressed herself, heading up topside.

When she surfaced, she saw that it was perhaps a couple of hours past midnight. Gwen felt the cooling night breeze sweep past her forehead, and enjoyed the feel of it through her freshly washed hair.

She looked out at the surrounding hills, and her heart sank as she saw a large movement off to the north. "More raiders," she wondered aloud. She looked up at the crow's nest, and saw that the navigator was busy looking south with his spyglass, in the direction that the Khan had come from before. She hustled to the pilot box, where the first mate was at the helm. "Possible raiders, from the north," she panted as she burst into the box.

"Right." He barked out orders in his people's tongue, and the top deck turned into a roiling flurry of movement as runners were sent below to summon the rest of the ship's defenders.

In minutes the Jaft warriors were all set to defend their ship from either side, and the navigator suddenly barked something loud from above. The first mate shouted something back that Gwen still couldn't understand, and the men on deck drew their weapons and shields.

When at last the first Simpa flew up onto the low deck of the ship, he carried an air of authority and nobility. "Groma sudnamei," he said, using the Jaft speech and holding his empty hands out toward them. "Summa su nocknet shumpatha, eh?"

The Jafts on deck lowered their weapons, but kept them in hand. A runner was sent below, and Gwen cocked her head toward the first mate, who scowled suspiciously at the large Werelion.

"What did he just say," the Half-Elf Aeromancer asked the first mate, not taking her eyes off of the big, golden-furred man.

The Simpa wore no upper clothing, but only a set of black baggy trousers over his legs. He bore no weapons, and a moment later, two more armored and weapon-bearing warriors landed next to him. They were each about a full foot shorter than he, who stood easily as tall as Gronen at seven feet.

"He asked us to stay steady," the first mate replied, signaling for the men closest to the main mast to furl the main sails, so as to slow the ship's pace. "He then asked us to bring up the captain, for he assumed that he was not among us."

Good assumption, then, Gwen thought. She was glad that at least there seemed to be no hostility in the Simpa. They were not only huge, much larger than their hated Khan enemies, but they appeared much more disciplined and trained.

Gronen came up on deck then, and he stalked directly to the leader of the Simpa group. "My runner tells me you speak our tongue, lion man," Gronen said aloud, so that all could hear. "Why is that?"

"Because," the Simpa leader said, his thick, tempered voice rumbling from his chest. "My tribe does regular business with the sailors of your Race that pass through these hills on this river. Would you do trade with us?"

"We have little aboard for regular trade. We take orders from afar, and ship the requested goods directly." Gronen motioned behind him for his men to sheath their weapons and return to their assigned duties.

Those who had been summoned from rest remained in place, their weapons put away for the time being. Gwen stepped out of the pilot box, and approached the captain. She had an idea, and thought she might be of some help in this situation.

"Excuse me, captain?" She approached the group skipping, making light of her presence here in these clearly serious and tense negotiations. Gronen gave her a worried and disturbed look, like she'd lost her mind. "I may be of some help!"

"How say you in this, Elf?" The large Simpa turned his leonine head to look at her.

"Half-Elf," she said, pulling back her hair and pointing to her partially pointed ears. "Well, I'm an Aeromancer. I could lock some spells on your weapons in exchange for whatever you can offer the captain."

Gronen smiled at her warmly then, and nodded at the Simpa chieftain.

"Is she skilled?" the Simpa asked, turning his attention back to the Jaft captain.

He nodded silently, and the Simpa turned toward her again. "Very well. These men are two of my personal guards. There are five more awaiting my order to board with pelts, weapons and armor. Lock some of your most potent spells on their swords and axes, and we have a deal."

The Simpa and Gronen shook hands on the matter, and one of the two guards handed Gwen a long bladed sword. She sat down on the deck, and locked one of her Wind Cutter spells onto it, handing it back.

She repeated the process with each of the guards' weapons as they came on deck and approached. By the time she was finished, Gwen felt ready to fall asleep on the hardwood deck, her physical energy drained from the earlier combat and sexual encounter, her mana depleted from locking spells on weapons. She used twice the normal mana to lock a spell than to cast it instantly, and she gave each weapon a few uses of magic. She bowed to the captain when he thanked her, and she headed back below decks for Aaron's chamber.

When she stepped inside, she found that he was nowhere to be seen.

* * * *

Aaron Horn watched the guard leave the cargo hold from the doorway to Gwen's quarters, and slipped inside as soon as the Jaft was up to the second deck. He closed the door softly behind him, and looked around at the ship's cargo. He headed to one of the crates, opened its hinged top, and peered inside. "Well, that's interesting," he said, shutting the box on its contents. "Wonder who ordered this stuff."

Inside of this second crate, he found something infinitely more interesting, and more importantly, valuable. "Ah, here we are. I knew this was going to be worth it." He threw the lid open and pulling out two large gemstones. Gronen had taken them aboard to be shipped and taken to a Gnome jeweler in Ja-Wen who was to set them into a necklace for someone's mother. The estimated value, according to Aaron's eyepiece and his little jeweler's book, was around six thousand gold pieces per gem. "Oh, this was so worth it."

* * * *

Gwen was so deeply asleep that she almost didn't notice when Aaron came back into bed fully dressed. She didn't come fully awake, and didn't say a word to him until the next morning. "Hello, dear," she said as she woke with the sun. Aaron Horn was sitting on the edge of the bed, making notes in a small notebook, which he swiftly placed in an inner pocket of his blue leather vest.

"Good morning," he said with his trademark grin. "So, you think we'll be much longer in the Allenians?"

"Gods, I hope not," she joked, standing up and stretching. "I'm going to go fetch something to eat. Do you want anything?"

He told her no, thanks anyway, but he had some reading to catch up on. His tone was distant, distracted, and Gwen worried that perhaps he was regretting what they had done the evening before. She exited his quarters, and made it halfway to the kitchen when Gronen called down the hall to her.

"Hello, captain. A fine morning, yes?"

He gave her a quizzical look, and glanced at Aaron Horn's door.

"You slept with him, didn't you?" he asked rather bluntly, his expression flat and devoid of humor, or any other emotion for that matter. He looked tired and haggard, with heavy bags under his eyes. *Probably stayed up all night to steer the ship,* she thought.

"Yes, as a matter of fact, I did," she said, bristling at his inquiry. "I don't see as it's any of your business, Captain. I paid for the ride, not the company of the crew," she said in a huff, and retreated down the hall away from him. *How dare he,* she fumed internally. *He has no right to ask such a thing! And he doesn't know Aaron like I do,* she thought, suddenly defensive and possessive. She entered the kitchen, and found Thelma behind the counter, handing a platter of food to one of the crewmen.

"Ah, I see you're awake," Thelma said from her side of the counter. She spooned eggs and oatmeal onto a plate and bowl, and then placed three sausage links on her platter alongside. "Here, a hearty meal for you. We're almost through the Allenians, making record time, Miss. We're stopping at the trading outpost this morning, and then we'll be off again. If you need anything from the town, get yourself ready when you finish breakfast."

"Thank you." Gwen gave her a small grin and took her tray down to Aaron's room. When she tried the knob, she found that he had locked the door. She knocked twice, and called out to him. "Aaron? Can I come in?"

"I need some time to go over a few things in my books," he called through the door.

Her heart sank a little, but she cheered up right away when he said, "I'll come get you when I'm done in here, okay?"

"All right." She headed down to her own quarters.

After she finished, she headed up to the top deck, and felt the ship slowing as they came upon a small docking area at the trading outpost that was the Allenians' only neutral territory. She spotted several dozen Humans, Elves, Dwarves and Jafts from the crew already milling about in the streets of the small trading town.

She readily walked down the extended plank off of the ship, glad to be on dry, solid land for the first time in over a week.

She looked back over her shoulder, and hustled into the trading outpost when she saw the captain preparing to disembark.

* * * *

"Stupid girl," Gronen said to himself as he set off on dry land into the trading town. She had seen him and scowled, sprinting off into the trading outpost away from him.

"Brendon?"

One of the ranking veterans of his crew came up to him and saluted smartly.

"Keep an eye on the ship until I get back. Get that guard back down to the cargo hold too. Myself and another crewman will relieve you when we're done in town."

"Aye sir." The other Jaft saluted again.

Gronen waited for Thelma to join him, and when she did a few minutes later, he was pleased to see that she had changed from her cook's uniform into her battle raiment. Her war mattock was slung on her hip through a simple leather loop.

"Why dear, you look good enough to take out on the town," Gronen said with a broad, loving smile to his wife.

"And after our business with the Watch, that's just what you're going to do." She took him by the hand and led Gronen directly down the dock steps toward the trading town proper.

It took only five minutes for them to force their way through the clustered throngs in the narrow streets to the Office of the Watch. The building itself was squat and narrow, only two stories high, housing a total of only twenty lawmen. Gronen knew, however, that this Office of the Watch routinely received transcriptions and reports of major criminal activity from both the Ja-Wen region, and the Desanadron city-state.

A familiar Dwarven gent in chain armor and coif sat at the sign-in desk, and when he looked up from his paperwork, he and Gronen smiled and clasped hands over the desk.

"Gronen, it's good ta see ya, mate," the Dwarf said.

"Likewise, Thromir," the captain said. "You remember my wife, Thelma?"

Thromir nodded, shook her hand as well, and lowered himself once more to his seat.

"Thromir, we need a favor from you. We need you to look up a man by the name of Aaron Horn. He's an Aquamancer on board our vessel, and I'd like to know if he's got any warrants."

"Wot's 'e look loik?"

The Dwarf jotted down Gronen's description of the man to the last detail. He tore off the sheet from his pad, and shuffled off to the file room in the back.

When he did not immediately return, Gronen felt a pit open up in his stomach, and Thelma gripped his hand tightly.

Fifteen full minutes later, Thromir returned with a thick binder with an artist's rendition of their passenger on the cover. The name on the binder said Erin Thorn.

"This is yer lad, I believe," the Dwarf constable said.

Gronen didn't know how exactly to react; he didn't want to gloat, but at the same time, he had to confirm the whole thing and bring any relevant facts to light for Gwen.

Gronen opened the binder to the first page. When he saw the hotsheet, which posted the criminal in question's most frequent crime, he showed it to Thelma. The two of them set the binder down, thanked the Dwarf, and sped out of the station. As soon as they were back out into the crush of people, Gronen stopped to take a deep, steadying breath. "Piracy," was the only word he uttered.

* * * *

Gwen agreed to go into the town with Aaron, and instead of taking her directly to a diner for a decent meal, he told her that he had to hit up a pawnshop first, in order to get money for the meal. "I spent most of my money on my quarters, dear," he explained sweetly.

She understood, of course; he wanted to travel in comfort while he thought over his poor brother's situation in Palen.

And so she smiled amiably at traders as they passed by her on their way here and there, many of them filled with anxiety to get out of the Allenian Hills region on the safe roads as fast as possible. She waited patiently while Aaron conducted his business inside, and even managed a small smile to captain Gronen and Thelma when she saw them dash past her on their way back to the ship. *Probably off to enjoy some 'alone time',* she thought. *Perhaps I should apologize to Gronen. I'm sure he has my best interests in mind.*

No sooner had the Jaft couple disappeared than Aaron came out of the rusty screen door of the pawnbroker's store. He had two heavy sacks of coins on his hips, and he positively radiated as he smiled at her.

"Come along, dear Gwen," he said, twirling her unexpectedly, eliciting a high, trilling laugh from her as he dipped her toward the street.

Passersby smiled and pointed warmly in their direction, and Gwen blushed a deep sanguine color. He lifted her up to him then, and gave her a strong, smooth kiss. "We're going to have a fine meal, and perhaps some entertainment. And you know what else?" he said.

"What's that?" She draped her arms over his strong shoulders. *For a magic user, he's very burly,* she thought. *Maybe that's my attraction to him. He's so, well, safe.*

"The trade roads leading out of the Allenians only take a couple of days' travel from here, Gwen. You and I should enjoy each other's company and make the rest of the trip out on foot."

Gwen gasped at such a proposal, because she wanted to make quick time to Palen, and shouldn't Aaron do so as well?

"We can hire a coach at the nearest village out of the region, and have it take us all the way to Palen! It would take about a week's extra time, but it would be time well spent."

Gwen wondered why he would suddenly want to travel for a week over the road with her, when he had seemed so distant the day before and that morning. But he was her first love, and she truly hoped, in her youthful ignorance, that they could stay together for a long, long time.

Before she could think her response through with any degree of certainty, she blurted out, "Of course, my love! Let's do it! Those Jafts are getting into some heavy traffic anyway, and they're all a bit stiff, aren't they?" She was ashamed as soon as she let the words fly. "Oh, but our luggage! It's still on board!"

"Not to worry too much, dear." Aaron wrapped an arm around her waist and led her to the only diner in the port town that didn't look excessively dingy.

When they were seated, they each took up a menu, and Gwen's heart fluttered away again as she looked at his handsome face around the corner of her menu.

"I'll tell you what; when we finish the meal, I'll wait outside of this diner for you. Head back, grab your luggage, and return to me here. Then I'll go back and fetch mine," he said. "While you're fetching your things, I can make arrangements for travel or maybe post inquiries to the local inns about short-term stays, just until we can find something more permanent."

Gwen quickly agreed, and they ordered the most expensive items on the menu, Aaron assuring her that they had plenty of money to spend now.

Now, she thought as she started to eat her meal slowly. *He said we had plenty of money now. What did he pawn off that could have taken him from being destitute, to having plenty of money to eat, get entertained, and then hire a coach to go to Palen? Something of great value, I'm sure. But what?*

* * * *

"I don't understand." Gronen opened yet another crate in the cargo hold.

The guard had received orders to only let him and Thelma in, and when they had rushed the hold, he'd flung the door open and stood aside. The married Jaft couple had gone through almost every crate, and had narrowed down their search to two crates, each one holding the items they had been paid the richest fee to transport. Thelma pried open the crate containing several well-preserved body parts for a Necromancer in Ja-Wen, who had ensured the safe shipment of them with an arranged payment of twelve-hundred gold pieces upon delivery. However, the items in the other crate worried Gronen the most.

Two Gems of Entombment, magical items that could imprison the souls of living creatures upon their death, had been placed in his care to transport to Ja-Wen, where a gifted Enchanter expected to receive them. False orders had been planted in the shipping crate to conceal their true purpose, a careful code arranged by the client in the event some half-wit should get their hands on the shipment. Such a person would only think they were nabbing some very pretty jewelry pieces, but Gronen's client had greater intentions for the bits of sparkle. He planned to set the gems, with the help of a skilled smithy, into a sword for a very special client. Gronen had been promised ten-thousand gold pieces and a fleet-class vessel of his own, which would be waiting for him on the eastern shore only a short way from Ja-Wen.

When he opened the lid of the crate, he found the Gems of Entombment gone from their protective casing. "Fucking pirates," he groused.

* * * *

Aaron Horn stood just outside of the diner as Gwen disappeared into the crowds heading toward the docking area of the trading post. A thick fog started to bank into the town from the north, and as soon as he felt certain she couldn't look back and see him, he sprinted off toward the land exit of the town.

Aaron Horn, using his real name for the first time in many years, had arranged for his own crew to wait for him just outside of this very port town on the river. He assured them via messenger pigeon that the ship would stop in the trading outpost, and that he would take something from onboard of value. He'd quickly pawn it, hopefully garnering a nice sized profit from the exchange. He'd spent a great deal to get the private cabin, but in return, he'd been given fifty ryo, coins worth one hundred gold pieces per coin. Considering the payment of only seven hundred gold for the private cabin, he felt pretty good about his profit margin.

The pirate darted through the streets, and made his getaway as fast as he could.

* * * *

When Gwen returned to the diner, panting and out of breath, barely having avoided delay with a conversation with Gronen and Thelma onboard the ship, she was puzzled by Aaron's absence. *Perhaps he's gone inside to use the privy,* she reasoned. *He'll be out soon enough. I'm sure he will. Mayhap he's gone to make those inquiries at the inns.* Yet when fifteen minutes passed with no sign of his return, Gwen finally began having solid doubts.

Before she had the chance to check inside, a powerful, familiar hand grabbed her by the shoulder. Pain lanced through her as Captain Gronen dug his fingers into her.

When she looked up to yell at him to let her go, she froze. In his eyes she saw such unmatched fury that nothing she said, shouted or hollered would be able to match the malevolence.

"Captain Gronen, I, I," she stammered.

Gronen heaved off on her, pinning the Half-Elf Aeromancer against the wall of the diner as Thelma came up behind him from the direction of the ship.

"Were you working with him, girl," he growled, pressing his horrid smelling, blunt face only an inch or so away from her nose. He had a hand on either side of her head, leaning forward menacingly. "Tell me!"

"Gronen," Thelma gasped as she finally got up next to her husband. "Stop this now, of course she is not working with him."

Gwen's heart and mind twirled away in an internal cyclone not of her making, but tempered with her own sudden realization of her foolishness. When she spoke finally to the big Jaft captain, she burst into uncontrollable sobbing.

"I gave myself to him." She unleashed the flood of tears that had welled up within her.

Gronen, shocked and very awkward, looked to his wife, who was glaring daggers at her husband.

"Oh Gods above, what was I thinking," Gwen sobbed as Thelma pulled her close and started stroking her hair, patting her back to console her. Gwen pressed her face against the ample chest of the blue-skinned woman who rocked her easily back and forth.

Gronen, flushed but still wary and in a mild panic, looked around at the faces of the scores of men and women bustling by. He rubbed the back of his bald head, and shifted back and forth on the balls of his feet, trying to think of what to do next.

A few minutes later, when Gwen had finally released most of her despair, she felt greatly relieved to be rid of her emotional torrent, and in the presence of two capable people.

They can tell me what I should do now, Gwen thought, wiping the last of her tears away and laughing a little at the pattern of dampness on Thelma's vest.

The Jaft woman looked down at her vest and blouse and shook her head, grinning. "It's nothing to worry about, dear. I don't wear these clothes that often anyway. Now, my husband should probably apologize," she said, kicking back at Gronen's shin, barking him a good one and making him growl as he hopped on his other leg for a moment.

He bowed slightly to Gwen. "I am most sorry, Ms. Surefire," he said, straightening out again quickly. He scanned the crowds once more for some sign of the pirate. "Gwen, we need to find Aaron. He is not who he seems."

"I'd figured that much," she said, her breath hitching up one last time in her chest. "He's some sort of criminal, isn't he?"

Thelma and Gronen nodded, and Gwen felt a sudden surge of inspiration. "Wait a minute! He said he spent most of his money on getting the private cabin onboard the ship, but he went into that pawnshop and came back out with two heavy sacks of coins," she said, pointing up the street a short distance to the pawnshop.

Gronen, his face suddenly alight, nodded to Thelma, and darted through the crowds toward the store, pushing and shoving people out of his way.

"What are we going to do now?" Gwen asked Thelma, her voice still quavering.

"Well, that partially depends on you, honey,"

Thelma's words sent a cringe through Gwen. She didn't like being addressed like a child, though right now, she did feel about as foolish as one. *Besides,* Gwen thought, *I'll bet she talks to everyone like that. I wonder if they've ever had any children?*

"Gronen will probably want to just get the gems back and head out of port. Of course, we've never been stolen from before so stealthily, or handily. He's just as liable to want to go after the man, especially since he's going to have to pay out of pocket to recover our stolen shipment."

"What did he steal," Gwen asked, curious about what could have garnered Aaron so much money. He'd paid for their meal with a coin worth one hundred gold pieces, a type of currency she'd only seen once before, at the Guild.

Thelma looked away from her and cleared her throat, reluctant to answer her question.

"It's okay, you don't have to tell me," Gwen said in a rush.

Thelma turned her smile back on Gwen, and patted her on the shoulder.

"Business has to be kept discreet, right?"

"That's right, honey. Now hush up for a minute, and let's listen to what the captain has to say. That's him barreling back toward us."

* * * *

Captain Gronen always kept a handy supply of money on hand for his business trips, for expenses incurred during travel. Most often these reserves of coins purchased repairs for the ship, supplies of food for the men, or helped go toward damages caused by his men in the rougher taverns of port townships and villages. Now, thanks to the machinations of a low life pirate by the name of Aaron Horn, the entirety of his reserve fund was being spent to re-secure items for shipment to Ja-Wen.

At first, he had offered the Lizardman shop owner half of his reserve fund, a full three thousand gold pieces. The reptilian man had laughed, and told him that he wouldn't accept double that price.

As the Lizardman cackled, Gronen's face split into a wicked smile of his own. As with most pawnshops throughout Tamalaria, this particular businessman had a thick wooden wall and a set of iron bars separating himself from the customers, in case they should get volatile. The problem with this arrangement was that, although it kept sore customers out, it also kept the shopkeeper in.

Gronen didn't know where the back door to this place might be, and at the moment, he didn't have the time to care. Instead of going outside and searching for it as the Lizardman laughed one last burst at him and returned to his chair off to one side of the transaction window, Gronen hefted his war hammer off of his back. He glared balefully at the wooden wall next to the window, opposite the Lizardman, who buried his nose in a book of some kind, his back to the area that Gronen was looking at.

The Jaft turned around, engaged the deadbolt on the front door softly, and flipped the sign silently from 'Open' to 'Closed'. He'd done this sort of thing before.

With the shopkeeper's back to him, Gronen hefted his war hammer, and switched his grip, the head of the stone weapon just over his left hand. He brought the weapon back low, at around his hip level, and gave it a swift, powerful torque, smashing the wooden retainer wall apart. Wooden splinters flew into the back wall of the shopkeeper's area, and he gave a startled yelp, jumping up from his chair and facing the monstrously muscled Jaft sailor who was even now kicking the lower wooden shards over as he stepped through into his area.

The Lizardman put his hands up in a pathetic defensive plea for mercy, waving them back and forth as he stumbled back into his chair. "Hey buddy, take it easy," the pawnshop owner/operator said as Gronen, his mind an utter blank now that he'd decided on a course of action, took two gaping, stalking steps forward, holding the war hammer with its head down near his left knee.

Dust swirled through the air, giving him a hazy, otherworldly appearance, like Death given flesh and purpose.

"Look, I'll give you anything you want, just don't kill me," the Lizardman bawled, curling up his legs and covering his head with his hands.

His reptilian eyes squeezed shut, he didn't see Gronen put the war hammer back in its holster on his back, but he did hear the heavy thud of something on his side of the transaction window. When the shop owner opened his eye to see if he had been struck without feeling it, he saw the Jaft's money pouches on the counter.

"I want those Gems, now," Gronen rumbled, his chest heaving, his hands clenched into gnarled fists. "I'm going to pay you, because I'm not some thug or thief. That's all the money I have on me at this time, six thousand and two hundred gold pieces."

The Lizardman did not doubt him. There were three huge sacks of money on his side of the window/counter, and he felt certain that it would cover his losses for purchasing the Gems of Entombment, and the repairs to his retainer wall. He looked up at the blue-fleshed humanoid, and took in once again his thickly muscled frame.

The Lizardman dropped off of his chair and rolled it aside, fumbling with the lock on his stash safe, where he'd placed the items. He should have known that the Human could not have gained such priceless magical items through honest means. He should have known, and now his ignorance had cost him his wall. He'd have to close up shop and pay the nearby carpenter to repair the wall, which would lose him time and business as well.

He opened the safe, handed the Jaft the Gems of Entombment, and when Gronen was gone, the Lizardman breathed a heavy sigh of relief.

* * * *

"I've got them back," Gronen said to Thelma and Gwen, who both smiled gently at this news. Gronen saw something in the girl's eyes, however, something that unsettled him greatly. Pain coiled in her soul, a pain that was plain to him, and which would eat away at her until the cause of her pain could be dealt with. *Aw, crap,* he thought, rolling his eyes at himself. *Looks like we're not going to be on schedule anymore.*

"We're ready to get going again, dear," Thelma said, putting her arms around one of Gronen's well-sculpted biceps. But he shook his head, and handed her the Gems of Entombment.

"What's the matter dear? Oh, did you still want to have a little fun in town with me first." Thelma squeezed his arms before taking the Gems from him and stuffing them into one of her pouches.

"No, dear," he said, grumbling even as he spoke. "We're going to take those back to the ship, and we're going to tell the first mate to depart without us."

His words elicited gasps from both Thelma and Gwen.

"The three of us are going after our absent friend, Mr. Horn, and we're going to take back what he owes us... in blood," Gronen growled.

Gwen's heart lifted at the idea, and she felt her magic twitching in her blood to be released, to be brought fully to bear. "What he owes all three of us."

* * * *

"Oh, don't bitch about it," Aaron Horn said to his men as they made camp by the side of the trading road through the Allenians. They were still in safe, neutral territory, and Aaron was trying to divide up the profits among himself and his five men fairly. "We all put in about a hundred gold pieces toward this little enterprise, and we're coming away with almost a thousand apiece. You men have nothing to complain about."

He leaned back against a tree log and tore into a piece of dark bread, enjoying the warmth of the fire, the closeness of his comrades, and the feel of a job well done. "So, did ye take anything else of value, captain," one of the scruffy, gangly Humans of his crew asked with a nearly toothless smile. Aaron sat up, and smiled broadly at him.

"Oh yeah. I took myself a sweet little thing, Salty Jim, a perky little Half-Elf girl," he said, enjoying the harsh laughter of his mates. "Nothing much for tits on her, but she felt great I'll tell ya." He chuckled a bit himself. "I think I may have popped her cherry, gentlemen!"

"Three cheers fer the cap'n," Salty Jim said, and they all hip-hip-hoorayed the Aquamancer. On the third and final hooray, Aaron's heart nearly leaped out of his chest as the stone head of a war hammer came down atop Salty Jim's head, spraying bone, brains and blood all over the rest of the company of pirates.

"Holy shit," one of the men screamed, turning to see a tall, muscular Jaft man holding the weapon that had just killed one of their team members. A woman of the same Race brought a heavy axe down at an angle into this second man's face, finishing his last thoughts, which had been *We're all gonna die!* Truth is greatest in the face of death.

"Magra vak shu," a high, feminine voice chanted, a voice that Aaron had become intimately familiar with.

A wall of wind force slammed into him, sending him flying several dozen yards from the fire, into the side of the nearby hillock.

When he landed with a groan, he pried his eyes open, and found Gwen Surefire using the spell of Limited Flight to fly through the air toward him, an expression of pure hatred on her face. He grinned his disarming little grin, and thrust his own palm out toward her as she closed the distance.

"Noseum ishrack! Ice Needles," he cried, summoning a fleet of tiny shards of razor-sharp ice to fly from his palm into her.

Gwen cried out in pain as the first of these tore into her cheeks and legs, causing her to crash hard into the ground to avoid further damage.

Aaron got to his feet, looked down the hill, and waved his right hand up to the side of his head, and then whipped it in an arc down toward her. "Wash Away," he murmured.

A flood of water charged up from mystical space behind him, and it struck Gwen as she got haltingly to her hands and knees, carrying her down toward his men and the Jafts, who had dealt death to at least three of them already.

Got to get away, was Aaron's only thought now, and he listened to it carefully, running east and back down to the trading route.

No good to get away from them and run into a Khan or Simpa in non-neutral territory. He sprinted as swiftly as he could, lamenting the loss not of his men, but of the money they had on them.

He could always go back to their corpses later, he reasoned, and pumped his arms and legs.

Gwen finally finished up a few yards away from Gronen, who had backed away from the magically charged water as he smashed another pirate in the knees, breaking his legs cleanly and felling him.

Gronen reached down, and Gwen took his hand, sending a Wind Cutter just past his left ear to cut into the pirate who had taken the opportunity to try to get him from behind.

Gwen nodded to Gronen, who smiled. "Go, get him," Gronen said to her, and turned back to the last two pirates, who were assailing his wife without quarter. They'd drawn blood in a couple of places, and Gwen hesitated. She wanted to help the married Jaft couple, who had done her no wrong, in the end, but Gronen's words stuck in her mind. *Get him.*

Using her spell of Limited Flight again, she gave hot pursuit, following the road as it turned, curved, and bent here and there around hills and small, sudden rises in the landscape.

It took her ten full minutes to finally catch up, but when she did, she was ambushed by a flying spear of ice. It clipped her side and knocked her out of the air, crashing once again into the road.

Aaron Horn had stopped a few minutes before, and waited for her, because he knew that washing her away wouldn't finish the job. He watched her crash land, and thought vehemently, *Shit, that should have taken her in the fucking head! What's wrong with my aim today?*

"Oh, I'm so sorry, Gwen," he cooed, mocking her as he backed away up the road, bringing more of his magic to bear as she got to her feet, clutching the bleeding wound in her side. "Did I hurt you there? I assure you, I didn't mean to." He formed another spear of ice magic to hover next to him. "I meant to kill you!"

When she saw the second spear forming, Gwen looked down, hearing his words but not really registering them. Her own magic acted partially on its own, forming a barrier of wind in front of her, and when the spear flew at her, she looked up, and saw it stop, held perfectly still in the air.

Aaron's face was a bloodless mask of shock, and he started backing away again down the road.

Gwen twitched her magic, and used the simplest Aeromancer spell ever learned to send the weapon back at him.

"Push Off," she muttered, sending the spear flying at blinding speed through Aaron Horn's chest. Blood sprayed out around the magical weapon, which began to melt as soon as it pierced his heart, killing him almost instantly.

Satisfied, Gwen stalked on foot back down the road toward Gronen and Thelma. When she arrived, she found them sitting around the pirates' fire, eating from their supplies.

She sat down heavily across from them, and Thelma dressed and bandaged her wounds.

"Well, I guess we'll be on the road together for a few days," she said weakly.

"Yes indeed, but at least the company's good." Gronen dug into a container of some sort of potato-based salad. He made a face, at which both of the women present laughed gaily. *Yes,* Gwen thought, *at least the company's good.*

Tale Six: The High Road

877, A.F. A man in splendid silver armor stood over an unmarked grave, staring down at the soil and grass that had grown a strange shade of blue over it, and the wild, crimson roses that grew just over this patch of ground. He stared down with a heavy heart, and heaved a sigh. "Has it really been thirty years, my friend?" The man's voice formed a strange, garbled harmony of two voices, one husky and pleasant, one deep and filled with a darkness of the soul.

The man bent down on one knee, the metal plates and joints of his armor creaking and clanking as he did so.

The roses smelled wondrous to his strange nostrils, which he presently hid beneath the faceplate of his helmet. The man's horse, a black roan of amazing size and strength, whinnied nearby, and he looked over at it for a moment, trying to decipher what could possibly give it such discomfort.

"Probably this place," he mused aloud. "Or perhaps this unscheduled visit."

The man removed one of his mailed gloves, and beneath, his flesh appeared stretched and blotted with patches of black skin here and there amid his predominantly pale hand. A second look would reveal that the black spots were actually moving, writhing shadows, wisps of darkness flowing out from beneath his armor and clothing.

The creature, for he wasn't truly a man, reached down and touched the grave, wondering how so much time could have passed without his returning here to visit the man he'd once called friend.

He withdrew his hand, and put the gauntlet back on, rising to his feet. "It has been ten years since I last visited your final resting place, Byron." The creature's voice now was that only of a Human, one who still mourned the loss of Byron Aixler, best known near the end of his un-life as Byron of Sidius. "And for that I am sorry. But I have been very busy."

He looked south and east, toward Mount Toane. "I have been hunting down those demons who escaped during the final battle, and it has been a long, dark road I have traveled. But I feel I owe it to you, since I could do little else during that war to help."

The creature looked down once more at the roses and strangely colored grass. "I pray you are resting well with your God, Oun. I myself must go now." The creature moved toward Thunderstorm, his steed these last six years. "I have unfinished business to tend to."

The half-demon Grigory Molis mounted his horse, and rode off, away from the grave of the land's most celebrated hero in recent memory.

* * * *

A week's hard riding, with little rest and almost no food, brought Molis to the Elven Kingdom's eastern border. There, a patrol of the kingdom's troopers formed a barricade across the road.

The half-demon reined in his horse, and dismounted slowly, keeping his hands open and loose at his sides as one of the Elven Knights approached, sword in hand.

"Hail, traveler, and well met." The trooper stopped perhaps five yards in front of Thunderstorm. "Please name yourself, and tell us your business within our kingdom's borders."

Molis raised his right hand toward the sky and brought it swiftly to his chest, pounding his armor just over his heart. "I am Grigory Molis, goodly Knight of the Elves," he said, his voice booming and clear of the demonic taint. "I am here in search of a demon, that I may destroy it and send it back to the Pit."

The Elf gave him a brief up-and-down look, most likely trying to size him up.

Damnable Elves, Molis thought. *Always so suspicious.*

"You speak truth, for I can tell it in your words," the Knight said. "Such is one of the powers of a Knight. I will not ask you to remove your helm or your armor, but I must ask you this; what is thy Race, man?"

Ah hell, Molis thought. *This is going to cause some difficulty.*

-No it won't,- the voice of the demon within his soul said inside of his mind.

Are you so sure? the voice of Edgar Cesar replied internally.

-Yes, I am sure. Besides, if they give you trouble, you could easily slaughter the lot of them, all ten made into corpses at our feet!-

The minds and souls merged once more, and Molis replied to the Elven Knight's question.

"I am a half-demon." Molis dropped the fake tone of reverence and friendliness altogether.

The Elven man took a few steps back, and raised his sword a little, more out of reflex than out of menace.

"I know, this seems strange, but you heard the truth of my claim when I said I have come to slay a demon," Molis said abruptly.

The Knight returned to his group, and they huddled together, speaking in whispered tones in the language of their people. *I really need to learn a few languages,* Molis thought bitterly.

As the Elven border guards had their little pow-wow, Molis lifted the faceplate of his helmet and let the cool breeze coming from the south pass over his shadow-drenched face. He squeezed his eyes shut, and welcomed the chill that ran down his spine. When he opened his eyes again, he could see far off into the distance, almost down to the beach. He gasped at the sight of it, for the sand he saw there was pitch black. He was not seeing what was really before him, but once again saw where the demon hid from him.

The beach, he knew, was actually along the western edge of the land, through Elven lands. He needed more than ever to get past these guards and through the kingdom.

His vision blurred for a moment, and he smelled the flowery perfume one of the guards wore as their group approached him as a whole.

He turned toward them, not bothering to pull down the faceplate of his helmet. Four of them were approaching, and they stopped dead in their tracks at the sight of his blackened face and yellow, gimlet eyes. He heard their breath catch in the their throats, and felt a sick surge of glee at their discomfort and fear. The Elven Kingdom, particularly the capital of Whitewood, had been ravaged by demons with eyes such as his thirty years before, and the natural distrust and fear they held for him could be easily explained.

"Grigory Molis," said the Elven Knight, who had lieutenant's bars on his armor. "We shall let you pass into the Elven Kingdom, if you can give us some show of good faith."

Molis barked harsh twin laughter, and planted his hands on his hips, shaking his head as he looked at the ground. He then turned his blazing eyes on the Knight.

"I am a half-demon, my friend. Asking me for a show of good faith is much like asking a fish, very politely, if he'd like to come out of the river and enjoy the fresh air! Do you understand what I mean?"

The Elven Knight gave him a curious look, and conferred with the men closest to him.

He turned back, and shook his head. "Oh man, you guys are dense." Molis pulled down the faceplate and smacking the forehead-plating of the helmet. He folded his arms over his chest, and pulled on his goatee, concealed under the shadows of his head.

The Elves made no move, either away from him, or toward him. He could, however, smell the cold sweat forming on their brows, and he heard the stretching tension of a bow string somewhere off to his right, to the north.

Snipers, in case things don't go so well here, he thought.

He looked briefly past the four men clustered a few yards away from him, and saw that the other six men had all taken up posts to the north and south of him, placing themselves at diagonals to avoid a crossfire should they loose their arrows on him and Thunderstorm.

The horse neighed at him briefly, and he sensed its boredom and malcontent.

"I know, boy," he whispered, leaning toward the roan's head and floppy ears. "We'll be moving again soon, not to worry."

As he finished speaking to his mount, one of the other Elves with the lieutenant broke from the group and charged at Molis, a spiked mace in hand. He issued no war cry, no warning, but his movements were hasty, rushed. Molis slapped Thunderstorm on the side, sending him into motion, and dropped into a crouch, ducking the sidearm blow aimed at his shoulderblade.

Molis heard the Knight crying to his man to cease his attack, to drop his weapon and remove himself from harm's way.

The trooper had just missed his swing, and Molis brought his hands up as he rose, grasping the man's wrist in one mailed hand and bringing his other armored forearm into the man's shoulder joint, hard.

He didn't break the Elf's arm, but the trooper cried out, and his hand went limp, dropping the mace to the ground.

Molis whipped the man around into a figure four armlock, dragging him along through the dirt back toward the other three Elves nearby. He dropped the Elf roughly to the lieutenant's feet, his saffron eyes blaring in his shadowy face. With a grunt, he turned and headed back to Thunderstorm, who had resumed his post in the road.

"Good boy," he said to the horse, who nickered and nipped at him.

"Hey, take it easy, I'm praising you, not being sarcastic." He brushed his mailed hand along the horse's side.

"We shall let you pass," the lieutenant said suddenly, despite the protestations of his kinsmen in their tongue.

He held a silencing hand up to the them, and approached Molis and his steed slowly, bending down and tossing the other trooper's mace back to him lightly. "That was rather remarkable, and I apologize for the brashness of my corporal."

"A corporal, eh?" Molis asked, intrigued.

He mounted Thunderstorm, and cantered up next to the group, watching the archers lower their arrows and put their weapons away. He pointed his mailed fist down at the corporal who had attacked him without provocation. "I suggest that whatever duty the lieutenant assigns you for punishment, you do it well and you do it without complaint, little man! The military is no place for rash action and misjudgment, corporal. When your contract comes up for renewal, remember this day, and think carefully about your career and its possible outcomes. Good day, gentlemen." He smiled to himself as he rode Thunderstorm at an easy clip into the great forest that was the Elven Kingdom.

* * * *

Later, during the evening, Molis took himself and Thunderstorm off of the main road into the woods themselves, and found himself a comfortable little area to make his camp.

He traveled alone most of the time, but just lately, it had become a very oppressive loneliness. He wondered, very briefly, if he was doomed to be alone for the rest of his twisted, dual existence. He also wondered if, in the beginning of his freedom, Byron of Sidius had felt the same way.

"You're the only true friend I have, partner," he said to Thunderstorm, who rested across the small fire he used to cook from him, legs locked upright.

Molis let out a long sigh, and skewered the rabbit he'd hit with a thrown rock an hour before on a whittled stick. The meat cooked quickly, and he devoured it in a few bites. He needed some real food, and soon, because subsisting on meat alone grated on his nerves, and his stomach.

He took a brief inventory of his saddlebags, and laid down, pulling a blanket over himself and drifting off to sleep.

The half-demon came to at the sound of approaching footsteps perhaps an hour before dawn. His eyes fluttered open slowly, and he groaned as he sat up, looking around with sleep-fuzzy eyes. He listened closely for the sound of the footfalls, and got to his feet in time to see someone duck behind a nearby tree.

A brigand, he wondered?

"Whoever you are, you'd do well to show yourself, right now!" A head covered with long, golden hair poked out from behind a tree, and Molis found himself looking at a young Elven girl, not even old enough to be into puberty.

He took a step back, his face twitching, his mind racing. In all of the years he'd been on the road, he'd never spotted a child on their own, certainly not out in the wilderness like this. *How close am I to a village? Must be pretty close for such a young girl to be here. Oh, man, what do I do?*

"Are you lost mister?" The girl came fully out from behind the tree. She was dressed in a simple yellow dress that flowed down to her shins and clutched a rumpled-looking teddy bear. Her voice was high-pitched and a little whiny, but otherwise, unsettlingly child-like. Edgar Cesar hadn't had children in life, and the demon within him didn't have any experience with kids, so he wasn't exactly sure how to proceed.

"Um..." He crouched so that they might be at eye level.

Molis summoned up his powers, and changed his countenance to resemble that of a Human. He removed his helmet slowly, hoping against hope that he had succeeded. He assumed he had, since the little Elf girl wasn't running away in total fear.

"I'm not lost, little one. What is your name?"

The girl trilled youthful laughter, and the sound of her laugh lifted his heart; at least, that part of it that belonged to Edgar Cesar.

"I'm Samantha Longleaf." She put her hands behind her back and twisting back and forth on her feet. "What's your name, mister?"

"I am Grigory Molis," he said gently, giving her a soft grin. "You can call me Mr. Molis if you'd like. Where are your parents, little one?"

As soon as he asked, Molis noticed the layers of dirt and grime on the girl's dress, face, and bare arms. She looked a tad emaciated as well, he noted. She also wasn't smiling any more.

"My parents aren't around, Mr. Molis," she said, her tone saddened and honest in that way only children can manage. "We were walking in the woods when a bad man came along, and they told me to run as far as I could," she said, tears welling up in her eyes.

-Way to go, numbshit,- the demon within said to him. -Now she's going to cry, and you want to help her, don't you?-

Well yes, of course I do, Edgar Cesar replied. *She's lost, alone, probably starving, and there's little shelter around here from the look of things. We're a good four days from Whitewood if we walk, and I'm not going to leave her here, alone and unprotected.*

-What about the demon, Edgar? What of our mission?-

The mission be damned, it can wait, Edgar thought back.

Once more the two minds merged into one, with Edgar Cesar's consciousness taking the forward position. "So you're all alone out here, Samantha." He stood and took a tentative step forward.

The girl didn't even flinch, or make any move to get away; she looked too frail to run any further.

"When did you eat last?"

"I think it was two days ago," she replied.

Molis traipsed back to his bag, and took out a hunk of bread, and the little bit of cheese that was still edible, returning toward the girl and offering them silently.

Quick as a bullet she darted toward him, snatching up the food and tearing into it like a little savage.

Molis knelt and ruffled her hair lightly with one of his mailed gloves, and she flinched.

"Your gloves are heavy, Mr. Molis," she complained, using her left hand to straighten her hair now that the cheese was gone.

He chuckled a little and stood up.

"Yes, they are. Listen, I'd like to take you to the nearest town or village. Do you have any family other than your mother and father?"

The girl wolfed down the last of the bread he'd given her, which he realized with some dismay was the last he had on him, and cocked her head to one side, appearing to think about his question.

"My uncle Silva and aunt Margaret live in the big city, Whitewood," she said, her face lighting up as she mentioned the name of the capital. "I haven't seen them in years! Can you take me there?"

Molis nodded, smiled at her again, and put his helmet back on, pulling the face guard down once more. He packed the rest of his belongings in Thunderstorm's saddlebags, and led him over to the girl, Samantha, by the reins.

"She's pretty, mister," the girl said, at which the roan harrumphed.

"Actually, Thunderstorm here is a boy." Molis watched with dismay as the girl crouched down and looked back at the horse's underside.

"Oh, right. I didn't see that before." She giggled before standing again. "Can I ride him, Mr. Molis?"

Molis looked at the horse, who turned his long, equine face toward him and seemed to cock an eyebrow questioningly.

"Sure thing, Samantha," he said, glad to relieve himself of the magic that had been hiding his demonic visage. He led the Elven girl to the horse's side, and turned to Samantha, who had her arms out toward him, ready to be lifted up.

She still clutched the teddy bear in her right hand, and he wondered how old precisely she was.

He scooped her up, cringing a little at how light she was, and set her in the saddle. "Hold onto that horn at the front of the saddle, and I'll lead him with the reins." He stepped in front of Thunderstorm and led the horse back to the road.

"So how old are you, Mr. Molis," she asked, and immediately the demon inside interrupted him.

-Oh, wonderful. She's at that curious age. You sure know how to pick them, Edgar.-

Oh shut it, you, he replied internally. "I am fifty-seven years old," he said aloud, which was technically accurate.

"You don't look it," she said sweetly. "Aren't Humans supposed to get all wrinkly and stuff when they get that old?"

Molis hunched up his shoulders at this, irritated on the surface with the girl's statement, because, well, it was true.

"I take very good care of myself," Molis said. *Okay, maybe she'll stop asking questions now.* None such luck, as it turned out.

"Are you married, Mr. Molis?"

The half-demon cleared his throat, and shook his head no.

"Do you have a girlfriend," she asked, drawing out the 'ir' sound like a little schoolgirl teasing some boy in class.

Molis growled low in his throat, and once again shook his head in the negative.

"Do you have a boyfriend," she asked, giggling uncontrollably.

Molis sighed, pressed his hand where his temples would be under the helmet, and shook his head again, restraining the sudden urge to stuff a cloth gag in the girl's mouth.

"Where are you from," she asked now, as they came to a fork in the road. Molis took note of the heavy wheel tracks and hoof prints on the right road, and led Thunderstorm that way.

"I am from a place far, far to the east, Samantha," he said, using his pleasant, husky Human voice again. "A place you may have heard of, even."

"Is it Ja-Wen," she asked quickly, and when Molis looked back, she was rocking back and forth excitedly in the saddle, one hand on the horn and one on her teddy bear.

"No, it's--" he said, unable to finish due to another interruption from the little girl.

"Is it Palen," she asked, rocking faster now. What was she so excited about? *Are all little girls like this?*

-Actually, in my limited experience, yes.-

Ah, hells, Edgar thought. "No, it isn't Palen. I come from--" he said, yet again interrupted, much to his rising fury.

"Is it Arcade? Because my mommy and daddy told me once that Arcade is a bad, bad place. My uncle Silva went there once, and he told me it was all full of Wererats and Gnomes who were thieves, and they tried to rob him, and he told them he wouldn't give them his money, and--" she prattled at high speed. Molis, who had just about had enough of her nonsense, twitched the horse's reins, bringing Thunderstorm to an abrupt halt.

"Will you please SHUT UP and let me tell you," he roared, his saffron eyes blazing inside of his helmet. He spun on his heels and glared up at the girl, and saw to his horror that she was doing something he'd never seen before, but instinctively knew was bad news. Her lower lip trembled up and down, and her breath seemed to be hitching in her chest.

"Oh, oh Gods in the heavens above, Samantha, I, I didn't mean to yell at you," he stammered, and the dam holding back her fragile emotional control broke wide open, and she started to babble and bawl, tears streaming in twin rivulets down her dusky, dirty cheeks.

What do I do, Edgar asked the other who resided in his soul, as their combined whole brought his hands to his head, looking around as if from help from some third party.

-You expect me to know? I'm a fucking demon, not a wet nurse! I have zero idea of how to handle children! You got us into this mess, Edgar, so get us out! And for pity's sake, get the girl to stop making that noise! She's going to make my (our) ears bleed!-

Molis, hands up toward Samantha, pleaded with her silently to stop crying, to at least cry more quietly, when Edgar spotted something through his shared eyes, off on the side of the road. Molis walked slowly over to a cluster of wild growing flowers, and plucked a beautiful yellow flower from the bunch.

Samantha continued to babble unintelligibly, but somewhere in there, Molis thought he heard something about a bad man making her parents scream, and for the time being, he chose only to log this bit of emotional flotsam away in his memory for later. He walked slowly up to her, and snapped his gloved fingers right in front of her nose.

She stopped crying and babbling just long enough to hand her up the flower. Her eyes opened wide as she took it with her left hand, marveling at its simple beauty. "For, for me," she asked between sobbing gasps.

"Yes, for you." Molis pulled off his helmet again. His Human facade held best when the demon let go of some of its hold, as it did now, and he saw his own handsome face reflected in her wide, wondering eyes. "I am sorry, Samantha. I didn't mean to lose my temper with you."

Helpless to do anything else, he caught her in his arms as she flung herself from the horse toward him, holding her against his heavily armored upper body and patting her back as she cried against his neck.

"I'm so sorry Mr. Molis, but I'm so scared, and I've been lost for days, and nobody looked friendly enough to help me, and there were these evil Orc people, and I almost got caught by them yesterday, and I think maybe the bad man is still out there, and," she stammered, trying to tell him everything in one huge rush.

"It's all right, it's all right." Edgar left the demon and Molis aside for the moment being as he stroked her hair gently. "I'll get you to your aunt and uncle's home. There should be a hostel somewhere down this road, and we can rest there for the day. What do you say, does that sound good?"

Without waiting for an answer, he set her back on Thunderstorm, who was giving him an odd look for an animal.

Is he grinning at me?

The Elven girl wiped away the last of her tears, and looked back and forth between her teddy bear, the flower, and Molis, who was putting his helmet back on again now that the demon within was resurfacing, merging to make him the half-breed once more.

"Yes, that sounds good. I could use a bath," she said, laughing at herself. "I don't mean to be a burden." She blushed as he smiled at her before he pulled down the faceplate.

"You're not a burden, Samantha, I assure you. You know, I could put your teddy bear in one of my saddlebags." He took the stuffed animal when she handed it to him.

For a moment, Molis hesitated, looking at the stuffed toy. There appeared to be some sort of trace memory held within the toy, some amount of empathic runoff. *I'll inspect this more closely at another time,* he thought.

Samantha tucked the flower behind her left ear, and he took a moment to think, *If she survives long enough to mature, she's going to be beautiful.*

Once again he took Thunderstorm's reins, and led the way at a nice brisk pace, enjoying the scenery of the forestlands around him.

Samantha let her questions go for the time being, but Molis decided to open up conversation after an hour's pleasant silence. "I hail from Mount Toane, Samantha. Do you know of it?"

"Only a little. Isn't that an evil place?"

"It has been, in the past." Molis sniffed the air periodically for any trace scent of the demon he presently pursued. "But not everything from that area is wicked or evil. I'm not directly from Mount Toane. I'm from an area, south, of the mountain." He smiled at his little jest.

"How far south," Samantha asked, completely innocent of the half-demon's origin.

Molis almost overflowed with mirth at her question, but waved a hand to stay off the questioning glance she gave him as he chuckled.

"Very far south," he said. "Now, I'll answer any questions you have at all, Samantha, but you must ask them one at a time. Okay?"

She smiled widely at him, closing her eyes to emphasize how honest her smile was. They walked on in comfortable silence for a while, and then Samantha's youthful curiosity got the better of her once more as they started crossing a short clearing.

"Mr. Molis, why do you wear all that funny looking armor? And that sword on your back? Isn't that uncomfortable?"

"Not really, Samantha," Molis said, cursing her last questions. As soon as she asked it, he felt the inevitable chaffing of his inner thighs inside the suit of armor's leggings. Without such probing, he might have been able to ignore his discomfort for a while. "Now and again I have to go a day or so without the armor, but as for the sword, I always wear it on my back. It is where most Knights learn to draw their blade from," he said.

"So you're a Knight? A for real Knight." Her voice sounded awed and a little whispery.

Molis cocked a shadowy eyebrow and looked up at the girl for a brief moment, noting the way she had her hands clasped together just under her chin.

"Yes, though not the sort you've probably read about in fairy tales and such." Molis turned his attention back to the grassy field.

As they passed out of the clearing and into the forest again, Molis's spine tingled, warning him of some coming danger. *The Great Forest houses the Elven Kingdom, but it contains many other things as well, Molis,* he reminded himself. *That's why they have walls around their towns and cities, remember?*

Molis stopped with Thunderstorm's rear end still in the clearing. "Samantha, stay on Thunderstorm," he said quietly, slowly.

He turned around and pointed his left hand back to the clearing as he drew his bastard sword with his right.

The girl's hands flew to the saddle horn, and her face fell into a look of mixed curiosity and innate fear.

"If there's trouble," Molis said, "he'll run you off to someplace safe."

"Does he know to do that?" Truly afraid and hushed, she seemed even smaller than when he had first met her.

So vulnerable, Molis thought, his blood boiling in his veins. *And someone destroyed her parents. Something that would show no mercy even to this small child! Not that I should be too surprised. These realms are full of those with dark hearts.* He turned his attention back to the forest path ahead, which seemed to have grown preternaturally dark.

"Yes, Samantha. Thunderstorm is a very intelligent animal, not some beast of burden," he said, pointing behind himself to the clearing again. The horse nipped his mailed glove once quickly, to tell him it understood its charge. "Wait with him until I come for you, and do not go off on your own. Do you understand?"

"Yes, Mr. Molis, sir," she said demurely.

Molis nodded, and assumed a crouching stance as he headed back into the forest. *Something is out there.* He darted his saffron eyes left and right through the trees, seeking out the source of his discomfort. *Something not of the Races. Some beast or creature of malcontent, I can feel it, almost a kindred spirit. But what is it, and more importantly, where?*

The crack of branches splitting underfoot took his attention northeast, forward and to his right.

No paths led off that way, so he felt sure his assumption had been correct, and his soon-to-be-assailant was not a man or woman of the known and civilized Races. A primal grumbling, a growling of sorts, sounded off in that direction, and Molis ducked behind a tall, strong oak tree, pressing his back to the ancient bark and rolling sideways to peer around from cover.

As he poked his head from behind the tree, he spotted the massive body of some strange monstrosity a moment before a blob of green fluid smashed into his cover and started eating away at the tree.

He ducked back and listened as the pop and sizzle of the tree he was backed against ground in his ears, eating away at the tree's insides.

Some sort of projectile acid, he thought.

Molis leaped out from behind the tree, tucking his arms and his weapon in to avoid stabbing himself and rolling to miss another blob of the acidic fluid that hit scant inches away. Springing to his feet, he turned and squared himself with the creature.

The monstrosity had the body of a fully-grown lion, with an eagle's head jutting from its long, powerful neck. Great black wings, leathery, bat-like, extended up from its back, and it loosed a garbled, strangled cry as it started hawking something up from its throat.

Another of those blobs of acid coming, Molis thought. He lashed his left hand forward, bringing up a shield of shadows, and held it before him, charging forward with his sword held in his right hand, at the ready.

A blob of the thick, viscous fluid splashed against his demonic shield and started to disappear into the blackness. Molis leaped, bringing the bastard sword down on the creature's neck, decapitating it cleanly and with little effort.

The sinew and muscle in its neck turned out to be the only thing holding its head in place; no spinal column had been connected to the base of its brain, apparently.

What sort of creature was this, he thought as he whipped his sword to his side, shedding the blood and gore from its surface.

"No matter," he muttered aloud. Molis didn't sheath his blade just yet--there might be more such creatures nearby. The half-demon brought forth his demonic nature, letting the creature from the Pit within him come forward and take fuller control of his body.

The demon sent tendrils of shadowy magic through the woods, seeking out all life forms for identification. He surveyed the area in perhaps a mile radius from himself, using his own body as a central point for a circle of observation. He spotted Elves, a handful of Cuyotai hunting several deer, and other natural animals. This creature had apparently been on its own.

Molis sheathed his blade and withdrew the demon inside, bringing himself back into balance. The tendrils of darkness receded back into his helmet and armor, and he checked himself to assure that he didn't frighten Samantha when he returned to her.

Back to the main path he stalked, checking left and right to make certain none of the Elves he had seen with his magical tendrils spotted him. When he exited the woods back into the clearing, he saw that Samantha had fallen asleep astride Thunderstorm, who glared balefully at him.

Molis chuckled, and headed over to the roan.

"Sorry, boy. I didn't mean to give you a fright." He patted the horse's flank, and looked at the girl's limp form. He opened one of the larger saddlebags and pulled out a wool blanket, wrapping it around the girl's fragile body, tying her to the horse and placing a small pillow under her stomach, so that the saddle horn wouldn't dig into her abdomen too badly.

Just before he took the horse's reins in hand, the girl's eyes fluttered open, and she looked blearily at him.

"Thank you, Mr. Molis," she mumbled, smiling at him before falling swiftly back to sleep.

The half-demon's heart skipped a beat, and he took the reins, leading the way safely into the forest once again.

-The girl is too much of a distraction, Edgar. We need to get her to a village and dump her off,- the demon within called to him.

We can't do that. She has no family, except in the capital, Edgar Cesar countered. These mental conversations often left him feeling drained and fatigued, but today, they just seemed to be fueling the mixed creature that was Grigory Molis. *We can't just leave her with strangers!*

-You're being too sentimental, Edgar,- the demon rasped in his mind. –There are bound to be Elves willing to take her in! There's a village not two hours west of here!-

And the capital is only ten hours farther north on this road. Edgar turned their collective head to look at a sign beside the road. It pointed in several directions, guiding passersby to several towns or villages. The bottom wooden sign bore the word 'Whitewood'.

If my calculations are correct, that is. Who knows, she may even rest the whole while. I don't think she's slept or eaten well in a long while.

-Cry me a fucking river, Edgar. Unless this gets us closer to the demon, it is a pointless, needless distraction.-

So you don't feel good about this at all? Not the slightest little bit good that we're helping someone who is much less fortunate, and far weaker than ourselves?

Dead silence met this line of questioning, and Molis's yellow, gimlet eyes flared with satisfaction. *Admit it, this is a good thing!*

-Yes, all right, this does feel good-, the demon admitted reluctantly. –It always makes us both feel good to help others. But I feel much better when we are tearing apart some black-hearted demon, Edgar. It makes me feel more alive!- The demon and Edgar's minds merged once more, and Grigory Molis continued on down the road until it forked in three different directions. Molis consulted the road signs, and took the right-hand fork, leading Thunderstorm, who seemed to have tensed up.

"What's the matter, boy?" Molis asked, and then received his answer in the form of three tall, gangly Wererats leaping out from behind bushes along the road and forming a makeshift roadblock.

"Ah, I see. What say you, fellows," he called to the Wererats, who had all crossed their arms over their chests, standing shoulder to shoulder.

They were garbed in simple black leathers, metal studs standing out in a block pattern over their chests. Molis wondered why they weren't intimidated by his silver armor, and then remembered that Wererats were allergic to copper, not silver like most other lycanthropes.

"Dis here is a toll road, buddy," the tallest of the three, the one standing in the middle, said, a hint of mocking in his tone. "You's gotta pay da toll ta get trew." The Wererat's thick accent rendered his common speech somewhat atrocious.

The large lycanthrope's little friends snickered and chuckled, and he gave them each a sharp slap on the snout to bring them back in line.

"And if I should refuse to pay?" Molis released Thunderstorm's reins and took a few steps away from the horse and his sleeping ward. "What then shall you do?" He drew his sword swiftly.

The large Wererat pulled out a pair of throwing knives, holding them deftly between the fingers of his left hand.

"Then me and da boys 'ere would have ta rough ya up a bit, ta teach you's some respect." The Wererat flexed his arms as he crossed his hand to his right shoulder, preparing a throw.

Molis gauged his chances of coming away unscathed from a confrontation as pretty fair, but what of his horse and Samantha? Wererats didn't know what honor was, in his experience, and might threaten to hurt her. It pained him to do it, but he sheathed his sword, and sighed. "Changed yer mind, have ya," the Wererat cooed.

"Do not misunderstand me." Molis fished in one of his pouches for five gold coins. He assumed it would be more than enough for these highwaymen. He clutched the money tightly in his hand, and slowly approached with his arms held out at his sides, fists clenched. "Were I alone, without the child to consider, I would lay all three of you out in shallow graves." He approached more closely, tendrils of demonic magic swirling out from the back of his helmet like long, pitch black hair blowing in the wind.

The saffron lights in his head blazed flaxen bright, and the Wererat in the center of the trio of bandits dropped his knives, his arms suddenly rubbery and weighted like lead. "However, in exchange for peaceful passage and the safety of the girl, I shall pay you your toll fee," he said, standing now only a foot away from the leader of this pack of rodents.

Molis reached out with his left hand, grasped the man's wrist, and pulled it forward, turning his hand palm up. With his right hand, he dumped the gold pieces into the upturned hand.

The Wererat stared with wonder at the money there. "Jeez, mister, dis is two and a half times more den we's usually ask fer." His eyes blinked rapidly at the half-demon, and Molis saw mortal fear reflected in his eyes. "As fer a girl, we isn't savages, man," the Wererat said. "We don't hurt kids."

"Right, right," the other two Wererats said in muddled unison. Molis still had use of his Knight powers, and now might be a good time to make use of them. If he asked anyone a direct question, he could tell if their answer was truth or a deception.

"Have you ever harmed a child," he asked the big Wererat leader. The man backed up a step, and Molis felt pretty certain he didn't even need to hear his answer; the man would lie and tell him they hadn't.

"No, not ever," the Wererat leader said.

A lie, and a bold-faced one, Molis thought.

"Well, we never did any real harm, dat is," the Wererat blurted. His two associates started to creep off into the surrounding forest, abandoning their leader to his fate.

Molis stomped forward, and grabbed the Wererat before him by his studded leather jacket, pulling forward and down to his own eye level.

"Look, mistah, we're Wererats, we've got a natural instinct to make profit!"

"What have you done," Molis growled, peeking back over his shoulder to ensure that Samantha was still asleep. He wanted to do something to the Wererat, but he didn't want her to see what, because she would immediately try to run away from him. He saw to his satisfaction that she was still fast asleep in the saddle. He turned his face back toward the Wererat, and used his left hand to lift up his helmet's faceplate.

The Wererat's eyes spread wide with silent horror as he looked into the darkened aspect of Grigory Molis. The half-demon smiled, revealing row upon row of razor-like teeth, and he flexed his demonic magic, letting the blackened aura of his body shimmer and flow from his body. Several tentacles of black magic took on the shape of black serpents, their tongues hissing out of their heads, eyes wide and filled with venomous intent.

"Tell me what you have done, and repent for your sins, foul creature," Molis growled in the pure voice of the demon who shared space with his soul.

"I, I, I smacked a couple a kids around a few times," the Wererat admitted, trying to grip Molis's arms and pry himself free of their iron grip.

In a full-blown panic, most Wererats went into their lycanthrope rage. Panic seemed to be the only emotion that brought the rage on in their particular Race. However, despite the Wererat's best efforts to engage this state of being, the hands that twisted into his leather jacket didn't seem to allow it. Some sort of magic blocked the rage from the Wererat's body, and he struggled harder to free himself.

"I've sold 'em to slavers, okay! It's a side business." The Wererat brought his knee up into the metal plate that guarded Molis's crotch, and cursed under its breath as Molis squeezed the jacket around his throat. "Oh Gods above, are you gonna kill me? I'm so sorry, I'll never do it again, I swear it!"

"That's right, you won't." Molis pulled the Wererat close enough to kiss the tip of his rodent snout. "I'll be keeping tabs on you, little man. If you ever harm a child again, I shall return, and slay you slowly and painfully. Now get from me." He tossed the Wererat into a nearby tree, bringing his demonic power back in check.

Molis returned to Thunderstorm, who seemed to be grinning at him. He took up the reins, and watched the Wererat run off into the forest, screaming bloody murder as he disappeared. "Well, that's another good deed for the day," Molis said to himself, and sauntered down the road toward Whitewood.

* * * *

About three hours later, Samantha awoke screaming from a bad dream.

Molis let go of Thunderstorm and dashed to her side, taking her down off of the saddle and holding her close again, stroking her hair and trying to assure her that everything was all right, there was no bad man around. He even told her that if the bad man came, he would send him away forever and ever, and when Samantha asked if he meant that, he smiled and said yes, he would send the bad man away. She hugged him fiercely around the neck, and clung there for a while, neither of them moving or saying a word. Finally, Molis asked if she wanted to walk for a while, and she agreed to do so.

Half an hour after that incident, Molis spotted a hotel up the road. It seemed to him to be perfectly placed, perhaps four hours away from Whitewood. Travelers on the long and winding roads of the forest would surely stop in to rest, but he didn't want a rest; he wanted to know if the hotel also served as a diner, which as he could see from here, it did. An outdoor patio area had been fenced off next to the hotel itself, and as they got closer, he saw waiters in white shirts and black pants moving between several patrons.

Molis concentrated, and brought his magic to bear once more, concealing himself in the guise of the Human, Edgar Cesar. He removed his helmet, set it on its hook on Thunderstorm's side, and pulled off his gauntlets, tucking them into his belt. He looked down at Samantha, who took his free right hand in hers, and asked, "Shall we stop and get something to eat?"

"That would be good, Mr. Molis sir," she exclaimed, letting go of his hand and sprinting ahead.

"Stay where I can see you, Samantha," he yelled after her, but she had already disappeared inside.

Molis tied Thunderclap to a hitching post once he got in front of the four-story hotel, brushing his side and telling him to stay put. Molis walked to the open door, and felt the cool air blowing past his forehead from the lobby. Samantha was standing in front of the check-in counter, trying to jump up and down and fetch the desk clerk's attention.

Molis stepped inside, and looked immediately to the right at some humming piece of metal. *A machine,* he thought. *What sort of Elves would have mecha in their hotel? I thought these people hated technology?*

The machine pumped cold air through the lobby, and though it felt good to his hands and forehead, he cringed from the piece of ancient equipment. He looked back toward the check-in desk, and saw a Gnome standing on some sort of stepstool.

Ah, that would explain it, he thought. *Pesky Gnomes and their tinkering.*

"Oi, what can I do for you and your little girl, sir?" The Gnome smiled down at Samantha, who stopped jumping up and down and waving her little hand in front of the Gnome's face.

"Um..." Molis considered telling the Gnome that the girl wasn't his daughter, but thought better of it. That would only raise questions, none of which he felt he wanted to answer. "We just need to grab some lunch, master Gnome. Do we need to pay for a room to get a meal?"

The Gnome laughed delightedly at Molis's ignorance and shook his head.

"No, just head through that door to your right into the dining hall. Someone will take care of you, sir. You and your daughter enjoy your meal."

"He's not my daddy," Samantha said brightly, and Molis quickly put his hand on her shoulder and squeezed a little. She looked up at him and he put his finger to his lips meaningfully. Molis then looked at the Gnome and smiled. He mouthed the word 'stepdaughter' to the Gnome, who raised his eyebrows in the 'oh, I see' gesture. He gave the little girl a smile, and the two travelers headed through the glass fronted double doors into the dining hall.

Molis told the young Half-Elf woman serving as hostess to seat them for two, and she led them outside to the patio dining area, handing them each a menu. Molis stared dumbly at the menu, which was written entirely in Elvish. "Um, can I have a common language menu?"

The girl eyeballed him suspiciously, looking at the girl. "She's my stepdaughter, but her and her mother still haven't taught me to read your language," he blurted by way of explanation.

The waitress gave him the same gesture as the Gnome innkeeper, and left to fetch him a menu.

"That was close," he murmured.

"Why did you lie to that lady," Samantha asked him abruptly. Molis gave her a stern, warning look.

"Because people wouldn't like it if they knew why you were traveling with me. They'd start asking some questions that I don't think you want to hear the answers to. Now let it alone, Samantha," he said, being stern but kind. "Do you want anything to drink, sweetheart?"

"I wanna have some cider," she said with a sweet, innocent smile.

When the waitress returned with his menu, Molis asked for a glass of apple cider for the girl, and an ale for himself.

"Mommy says ale is bad for you," Samantha offered, waggling her finger at Molis and imitating an older woman's voice in the manner little girls do.

Molis and the waitress shared an amused laugh at this, and the Half-Elf woman said she'd get their drinks and give them time to decide what to eat.

"Samantha, I think it's my turn to ask you a couple of questions," the half-demon said.

The girl perked right up and sat primly in her chair, waiting for his questions and bopping her head from side to side.

"How old are you, dear?"

"I'm twenty-four years old," the little Elven girl said. *Ye gods, she's still a young child,* Molis thought. *Elves don't even reach puberty until around sixty! On the Human scale, she's maybe six or seven!* Molis cleared his throat, his mind, and continued.

"All right, you're still very young. Samantha, dear, I have to ask you a few questions that are going to make you a little sad, okay?"

She gave him a puzzled look, and he proceeded. "I have to ask you about the bad man."

He noted the sudden shift in her eyes, the way she clutched the front of her dress in one hand. Her bottom lip started to quiver ever so slightly, but to her credit, she didn't start bawling again or anything so theatrical. "Are you okay with that?"

"Uh-huh, I guess so," she said, grinning much less happily as the waitress brought them their drinks. "I'll have the munch-munch platter, miss," she said to the waitress, who jotted down her order.

"A portion of meatloaf and broccoli for me, miss," Molis said, savoring the idea of a well-prepared but simple meal. He had a moment to once more wonder how long it had been since he'd enjoyed a good, solid meal. *Weeks, it must be.*

"Samantha, can you tell me what the bad man looked like," he whispered, leaning slightly over the table so as not to air out their conversation.

Samantha averted her eyes from his for half a minute, and then stared him right in the face.

"He looked all, weird," she said, clearly struggling to think of a way to describe the bad man. "It was like he was a shadow, but not one on the ground," she said. "Like a walking shadow, you know? And his eyes, he had four eyes in his face, and they were all yellow, like yours get sometimes," she said, giving Molis a start and making him choke a bit on his ale.

She's seen my eyes? Oh boy, that's no good. She'll start asking troublesome questions, and then I may as well do like the other one suggested and drop her off at some random village!

"Samantha, this is very important, do you understand," he whispered, looking around at the three other patrons on the patio. They all seemed to be minding their own business. One had her nose buried in a book, one was using a spyglass of some sort to look up into the trees and jot down notes in a steno pad, and one was simply relaxing, enjoying his wine and reclining with his chair against the patio railing. "Did the bad man have a particular smell to him?" The four eyes had been one clue for him, something he had seen first hand when he began this hunt for the demon in this area.

"Yeah, he smelled funny too." She scrunched up her nose and looking at Molis suspiciously. "Did you come here to take the bad man away? I know sometimes nice people like you do that to bad men and women. Daddy calls them Crusaders. Are you a Crusader?"

The Crusaders were a loose Guild-like affiliation with several chapters throughout the lands of Tamalaria. Their sworn purpose was to deal with criminals and monsters for the well-being of the peoples of the lands. Unlike Bounty Hunters or mercenaries, this order operated freely, with no expectation of payment or compensation. *A bunch of do-gooders,* Molis thought a tad harshly.

"Not precisely, sweetheart, but I do similar work," he said to put the child's mind at ease. "Now, what exactly did he smell like?" He took a swig of his ale to prepare himself, though he felt positive he already knew what the bad man smelled like.

"Cinnamon," Samantha said, confirming his suspicion.

The very demon he came to the Elven Kingdom to hunt down had slain this girl's parents. *Fate is a strange, large wheel,* Molis thought. *It mows down everything in its path, and spits it back out again later.*

"He smelled awfully nice for such a bad man. I, I think I saw him hurt my daddy," she mumbled, her words barely audible.

The two of them sat in silence until the food came, and both of them quickly devoured what was on offer.

Molis paid the bill with six tin coins, and then the two of them headed back to Thunderstorm, who was happily drinking from the water trough near the hitching post.

As he lifted Samantha up into the saddle, he felt obligated to ask, "How do you know the bad man hurt your father?"

"Because he used some kinda spell, and my daddy started screaming.

That's when I ran."

Molis took up Thunderstorm's reins again, and started down the road. If they didn't come across any more interruptions, they could make Whitewood in a few more hours. Of course, in his experience, trouble seemed to follow him like a dog that refused to go away after its been given a handout.

* * * *

Three hours later, Grigory Molis once more came with Thunderstorm and Samantha to a fork in the road. This time the intersection came with a four-way split, with two roads, the one furthest left and furthest right, both labeled Whitewood. However, on the left-hand path, underneath the fine cursive print, stood the words 'low road.' On the right-hand path, the words said 'high road.'

For a long pause he stood there, the reins of Thunderstorm in his hand, his senses tingling. His quarry could not be far down the path marked as the low road, because its scent tickled his nostrils. The sunlight streaming through the forest was still strong, and that meant his target would be weakened.

-We should go for it, now! It is weakened, we've just eaten to recover our power, and we have the drop on him! We must do it now, Edgar!-

The part of Grigory Molis that still belonged to Edgar Cesar recognized the strategic wisdom in what the demon said to him. However, it didn't account for Samantha's safety in the slightest.

We can't, he thought back regretfully. *Samantha could wind up in harm's way.*

-She could, I suppose. But what does that matter, Edgar? The demon tried to kill her once before already, and will surely go for it if we use her as bait.-

I will not. Edgar's rage surfaced close to the outermost shell of his body.

-And why not? We have used people as pawns in our hunts before.-

They always knew the risks. They were adults! This girl is a child! I refuse to put her at risk to put down another demon. We'll come back this way when we drop her off at her aunt and uncle's.

While the demon within didn't care much for the idea of letting the demon they hunted live for any longer than needed, it understood Edgar's request. Grigory Molis was not a full-blooded demon; he was a half-breed, and had to remain somewhat mortal in mind and heart. It conceded to the mortal half's wishes, and they started toward the high road.

The dirt path of the high road showed no clear evidence of being often traveled, unlike most of the roads they had come down since he had picked up Samantha on the road that morning. It seemed strange to him that he had only traveled with the girl for three quarters of a day, for he had become highly protective in a very short period of time. He supposed it was only natural, in a way. Knights protected people, it was their job. But more than that, he had traveled from coast to coast, region to region, kingdom to city-state for the last thirty years trying to exterminate the last demonic vestiges of Richard Vandross's unholy army. *And why have I been doing this? To protect the people of Tamalaria from the threat of them forming a force again, because if they do, they'll stir up worse trouble than the land has seen in half a century.*

And was that not what he felt most afraid of, in the end? The company that had defeated the armies of the warlock thirty years ago were scattered to the four points of the compass. Shoryu and Ellen Tearfang lived as a married couple in the city of Whitewood, where he was heading. The Cuyotai husband of the pair served as a Councilor, last he'd heard. Ellen busied herself with the rearing of their two children.

Morek Rockmight, the Dwarven Boxer who had accompanied the legendary hero Byron, had returned after the war to the city of Traithrock, capital of the Dwarven Territories. He too held a position of leadership, and was a very busy man in his elderly years. James Hayes had passed away four years ago, having served his living years after the war as a Cleric of peace. He had sired one son, Christopher, who served as a Knight in the Order of Oun. Selena Bradford had perished before the final confrontation, as had Alex, the Ki Fairy. And Bael, the proud leader of a tribe of Lizardmen who resided in the Elven Kingdom, had also been rumored to have died not too long ago. In short, the lands of Tamalaria had no heroes to stand against an army of demons, and Molis had taken it upon himself to reduce their ability to form such a force. As of the moment he finally spotted Whitewood in the distance, he had only fourteen demons left from Vandross's armies to destroy.

The high road turned out to be littered with long, loping curves and twists, but on both sides of the path, various beautiful breeds of flowers grew in large beds and clumps formed by the naturally rich Elven lands. Samantha and Molis enjoyed a comfortable silence until finally, with Thunderstorm in hand, Molis came to a halt a dozen yards from the southern gates of the Elven Kingdom's capital city.

Four guards in heavy plated armor came forward, all four of them handsome young Elven men. A fifth guard, a Cuyotai, kept his distance despite his iron plate armor. Molis's silver armor clearly set him ill at ease.

One of the Elven guards smiled warmly at Molis after looking up at

Samantha, who had inclined her head slightly toward him and lifted the hem of her dress half an inch in a mounted curtsey to him and his men. "Greetings, sir, and hail. Welcome to Whitewood, fair capital of our kingdom," the guard captain said, spreading his arms wide to indicate the whole of the city behind him. "Might I ask what business brings you here?"

Molis decided that, so close to the home stretch, honesty was going to be the best policy. At least, a dash of the stuff would do.

"Might I in turn ask to speak with you aside, sir." Molis bowed low with his hands held together in a triangle in front of him, in the traditional salute of good tidings that the Elven folk used with one another, particularly when formal matters were to be discussed.

The captain of the guards raised an eyebrow, but his grin didn't fade in the slightest.

"And may the girl and horse approach your men closer?"

"Surely," the captain responded rapidly, moving off to one side of the guards, twenty feet away and with his back to them.

Molis watched Thunderstorm stalk dutifully closer to the other guards, and now even the Cuyotai approached Samantha. The Werecoyote cast an Illusionist spell before her eyes, setting off an imaginary firework from his palm to explode into a starburst pattern overhead.

Samantha giggled excitedly, clapping her hands and asking the Cuyotai to do it again.

The captain leaned in close to Molis, and his smile faded away to nothing. "What is so important that you would use the formal greeting of my people, Human?" The captain sounded a little offended.

"I have come to this great forest to hunt down and destroy a demon," Molis said rapidly, whispering his words so that they wouldn't reach the girl. All she knew was that the demon was a 'bad man', and didn't need to be terrified further by finding out just what had probably killed her parents. "I awoke this morning to find that girl spying upon my camp. She was alone, and lost, sir." Molis shrugged his shoulders. "I couldn't leave her to starve or fall prey to worse fates."

The Elven captain of the guards looked back over his shoulder for a minute, and seemed to communicate silently with one of the other Elven guards, a sergeant from the stripes the man wore on his light green uniform tunic.

"I see." The Elf said, turning his attention back toward Molis. "I also see, from your changing eyes, that you yourself are of a demonic nature."

A chill went down Molis's spine. *Oh shit, I lost my focus! Great, now what? Will he trust me?*

"Some of us know of your work, Grigory Molis," the captain said, smiling at him and sending a different shock through Molis, one of gratitude. "I myself was with the contingent of men that went with mighty Byron through your tunnel into Mount Toane, sir."

Molis bristled with pride at his past accomplishments, and the doors they sometimes seemed to open. He pulled his faceplate down anyway, in case the other men on watch didn't share this captain's high regard for him.

"She says she has an aunt and an uncle here in Whitewood. I would ask that you take her to them. I shall say a farewell to her, and then return to my quest. The demon is not far from here," Molis confessed.

The Elven captain of the guard's eyes lit up brightly, and his body seemed to tingle with anticipation.

"Shall I accompany you, sir?"

Molis stayed him with a mailed hand.

"No. When I say my farewells, take her inside the city and get her to her relatives. We were fortunate enough to have had that high road to travel on, or I may have had to risk her safety getting here."

The Elven captain gave him a queer look then, confused and a bit wary. However, he said nothing, merely nodding and clapping Molis on the armored shoulder.

"Very good, sir. We shall take the best of care of her."

Molis and the captain of the guards approached the others, and Molis reached up, setting Samantha down gently on the ground. Samantha had a smile on her face as he lifted her out of the saddle, but when the half-breed lifted his faceplate, her smile started to fade.

"You're leaving, aren't you," she asked very quietly.

Molis hunkered down to her eye level, and nodded.

"These nice guards are going to take you to see your aunt and uncle. But they'll need your help, Samantha," he said, lifting her drooping head with one crooked finger under her chin. "They don't know where to look for them. So you have to tell them where to go, okay?"

The little Elven girl nodded, and then threw herself around Molis, arms wrapped around his powerful neck and armor.

He returned her embrace lightly, not wanting to crush the poor little girl, who was now sobbing against him. "It's all right, Samantha, it's okay."

He held the little girl out at arm's length, and marveled at the tears that streaked down her face. He'd known her less than a day, and yet she didn't want him to leave her. *I've probably been the only person to show her kindness in the last few days, since she started running.*

"When I'm done with my business in the area, I'll come back and visit you, okay? Does that sound good?"

"Uh-huh," she managed, trying to press forward on the hands he held her shoulders with. "But you shouldn't go, Mr. Molis, sir, that bad man will hurt you!"

"No. He won't." The half-demon wondered if he'd spoken a lie. "I'll make him go away, Samantha, I promise. Now, you have to go with these men."

He let go of her shoulders and rose to his full stature.

Grigory Molis was not impressively tall, only topping out at around six-foot-two, but to the little Elven girl, he must have appeared to be a colossus.

The captain of the guards put one hand on her left shoulder, and led her inside the city gates. Samantha looked back over her shoulders until the wrought iron gates closed shut, and even then, Molis felt her eyes upon him through the heavy metal doors.

He sauntered to Thunderstorm, mounted, and turned the roan around with a tug on the reins.

-Well, that burden is behind us,- the demon spoke within the shared mind and soul of Molis. -Tell the truth, I feel much better now that she's safe inside the city. What about you, Edgar Cesar?-

Indeed, I feel much better, Edgar replied, working his way back to the branched road he expected to come upon. *Still, I feel like I've forgotten something. By the way, where the hell is the split in the road? We came here by the high road, so where's the spot where we came off?*

Molis looked around, having only come five minutes away from the capital's gates.

-I'm, not sure-, the demon murmured.

"It should be right here," Molis said aloud, looking left and right astride Thunderstorm. Molis clicked his tongue, and the horse trotted along once more, getting up a decent pace as the elms, oaks, and spruces passed by on both sides of the half-breed.

He continued on in this fashion for perhaps fifteen minutes when he felt the tingling sensation near the base of his spine that warned him of looming danger. "Whoa boy, whoa," he said to Thunderstorm, who stopped immediately in the middle of the widening road to let Molis dismount cleanly.

He took several steps north, back the way he had come, scanning the surrounding bushes and bunches of trees and saplings around him. He smelled the demon, the hint of cinnamon, and he heard something rustling around to the west, his left.

Grigory Molis drew his sword, and a moment later, with his arm still slightly upward with his weapon, a three-tailed flail whip, tips aglow with arcane power, wrapped around his wrist and sent power and pain exploding down through his arm to his shoulder.

The half-demon voiced a cry of pain, his body jerking in the direction of the whip's wielder, and he was pulled to the ground.

"I don't know how you avoided me on this road before, huntsman, but rest assured you shall not avoid me now," a curdled, gurgling voice said from behind a set of tall, berry-bearing bushes.

Molis looked up from the ground as the whip came off of his wrist, taking his sword with it, and saw the demon he'd been so close to catching twice. Now it stood less than twenty yards away, and it reminded him of just how ugly one half of his makeup could be. The creature before him stood at least eight feet in height, with a body that was angular, scaled, and as gray as cement. Thin, hooked white blades covered its arms, which segmented into three jointed lengths with two elbows apiece.

The demon's head sat on a squat, powerful neck, and held a triangular, pointed chin. It curved out toward the top, resembling a sort of craggy crown. No discernable eyes peered from its flat face, which was a plain surface only broken by the small mouth that opened almost directly on its chin. In its right hand it held the handle of its flail whip. In its left hand it now held Molis's sword.

He could take the demon on without the weapon just fine, but he preferred not to use his demonic powers so close to the city. If the guards should hear their confrontation and come to the scene, they wouldn't be able to tell which was the threat.

Molis assumed a crouched fighter's stance.

"Oh, what's this?" the demon called haughtily. "Planning to have a little fist-ee-cuffs with me are you, Grigory Molis? You're welcome to make the effort, little man, but I'll shred you to pieces with my whip before you get close enough to land a single blow!"

"I don't think so." Molis grinned. Bending his legs, he leaped into the air, using all of the physical power his half-demonic blood could supply him with to jump at the demon.

He flew a good twenty feet up in an arc, staying out of the whip's direct line of attack until the last bit of the jump carried him down almost on top of his prey.

He brought his arms up around his head as the flail whip lashed at his silver armor, tearing long rents in its exterior as the demon tugged it back over his head, preparing another attack.

Molis plunged up and forward, delivering an uppercut that would have taken any other humanoid's head clean off of its shoulders.

The demon rocked back on its heels, grunting as it pin-wheeled its arms for balance.

Molis took advantage of its startled state and lunged forward again, volleying an overhand punch square to its chest.

A large chunk of its body flew off on impact, and Molis learned something new about this particular demon--its body was a thick exoskeleton surrounding a much softer sort of black jelly underneath.

As Molis's saffron eyes blazed, locking on the writhing underbody, the demon brought the stolen sword down over the small opening protectively, and backpedaled away from the half-breed.

Molis growled low in his throat, summoning up his demonic energy and magic. He had thrown everything he had into the second punch, but it had barely made a small opening in the demon's hide. He would have to use his powers to finish the demon off because his gauntlets would break if he tried to pummel it to death. He couldn't be certain his sword, which the demon discarded to the forest floor with a twitch of its arm, would even scratch the rock-like exterior.

Molis clenched his fists at his side, assuming a spread-legged stance, crouching low and continued drawing up his power.

The demon tucked its right leg up behind the crook of its left knee, and also began to growl, drawing up its own magic.

I've never seen that posture before, Molis thought. *Certainly not from any of the others I've tracked down. This is no Shadowbeast; this demon is something different.*

Molis gauged his power as sufficient, and brought himself up into a straighter stance. He wove his left hand through the air, carving out arcane runes in the air. "Moluk an tabo tenia, ush uo locka! One Thousand Needles, Strike Mine Enemy," he invoked.

Shimmering lights blinked above and behind his head, forming a thousand needle-thin projectiles. Molis thrust his left hand, pointer finger out, toward the demon, and the needles flew at the creature.

The demon, still in the midst of pulling on its demonic mana reserves, didn't move an inch as the first couple of hundred needles bounced harmlessly off of its carapace. However, it screamed like a dying animal as twenty or so landed squarely in the open wound on its chest, burying themselves into the soft, black, gelatinous flesh underneath.

Thick red blood spurted out of the wound, and the demon flew back, flailing its arms as it landed with a heavy thud on the collected leaves, branches and moss on the forest floor.

"How did that feel, you cocksucker," Molis shouted at the creature from the Pit, spitting in its direction.

Molis tore his helmet off, the inside of the faceplate now lined with phlegm, the shadowy tentacles of his head making it nearly impossible to see through his closed visor.

"Just, terrific," the demon groaned as it rolled over onto its stomach and pushed itself up to its feet. "Molag shurak anamemnon! Fist of Ruin!" The creature clapped its hands together before its chest, and a small black fist of magic streamed from his joined fingertips, punching Molis hard in the shoulder as he rolled it in the way, avoiding taking a blow directly to his armored chest.

The shoulder plates the magical fist struck immediately spread with rust from the point of contact, and Molis ripped the plates free, tossing them aside.

"How about you, half-breed?" The demon poured as much malice into this last term as he could, and rose to his full height, assuming the stance of power collection once more.

"Enough of this." Molis brought forth his black shadow shield and pumped his legs hard, hoping to span the thirty yard distance before his prey could unleash anything nastier than the Fist of Ruin. *That spell is only practiced by Gaiamancers, Necromancers and Q Mages,* Molis thought. *Clearly this demon has some interesting powers at his disposal. I wonder if he has anything like mine?*

It took only moments before the demon provided him with evidence that he indeed had similar abilities.

"Mula ensomanon! To me, spirits, to me!"

When Molis got to within ten yards of the demon, cocking his free right hand up to deliver another powerful punch, a Wraith, charging from seemingly nowhere, blasted into Molis's right side, sending him flying into a huge pine tree.

The trunk cracked thunderously, and the back plate of his upper armor bent cruelly inward, pressing against his spine.

He opened his blazing gimlet eyes for a moment, and watched the Wraith depart, its business here done.

"Not even the most skilled Necromancer can summon a Wraith, I'm sure you're aware. At least, not those that have none of the Sage Powers. You are outclassed, half-demon." The creature threw back its crown-like head and cackling madly. "Run along home, and I might spare y-," it began, breaking off as Molis stood from the ground where he had crumpled.

"We, who stand against the darkness, shall see banished by our holy light. No matter the cost." Molis's chin touched his chest, the tentacles on his head took snake-shapes again, hissing at the demon, thick vitriol dripping from their fangs. When Molis looked up, his eyes were no longer the yellow, saffron shade. They held instead cobalt light that shone brilliant and deep like the ocean of time itself. "These words have been spoken before by the greatest hero this land has known in this era, demon," Molis said, stalking forward. "I have none of that man's holy powers, or his righteousness," he growled, advancing on the demon, who now quivered visibly, fearful as a demon could be. "But we did share one thing in common, one common goal."

He batted aside a blast of black power the demon sent at him with ease. "To see creatures like you banished back to the darkness and flames of the Pit," Molis growled, now only ten yards away.

The demon lashed out with its whip again, wrapping it around Molis's left ankle and hauling back on the handle, trying to trip him. Molis held firm to his position, and kicked backward, pulling the demon to the ground at his feet.

The demon whipped itself up onto its knees, and put its hands before its face, pleading for a stay of execution. "Please, wait! I can help you! I know where the others of my kind are! I can guide you to them, Grigory Molis! If you grant me quarter, I shall take you to them, one by one, and you can destroy them! I have no great love of my kinsmen."

For a moment, Molis considered sparing him long enough to question him on the other demons he had yet to find and destroy. However, he noted the way the demon's aura seemed to be fluctuating, and looked over the creature's shoulder to find he had tucked his right leg over the crook of his left knee. *He's summoning power for another spell, and he thinks babbling will stall me. I think not.*

"You know, maybe you're right." Molis rubbed his black, shadow-drenched chin. "Maybe I should consider your proposal." He smiled wickedly down at the demon, who grinned madly right back. "Maybe I should, but I won't."

Molis grasped the left side of the demon's head. Sinking his left hand into the small opening in the exoskeleton, he tore his hand back, ripping a huge chunk of the stone-like flesh free, and then thrust both hands inside the wound.

Molis used the last of his summoned mana reserves to bring spiders streaming out of the darkness wrapped around his fists inside of the demon's breast. The arachnids were of a horrible, carnivorous bent, and set straight away to devouring everything inside of the demon's hide as it screamed and twitched, flopping to the ground and writhing about in sheer agony.

Molis picked up his sword and sheathed it, heading back for Thunderstorm as the demon perished slowly behind him.

The roan seemed more than happy to see him, and Molis retracted his demonic power and aura. He picked his helmet up on the way back to the horse, cleaned it, and planted it on his head. He opened one of the horse's saddlebags, reaching in for some of the strips of jerky he always kept on hand, and his mailed glove came upon something soft and plush. He drew the object out, and stared dumbly at Samantha's teddy bear.

A little smile crept over his face, and he patted the horse's side lightly. "Better turn around, old friend. We forgot something when we dropped off Samantha."

Molis mounted, and headed down the long, narrowing road toward Whitewood. Once more he held an internal interview regarding the missing split in the road, and when he came upon the gates, his heart lifted at the sight of the Elven captain he'd spoken with before.

Good, he's still on watch.

He stopped Thunderstorm a few yards from the captain and handed the reins to one of the other watchmen, who took the roan aside to be fed and watered.

Molis walked directly to the captain with the teddy bear clutched tightly in his left hand. "Captain, the little girl forgot this in my saddlebag. Might I go inside the city and deliver it to her?"

The captain smiled broadly, warmly even, at the half-demon. He nodded, giving the signal to open the gates for the traveler. "You're lucky," the captain said. "We've had reports of a demon attacking travelers on that main road for the last week or so. Did you come upon him?"

"I did," Molis said quietly to the captain. "And I sent him back to the Pit, Gods willing. Do Samantha's aunt and uncle live close by the gates?"

"Only a few minutes away. I'll have one of these men guide you there directly." The captain waved another Elven guard over. Before they headed inside of the city, the half-demon decided that the captain would certainly be able to settle the debate inside his mind.

"Captain, how do I get back onto the high road to and from the city? I took it to get here with Samantha, but I wasn't able to locate it again. There were some lovely flowerbeds along that path," Molis asked. The captain of the guards gave him an openly befuddled look, and shrugged his shoulders. "What's wrong?"

"Sir, there's only the one main road to the south leading here."

Molis's eyes shot wide open, and he shook his head slightly. The

Elven captain seemed to understand his confusion, and placed one hand on his bare shoulder. He whispered to Molis, "Sometimes, the Gods watch over the innocent in odd ways."

Molis immediately remembered what the demon had said to him when they first engaged in combat; *I don't know how you avoided me, but you won't avoid me again.*

There had never been any low road or high road, he realized. Molis looked up through the canopy of trees at the skies above, and thanked the Gods for seeing Samantha safely to her new home.

Tale Seven: The Old Stomping Grounds

"This is awfully sudden, Lain," Thaddeus Fly groused as he stood in Lain McNealy's chamber doorway, watching her pack her rucksack for travel. "Besides, I thought you were enjoying your time off in the city." He tried not to push her away by arguing too much with her. He'd told Markus Trent during their quest for the Glove of Shadows that Lain was meant for bigger, better things than serving in the Midnight Suns, one of the two large thieves' Guilds that operated in Desanadron. Still, he hoped against hope that this wasn't her final good-bye.

"I have been."

Her light, sultry voice called out to the more primal impulses in her boss's head. He wondered if it was healthy for him, a Black Draconus, to sleep with a Human woman, but neither of them questioned it much when they were alone in his bedroom.

She tossed her head to one side, whipping her long, raven black hair out of her face as she stuffed the last few articles of clothing she'd be taking into the rucksack. She looked up at her leader and lover, and gifted him with a blown kiss. "I just feel the need to go back, if only for a few days. The trip will take longer than my actual time there, Tad." She used this pet name knowing that he hated it when she used it anywhere other than in private. She giggled as he flinched at the sound of it, but he squeezed his eyes shut, and heaved a heavy sigh.

"I see I'm not going to be able to talk you out of this." He crossed his arms over his broad chest once again. "You're taking someone with you, aren't you? Don't tell me you're going to be going alone." He pointed one long, scaled, talon-tipped finger at her in warning. "Because if you are planning on doing this on your own, I forbid it! Even for one such as yourself, those marshes are dangerous business."

Lain planted her hands on her hips and leaned to the side slightly, giving him her patented 'Do I look like an idiot' look.

"So someone else *is* going with you. From the Guild?"

"No, dear." She hauled her rucksack up onto her back. "I met an interesting fellow at one of the local magic shops a few weeks back. You may remember me mentioning him, a little Kobold fellow."

Fly turned his eyes upward, thinking back to their recent conversations. Then, he snapped his fingers and pointed at her.

"Right, that Kobold mage fellow, what was his name?"

"Kobuchi." She curled one hand up against his rough, scaly cheek, and gave him a short, hard hug. "We'll be perfectly safe, dear. Don't worry so much." She felt something pressed into her free left hand. She looked to her left, and saw the white clad Ninja, Akimaru, standing there. He had pressed a small cage into her hand with a messenger pigeon inside.

She uttered a little laugh and thanked Akimaru, who saluted her and darted off back down the hallway after bowing to Fly. "I think you're being ridiculous, but thank you dear," she said, planting a kiss on his mouth.

He stepped further out into the hall, and patted her on the shoulder.

"Have a good time, Lain, but be careful and write me at least every other day. I want to know if there's trouble. That pigeon's enchanted, he can get back and forth from here to Ja-Wen in a couple of hours. You're not going that far, so it'll only take about an hour." He turned his back on the Human Necromancer and starting slowly away from her. "Have a safe trip, Lain."

"I will, dear," she called after him, then started down the long, narrow hallways for the exit out of the abandoned apartment complex that housed the Midnight Suns.

Already her mind flooded with memories of her old training grounds, the strange temple they housed, and the quirky, cute little Kobold fellow she'd met in the magic shop a few short weeks ago. He had told her he was in the area because Desanadron and Palen were the only two cities that carried the sort of magical items he required for his research, and Palen was fresh out. The Kobold had also told her, before Lain even had a chance to introduce herself, that he had approached her because he sensed a powerful magical aura about her. He'd been able to identify her Class just by being near her.

Kobuchi himself possessed an interesting amalgamation of magic and spells from several different schools of magic. He claimed to have two of the Ancient Spells under his belt, though she highly doubted it.

Probably just puffing himself up, she'd thought, but she also found herself quite liking the little man. With so few other magic users in the Guild, she found herself wanting some like-minded company for a while, and she'd already planned a trip to the Lucara Marshes. She impulsively invited him to accompany her, and he had agreed just as impulsively.

Lain exited the Guild's building into an alley, and then guided herself between the various Wererat and Human drug dealers in the alley to the main street out front of the Guildhall. The bright, midday sun streamed lovely light down on her, and she took a deep breath of the open air. She regretted for a moment leaving her Permanent Attendant behind again, but then realized that she didn't really like having him around much these days anyhow. He had become very strange as of late, and seemed to be growing more independent of her control and suggestions.

He's evolved too much, that's all, she thought. *I should have put a stop to it a long while ago, but what can I do about it now? I'll just have to create a new one.*

Permanent Attendants were usually the first undead creature that a Necromancer raised from the dead, and they did anything and everything the Necromancer ordered them to. The undead, under the careful control and crafting of a skilled Necromancer, could 'evolve', as it were, into larger, more powerful undead creatures. When first starting out, Necromancers could raise a skeleton or a zombie, but nothing else. As they became more powerful, and reached new levels of mana growth, they could conjure up more powerful undead, such as Uberzombies, Skull Warriors, and Red Bone Warriors. These creatures could then, in turn, 'evolve' either on their own or with the aid of a Necromancer into Dread Knights (for Uberzombies or Skull Warriors), or, with an old and nearly forgotten ritual, into Wraiths. Only the most powerful Necromancers could summon or create a Dread Knight from scratch, and none could tame a wild or natural Wraith.

Lain had the ability, if she had the inclination, to raise or create any of these creatures if she wanted to. She had once constructed a Dreadnaught all on her own, and brought it to life, nearly sending herself into a weeklong coma. She had come in and out of consciousness during that time, and her Personal Attendant had been forced to destroy the Dreadnaught, since it went berserk after coming to life. She hadn't been too happy about that, but knew why he'd had to do it. She had used body parts from several different brutal Races, and hadn't used anything with less than a moderate degree of brute power at its disposal. Having erected it, though, she knew it would be a snap to create a new Personal Attendant, but she didn't want to at the time. For now, she was content.

The Human Necromancer, pale and slender to the point of being sickly-looking, headed off down Quarter Street toward the nearest magic shop, where she'd agreed to meet Kobuchi. From a hundred yards away, she could barely spot him, since he only stood at three feet (if that) in height. The Kobold mage wore a plain white button shirt over blue jeans, with a tan leather duster over the shirt and a rancher's hat on his head. He'd been wearing it on the day they met, and he'd called it a 'cowboy hat', or something equally odd sounding. He spotted her as she got closer, and waved her over.

"Wonderful day to head to someplace like we're going. Seriously, though, it'll be interesting I'm sure." His high, reedy voice lifted up to her ears over the noise of someone haggling with a street vendor nearby.

Lain looked over, waved to the vendor, Harold Deus, and returned her gaze down to Kobuchi, who wore a long duster and his cowboy hat despite the hot sunlight.

"You look ridiculous, but I guess it's fitting." She tapped the wide brim of his hat with one long, slender finger. "It rains a lot in the Lucara Marshes. I suppose you already know that, though." Kobuchi struck her as the sort of fellow who does much research on an area before going there. She thought that probably applied to people as well.

"Indeed, I do," he said, confirming her suspicion. "Now, I have never been to the Lucara Marshes myself, but I can teleport us to someplace reasonably close by." He drew mana into his body. "It'll only take us a day and a half to walk to the southern front of the Marshes."

Lain considered this, and then grinned and nodded.

"Please place your hand on top of my head," Kobuchi said quietly, and Lain complied.

"Condura, condua, condura, condua," he chanted, bringing his palms together.

An emerald sigil appeared on the ground beneath them, and a matching one formed in the air just over Lain's head.

She stared in wonder at them, shifting her eyes first down, then up, then down again. The circles rotated in opposite directions, first slowly, then faster, to match the quickening pace of Kobuchi's chants.

"Condura, condua, condura, condua! Fly us through space and time, hurl us forth! Teleport!"

Blinding white light flared all around Lain, obliterating her view of the city around her, and a vacuum of air popped her ears as she felt herself pulled into emptiness, nothingness. Magical power thrummed all around her body, and she then had the sensation of flying, weightless, down some sort of corridor. She had been through Alchemy teleportation, which wasn't a pleasant experience, but this was something far more terrifying. With Alchemy, she at least felt *whole.* With this magical Teleport spell, she felt as if her body had been pulled apart into its smallest components, and was being delivered piece by piece someplace else.

She prayed to Necros that she would be reconstructed in the proper order. *Head, neck, upper torso, lower torso, legs,* she thought. *Oh, and make sure you remember the arms along the way!*

Another loud explosion erupted in her ears, and behind her eyes, as she crash-landed into the ground, which she could vaguely see and feel was soft and grassy. She groaned and curled up into a ball, hugging her knees to her breasts and moaning loudly.

"It's always nasty the first time, but you get used to it over time,"

Kobuchi said from somewhere nearby.

Lain McNealy opened her eyes slowly, letting them come into focus, and found herself looking at a jean-clad pair of legs. Short legs at that, and she realized she was looking sideways from the ground at Kobuchi, who didn't appear in the slightest affected by the whole process.

"Why did it feel like that?" She groggily rolled into a sitting position, still hugging her legs. The tall grass around her stood a few inches under Kobuchi's head, and she almost laughed, but held it back for fear that she would vomit if her stomach tensed up any more than it already had.

"Oh, well, that's simple enough to explain." Kobuchi waved a hand almost as if to say 'everyone knows that'. "Teleportation of the magical sort requires that we travel directly through the realm of Time itself. We travel through what is called, in the ancient scripts, 'The All,' you see. Mortals such as you and I were never intended to do such a thing, and the magic required makes us sort of, well, less *real* for a few moments."

"A few moments." She clutched her chest, feeling her heart still racing. "It felt like we were in that, that tunnel, for hours!"

Kobuchi shook his head and chuckled.

"What's so funny about that?"

"I'm sorry, dear Ms. McNealy. It's just that only a few seconds have actually passed between our leaving Desanadron and our arrival here. We're just north of a town in the Fiefdom of Lemago, a little farming village called Suikosu. We could go there and purchase horses if you'd like, but I think that would be a waste of time and money. We're only a day and a half south of the Lucara Marshes."

"How can you know that if you've never been there?" She slowly got to her feet. She experienced a moment of vertigo, and then mastered herself.

Kobuchi gave her an indignant look, one that, to her, appeared very natural for him.

"I know where it is because I have very purposefully avoided it," he said. "I'm not big on places like that, Ms. McNealy, because they're terrifying and full of monsters. Demons still roam the lands, and they are said to often travel through that region. I'm powerful, I assure you, but little match for a full-blooded demon."

Lain nodded, and hitched up her bag on her shoulders.

"Not many folks other than Necromancers and Anti-Paladins roam within the Lucara Marshes. At least, not normal folks, you understand." She headed north, leading the short-legged Kobold with ease. She sent invisible tendrils of magic into the ground around her, and scouted outward for several hundred yards in every direction, marveling at the sheer quantity of dead bodies buried in the ground around the area. "Kobuchi, is Lemago a war-riddled region?"

"Oh, goodness yes." Kobuchi's tone was light and conversational. As a scholar, she supposed he knew a good deal of the different regions' histories. "Lemago is a fiefdom that has been established by spilled blood, you see. The empire started off as only one large city and a handful of surrounding townships. Through military campaigns, they have acquired much more land, accounting for about three-quarters of its entire circumference. Not only that, but different towns and villages are ruled by sub-leaders who take direct commands from the Emperor himself, and they are allowed to wage internal war on one another for control of more lands. Sometimes, when one of these 'warlords' gains too much power and influence, the Emperor employs Ninja to assassinate the warlord, and reassigns his lands and districts to other men in his employ," Kobuchi went on. "Why do you ask, Ms. McNealy?"

She grinned hugely, keeping her toothy visage facing forward, away from the Kobold. "Because, we're surrounded by hundreds of potential servants."

Kobuchi drew up short, looked around over the top of the high grass, and then sprinted after Lain to catch up.

"You name it, it's under our feet. And I think that will prove quite useful," she declared, stopping in her own tracks.

She only budged about an inch when Kobuchi, looking down at the ground with a little trepidation, bumped into the back of her, his forehead planting hard into her buttocks.

"Do you mind," she asked curtly, turning around to look at the Kobold.

"Sorry." He shook his head.

Lain sent down her tendrils again, locating a buried horse. She tried to probe whatever might be left of its mind without raising it, but that proved too difficult. It had been dead too long, which she supposed would work to her advantage.

She drew forth her mana and sent a fork of black power into the ground.

The soil three feet ahead of her started to stir, splitting wide open, throwing dirt and rocks in every direction but at her and Kobuchi.

The completely skeletal remains of a horse, a large beast from the look of the bones, rose to its four feet in its shallow grave, its head standing a good foot above the unmarked path they traveled upon. It made a strangled whinnying sound, and shook its head, emptying its eye sockets of dirt.

Lain stretched out her hand, and patted the horse skull on the side. "Good. Get out of there," she said to it.

The undead horse complied immediately.

Trembling, Kobuchi slowly backed away. She had raised the undead so easily, so effortlessly, that he worried for his own safety. She might prove to be more of a threat to him than anything they met in the Marshes.

Lain strapped her rucksack onto the spine of the skeletal steed, cinching the straps down tight. She then turned, her shadow streaming out over Kobuchi's eyes as she took two steps toward him.

"What do you want?" he asked as she reached out one hand.

"Give me your bag. He'll carry our things." She used Kobuchi's own 'don't you know that' tone on him.

He huffed, and took the bag off, handing it up to her and watching with disgust as she tied his pack down behind her own, closer to the rear end.

"Don't worry, he won't run off. He is bound to me." She started off once again northward.

Kobuchi followed right behind, and soon they were walking side by side, Lain taking her time, sniffing the fresh grass and the clean air, looking out far to the east and west at rice paddies and other vegetable crops growing not far away.

They walked on in comfortable silence until late afternoon, when they stopped to dine on a quick meal of salted meats and fruits that Kobuchi had packed.

"How late are we going to travel today," Kobuchi asked Lain, who busily munched away on an apple.

She cocked her head up, considering his question, and then swallowed.

"Probably until around midnight. I've got a good internal clock for the late hours."

"Right," he said. "You Necromancers have your largest mana pull at midnight, right?"

Lain baffled him, though, by shaking her head and chuckling.

"Am I wrong?"

"Misinformed, more likely," she said. "It's a common myth that Necromancers hold all of our rituals at midnight like the witches of old. We actually can gather the most mana about an hour *after* midnight has come and gone. And don't apologize; like I said, it's a common misconception." She took another bite of apple.

The sun cast long shadows in the dirt and grass, which had visibly shortened the father north they traveled.

"We'll have to start bearing more eastward in a couple of hours or we'll completely miss the Marshes. Come on." She finished off the apple and tossed the spent core into the grass. "We've still got a few hours of daylight, and something tells me you don't like the idea of traveling at night."

"It's only natural," he said defensively. "My people don't see very well in the dark, and I suffer terribly from it. I have to make use of my other senses to make up for my near-sightedness. You know, I once met a fellow whose senses sharpen the longer he remains silent," he said as a conversational bit.

"Portenda the Quiet," Lain said, nodding. "Never met the man myself. What's he like?"

"A bit of a prick, actually," Kobuchi said grumpily, sallying forth behind Lain and the undead horse, which followed her every direction. "A bit droll, and sort of moody, I'd say. The very first time I met him, he was in the process of saving a friend of mine, and freeing me from magical bondage." He didn't want to get into the specifics of his imprisonment. "However, I met him another time, with a young Alchemist, Mister Jonah Staples. He's got a shop in your city, did you know?"

Lain nodded, knowing very well of Jonah Staples and his rather popular Alchemy shop. The young Human did a lot of business, and had a gorgeous Elven wife who helped him run the place. Lain had stopped in a few times to purchase healing potions, and found the shop empty and silent, with the exception of noise overhead. The two of them had a small storage room over the main shop, and apparently they used it for more than inventory.

"You were saying something about Portenda," she prompted.

"Ah yes, meeting him the second time. It was a few days before young Jonah's wedding." Kobuchi once more checked the ground around them. His own shadow was lengthening still, telling him that the day was passing on and that evening, and then true night, would be upon them in only a couple of hours. "Portenda and I met with the groom's other invited guests at one of the city's banquet halls for a rehearsal dinner. The man groused through the whole thing, and didn't have much of anything pleasant to say about anyone with the exception of the groom, his family, and myself. Everyone else seemed to somehow rub him the wrong way, and he let it be well known."

"Really?" From everything she'd heard about the Bounty Hunter, he rarely spoke at such social gatherings, if he bothered to attend them at all.

Unbeknownst to either of them, said Bounty Hunter was presently getting a beating from a particular Red Tribe Werewolf whom Lain had enjoyed the company of not too long ago.

"Oh yes. He was rather ill-tempered the whole while, with the exception of the time he spent speaking with Jonah's parents. He seemed rather fond of them. I wonder if he has any family of his own?"

Lain didn't offer an answer to his question, and they continued on in companionable silence until sunset.

Kobuchi closed the gap between them as soon as evening settled in, big and dark and threatening. Kobuchi knew that certain creatures in this region of Tamalaria were strictly nocturnal, and some of them came in varieties that he'd only ever read and seen paintings of.

Lain, on the other hand, looked forward to the coming of true night with an eagerness she hadn't experienced in a while. She had been stuck in Desanadron for nearly three months, and hadn't truly experienced the darkness of night for some time. She did feel a twinge in her heart, missing the closeness she usually shared at night with Thaddeus Fly, but she brushed the feeling aside. *Got to stay focused,* she thought.

A few hours later, as they approached a broad, flat valley just outside of the fiefdom, Lain and Kobuchi both heard the approach of heavy footsteps. They came to a halt, and Lain drew forth her magic, conjuring up another corpse from the soil, this one a zombie still clad in the armor the man had been wearing when he died.

She poured extra power into the creature, instantly evolving it into an Uberzombie.

The undead creature turned toward her, and bowed, its left eye hanging down from the tendon that held it in its head.

"What is thy bidding, my mistress," the creature droned, standing up again.

She gave it a critical look, identifying it as having formerly been an Elf. *A Solider Class or Knight Class. Not what I'd hoped for, but he'll do.*

"Scout ahead to the east, and see what you can see. I shall look on through your eyes." She stepped forward and popping the loose eye into the creature's socket.

Kobuchi felt his stomach clench up, and barely withheld the urge to vomit.

"Listen for my command, and follow it. Do you understand?"

"Yes, mistress." The creature drew a rusty scimitar from its sheath. Off to the east it stalked with surprising speed.

"I say, that thing is awfully fast and intelligent for something you just raised," Kobuchi said.

"I evolved it, that's all." She connected herself magically with the Uberzombie, seeing through its eyes as she closed her own, smelling through its half-rotted nose. She could almost hear its reanimated thoughts, but she pressed a barrier between her own mind and the undead servant's, not interested in that just now. She listened instead to what it could hear, and as it plodded toward the east, she detected that it was closing on something heading in her own direction.

Watching through the Uberzombie's perspective as it came to the upper lip of another hillock, she was startled to find a band of six Greenskins in heavy battle armor heading their way with weapons drawn.

Three Orcs, and three Hobgoblins, she counted, hearing the war cry they loosed as they spotted the Uberzombie.

Lain immediately cut the connection, and raised up ten more similarly clad undead Elves, casting her magic into them and making Uberzombies of them all.

Kobuchi watched her do this all with astonishment, awed by her pure lack of visible effort and the calm, collected way she commanded them all to head east and engage the Orcs and Hobgoblins.

They all saluted her haphazardly, one of the undead creatures burying its short sword into its forehead, since it only had one arm still attached to its body. It pulled the blade out of the shallow wound with a loud sucking sound, long coagulated blood running free again.

The collective stench of rotted flesh finally dragged an eruption of vomit from Kobuchi, who could bear the smell no longer.

"Oh Gods, are you all right?" Lain looked south at her diminutive companion.

He held up a hand at her, still bent double, feeling another wave of the stuff roiling around in his stomach and throat. He vomited a second time, and felt much better for it. "Better out than in, I always say," he joked, laughing nervously. "What is it you said was out there again? Greenskin raiders?"

She nodded, and looked off to the east again. They heard the roars of battle, steel meeting steel, and the strangled, gargling sounds of Orcs and Hobgoblins dying painfully. Curses in a foreign tongue lashed the air, and Kobuchi flinched just a little. "Couldn't you have told your men to just hurt them, or scare them off?"

"Greenskins are too dumb for that. Superstitious buggers, but that would only send them packing for reinforcements. Come along," she said, clicking her tongue at the horse and moving northward again. "They've received my command to do as they like when they're finished with the Greenskins. The first one shall return to us, however, and stand watch when we make camp tonight."

Kobuchi shivered, revulsion at the idea of being guarded by an undead creature running up and down his heart and mind.

"Can we trust him enough to do that?" he asked tentatively.

Lain stopped marching and spun on her heel, ducking down to look him square in the face.

Uh-oh, the Kobold mage thought.

"My creations are not mindless drones, Kobuchi. Not even the simple zombies and skeletons I raise. He will do us no harm." She stiffly turned on her heel again and marching northeast.

An hour later, the first Uberzombie indeed returned to them at a trot, holding an Orc's severed head in one hand. He held it up to Lain, who smiled and patted him on the head like a dog. "Very good. Now, do you have a name?"

"None that I recall from life, mistress. What name do you wish for me to have?" the undead trooper asked as they walked.

"Your name shall be William. Now, William, scout ahead of us, northeast, and ensure our safe passage. When I call to you with my mind, return to us and stand watch while we rest. Understood?"

"Perfectly, mistress." The trooper saluted after he sheathed his scimitar.

Another hour passed in silence, and Lain called to the undead warrior, whom she'd identified as a former Soldier Class Elf.

Kobuchi lit a fire for their camp with a simple spell, and they enjoyed a small meal of ration packets. The undead Soldier, William, patrolled in a wide circle around their tiny camp, and Kobuchi could, here and there, feel its dead eyes upon him.

"Something the matter?" Lain asked, unrolling her sleeping bag and pulling a small pillow out of her bag on the skeletal horse's back. She pulled down Kobuchi's bag, and handed it gingerly to him. She could see just from the look in his eyes, and the aura of fear he was giving off, that he felt completely out of his element. *Not really surprising, is it,* she thought. *Any normal civilian would have shit their pants when I brought up the horse. And then William, and then a whole battalion of Uberzombies. I'm amazed he's still sitting here with me, instead of hightailing it back to Desanadron or Palen.*

"Oh, it's nothing, really." He tried for a smile but came away with a grimace. "I'm just a little nervous, you see. William, as you call him, is your completely willing servant. I myself wasn't much unlike him under Genma, my captor."

"One big exception," Lain said softly, looking at her undead servant. "You had a pulse and a soul. William talks and interacts, and he has a personality, but no soul, Kobuchi. He is not the same man he was in life."

"How does that work, exactly?"

Lain explained. Any undead creature, be it a simple skeleton or zombie, or something like a Dread Knight or a Lich, had no true soul. The only exception in history, so far as she knew, had been Byron of Sidius. The undead creature, more often than not, was raised with a basic grasp of some of its living memories, and the influence of the Necromancer who raised it. The memories and the Necromancer's will formed a personality for the undead servant, and thus, a new being was created, completely devoid of soul.

"I see, I think," Kobuchi said.

"The undead servant's Class, if they were an acknowledged Class at that, also weighs heavily in the personality makeup," she said, sipping water from a skin. "You know, not all Necromancers are evil," she said.

Kobuchi regarded her gravely, then looked into the fire. "I'm aware of that," he said. "You don't seem so bad, after all. Besides that, one of my pack mates was a Necromancer."

"Pack mates?"

"It's what we call our closest friends and family in Kobold society." Kobuchi's voice dropping in volume. "Kobolds are very tightly knit in family until our adolescence when we leave our parents," he continued. He fell silent for a minute, until Lain asked him to continue. He told her of how between the ages of thirteen and sixteen, a Kobold leaves his parents, usually with his closest friends. They formed a pack, and referred to one another as pack mates, or in their native tongue, 'surenmo.' The pack would then go on a pilgrimage to another town or city, somewhere far from their parents. They could not remain within the same kingdom, city-state, or fiefdom as their parents for a period of no less than three years. After that, they could return, but most times they did not, and often times they picked up new pack mates along the way.

"So Kobolds rarely travel alone, I take it," Lain asked.

"Nope. We're pack creatures by nature, and only a few travel without at least a few others. My first pack had a Necromancer in our group, a great scholar of the undead. His name was Theodore Lagil, and while he didn't wield a great deal of influence, he was very thorough in his studies. One day, he raised a Dread Knight, quick as a whip, and there it stood before us. Unfortunately, Teddy didn't have much control over it, you see. As sometimes happens with raised dead, it went completely berserk, and tried to kill us all. Teddy had already used too much mana raising the creature, and then he went and traded his life force for more mana. He destroyed the Dread Knight." Kobuchi heaved a sigh and wiping away the lone tear that betrayed him. "But it cost him his life, in the end. That's mostly why I'm uncomfortable around the undead. Bad memories."

Lain offered her apologies, but Kobuchi simply waved her off. "That's life," he said before curling up into his sleeping bag.

Lain lay down in her own, and they were both quickly asleep. That night, they each dreamed of failed experiments.

* * * *

At dawn, Lain felt something kicking against her feet in the bag. She rolled her eyes open, and saw William standing over her legs, preparing another light kick. "I'm awake, William, thank you. Could you think of a slightly nicer way of rousing me next time, please?"

"Sorry, mistress," William groused. "Old habits die hard, as they say."

"William, before we wake up Kobuchi, I want to know about your past, as a mortal." Lain sat and rolled up her sleeping bag. "Tell me what you can remember thus far."

"Hm, let's see." The Uberzombie removed its horned helmet and scratching the right side of its head. She could see now, in the daylight, the wound that had done him in as a mortal--a deep, horizontal slash across his throat stood out, caked with dried blood. It must have been a light sword that dealt the blow. A heavy sword, hatchet or axe would have decapitated a frail creature like an Elf.

"I served as a Soldier in the territory of Lord Ukitoki in the fiefdom you raised me in. He was a warlord of the southern districts, and waged internal war on his neighbors in the northern and eastern districts. I was felled in a battle against Lord Uzumo's forces, who were among the most elite Samurai warriors I'd ever seen. My throat was slashed by one of their generals as he rode past me. As of now, that's about all I recall, mistress," William said.

"All right. Try to remember more, if you can." She tucked her belongings into her sack and re-strapping it to the skeletal horse, who she had dubbed Bones. "I can probe your brain, but I'd rather not for now. I might make you my Personal Attendant eventually. Would you like that?"

The undead Solider merely grunted, and shrugged his death-stiff shoulders.

"Whatever you will, mistress, I shall obey." He bowed to one knee.

Lain headed over to Kobuchi, and lightly shrugged his shoulder, which did the trick just fine.

"Come on, sleepy head. Time's a-wasting," she said.

Kobuchi helped her pack the rest of the camp, and then they were off again, with William ranging about half a mile ahead. One, at about mid-morning, the Uberzombie sent a mental warning back to Lain, and she and Kobuchi waited until he said it was safe to proceed again. When the two mages came by the spot where he'd sent the warning from, they found a slain thresherbeast, one of the land's nastier monsters, laid out on the ground. William had apparently used his bare hands to rip the creature's head off, and Lain smiled at the sight of it.

"He's good," Kobuchi commented.

"Yes, he is. He's got potential to be something much more than he is. We'll have to see in the next few days."

An hour after this, a little before noon, Lain called a halt to their march and brought William back with a summons. She took their break as an opportunity to write a letter to Fly, sticking it to the bird's leg.

She had attached the pigeon's cage to Bones, and opened the cage to stick the letter in the little tube, and send the bird off. It was a dot on the horizon to the west in only a minute's time. They ate a short meal, and headed off again.

Forty minutes later, she smelled the marshlands through a brief connection with William, who now ranged a full mile ahead of them.

"We're very close. Only a couple of miles to go, I think," she said, navigating through a tall, wild wheat field amid the vast south-central plains. She called for William to stop his progress, and twenty minutes later, they exited the wheat field together, with the Marshes in plain sight ahead of them.

One dirt road off to the east of their position led into the marshlands, and Lain didn't care much for the several sets of relatively fresh tracks on the road leading in.

"Those tracks." Kobuchi headed over to the road, stood over a set of the tracks, and chanted several words under his breath, sending a wash of yellowish light over the footprints.

The light returned to his palms, and he closed his eyes for a moment concentrating. Lain walked over to the Kobold with William and Bones in tow, and stood to his side, waiting for a report.

"Two days old. There's been no rain in the area for about a week," he said, looking up at the gray storm clouds hovering closer and closer from the north. "My best guess is that there were four armed men, probably Paladins from the aura they left behind." He plainly mulled over the reading. "Two Humans, one Elf, and one Sidalis."

"Great. A mutant," Lain grumbled miserably. "I don't suppose that spell you used could tell us what powers he possesses, outside of his Paladin magic?"

Kobuchi shook his head regrettably.

"I thought not. It doesn't matter. William?"

The undead Soldier stood straighter than before.

"If we come across them, I want you to wait for my command, understood? Do not respond to any of the Paladins' threats unless I tell you to. Now, Kobuchi," she said, addressing the Kobold as she looked to the marshlands. "Do you have any spells that will render us undetected by the Paladins?"

"I do indeed, but might I suggest that I look for them first," he asked, smiling up at her.

"You can do that," Lain asked.

"Yes indeed. I have the soil here, disturbed by their feet and not yet by our own. I can use this trace of their auras to track them down. It'll take a while, though, I'm afraid."

"That's fine." She sat and motioned for William to do the same. "Do your thing, Kobuchi, and tell me everything you find in the Lucara. I'm most interested in these Paladins." Already, she was forming a strategy.

And so the two mages set about their separate tasks.

* * * *

Kobuchi summoned up the magic from within, and cast his Aura Tracker spell out from his forehead, sending it whipping over the ground into the marshes.

His field of vision was narrow in this initial tracking phase, and would be until it slowed down upon approaching the targets of his search.

He saw thick, gnarled black trees whiz past, sickly looking coyotes, thresherbeasts, roaming undead creatures, and caught brief glimpses of monsters he'd never seen before in all of his travels. Some of them were downright nasty looking, and some of them he thought might be abominations, creatures never meant to dwell in the realms of Tamalaria.

At one point, his tracker wove around a tree, and almost directly into the body of a Wraith, its pitch black writhing away from the magic, which was good. Such a creature might have been able to send the Aura Tracker spell back at Kobuchi, and ride along its tail to the Kobold and Lain.

Finally, after almost a half-hour, he felt and saw the tracker slow, turning this way and that. It came into a small clearing, if it could be called that, in the murky, muck-riddled marshlands.

Three of the Paladins had been fixed to giant stakes stuck in the ground, and they thrashed weakly against thick steel bindings. A creature danced and capered among them, each Paladin staked at a different point of a sort of triangle. The creature wore a garish black and white jester's outfit, with a large, triple-pointed hat with bells on the tips jingling and jangling.

Kobuchi tried to focus more power into the tracker to gain an audio input, but found he could not. The tracker was pulling away, seeking out the fourth and final Paladin, somewhere out in these marshes.

The tracker found the fourth Paladin not far away, his breastplate and chest torn wide open. Kobuchi could see that the plating and flesh and bone had been blasted apart by some sort of spell or weapon, though what, he couldn't say.

It was the Elf, that much he could tell from the pointed ears, which meant the Sidalis was among the imprisoned Paladins.

He snapped the connection with the tracker and let the magic fade away.

He had a proposal for Lain, though he didn't think she was going to like it very much.

* * * *

"They're helpless, Lain," Kobuchi beseeched her, once again to no avail.

She stomped and paced back and forth in a straight line, wanting nothing more than to simply go into the marshes, locate the temple, and spend a couple of days studying its inner mysteries.

"We have an obligation to help them!"

"Why," she raged at the Kobold, wheeling on him and grasping the lapels of his duster, hauling him easily up into the air to flail and kick out at her. "Do you really expect them to thank me? Hmm? Because they won't, Kobuchi. Paladins are self-righteous assholes, every last one of them. They'll try to convert me or kill me the second they're freed! I won't waste my time on them! They're out of our way, they're no threat to us, and that's all I have to say on the matter!"

She set him down, and spat into the distance, settling the matter as closed in her book.

Kobuchi straightened his jacket, and harrumphed loudly.

"Fine! If you don't want to help them, I will." He started off for the Lucara Marshes.

William, Bones and Lain remained where they were for a full minute after the Kobold disappeared into the woods of the marsh.

"He'll get himself killed, mistress," William finally offered.

"Oh I know that," she said. "I'm just trying to figure out if it's worth saving the little bugger."

Then the matter was settled for her. Arcane words of magic were shouted not far into the Lucara Marsh, words shouted in Kobuchi's voice, and they were followed by a sudden, violent burst of blue light.

"All right, let's go boys," she said, and the three of them, Necromancer, undead mount and undead servant, sprinted toward the marshlands.

* * * *

"I'm impressed," Lain said as she came upon Kobuchi, who was examining the bodies of three thresherbeasts. They appeared to have exploded from within, a neat display of power as far as Lain was concerned. Kobuchi stuck a small dagger into the ragged opening in one of the monsters' bellies.

"Oh, this? Nothing much, really," he said. "I simply raised the temperature of the acid sack in their bodies that they use to excrete their metal-eating saliva." He poked the exploded organ he had just mentioned. It was a tiny thing, little more than a flattened balloon in appearance, with a thin, brown skin coating. "To tell you the truth, I'm a little more worried about the Wraiths and other denizens of these marshes. I'm sure there's stuff living in the ponds and swamps themselves that could give us a nasty scare."

"You're probably right," Lain said. "William, stick close. No ranging ahead. You'll serve as a rearguard from here on out. Stay no more than fifteen yards behind me at all times, until there's trouble. Then you come forward, sword a-swinging, got it?"

"Of course, mistress. Master Kobuchi, must you poke at that thing," William growled, his voice suddenly thick and phlegm-laced.

The Kobold gave him a wry smile, poked the sack one more time, and then stood.

The three of them continued on, Kobuchi leading by just a little.

Lain felt the presence of the Wraith as they passed by, and sent a small streamer of her magic in its direction, letting it know that she was not a threat to it in any sense. While it did not respond, it also did not come any closer.

Kobuchi suddenly hissed through his teeth and crouched, signaling for Lain and William to do the same. The undead warrior had the horse with him, and he clouted it aside its head to get it to drop to the murky forest floor.

Between several trees, perhaps thirty yards ahead, Lain saw the trio of Paladins on their stakes, and the strange creature that pranced about between them.

Lain, Kobuchi and William all listened as the creature sang and pranced about, a wicked-looking curved dagger in its hand.

"Diddly-dee, diddly-do, I'm going to kill, all of you, ahahahahahahahaaaa." It leaped toward the Paladin to the right of the triangle and stabbing him hard in the armored leg.

The trio hidden in the bog watched the dagger stab through the armor with ease, and glide back out, dripping blood. To their surprise, no mark was left on the armor itself.

"How do you like that, Paladin? Do you enjoy the pain? DO YOU?" The jester-creature danced around in front of the Paladin like a loon, finishing his little number by performing a headstand and splitting his legs apart, twirling on his jester's cap in the brackish mud. "Of course you do, of course you do! Hee hee hee heeee!"

"What the hell is it?" Lain was unable to identify the creature as anything more than a very pale man in a jester's outfit.

When it turned and pranced over to the Paladin whose back was to the three of them, she saw that there were no eyes in the creature's pale, grease-painted face. A huge, smeared smile had been painted or tattooed on its face, and two large red blotches graced its puffy cheeks, but she couldn't say if it was truly humanoid.

Kobuchi squinted hard, and thought he knew what it was.

"It is a Grim," the Kobold mage said. "They are strange creatures indeed. Not much is known about them, but they are something between a spiritual creature, and a demon. Not truly either one, but that's basically how to best describe them."

"How does one kill a Grim," William asked, having come forward at Lain's beckoning.

"I'm not entirely certain," Kobuchi said. "The only recorded encounter with a Grim that resulted in the creature's death was rather, well, odd. The Grim in question wasn't hostile. It wandered into the city of Palen, and asked a Bishop to accompany it to its home, which as it happened was a small cottage north and east of the city. When they arrived, the Grim asked the Bishop to stand outside, and when he entered, he asked the Bishop to burn the cottage with the Grim inside. The Bishop was reluctant, but he did as he was asked, and the Grim was no more. It had simply turned into a pile of salt inside the blaze," Kobuchi said.

"So we're going on basically, what? Nothing?" Lain sounded pissed, but when Kobuchi looked her in the eyes, he saw a mischievous glint in her eyes. She looked him in the face, and he saw that she'd already formulated a plan of action in her head.

"Follow my lead," she said, standing up to her full height.

She spoke to William out of the corner of her mouth and over her shoulder. "William, remain hidden until you receive my signal, understood?"

He didn't respond audibly, but she felt him agree internally.

"All right little man," she said, putting one hand on Kobuchi's cowboy hat. "Let's go."

She led the way into the range of the Grim's vision, if he had sense of sight. She assumed it did, since it seemed to now be staring right at her.

It twirled the knife in its hand gracefully, and thrust it quickly into the Paladin's leg.

The Human screamed in agony, and tried to look around the gigantic stake he was bound to hand and foot.

"My my my, what have we here, dear." The Grim shucked and jived, pumping its fists up and down and kicking its legs out from side to side like a man at a ho-down.

"Greetings, sir." Lain spoke sweetly, bowing just enough to reveal some of her cleavage.

The Paladin to the left of the triangle glared at her, but she didn't sense any malice in his stare. She could see him mouthing something at her, and when he repeated it, she could read the words on his lips; *flee, run for your lives!*

"I am Lain McNealy, Necromancer, and this is my associate, Kobuchi. He is a mage of many schools of magic, sir, and we were wondering what you were doing with these Paladins." She tilted her hips to one side, planting her right hand on her hip. It was a stance she knew drove Fly crazy, along with most other men of her Race, and she felt a moment of triumph when the Grim leered at her and licked his lips with a forked, reptilian tongue.

"Why, my dear lady Necromancer, I'm having some fun with them! Yes, yes, some fun indeed, my dear lady." The Grim performed four back-flips, and then a tumble roll, finishing off with a split, raising his arms to the sky.

He's so, wiry, she thought, looking at the graceful jester's movements.

Without using its arms at all, the Grim slid its legs in, scissoring them together and standing up. She looked to each Paladin's face as she entered the triangle of stakes, and saw the disapproving scowls on each visage.

Hopeless buffoons, she thought. *Do they really think I'm so bad? Never mind, I know the answer to that.*

"Tell us," said Kobuchi. "Why are you torturing these men?" The jester-thing, the Grim, waved its free hand over its face, and when it passed, two large, goggling purple eyes had been painted onto its formerly blank forehead.

"Why? Because I can, and because I hate Paladins." The Grim did several cartwheels over toward one of the Paladins, the one on the left. This one hadn't appeared to be very damaged, but Lain reminded herself that the Grim's dagger didn't touch the armor at all. "Always poking their noses where they don't belong, forcing their religions on other people." It poked the dagger into the underside of the Paladin's foot.

The Sidalis, Lain thought, listening to the mutant scream.

The Sidalis looked mostly humanoid, with the exception of what appeared to be a row mouths along his bare forearms. These mouths all snapped and bit at the air, and she saw rows of jagged teeth in each mouth. One of the mouths shot some sort of spider webbing into the air, hitting nothing of use.

"They think they're so holy, so righteous! Yet I challenge any one of them to say their own souls are completely untainted! You, however," he said, turning and pointing his dagger directly at Lain. "You are a Necromancer! You not only acknowledge the darkness and sin in your soul. You embrace it! And that, my dear, is the whole point of this little exercise. To make them realize they aren't so high and mighty!"

Kobuchi cocked his head to one side, and looked up into the miserable face of the Human Paladin who was suspended, bound with iron bands, to the stake nearest them. He looked young, even for a Human, and Kobuchi wondered what someone so clearly wet behind the ears had been doing in the Lucara Marshes in the first place.

Blood oozed out from the joints in his armor where the plating didn't link together, and Kobuchi worried that the boy might bleed to death before they could save him. With their hands pinned down, palms facing the wooden stakes, they couldn't cast any spells that would help them in any way. Aside from that, a sort of magical barrier seemed to be fixed to each binding.

Can I counteract that, I wonder? He might just have to try it.

"And if they admit the tarnish on their souls," Lain asked coyly, bringing her arms up under her ample breasts, accentuating them.

The Grim leered at her again, and she could *feel* its vision fixed to the swell of her tits.

"Why, then they are free," the Grim said. "Yes, I shall free them upon their words, I shall," he shouted, cackling madly and doing another back flip. "Yes, just like I freed the other one! Ha ha!"

"You killed our fellow man," the Sidalis Paladin shouted, spitting in the Grim's direction. "He admitted the taint of his sins, and you destroyed him!

You there, woman," the mutant called down to Lain. "You are to leave! Flee while you can, for this creature shall surely do to the two of you what he has done to us!"

"And how did he do this?" Lain bit the end of one finger teasingly, looking at the Grim. She could see a bulge in the front of its jester's pants, and once more felt a moment of slight triumph. *Living, dead, spirit, demon, or mortal, a man is still a man.*

"I'm delighted you asked, my dear. You see, it was a simple matter of magic and conjuring." The Grim waved his empty hand. A fourth wooden stake, enormous in size, shot out of the ground across from Lain and Kobuchi, complete with metal bonds. "After raising the stakes, I used other spells to affix them each to their own stake. You see, simple! Ha ha ha." The creature tapped one of the bells on its hat with the tip of its dagger, and it jingled merrily. "Now, would you like to take a few free shots at these men, my lady Necromancer? I know how much their kind have bothered Necromancers throughout time, and this would be the perfect time to get some much deserved revenge! What do you say?"

"Oh, can I?" Lain put her arms behind her back and twisted side to side like a little schoolgirl. Kobuchi couldn't help but wonder why she was acting this way, but then he looked at the Grim and saw the same bulge she'd spotted a minute ago. *Criminy, some people have no shame,* he thought. *This might turn out to be easier than I thought.*

"Of course, my dear lady! Do as you'd like to any of them! I shall remove myself from the stage for a moment, and you can have your way! Oh, do you know what would be magnificent? Their friend is only about fifty yards away to the east! Raise him, and use him to assail them! That'll be a real treat." The Grim laughed so hard that it dropped to the ground and started rolling, howling uncontrollably.

Lain didn't want to do any such thing, especially if she expected any thanks from the living Paladins. Instead, she sent magical feelers into the murky soil, finding many bodies available, most of them animals.

When she'd located a few wolves and coyotes, her favorites, she raised them from the loose mud and muck, twelve of them in all. They all snarled deep in their rotted throats and stomachs, save for one that appeared to have no flesh left in its neck. This one, however, was so thickly muscled that she thought it might be some sort of freak of nature.

"My, my, that's nice," the Grim said. "But these gentlemen have armor on, in case you didn't notice."

Lain turned to Kobuchi, and smiled sweetly at him.

He took his cue, and started to bring forth his mana, pulling up a set of spells just for such an occasion. The bindings on the Paladins' wrists and ankles might have been magically protected or binding, but the stakes sure weren't.

Lain then turned and smiled angelically at the Grim, and sent a mental summons to William, who came charging out from his hiding spot.

"I know that. The animals and my servant here aren't for the Paladins. They're for you."

She pointed one extended finger at the Grim. "Attack, my minions! Tear him apart!"

The Grim's smile melted into a look of pure panic as the first of the undead wolves leaped at him, knocking him sprawling to the mud.

Kobuchi sent out several spells to eat at the wood of the stakes, and after less than half a minute, the Sidalis Paladin tore himself free.

He landed heavily in a gasping heap on his hands and knees, and Lain sprinted over to the right-hand Paladin, helping him down as best she could. The Paladin rested against her and the stake, and she panicked, hardly able to support even half of his weight. "Please, I'm going to drop you in a minute," she panted.

"Go, go now, before he recovers," the Human said weakly to her, his long, lank hair screening his pale face from Lain.

The Necromancer looked over at the Grim, and saw that he had managed somehow to regain his feet, and was hacking mercilessly at her undead animal servants, sending lines of crimson energy into their faces, splitting their heads cleanly in half.

Only half a dozen still remained, including the big fellow, who hadn't yet taken a lunge at him. However, much to her satisfaction, the Grim had dozens of bleeding claw wounds and bite marks, and he seemed to be flagging quickly.

Kobuchi used a Slowfall spell on the Paladin they had emerged from the woods near, but knew right away it was a lost cause. The young Paladin had indeed bled to death while Lain used her feminine charms on the Grim, and he shook his head, saddened by the loss.

The Sidalis, he saw, had gained his feet, and was shambling over to Lain and the other survivor.

Kobuchi used his Rush of Might spell on the Sidalis, and as soon as the magic speared into the mutant's chest, he stood upright and marched hurriedly over to Lain and his ally. The Kobold sprinted over to join them, and turned to see William leap over the last four undead animals, scimitar plunging down into the Grim's head, splitting it clean to the chest.

The air stilled for a long minute, and the Grim dropped to the ground. As soon as it hit, there was a loud, ear-shattering explosion of noise accompanied by a flash of darkness. What was left in the Grim's place, was a high pillar of white salt.

Three of the undead coyotes perished in the blast, but the big, freakish undead wolf remained, as did William.

Kobuchi and Lain backed a few paces away from the Paladins, and Lain summoned William, Bones, and the huge wolf zombie to stand behind her.

The Sidalis and surviving Human stood arm in arm, staring at Lain like she was some new species of wildlife.

"We, are eternally, in you debt, Necromancer," the Sidalis said. "And yours as well, Kobold. Tell us, what, are your names?"

"I am the Necromancer, Lain McNealy." Lain gave them a shallow curtsy, lifting invisible skirts.

"And I am the mage, Kobuchi." The Kobold gave them a sweeping bow, taking off his cowboy hat and swinging it to one side.

"We were happy to be of help," Lain said.

The Sidalis did something rather unexpected then; he came forward, and embraced her, wrapping his huge, many-mouthed arms around her.

She felt strange tongues press against her exposed neck for a moment, and realized they were *kissing* her. The Sidalis let her go after a mighty clap on the back that almost knocked the wind out of her. "Um, you're welcome," she said awkwardly.

The Paladins looked at one another, and then once more at Lain McNealy.

"Miss, we cannot thank you enough for what you have done. We surely would have died a very slow death at that creature's hands." The Human Paladin said, using a healing spell on himself, and then the Sidalis. "We are Paladins of Sunemo, the great and mighty God of quest and discovery, cousin God to Aeros, the wind Goddess." The Human put one last spell on himself.

"What were you doing out here, if we might ask?" Kobuchi patted the hulking wolf-zombie on the head. It made some sort of satisfied sound in its diaphragm, the rumble vibrating all the way up to its partially rotted head.

The Sidalis cleared his throat, and spoke up on this subject.

"We were sent by our headmasters to this marshland in order to map it for our order," the Sidalis said. "You may or may not be aware of this, but there are no existing maps to be found of the Lucara Marshes. Our mission was handed down to us by the headmasters in the township of Munasinto, to the east and south of here. The idea for the mission, however, came to our eldest in his dreams a week ago. Sunemo speaks with his children in this manner, miss," the Sidalis said, a tad embarrassed.

"I'm sure he does," Lain replied with a gentle smile. "Necros and Necrophite speak with their followers in much the same fashion, only we go into trance-like states when they speak. It's part of why we always keep a couple of guards on hand while we travel." She indicated Bones, William, and the wolf zombie. She decided, rather suddenly, that while she would certainly get rid of Bones before returning home, she wanted to keep William and the mutt around.

She sent a mental message to the undead wolf, and informed it that its new name was to be Patches, since he was missing large patches of flesh and meat.

The wolf made a strangled growling noise, as if to disapprove, but she gave it a stern, warning glance and it lowered its head, defeated. *Have I ever evolved an undead animal,* she wondered? *I think I shall, after our business at the temple is done.*

The surviving Paladins stood apart, and adjusted their armor, scanning the ground for something or other.

Kobuchi found what he thought they might be looking for, and pointed to two large spears lying near the murky forest around them, to the east where their other dead companion lay at rest. They thanked him, and strapped the weapons to their backs, popping them into metal hoop attachments on their armor.

"We once more give you our thanks, but we must leave this place, at once," the Sidalis said. "We must inform the elder and our headmasters that this place is too dangerous for initiates such as ourselves. We don't even have a good deal of offensive spells at our disposal yet. Peter did," he said, speaking clearly of the dead Elf. "But that, jester-creature did away with him before we had a chance to respond to his hijinks. Come, Galler." He put his arm around the Human once again. "We must go and report the loss of our kinsmen. The best of luck to you, Miss. May your Gods smile upon you."

That was a phrase Lain didn't usually hear from Paladins. Usually they said 'may *our* God smile upon you', replacing the words our God with the name of said deity, and their tone was usually condescending.

With the Paladins disappearing into the gnarled, murky woods to the south, Lain looked off east, through the thicket. She glanced down at Kobuchi, who was asking William to hand him his bag, which the Uberzombie did without complaint.

Kobuchi rummaged around, took out a small wooden box and handed the bag to William. "Hold onto this for a moment," he said, and headed over to the pile of salt that had once been the Grim. He put on a leather glove he had tucked into his belt, and scooped up a small sample of the salt, pouring into the wooden box and then locking it shut. He came back, stuffed the box into the bag, and slung the sack onto his back. "Thanks a bundle, Big Bill," he said.

"Don't call me that," William replied darkly. "My name is William."

"Oh come on," Lain said, giving her servant a companionable shove. "I think Bill would be acceptable at least, right?"

The Uberzombie sighed, sagged his shoulders, and nodded, closing his lids over his eyes for a second.

"But no Big Bill, Kobuchi." She waggled a finger at him as the sun shone for a moment through the gathering clouds overhead.

The first droplets of rain pattered down on the clearing, and Lain started into the woods. "Come on, we don't want to stick around out of cover with the rain coming. It looks like it's going to be a big one."

She led the way with Kobuchi next to her on the right, Patches on her left, and William leading Bones in the rear.

****

The rain pounding down on the Lucara Marshes seemed to be able to ignore what little coverage the bent, blackened walnut trees were able to provide. In less than an hour, Lain McNealy was completely drenched, her long blue jeans and black short-sleeved shirt plastered to her curvy body.

Kobuchi shivered a little in the rough wind coming out of the north, but his duster kept the rain off of skin, and the cowboy hat kept it from his head. He'd applied special oil to them both, and the water simply ran and pattered down and off of his exterior clothing.

He wondered for a moment how Lain dealt with the rain and the cold, and looked up at her to find she was shivering ever so slightly. Her nipples bulged out from behind the thin material of her shirt, hard and large in the deep chill of the wind and rain.

"You know, I've got a wonderful spell to keep the rain off of you, if you'd like," he offered weakly, his eyes locked on her feminine assets.

"No, thanks," Lain replied, rubbing her exposed forearms for warmth. "I haven't been out in weather like this in a while and I actually rather enjoy it." She flipped a hand against her long bangs to clear them from her eyes. "Besides, I've got a change of clothes and a slicker in my bag if I need them. The challenge there is getting someplace dry to change. It shouldn't take long, though," she said, turning their small company northward once again. "The temple is nearby--maybe a half an hour away."

Kobuchi nodded, then turned his attention to the path once more.

Scraggly looking coyotes, half-starved and possibly rabid, lined up along the sides of the path up ahead, but they didn't seem too interested in the mages or undead.

The group passed by them without incident, and he let out a sigh of relief. He didn't care for canines of any breed much, with the possible exception of Patches. The undead wolf seemed rather amiable, now that there was nothing threatening its master.

Half an hour later, the company came upon a vast clearing, in the middle of which stood a two-story stone structure.

Kobuchi felt arcane power emanating from the structure. "It's the Temple of Unaki." He recognized the temple's front from a sketch in a book on the various religions of Tamalaria written by Vandabar Swellskin.

"Yes, it is." Lain pouted and nodding at the Kobold mage. "I'm impressed by your wealth of knowledge. I've been here twice before." A vaguely confused look came over her face. "I don't remember it being so centrally located, though."

"What do you mean," Kobuchi asked.

"Well, it's almost like it's moved from the last time I was here. Of course, that was almost six years ago," she said. "And the time before that, I was only fourteen, six years before that I think it was. The place seemed a lot bigger then."

Slowly, reverently, she moved forward.

She beckoned to her servants to come with her. Kobuchi stayed at her right side a foot away. He stared upward at the stone structure, and saw a tall spire rising atop the back end of the building. This spire reached a good hundred yards up into the sky above the roof.

"I came here to complete my initial training the first time."

"When you were fourteen?" Kobuchi could hardly believe it, because as far as he knew, most Humans remained with their parents until the age of eighteen or so. "How long ago did you start practicing Necromancy?"

"Oh, when I was about ten." She led him and her servants to the large double doors at the front of the structure.

Kobuchi stared at her with wide, awe-filled eyes.

"I went with my mother and father to my aunt Kate's funeral, and when I touched her arm in the casket, I felt some sort of pulse in my head. I didn't know what I was doing, and I inadvertently raised her from the casket."

Lain laughed a little at herself, and the memory of what had happened on that warm September afternoon. "It caused quite a commotion, and nobody knew what had happened, exactly. I think my mother may have suspected, but she never said anything."

"What exactly happened," Kobuchi asked quietly.

"Well, aunt Kate sat up in the casket, and then lifted the lower part. She flopped out onto the floor with this thick, wet, smacking sound, like raw chicken hitting the kitchen floor after it's been soaking in marinade." She made it a question with the lift of her tone near the end.

Kobuchi nodded, familiar with the exact sound she was trying to convey.

Lain laughed, and proceeded with her story, just staring ahead at the double doors that lead into the Temple of Unaki. "Well, she stood up and started shambling toward the preacher that was giving the sermon, and she grabbed his robes up and threw him over the casket into the back of the pulpit area. Then my dad, who mind you was a trained Soldier in his day, and a guard in the town, he ran up and cut Kate's head off. There was all kinds of blood, and everybody screamed and threw up, including my father. They put her back in the casket and used tie-downs to secure it, and they carried her right out back to her grave. They didn't even have a eulogy of any kind, which was too bad," Lain said. "I'd written a really nice one."

"Really?" Kobuchi asked.

Lain reached out and touched the doors, which Kobuchi saw had no visible handles or knobs. The left one gave off a purplish glow, and opened smoothly, soundlessly.

"Oh yes." She headed back to Bones and gathered her bag. "I wrote a letter blaming her for all of the crappy presents and slobbering kisses she planted on me." She hitched the bag onto her shoulders, and looked at Kobuchi, whose jaw hung stupidly open.

"What? I was ten and I was selfish. Still am, for the most part," she amended, dropping her volume a little. "Bones, Patches, you shall remain out here. Patches, if anything out of the ordinary comes along, you get in here and warn us, okay?"

The zombie wolf yipped happily, and lolled its maggoty tongue. Little white insects crawled around in its mouth, and she decided she'd have to do something about that. "Go get some water first, wash out your mouth. Okay?"

Once more the wolf yipped, and headed off to look for a puddle.

Lain walked inside, followed by Kobuchi, and then William in the rearguard position once again.

The main entrance hall was large and plain, stone columns reaching from the floor all the way up to the ceiling, two stories above. They flanked a long, golden carpet that led down the center of the aisle, and at the far end, about two hundred yards away, stood a large altar of some sort, with a stone sculpture of some odd creature.

Unaki, Lain thought as she gazed upon its countenance. A knee-high pedestal stood before the statue, with a nine-candle candelabrum set in its center. There were no actual candles in the holders, but Lain knew where there would be some.

"It hasn't changed a bit," she said quietly, somberly. "Not in six years." She then thought better of this, because when she had left the temple six years ago, she had left nine half-burned candles on the altar.

"Well, there's the one thing," she mumbled. She stalked forward, and then turned to the left when they actually made it about twenty yards down the aisle. There was a small changing room of sorts there, and she headed toward it. "Hang tight right there," she said. "I'm just going to change. William, keep watch over Kobuchi."

She headed over to the little room, entered, and set her bag on the one wooden bench inside. A full-length mirror stood on the door behind her, and she stripped off her sopping clothes, turning to take a look at herself in the mirror. She turned this way and that, appreciating the way her body curved in all the right places. She turned around again, and reached into the bag, pulling out one of her long, flowing black evening dresses, the typical garb for a female Necromancer.

She pulled it on over her head, and smoothed the front of it. She turned back to the mirror, and blew herself a smooch in its reflective surface. She grabbed a separate bag from within her rucksack, treated with oil like Kobuchi's hat and coat, and stuffed the wet clothes inside, setting the whole ensemble back into her rucksack.

She came back out into the temple, and found Kobuchi standing where she'd left him, craning his neck to peer up at the ceiling. He appeared to be looking at one thing in particular, and when she looked up to see what it was she stopped in her tracks.

Hanging perhaps one hundred feet over Kobuchi and William's heads, suspended on some sort of thin length of thread or webbing, was a creature with the heavy body of some sort of man-frog. Its flesh, green and spotted all over with brown ovals, looked slick in the light of the torches that burned eternally along the walls of the temple. Four arms poked out of its sides, and in each one it held a blunt wooden club with spikes driven through them. Wide, amphibian eyes stared down at the Kobold, eyes full of malice and hunger.

"Get out of the way," Lain shouted, and that finally seemed to break whatever paralysis had come over the Kobold and the Uberzombie.

Kobuchi broke left, toward Lain, while William leaped the other way, standing across the wide aisle from his mistress and the Kobold mage. The four-armed monster landed heavily on the floor's golden carpet in a crouch, each arm waving its weapon defensively to keep the three of them at bay.

"What the hells is that thing," Lain asked, finally seeing the long line that it had suspended from was actually some sort of retractable tail, thin and scaly. She shivered at the sight of the forked tip of the tail as it pulled back toward the body of the monster. A segment of the stone ceiling had come with it, and stone dust still drifted down from the pierced ceiling.

"I'm not sure, I've never seen anything like it." Kobuchi summoned his mana and cast a defensive barrier spell in front of himself and Lain. "Some of Genma's Alchemy beasts were rather strange, but I could identify them at least from their components."

He winced as the four-armed monstrosity charged at them and slammed all four of its clubs into the force barrier two feet in front of them. "Whatever it is," Kobuchi said, feeling the barrier waver and tremble, "it's strong!"

William charged up behind the creature. Without even rolling its side-mounted eyes back, it lashed its forked tail at him, knocking the Uberzombie back with ease as it crashed into the barrier once again.

Kobuchi prepared an offensive spell, an Aquamancy burst that he hoped would discourage the creature from attacking them so menacingly. Before he could release it, the creature struck once more, and the barrier shattered apart like glass.

Lain, her mind flooding with possible solutions, backed away as Kobuchi planted his feet in a wide stance and cried out. "Asa mencrifer! Rolling Bubble!"

Kobuchi slapped his hands once and raised them toward the ceiling, where a bubble of water formed and dropped atop the amphibian menace.

There was a loud splash as the bubble surrounded it entirely, and as it thrashed against the exterior of the water bubble, it started to swirl and roll toward the wall at the back of the temple.

Lain, Kobuchi and William sped to the center aisle, and watched as the creature crashed headlong into the stone wall next to the altar. There was a cacophony of sound as the splashed to the floor and the monster roared in pain and frustration. However, it kick-flipped to its webbed feet, undeterred, and started to charge at them again.

William stood before Lain and Kobuchi, who opened his mouth as he shook his head. "That should have killed it," he whispered.

"Well, clearly it didn't," Lain exclaimed as William shoved her and Kobuchi back, engaging the amphibian in melee combat as the mages thought over their next move.

Lain watched as William was pummeled time and again in his exposed sides by spiked clubs. He might not feel pain, but his scimitar didn't seem capable of cutting into the monstrosity.

"I think it may be immune to physical attack." Lain backed quickly toward the door, where Patches had stuck his head in and was growling at the creature menacing its master.

"Then we've got to use magic," Kobuchi said. "I'm reluctant, though, Ms. McNealy, because I don't want to damage the temple. Unaki is said to still reside within this structure, possibly in that statue." He pointed across the temple to the sculpture at the altar.

Lain could almost feel the presence of the old, forgotten God of the undead and Necromancers, and wondered if Unaki might be watching this conflict right now, from the spirit realm.

"I'd hate to have a God angry at me, old and forgotten or not," he added.

"Don't worry too much about it." She flinched as the monster knocked William roughly aside with two left-handed roundhouse strikes. "I don't think Unaki will mind too terribly."

Kobuchi nodded, and yelled to William to stay out of the way.

The amphibian creature closed the gap between them at startling speed, its forked tail lashing behind it at William again.

Lain watched with wonder as her Uberzombie servant caught the forked tail in his hands, and started to drag back on it. The tail extended behind the creature as it closed in on her and Kobuchi, but after twenty yards, the creature was jerked back, shock registering clearly in its alien face.

Kobuchi stepped forward, and muttered darkly under his breath. "Su, na, ka, fa, su, na, ka, fa." He made odd gestures with his fingers. To Lain they appeared to be little diagrams. Each shape flashed in the air over his head for a moment before disappearing.

"Su, na, ka, fa, su, na, ka, fa." Kobuchi thrust both hands, fingers spread, toward the beast, and roared, "Fly forth, arrows of fire, ice, wind and rock! Fly forth, and destroy mine enemy!"

Hundreds of shimmering, elementally charged magical arrows flickered into existence, firing in a steady stream from his outstretched fingertips and piercing the monster's body. Jets of spurting blood streamed from it and in no time, the amphibian menace was reduced to a pockmarked, hole-riddled mess of blood and gore.

"Sulu maten, anso," Kobuchi growled, and a forearm blade of ice formed over his right arm. Kobuchi darted forward as the creature, still managing to stay mostly upright despite its damage, dropped to its knees, and he sprinted past on its right side, tearing the forearm blade right through half of its torso.

The creature vomited blood and chips of ice, and fell dead to the stone floor.

Panting, Kobuchi dropped onto all fours, and stayed there for a moment as the blade on his arm melted into a harmless puddle on the stones. "Kobuchi, are you all right?" Lain was frankly amazed that so much magical power resided in such a small creature.

The Kobold got up and shuddered. He picked up his hat, which had fallen off when he fell, and popped it back onto his head.

"I'll be fine. Look, let's just do whatever you came here to do, and get going. This is one marshland I don't want to hang around in much longer. You say you trained here at fourteen?"

"Yup." Lain moved now toward the altar and reached under the pedestal for the box of candles she knew would be there.

She pulled out nine plain, long white candles, and set each one in a holder in the candelabrum. She searched in her dress pockets for the book of matches she usually kept there, coming up with bupkes.

Kobuchi approached, and leaned forward, touching the wick of each candle with one fingertip, setting them burning.

"Thanks, Kobuchi. Yes, these used to be my old stomping grounds, I guess." She knelt before the altar, bowing her head slightly. She kept her hands planted on her knees, and listened for the tiny voice she heard each time she'd come here, presumably the voice of Unaki, the forgotten Necromancer God.

"I see. Look, do you, um, want some privacy?" he offered awkwardly. "I just, well, don't feel right being here while you do your thing."

Lain kept her head down but smiled wryly.

"Go ahead. Send in Patches when you go out, but keep Bones outdoors. He shouldn't be part of this."

The Kobold mage headed down the aisle, the golden carpet slick and wet where the monster's blood had soaked through. He spat harshly on the corpse, and a few minutes later, Lain felt Patches nuzzle her neck with his cold, wet snout. Muddy water clung to the matted fur of his snout, and she thought it might be trying to smile at her.

She patted his head, and cooed at him, "Who's a good boy? Who's a good boy?"

Patches yipped aloud, and waggled his tongue at her. The maggots had been washed free, but his breath still positively reeked.

No helping that, she thought belatedly. *He's a dead wolf for goodness' sake.*

She returned her attention toward the altar, listening for the voice of Unaki.

Pleasantly, she wasn't disappointed.

'Greetings, believer,' it said in her mind.

She felt the power of the forgotten God swell within her breast, and she let the power waver up and down her body, searching her body and soul.

'Why have you come,' it asked.

I have come to offer you mana, as is custom for my people, she sent mentally to the statue. She summoned up mana from her internal reserves, and sent it, formless, into the statue.

She felt more than heard the intake of the God's breath as the mana reached into the statue, finding its external, physical housing, and then weaving its way to the astral spirit of the God within.

'It is not a custom oft practiced by this new generation of Necromancers,' the voice echoed in her mind. 'Quite rarely, in fact. You have been here before, twice,' the voice said. 'The first time out of simple curiosity, the second time to offer mana, as now. Yet you have not asked me for anything in return,' she heard.

To do so would be an offense to your greatness, Unaki, she sent, with no trace of floor-licking for brownie points.

She genuinely wanted to keep in good with Unaki, because aside from her own primary God of worship, Necros, she wanted to have another greater being to draw power and wisdom from.

'I don't think it would be so terrible, Lain McNealy,' the voice of Unaki said clear as a bell. 'I recognize your power, your potential, and your purpose. Thou art not wicked of soul or mind, though, I sense you feel lost in your life's course,' Unaki said.

Indeed, I do, just a little. I can sense that a time of trouble shall soon be upon the lands of Tamalaria once again, and I worry greatly. There are no heroes left, it seems, to protect the lands.

'No, not since the Dread Knight and Paladin creature,' Unaki said. 'He was the last great hero of Tamalaria. Also, those in his fellowship are either dead, or much too busy with their own lives to deal with the coming threat. I know of it, Lain McNealy, and I tell you this; another hero shall rise into the light of the coming conflict. Rest assured, she shall.'

You already know who this hero is, Lain blurted, surprised.

'Yes, I do. I shall tell you her name, but you must keep it secret and to yourself. When her time comes, you shall have to be there to aid her in her quest. It is still several years off, and by then, your powers shall be unmatched as a Necromancer.' The temple around Unaki trembled with the God's presence and power. 'But be warned, as well, Lain McNealy. Yours shall not be a permanent place by her side. You shall give her aid, her and the other who shall accompany her, but then you must stand aside. If you do not, you shall be slain. Do you understand all that the great and forgotten Unaki has said unto you?'

I do, and I accept your wisdom.

The forgotten God whispered a name to her, and then Lain felt it begin to depart from her presence.

Wait, she called out to it. *Is there no way for me to take you with me? Must I constantly return here to hear your voice? These are dangerous lands, and I would take comfort in your closeness back at my home!*

"I cannot go with you," the voice said.

Lain opened her eyes, turning to face William, whose mouth was open. Unaki was using him as a vessel for his voice, she realized, and turned to face her undead servant.

"I must remain here, to hold down the spirit creature that is imprisoned beneath this temple. And though I am certain it pains you to do so, I must ask that you leave this creature behind. There is much use I have for it here inside the temple, to keep and ward this place from monstrosities like that which tried to kill you," Unaki said through William's throat.

Lain felt a pang of regret, but then felt Patches nuzzle her neck with his snout and whine softly. His eyes, so large and filled with a dim sort of intelligence, gave her a spark of hope. *He'll do,* she thought, stroking the big wolf's head.

"I understand your request, and relinquish command of William, Uberzombie raised by my hand and will, to you, great Unaki. I shall return whenever I am able, and give you my offering of mana."

She gave William, who currently housed the spirit of the great and forgotten Necromancer God, a low sweeping bow. "By the way, how will I know when to go to the girl?"

"You won't have to," Unaki said. "She shall be guided to you. The Gods above, those still remembered and worshipped, shall see to that. Now, go with my blessing, child of the dead. Remember why the Necromancers first came to the world of Tamalaria." The God left out the part about the other continent far to the south, Tallowmere.

Lain bowed once more and beckoned Patches after her.

He strode along contentedly at her side, head bopping from side to side as they exited the temple.

Kobuchi, sitting cross-legged a few yards away from the doors, had a heavy notebook in his lap, and was busily jotting down notes on their brief but interesting journey.

"Are you ready to head back to Desanadron," she asked him, and Kobuchi put up one finger to stay her.

The door slammed shut behind her, closing the temple.

"Almost," he replied, his voice high and squeaky. "I've just got to finish up the bit here about dealing with that, that frog-thing inside and I'll be ready to go. Where's William?"

"He'll be staying behind," she said, summoning Bones over to her. She sent a thin line of black power into the skeletal horse, and it collapsed into the mud, broken and truly lifeless once more.

"Patches will be coming back with us, however."

Kobuchi looked up from his musings, and gave the zombie wolf a considering look.

"He might not make it through the process of the spell, you understand," Kobuchi said. "When we show up on the other side, he may be, well, scattered."

Lain considered this for a long moment, and looked up at the night sky. She'd written Fly and told him that they had used a Teleport Spell to make for rapid travel. He hadn't written back yet, but he probably expected they'd travel back the same way. She had come out here seeking some time away from the Guild, but in truth, her heart called out for her home in the big metropolis of Desanadron.

She looked down at Patches, and wondered how her lover would take it, her keeping it around as her new Personal Attendant.

Something struck her as a bit odd then about Patches. When she had first felt him nuzzle her by the altar, he'd only had a brief spark of intelligence in his eyes. Now, however, he was looking back and forth from the Kobold to her, following their conversation.

'*A little gift,*' she then heard, the voice coming from behind her, through the temple's doors. '*I have evolved him for you. He shall serve you well. But the name, honestly.*' The forgotten god chuckled to itself inside her mind. *I don't think he's going to put up with that much any more.*

"Also, Kobuchi," Lain said aloud. "I think I'm going to give him a new name. Any suggestions?" Kobuchi finished his notes, and gave the wolf a long, hard look.

"Only one comes to mind," he said. He smiled ruefully at the undead wolf, and stood up, packing his notebook into his bag and slinging it over his shoulder. He started to make the mana preparations for the Teleport

Spell to take them back to Desanadron, and chuckled a little to himself.

"Oh," Lain said, approaching with the wolf. "And what's that?"

"I was thinking Brock," Kobuchi said. "That was the name of my Cocker Spaniel when I was little. But he was an idiot," Kobuchi said. "I think this fellow's a tad smarter than your average Cocker Spaniel. Besides, he's not even really a dog."

"What do you think, big guy," Lain said, looking down at the undead wolf. "Brock okay?"

The undead wolf seemed to smile, and gave them both a happy yip.

"Brock it is. Take us home, Kobuchi."

The Kobold summoned up the circles of light, and then came the flash, and the trio was gone.

* * * *

"You sure you spent enough time there?" Fly wrapped his arm under Lain's head in his bed, enjoying the feel of her pressed against his side.

"Yes, I'm sure." She kissed him once, quickly, on the cheek.

"That's good, that's very good dear. Now, can I ask you one more thing?"

"Sure, Tad. What did you need," she asked sweetly.

Thaddeus Fly sat up, and pointed at the creature lounging now on their feet.

"Get that goddamned dog off the bed!"

Tale Eight: Higher Council

In the heavenly realm of the world in which Tamalaria resided, there stood a grand palace. This grand palace was in fact the place where the heavens themselves could be accessed. Each of the Greater Gods resided within the Heavenly Palace itself much of the time, maintaining permanent offices so that they could, at any given time, confer with one another and reach the Lesser Gods when needed.

A few gods who no alliance as either Greater or Lesser Gods. One such trio, the Holy Triad, was considered an even higher authority than the Greater Gods. There was Truth, an ethereal woman of such unearthly beauty that no mortal could lay eyes on her, even if she were to take herself down to the crowded residential districts of Ja-Wen or Desanadron and declare her presence aloud. She was the authority to whom the Greater Gods turned when they had a dispute or question. The next was Power, for all purposes appearing as a sagely old man in a blue commoner's button tunic with a long white beard and plain pants, his face creased with more wrinkles than a hotel blanket after a newlywed couple's honeymoon night. His dominion was over all sources of mana and magical energy and might. And lastly of the Triad, there was Fate, he of the plain, angular golden mask with only two blackened eye slots to decorate his face, the keeper of the Histories and reviewer of the mortals' Keepers.

And he was the best and only true friend of another astral being, one who kept no offices in the Heavenly Palace, but made himself welcome anywhere and everywhere in it, no matter who had objections. He was most often referred to among the gods as the Honored Guest.

Death himself.

At that moment, this fellow was moving a knight into position on the marvelous jade chessboard set on Oun's work desk, carefully letting his bone fingers slide off of the piece soundlessly.

I BELIEVE, he said, THAT'S CHECKMATE, OUN.

As an astral being, Oun's appearance often changed in the perceptions of his mortal believers and followers. However, within the confines of the Heavenly Palace, he appeared in his true form; a tall, broad-shouldered man with a handsome, wind-worn face. A suit of full steel plate armor rode over his hypothetical 'body', and long, brown and blond hair flowed over his shoulders from his head. A neatly trimmed beard graced his face, and he exuded a presence of rightness, justice, and morality.

And, in this instance, confusion. "Um, well," he said, propping his hands up under his chin, surveying the board. "I believe you are correct. How did you manage that, and so quickly?"

IT'S NOT HARD WHEN YOU LEAVE YOUR KING STUCK THERE BETWEEN THE QUEEN AND THE BISHOP, Death said. THIS HAS BEEN RATHER AMUSING, BUT I AM AFRAID I'M HERE ON BUSINESS TODAY. THE LESSER GOD ROMINTO HAS NO MORE MORTAL FOLLOWERS, SO I HAVE TO COLLECT HIM. WILL YOU SPEAK FOR HIM?

"Certainly." Oun packed away his chess board and pieces. "Shame he has no more worshippers. I always thought his tenets had a lot of merit. Yes, he may come to my paradise. Perhaps in time I will introduce him to my lesser pantheon."

For the Lesser Gods, death was a possibility, and not a kind one to look forward to. Death himself would come to their personal astral realm and reap them, the souls of their long deceased worshippers either claimed by another god or reincarnated in some fashion in the mortal realms.

If the gods themselves were 'spoken for' by another god, they would be given the same access to that god's paradise as a mortal worshipper who perished. If nobody spoke for them, however, they were to be infused by Fate and turned into Keepers.

Waste not, want not.

The Alchemists of Tamalaria, if they knew of these intricacies, would be thrilled. It supported a theory from the late Fourth Age in which it was stated that energy cannot be destroyed, just converted into something else. As for the 'lesser pantheons' that Oun had mentioned, there existed within the hierarchy of the heavens sub-hierarchies, at the top of which sat the Greater Gods. Several of the Greater Gods had several Lesser Gods who were usually elements and representatives of a sub-sect of the tenets of the Greater God. One such example was Xerxes, one of Oun's sons. Xerxes was a Lesser God of justice and balance.

WELL, IT'S GOOD THAT SOMEBODY WILL BE SPEAKING FOR HIM. Death, rose from his offered seat and taking up his scythe. I SHOULD HEAD OVER TO HIS ASTRAL REALM AND DEAL WITH THE DUTY.

The Honored Guest cut a rift in the empty air of the office of Oun and stepped through the purple mist that flowed from the slash. When he was out of sight entirely, the slit sealed closed, and mighty Oun was left to his own thoughts and a stack of paperwork that he wasn't looking forward to.

"Prayers," he muttered to himself. "They just keep piling up."

* * * *

Marakesh, Great God of War, strode down the length of his grand hall toward the majestic double doors that would lead him out into a commons hallway of the Heavenly Palace A huge, brute of a man in manifested form, Marakesh wore full battle gear, complete with crimson armor, throwing pikes, axe, sword, spear and horned helmet. But for the moment, he wasn't thinking about his manner of dress. His mind was solely focused on the matter at hand, which was to get to the Grand Council chamber so that he might participate in the discussion and vote set to take place within the next few hours.

The issue being put before the Grand Council, which consisted of all of the Greater Gods, the non-pantheon Lesser Gods and the Holy Triad, was one that had been put before them once every five hundred years for the last four millennia, and always it ended in the same way. However, Marakesh, who once had been known as Ares, wanted to ensure that, at worst, the same result would come about.

The issue itself was a simple question, and the subject of the question would not even be present, hopefully, but it went like this--is Maragshet, the Mad God, to be declared a Greater God or a Lesser God?

Like a few of the Lesser Gods, Maragshet had once been nothing more than a mortal man a long, long time ago. However, he quickly became a folk legend, and that legend grew into a myth so potent that an astral being was born from the accumulation of belief, and it was Maragshet, the Mad God. Since nobody ever found out what happened to the physical body of the mortal man, it was further supposed that he had ascended to the heavens to guide over the mentally unsound.

That, of course, only solidified Maragshet as a god in the first place. However, it was never stated by any of the other gods which level of power and prestige he was to be afforded. Not even Fate, who had access to the Histories, could tell them where Maragshet belonged, and Truth could not decipher anything that came out of the Mad God's mouth as truth, lie, or anything in between. She only ever sensed that he drifted in and out of moments of clarity perhaps once every twenty or thirty mortal years. He was just too erratic to be figured out.

Marakesh stepped out into the hallway and almost collided with a tall, lanky figure in a flowing green cassock, carrying a book under one arm and a gnarled staff in the other hand. The two stopped inches from each other, and each Greater God smiled amiably at the other. "Ah, good Lenos." Marakesh stretched his arms wide to embrace his kinsman.

"Marakesh," said Lenos in his quiet, cultured voice. Lenos, the

Greater God of wisdom, tales and peace, appeared to have a narrow face that, despite his gauntness, glowed with an inner warmth and health that came from ages of immersion in the concept of togetherness. Along with being the primary authority of wisdom and stories in the mortal realm, he was also credited as having given the mortals of the realms below the first of the healing sciences and magics. Lenos also spoke for the whole of the Greater Gods to the Holy Triad, as his tenets were the only ones that accepted and honored the other Greater Gods. However, he also had a great distrust and dislike of anything that was too technologically advanced. This was only supported by the Fall of Mecha that nearly destroyed the whole of Tamalaria, his favorite collection of realms.

"So, any idea how you're going to be voting this time around, Marakesh?" Lenos asked.

"As I always do," the Greater God of War replied. "I say we leave him undeclared. Whoever wants him a Lesser God has my support, of course, but we both know the danger that presents. Our brother Sonamo would be quick to try and talk him into his own pantheon. We can't have that," said Marakesh.

Sonamo, Lenos thought. *Greater God of chaos and the random, the darkness. In essence, the polar opposite of Oun.*

That had led to a lot of bloodshed in the mortal realms. If Sonamo were given a crack at putting the Mad God into his own pantheon, then chaos and madness would truly and unilaterally be joined together, in the heavens as on the earth. None of the gods wanted that, with perhaps the exception, of course, of Sonamo.

Together the two Greater Gods made their way to the Grand Council chamber. An amphitheater arranged in a parliamentary fashion, Marakesh and Lenos entered to find that just about everybody else had already arrived. Death, the Honored Guest, stood down in the lowered central ring, a wooden box in his left hand, his scythe in his right. As in every Grand Council vote, he would only tally up the votes, remaining neutral to all matters. Lenos occasionally wondered why that was, and why Fate always seemed to have time to converse with Death, but not him. He didn't care for the possible meanings that could be attached to that friendship.

As the general hubbub died down, Death rapped the bottom of his scythe on the stone circle he stood in, the echo reverberating powerfully up through the seated ranks of the present gods and goddesses. LADIES AND GENTLEMEN, YOU HAVE COME HERE TODAY TO DISCUSS AND VOTE UPON AN ISSUE THAT MUST BE TENDED TO, AS IT HAS IN THE PAST, WITH CAUTION AND

GREAT DELIBERATION. IT IS THE DUTY AND PRIVELEDGE OF THIS GRAND COUNCIL TO DO SO WITH THIS ISSUE AS IT HAS BEEN WITH EVERY GREAT ISSUE THAT HAS FACED THE HEAVENLY PALACE. NOW, TRUTH OF THE HOLY TRIAD SHALL ANNOUNCE THE ISSUE TO BE DISCUSSED.

Death raised his scythe in the direction of the lovely Truth, who on this day was resplendent in a flowing golden kimono, lotus petals printed in rows that (no coincidence) ran right down the center of her breasts. "Thank you, Honored Guest," she announced as she stood from her seat between Fate and Power. "Today, we come together to discuss and vote upon the following; Is the Mad God, Maragshet, to be a Greater God, a Lesser God, or is he to remain undeclared until such time as the issue has had time to develop and become clearer? We shall begin the discussion with the Lesser Gods who wish to make any statements that may have bearing on the ultimate vote we shall conduct. Thank you."

She seated herself then, and a murmuring rippled through the assemblage of Lesser Gods without a pantheon. The reason for the lack of those Lesser Gods in the pantheon of a Greater God being part of the Grand Council was simple. They were under the governance of a Greater God, and so their Greater God spoke for them all. This insured that no Greater God had more say than any other, that their own personal agenda wasn't pushed forward without resistance.

Finally, a Lesser God whose appearance was that of a Simpa woman, nude from the waist up with arrows sticking out of her torso and a pair of tunic pants shredded about her lower body, stood from her seat. "I am Chandara, Lesser Goddess of the Simpa huntresses. I am concerned that, should Maragshet be granted the status of a Greater God, he will only introduce instability to the Heavenly Palace. Well, more than he already has. That is all I have to say," she said. She bowed to the chamber as a whole, and resumed her seat.

Some more murmurs rose, and then a Lesser God stood and cleared his throat. He appeared to be a man made out of stone, like a carving from the side of a mountain. "I am Torgata, Lesser God worshipped by the Minotaurs of the North-Central Mountains. It occurs to me that Maragshet has more disciples in the mortal realms than even I, who have entire clans of the Minotaur people to worship me. Even those who do not worship him believe in him, which is more than can be said for many of us Lesser Gods. I do not think he belongs among us. I believe, since he is so broadly known to the mortals, that he should be a Greater God. Thank you."

And so in this fashion the discussion carried on for nearly an hour, until everybody who had two cents to add in had done so. Curiously, however, Sonamo, the Greater God of chaos, had nothing to say on the matter. Little more today in appearance than a great, man-shaped shadow, he remained so silent throughout the entire process that Oun had to be just a little suspicious of his intentions.

The votes were written on strips of paper, which were passed around until finally Death collected them in his wooden box from the last person from each aisle in the circular chamber. He needed no time to actually review the votes, as the box's lid flashed once with a brilliant blue light, the faint scent of freshly cut grass carried along the wave of light. In curved script, the results of the vote were displayed on the top of the box. Death returned to the indented circle at the center of the chamber, and clacked the blunt end of his scythe on the marble floor three times to call order.

GODS, GODESSES, THE VOTE HAS BEEN CAST AND THE RESULT IS THUS; AT THIS TIME, THE MAD GOD MARAGSHET SHALL NOT BE DECLARED EITHER LESSER GOD OR GREATER GOD. THE VAST MAJORITY HAS ONCE AGAIN VOTED TO LEAVE THIS ISSUE REST FOR ANOTHER TWO-HUNDRED AND FIFTY YEARS, AT THE LEAST. IF, IN THE INTERIM, IT IS DECIDED BY THE MAJORITY OF THIS COUNCIL THAT THE ISSUE SHOULD BE VOTED UPON AGAIN, IT SHALL BE DONE SO. THANK YOU. Death removed himself then from the central flooring, and the various gods and goddesses began dispersing from the chamber.

After a few minutes, four astral beings remained in the Grand Council Hall. Seated in his heavy red armor, there was Marakesh, Greater God of War. A few seats down from him, arms crossed over his chest, sensing the lack of progress made this day and stewing about it, there sat Oun. At the end of their row stood Death, faint white lights in his eye sockets aimed up the steps toward the double doors leading out of the hall. And up several of the steps, the only remaining member of the Holy Triad, the golden-masked Fate.

SHALL I ASSUME BOTH OF YOU GENTLEMEN VOTED TO HAVE HIM MADE A LESSER GOD, Death asked of Marakesh and Oun.

"Aye, t'would be true to say of me," replied Oun in a sulking voice. He rolled his head on his shoulder toward the Great God of War. "Ares, old brother," he asked of the heavily armored god.

"Aye, me as well. I cannot abide the idea that that maniac might someday sit beside us here as equals," said the Great God of War, grabbing his thick black beard and pulling on it. "I hold no dislike of him, but he is just too unpredictable. He did not even show up to this meeting, and he has been told many times that he is welcome to vote on those issues brought before the Council."

"Fate," said Marakesh. "What of the Great Father? Has He made any voice on this issue?"

The masked astral being rose slowly from his seat, his white robes and cape fluttering against the marble floor with a soft swoosh. He turned his head slightly toward Death, who merely cocked his head slightly to one side, also interested in knowing the answer to this question. "He has not," said Fate. "At least, not to me. And no, nothing has as yet been revealed by the Histories regarding the matter, though there are things about the Mad God which have recently come to light."

"Such as what." Oun finally came out of his pensive contemplation.

"You both know that I may not discuss the Histories with you," said Fate, his usually soft voice hardening slightly, loud enough to carry throughout the entire chamber. "But I will tell you both this--I hope you have thought long and hard on another constant issue which must be reviewed soon, and that is the sentence of the exiled member of your ranks," said Fate.

"Ah, yes, the exile," said Marakesh. "How much time is left for him to remain among the mortals?"

"Let me see." Oun, reached down and pulling a small bag onto the bench before him. He drew from it a heavy leather tome, and opened it to a point only perhaps halfway through the pages. He ran a finger down the page, his eyes scanning his own handwritten notes quickly. "Here we are." He fixed his finger on an entry which changed every day on its own. "According to this, the exiled Great God of Adventure has eight-hundred and sixty-seven years remaining among the mortals. He has already completed two-thousand, six-hundred and seventy-four years in the mortal realm."

"Great Father above." Color flushed Marakesh's cheeks. He balled his hand into a fist and slammed it hard onto the bench, the vibration knocking Oun's tome from the table. "It has already been too long, I say! We should bring him back now, before we lose him entirely to the mortals! You know as well as I how attached he has become to some of them. He must watch them all age and die, while he carries on, eternal in life. It is cruelty to leave him as he is, Fate!"

AS I RECALL, YOU VOTED THAT HE ONLY BE REPRIMANDED FOR HIS ACTIONS BACK THEN, said Death to Marakesh, finally turning toward the Great God of War. BUT EVEN I

DID NOT THINK THAT WOULD HAVE BEEN ENOUGH, CONSIDERING WHAT HE DID. THE GREAT GOD OF ADVENTURE HIMSELF AGREED TO BE EXILED, THOUGH HE DID PROTEST AT THE LENGTH OF HIS SENTENCE.

"That could not be helped," said Oun quietly. "He has done much to cut time off of his exile, carried out our will when we needed to call upon him."

"And we shall have to call upon him again, soon," said Fate, which of course garnered the attention of all three other astral beings. "Twice, actually, and there shall be little time passing between the callings. That is all that I can reveal for now, fellows. Honored Guest," he said to Death, "if you would join me for a game of chess before returning to your duties?"

OF COURSE. Death followed Fate out of the Grand Council Hall.

When they were gone, Marakesh and Oun rose from their seats, and looked hard at one another.

"I still don't think he should have been exiled," Marakesh grumbled.

"There was no other choice, brother." Oun held his bag in one hand. "He had to be punished."

"But they attacked him," Marakesh fumed, throwing his arms wide in exasperation. "He only fought them off, and ensured they would not rise again to strike at him! I hardly see what was so wrong about that!"

"He didn't have to kill them, and you know it," Oun retorted. "And do you recall what happened when he destroyed them? Their mortal worshippers all perished, instantly. None of us knew it would happen that way, but it did, and he had to be punished for it, brother. It does not matter that they were Lesser Gods that he killed."

"One of them was a member of your pantheon, am I right," asked Marakesh.

"Yes," said Oun. "My second son, Ramilder. I tried to warn him, but he would not heed my words. Why?"

"Is that why you agreed to such a lengthy exile?"

Oun said nothing, knowing that he could not lie about the personal enmity he had initially harbored for the Great God of Adventure.

"It is, I can see that. Well, I can't wait for him to get back, then," Marakesh said. "I imagine you two will have a great deal to discuss upon his return."

Marakesh strode confidently out of the chamber then, leaving Oun alone to contemplate the coming years. Fate had implied that the gods would have to call upon the service of the exile twice more in rapid succession in the next few years. Would they agree to shave time off of the exile's sentence in return for his service?

Possibly, he thought. We've done it before. But how, he worried, did such things relate to the Mad God? After all, had they not been discussing that issue first? With Fate, Oun knew, there was no such thing as coincidence. So why would the masked member of the Holy Triad, the only one with access to the Histories, mention the two disparate gods in the same conversation?

With a chill of dread racing up his astral spine, Oun left the chamber hoping that Fate did not mean to imply anything.

* * * *

SO NONE OF THEM KNOWS YET WHERE THEY CAME FROM, IN THE BEGINNING, asked Death.

"No, they don't, although Truth, Power and I are aware. We have all, after all, spoken with Great Father. I believe that Odin has his suspicions, though."

HE WOULD HAVE TO BE A COMPLETE IMBECILE NOT TO. HE IS A GREAT GOD WITH NO DOMAIN, FATE. NONE OF THE OTHERS CAN SAY THAT, YET HE REMAINS AMONG THEIR RANKS. BUT WHAT BROUGHT YOUR BELIEF ABOUT, IF I MIGHT ASK?

Death sat at a simple oak table in Fate's personal chambers, though he knew it was not real oak. Nothing in the Heavenly Palace was too real, per se, because everything was constructed of the astral energy of the gods. But in order to maintain some semblance of order and permanence, the gods and goddesses kept some semi-permanent fixtures.

Fate's rather Spartan quarters had remained as they were since the middle of the First Age of Tamalaria. For five-thousand plus years, nothing had changed. Even Death was beginning to think about helping his friend do a little sprucing up.

"Well," Fate said, responding to Death's question after moving a knight to a new position, taking one of Death's bishops. "In general, it is the great distaste and dislike he seems to hold for Surt, Great God of Flames. Surt himself does not seem to remember anything, though."

YES, WELL, I DO TRY TO KEEP THAT IN CHECK. SPEAKING OF, CHECK.

"Ah, I see." Fate moved a rook into position to protect his king from Death's approaching pawn. "Will he ever remember the role he played?"

IT IS CERTAINLY WITHIN THE RANGE OF POSSIBILITY, BUT NOT FOR SOME LONG TIME YET, FRIEND. AND WHAT OF RATATOSK? DOES POWER KEEP HIM CAGED STILL?

"No, he just keeps the infernal little chatterbox bribed with fruits and nuts. You know, he's had to invent at least a dozen different new ones in the last millennium alone."

REALLY? THAT'S GOT TO BE ANNOYING. CHECKMATE, said Death, maneuvering his queen into a predestined position.

"So is losing four out of five games of chess." Fate gave a heavy sigh. "Aside from you, the only other person who gives me any challenge is Lenos, surprisingly. Marakesh won't play, of course, so I've never tested myself against him, but this is the worst."

DON'T BEAT YOURSELF UP OVER IT. Death patted Fate on the shoulder. UM, FATE? I KNOW I PROBABLY SHOULDN'T SAY ANYTHING, BUT I THINK IT'S SOMETHING YOU SHOULD KNOW. GREAT FATHER SHOULD KNOW, TOO, BECAUSE I DON'T THINK HE DOES.

"There is much Great Father doesn't know," Fate said. "You'll recall that he gave up his omnipotence. Hence the Histories." He removed himself from the table and sauntered gently over toward the lectern in the middle of the chamber that held the most recent tome of Histories, putting one gloved hand on the rough cover. "What have you discovered, Honored Guest, that it is so important that I should bring it to Great Father?"

IT'S FENRIS.

Fate, his eyes flashing wide in the narrow slits in his mask, darted a look at Death that showed clear panic at the mention of the name.

I HAVE LOCATED HIM. HE IS NOT IN THIS REALITY, FATE, BUT IN THOSE REALMS HE IS ABLE TO TRAVERSE, HE IS CAUSING A GREAT DEAL OF DAMAGE, SOWING CHAOS WHEREVER HE TREADS. WE MAY NEED GUIRDEJEF'S POWERS IN ORDER TO SEND SOMETHING TO HELP PUT A STOP TO HIM.

"We cannot do that, Grim." Fate looked away from the Honored Guest. "We had him sealed away for good reasons."

JUST LIKE YOU HAD THE OTHER EXILED FOR GOOD REASONS?

"Their circumstances were much different. Guirdejef's powers were making *our* reality unstable. How many gods vanished into other realities, gone from us forever? How much havoc did his descent into madness cause?"

A GREAT LOT OF IT. I RECALL THAT OUN TRIED TO WARN EVERYBODY ABOUT LETTING HIM SPEND TOO MUCH TIME WITH MARAGSHET WHISPERING IN HIS EAR. BUT HEAR ME OUT ON THIS. IF THE SEAL WERE TO BE

UNDONE TEMPORARILY, THE GREAT GOD OF PORTALS COULD CREATE A FEW RIFTS, JUST ENOUGH THAT YOU OR I COULD SEND SOMETHING USEFUL TO THOSE OTHER WORLDS WHERE FENRIS IS CAUSING SO MUCH TROUBLE. IT MAY NOT BE ENOUGH TO STOP HIM, BUT IT CAN HELP SOMEBODY ELSE DO SO. ALL WE NEED TO DO IS FIND A THIRD PARTY WILLING TO CREATE THE PROPER CIRCUMSTANCES.

Fate seemed to think this proposal over a while, pacing back and forth in his small chamber. "There is a way, but we should not deal with the situation ourselves," he said. "We have meddled once already, and look at what happened."

PORTENDA'S A FINE LAD.

"That's not the point. The point is, we never really know what's going to happen when you and I get involved, and that especially goes for you. We will leave this in the hands of somebody who's specialty is causing havoc," said Fate, going to his writing desk to form a letter.

WHAT ARE YOU DOING?

"I am writing Sonamo, Great God of Chaos and darkness, an invitation to take drink with me in the mortal realm," said Fate. "When he is inebriated, I shall put a rough parchment with our plan in his pocket, in his own handwriting."

CAN YOU DO THAT?

"Please, it's a simple thing. Besides, I can sense from the Histories that this is what must be done. He will convince a third party, a Lesser God, to do the dirty work of freeing Guirdejef, probably by invoking a miracle. However, we're going to have to use a mortal agent to seal up the portals right after they become a problem."

Death chuckled to himself, a low, disquieting sound.

"What's so funny?"

WELL, IT'S JUST THAT YOU SAID EARLIER THAT WE WOULD NEED TO CALL UPON THE EXILE TWICE, AND IN RAPID SUCCESSION, said Death. IT WOULD SEEM THAT YOU ALREADY SUSPECTED SOMETHING LIKE THIS WAS GOING TO HAPPEN.

"I don't suspect anything on my own." Fate stopped his hand's movement across the parchment. "I have those damned Histories to tell me what I need to suspect. You know, Sonamo won't move on the plan right away," said Fate. "He'll stew about it a while first."

THAT'S ALL RIGHT. WE WOULDN'T WANT HIM TO JUMP THE GUN ANYHOW. FATE, MY FRIEND, I MUST BE GOING. I

HAVE A DUTY TO PERFORM, AND IT DOESN'T EVER GET ANY EASIER. Death used his scythe to rip open a rift in the clear air, and stepped through it, out of Fate's chamber.

As Fate finished the letter, he realized something he had not stopped to think of in quite some time. Death wanted to use the portals of Guirdejef to move something, probably a spirit creature, to another reality to assist in fighting against Fenris.

Why didn't Death himself need such portals to move from reality to reality? It was a question that Fate would think over between the meeting and the next Grand Council. After all, it was one question he felt certain the Histories had no answer to.

Tale Nine Peace Treaty

Richard Tiverski sauntered out into the side yard of his woodland cottage, a steel bucket in his right hand, a long knife in his left hand. Elegantly garbed in black cotton gentleman's vestments, with a high collared white blouse, ruffled at both collar and sleeve cuffs, he appeared the perfect vision of a visiting statesman or ambassador. The pale skin, slicked back hair tied in a ponytail, and gorgeous, expensive rings on his fingers helped add to the overall image of the eldest of the Tiverski brothers.

Appearing to be a cultured man, however, was not all that went into Richard Tiverski's overall aura. He was well-spoken, thoughtful, and highly educated. Of course, he'd had years and years to acquire his wealth of knowledge and speechcraft. He was, after all, a Vampire.

Richard stood at the gate leading into the pen where he and his brothers, Trent and Simon, kept and raised pigs, chickens and every now and then, cattle. The animal blood was not as delicious or nutritionally bolstering for them as the blood of sentient mortals, but they had, all three, taken a vow to never again attack such people to sustain themselves. They were not related by any means, but they all took the name Tiverski to show their bond as a trio, and their commitment to the cause of not shedding innocent blood.

Portenda the Quiet, one of their once-in-a-while contacts, had been by only a few months ago, and had offered them a rather large donation of his own blood, bled out from a wound he'd made in his own wrist. The blood had been absolutely delicious, invigorating, and more importantly, powerful. The three Vampires had managed to sustain themselves for an entire week and a half just on what he'd given them, so potent was the man's essence.

"A pity he does not come to us more often," Richard mused aloud, selecting a nice sow for the bucket he had with him.

Richard opened the gate, walked into the pen, and marveled at the effectiveness of the spells that his brother Simon, the smallest and frailest of the three Tiverski brothers, had on the animals. They did not panic at the sight or presence of any of the three brothers, and would act exactly as the brothers wished. They didn't even panic when being bled, which was a ritual performed every couple of days to provide the Tiverski brothers with their necessary nourishment.

Richard crouched down next to his selected pig, cut a small gash along its side, and held the bucket under the flow of blood. He would only fill the one bucket tonight, in the hopes of using a spell from his own small arsenal to keep the swine alive after he'd collected their fill for the next couple of days. Whenever possible, they preserved the animal they fed from, so that they could sustain it and use it again. No sense in killing off your food supply, after all.

With the bucket only three-quarters full, Richard cast the sealing spell on the sow, and was pleased to see that it was very tired, but nothing more. It would sleep especially long tonight, but in a few days' time, it would perfectly healthy again.

"Thank you for your sacrifice." Richard patted the pig on the head before standing up and carrying the bucket back into the cottage proper, leaving the darkened forest behind him, on the other side of the door.

Upon entering the main den, Richard found his brothers engaged in their usual before mealtime activity. Simon, a short, gaunt figure, who wore a forest green robe with blue runes stitched into the fabric, was engaged in his newest novel. His head was completely bald, and his eyes were set deep in his face, the red irises barely visible amid the darkness of his hood. He sat on one of the two couches in the living room, completely absorbed in his story.

Trent, always a rather morbid-looking fellow in his black leather armor and cloak, stood in the open kitchen area, practicing unarmed self-defense techniques, his pointed, once Elven ears pricking up at the sound of the eldest Tiverski brother clearing his throat. Pale and tallow-skinned, like his brothers, Trent defied the stereotype of both Elves and Vampires with his physical presence and prowess. He was lean and muscular, well-toned for a man of his respective Race, and carried nearly as many weapons on him at one time as Portenda the Quiet. A combative and argumentative man in the best of circumstances, he was, nonetheless, as committed to the Tiverski cause as either Richard or Simon.

His eyes shifted down Richard's side to the mostly full bucket, and they then gleamed with a hungry darkness as he resumed a neutral stance.

"I belief it ist time for us to dine, ja?" Richard asked with a smug grin of satisfaction. "I efen managed to keep der sow alife dis time. Unlike your efforts, brother," he said to Trent, who merely grunted and took the necessary wineglasses out of one of the overhead cupboards over the sink.

Richard poured up an even amount into each glass, and took the bucket over to the Gnome-engineered icebox, setting the bucket inside to keep for another day's use. He turned around, and saw Trent carry Simon his glass, which the mage Vampire took without looking away from his book.

"Richard." Trent moved into the kitchen to join his elder brother, his thick leather boots creaking noisily as he moved to a drawer and withdrew a sealed envelope. "This was delivered to us today, about an hour after sunset, brother. It is addressed to you," Trent handed over the sealed envelope.

"Who brought it?" Richard turned the envelope over in his hands, trying to feel for latent traces of magic that might have been sealed on the envelope. He passed it to Simon, who closed his book for a moment, concentrated, and handed it back over his shoulder, not moving from his seat even a little.

"Allanso Itrivic," Trent spat.

Richard's guts squirmed at the sound of that name, knowing full well what this business would be about.

The Itrivic Clan, a long standing Vampire family, had its seat of power in the foothills north and east of these woods where the Tiverski brothers resided. They had harassed and harangued the brothers whenever they had the chance. However, with Trent as their bruiser, Simon as their magic user, and Richard as the diplomat and a nice average of his brothers' abilities, the Tiverski brothers had made their stand against the raiding parties routinely sent against them.

They also defended the nearby city of Desanadron from infiltration and attack by the Itrivic Clan, denying them access to the city's residents by warning the constables via anonymous letter whenever they learned that an attack was in the works. They had an informant in the Clan, but they hadn't heard from her in some time. Had she been found out, Richard wondered? Was that what this official business was about?

He walked into his bedroom, off of the kitchen, and went to his small writing desk, taking up a letter opener. He slit the wax seal on the envelope, and opened the flap, pulling out the folded letter therein.

The letter, which Richard Tiverski perused while sitting on the edge of his bed, read as follows:

Dear Richard Tiverski,

We of the Clan Itrivic understand your personal choice to ignore your noble heritage, and your superiority to the other mortals who inhabit this world. We acknowledge your free will to choose the sort of life you lead. We cannot understand, however, your repeated attempts to thwart our efforts to feed on the residents of the city of Desanadron. However, recent developments make Desanadron a secondary feeding ground for us.

We would like to extend an invitation to you to enjoy a hospitable evening at our primary stronghold, that we may discuss a peace accord between our Clan and your trio. We promise to visit no harm upon you at this meeting, as it shall establish peace between our two peoples. Also, at this meeting, we shall explain why we no longer view Desanadron as a primary target for our feedings, as long as you agree to the peace treaty. Thank you for your time and consideration. Upon your reply to this letter, for which we expect you shall use your messenger bird, we shall arrange and set a date for this meeting.

Signed,
Lord Vladimir Itrivic, Head of Clan Itrivic

"Damnation," Richard whispered to himself. They had his interest, something they seldom managed without also infuriating him. If Desanadron was no longer their primary target for feedings, then what was? Had the vampires discovered some other village closer to them and more vulnerable? And could he really expect them to visit no harm upon he and his brothers?

No, of course not, but if he wanted any kind of peace, the brothers would have to attend the meeting. It would be only three of them, the Tiverski brothers, surrounded by an entire family clan that numbered around thirty strong. They needed outside help if they were going to go, and Richard knew that Portenda's attendance was out of the question for the time being. He had other business matters to attend to.

Richard stood from his bed and entered the kitchen again, where Trent had resumed his unarmed exercises. "Trent, do ve have any friends in Desanadron?"

"Not many, Richard. Why?"

Richard explained the contents of the letter to Trent and Simon, and both of them mulled over Richard's suggestion that they bring some outside help. After a few minutes' thought, Trent snapped his fingers. "I think I may know someone who can help us. I'll send him a letter with Dirge." Trent referred to his own personal messenger bird, a raven he kept in his room.

"Vat sort of payment vill your friend expect from us," Richard asked as Trent stalked to his own room to form a letter for delivery.

"A few gold pieces, little more. The potential for violence will attract him more than anything, Richard." Trent bent over his writing desk and starting his letter.

"You're not thinking of Portenda, are you?"

"No, I believe he's off in Ja-Wen or something," Trent replied rather testily. "No, the fellow I have in mind is rather, unique. Like us." Trent waved his elder brother off.

Richard returned to his room, where he would read until almost dawn. At that time he would bring down the steel shutter over his window and sleep in total darkness.

A few minutes later, he heard Dirge's wings flapping away from the cottage, and he let himself relax. They would have a reply soon enough, he thought. *I wonder, however, who this man is that Trent trusts so much.*

* * * *

When the bird tapped on his window, the man Trent sent the letter to was frankly surprised. He had only seen this particular messenger bird once, and thus far, he had not informed his Headmaster that he'd taken work once from the client who owned the raven.

Clad in white Ninja's garments, the contact stood up from his kneeling position and headed to the window, opening it to allow Dirge into his room.

Akimaru pulled the envelope out of the bird's mouth, and checked the timepiece hanging on the wall across from the window. Four-thirty in the morning.

Akimaru seldom slept more than a couple of hours at any given time, but if this was important, he might not sleep at all until the request was either accepted or declined. If he accepted, he would inform Thaddeus Fly that he was going out on a scouting mission or something, for the Midnight Suns presumably. Depending on the severity of the situation, he might wind up taking Rage with him.

Ah, Rage-san, Akimaru thought. After the hunt for the Glove of Shadows, the lumbering Orc Berserker had been left blind in one eye, but with a strange new capacity for learning. He had become partially civilized, as intelligent as any Orc bruiser could be expected to be. Accepting the risks involved with entering a Vampire enclave, Akimaru formed a well thought-out response, and tied it to the raven's leg, sending it back to Trent Tiverski.

The white clad Ninja waited for two more hours, and then headed downstairs, to the weight room in the basement, where Rage had already begun his training regimen for the day. The broad-chested Orc presently worked on his bench presses, and had already accumulated a heavy layer of sweat on his gray sweatshirt. His left eye was sewn shut, and his right eye gleamed to match his smile as he looked up at Akimaru's masked face, upside down in his perspective. "Hey, Aki! Wanna' spot me?"

"Sure thing," the Ninja replied, spotting Rage until he finished his set. They set the bar with its attached weights onto the bracket, and Rage sat up, toweling off his forehead.

"Rage-san, I would like you to accompany me on a requested mission to the northeast. There may be much fighting, and your presence would be most useful."

"Oh, okay Aki," Rage said, getting up and heading over to the leg press machine. He settled himself in and started pushing the weights up and down. *One thousand pounds*, Akimaru observed. *Goodness, that's an awful lot of weight.*

"When we goin' then?"

"Today, Rage," Akimaru said. "Not until late this afternoon, so do not rush yourself with your program. I would not want you to hurt yourself, my friend."

"Hey, t'anks," Rage said, looking up between his bare feet as he pressed on the weights again and again, counting down from fifty. Akimaru left the Orc to his business, and prepared to make his request to Headmaster Fly.

* * * *

When the knock came at their cottage door, Richard looked up from the letter in his hands, informing him that the meeting would be tonight, at midnight. That meant that they would have to leave as soon as the guide showed up to take them to the enclave. Could this be the guide now, he wondered?

Trent came out of his room and stalked heavily to the door, one hand on the hilt of his long sword, as he grasped the doorknob. He pulled the door open, and there stood not a Vampire, but a slender man dressed in a white Ninja suit, and a lumbering Orc who easily matched Portenda the Quiet in terms of physical dimensions.

"Ah, Akimaru." Trent smiled, sheathing his sword and extending his hand to the white clad Ninja, who accepted it and shook.

Trent turned his fanged smile back to his elder brother. "This is the man who I contacted."

"Clearly." Richard stood and approached the Ninja with the graceful walk of a highly ranked diplomat. He gave Akimaru a half bow, and looked up at Rage, who flashed him a big, dumb smile. "Who then is this?"

"This is Rage-san," Akimaru said. "He is an associate of mine, and well suited for physical altercation. When are we needed?"

"Right now, Mr. Akimaru," Richard said. "Ve are expecting a guide from ze Clan Itrivic to escort us to zeir enclave in ze foothills northeast of zese voods. Please, vould you like to come in?"

"No," Akimaru said quickly. "We shall await the arrival of the guide, so that there are no surprises. Rage-san, sweep the area."

The Orc nodded and moved off heavily, surveying the surrounding woods. Every step the heavyset Orc took through the soft soil left enormous footprints, but Akimaru didn't figure that would make much difference. Anyone approaching, in fact, might be a tad more wary with such large feet tromping through the woodland, marking the passage of an engine of pure violence.

Akimaru decided, however, that he wanted to know something more about the Itrivic people. He would wait until Rage-san returned from his brief scan of the area, and would then ask Trent or Richard, since the latter seemed to be the leader of the Vampire trio, for the letter they had received in the first place. By holding the parchment, he might be able to ascertain something about the author of the letter's background or mindset.

Rage, meanwhile, was enjoying the deep, loamy scent of the woodland. Since the mission to obtain the Glove of Shadows, he had found the odors predominant in a large city like Desanadron (the largest in the world) to be overpowering and putrid. What was once the comforting smell of many people pressed into a tightly packed marketplace now assaulted him like a foreign chemical invasion of his nostrils' privacy. Out here, in the wilderness, he could smell the fresh pine scent of evergreens, the faint odor of a stream or creek that ran past just north of the Tiverski brothers' property, and the soil itself.

Additionally, his sense of hearing had been adjusted to the hustle and bustle of both the interior of the Guild hall, and the exterior, meaning the streets of Desanadron themselves. Out here, having developed a sort of fine tuning in the city, so he could pick out one particular strand of conversation, he could make out the passage of animals and other creatures that resided in these woods. His hearing wasn't on par with some individuals, but for the most part, Rage now operated with a heightened awareness outside of the sprawling metropolitan environment.

Rage made a full circuit around the Tiverski property, and returned to Akimaru's side. "Nadda," he rumbled.

"Very good, Rage-san. Now, Richard, was it?" Akimaru stood straight with one hand slightly extended out, and removed the white cloth glove with his other hand, revealing an extremely pale hand that seemed to plume with mist.

Richard cocked his head to one side, curious at this visual phenomenon.

"You have the letter that these Itrivic people sent you?" the Ninja asked.

"Ah, ja, ve haf it. One moment, friend." Richard gave a fanged smile before heading back toward his room. As he passed, he shot his little brother Simon a curious glance, indicating Akimaru with a flicker of his eyes.

As Richard headed toward his writing desk, Simon stood from the couch and positively dragged himself out into the walkway that went straight between the living room and kitchen, and all the way back to Trent's room at the end, with Simon's room off to the left side midway down.

Standing in his robes, with his hood up to cover his bald pate, Simon cycled through his encyclopedic knowledge of all things magical. However, upon seeing Akimaru's hand, he knew instantly what the white clad Ninja was, at least partially. For him, it was a no brainer, though he fully understood how his brothers might be confused.

"You're part elemental," Simon said very softly, his voice little louder than the wind that gently brushed past Akimaru and Rage.

"Hoi," Akimaru said, acknowledging Simon Tiverski's observation. "I am surprised by your statement, however. How did you know?"

Simon Tiverski's face took on no emotional reaction, but he did give a little half-hearted chuckle.

"The steam off of the hand, the sudden drop in air temperature, and a constantly running Inner Sight spell." Simon shrugged his shoulders before returning to the couch and picking up his novel.

Akimaru took an instant liking to Simon Tiverski, and to Richard as well, neither man having been known to him previously. Trent Tiverski, however, Akimaru had met once at a fighting tournament in Desanadron several years before, and the two men had hit it off splendidly. Trent had proven not only an efficient fighter, but clever as well. He had used a localized Dark of Night spell centered on his body in order to compete during the daytime hours, one of the few magical tricks he had in his arsenal. Sure, it made him clearly visible to an opponent, but it also allowed the largest of the Tiverski brothers to move about freely during the day, if he so chose.

So, Akimaru thought as Richard started to come back toward him through the kitchen, and then to the entryway of the cottage, *they have a good mix between the three of them. Simon the mage, Trent the brute, and Richard, an even blend of both, with a bonus of being very diplomatic and politically savvy.* Had they not been Vampires, Akimaru would have sponsored them for enlistment into the Midnight Suns. The Guild didn't have nearly what they needed in the way of magic users.

"This is the first letter, Mr. Akimaru." Richard graced the white-clad Ninja and the bull-like Rage with a little half bow again.

Akimaru snatched the parchment away and his eyes rolled back into his head as he used his Psychic-like powers to look into the mind of the author of the document. He had to sweep his mind first past a minor bit of information that Richard Tiverski had left on the parchment by handling it, but that took little effort.

Brief images and bits and pieces of partially audible conversations played inside of the mental theater house inside of Akimaru's head. At the moment they made little or no sense, but that would change with just a minor adjustment of his powers.

His body twitched here and there, back and forth, and Rage placed his heavy hands on Akimaru's shoulders to try to steady him.

The white clad Ninja moved out from under the hands, as their touch on even his clothed and covered shoulders was enough of a distraction to jumble what information he'd found, and this time Rage did nothing, merely standing aside and letting the mysterious Ninja work his gifts.

After a few minutes, the sights and sounds starting shuffling together again, making a great deal more sense than they had before. This Lord Itrivic was an interesting person indeed, and as a schemer, he was top-notch. Akimaru watched through the man's point of view, and listened with his ears as he carried on a conversation with one of his Clan members, informing him that when the Tiverski brothers arrived, they were to be offered blood and food, if they wanted any. Well, Akimaru thought, that clears up one myth. Apparently normal food is not as essential to the diet of a Vampire, but they still used some to sustain themselves, unless they absolutely gorge on blood.

Once blood and food were offered, Lord Itrivic informed this man of his, a 'strike team' was to place itself on the balcony surrounding and overlooking the main dining hall of their enclave. After a certain amount of talk, Itrivic would reveal to the Tiverski brothers the Clan's new source of blood for consumption. If the trio from the woods objected in any way to the Clan's plans, whether with subtle threats or outright promises to expose them, the strike team was to descend upon them and destroy the Tiverski brothers. Perhaps most interesting of all, Akimaru thought, was the fact that the blood offered was to be from their stock of diseased blood, weakening the three visiting Vampires. Also, there would be a Silence spell locked on the chair that would be assigned to Simon Tiverski, whom Lord Itrivic believed would not speak unless he tried to use a spell.

Akimaru slowly sifted back to the present, the here and now, and found himself staring into the concerned eyes of Richard Tiverski. Akimaru knew immediately that he could trust these Tiverski brothers, just from the look in the eldest brother's eyes. They spoke not to him of bloodlust, or dark desires; he was genuinely concerned for the white clad Ninja's well being. Any other Vampire would have lunged on the opportunity that Akimaru had left himself open to. Even a roadblock like Rage wouldn't have been able to stop all three of the Vampires from getting at Akimaru, because Simon could easily have scared the lumbering Orc Berserker off with magic while the other two assaulted the helpless Akimaru.

The white clad Ninja placed the parchment in his gloved hand, and handed it back to Richard, who took it gently, noticing how cold the document had become. Frost edged the paper, but the frost quickly melted into a dripping spot of water on the doorstep.

"Vell, vat can you tell us, Mr. Akimaru," Richard asked. His brothers came up behind him then, and all three listened to Akimaru's recounting of the trap set for them.

"He did not say precisely what their new source of fresh blood is, however," Akimaru said. "I apologize, but I could not delve deeper than that. The parchment was not handled long enough by any one man to get a good imprint."

Richard guffawed and clapped Akimaru amiably on the shoulder.

"No need to apologize, Mr. Akimaru," he said. "Vat you haf learned ist good enough. They are not expecting you and your large friend here to be comink along for ze visit. Vat did you say your name is, my good young Orc?"

Rage smiled broadly, and extended his huge, gnarled green hand to Richard, who took it and pumped twice, removing his hand so as not to lose it in that killer grip.

"Rage," the big Berserker said, offering his hand then to Trent, who returned the ferocity of the grip--much to the Orc's delight.

Simon, however, merely bowed, waving his own hand in deference. Rage raised an eyebrow and cocked his head to one side, confused. "I ain't got no germs or nuttin' mister," he said to Simon.

"Oh, please excuse our little brother," Richard said to Rage. "He ist physically frail, Mr. Rage, and I belief you rather intimidate him."

Rage took his hand back, grinned, and gave Simon a head nod of acceptance.

"Fair enough," Rage said. "So, when's dis jamoke s'possed ta come ta collect you guys?"

"He or she should have been here by now," Trevor grumbled... a little too soon. As Akimaru turned around, the five of them, three Vampires, one Orc, and one half-breed of sorts, saw a voluptuous woman smiling at them from some twenty yards away. She appeared Human, pale, with long, lank black hair all the way to her waist.

"Man, curved in all the right places," Trevor whispered after whistling at the sight of her. The woman was dressed rather provocatively, an affectation of the Clan Itrivic's women. Long, slender legs, bare despite the autumn chill of the region, stretched for what almost seemed eternity to Trent and Richard Tiverski.

"Brothers, if you'd pick your jaws up from the floor, I believe that's our guide," Simon uttered, his voice once more barely audible.

Richard and Trent cleared their throats, collected their wits, and tried to remember that this woman was most likely the enemy. "Am I to assume my brother is correct?" he asked of the woman, who smiled charmingly in reply.

"I am Nadia Itrivic," the woman said. Her voice had a pleasant reed to it, with an audible quality that reminded Richard of the middle-aged women he sometimes saw flitting here and there at the night markets in Desanadron. "I am indeed your guide to our Clan's enclave. We only expected there would be the three Tiverski brothers coming. Were we incorrect in that expectation," she asked, planting her hands on her hips.

"Ah, yes, allow me to explain," Richard said amiably, gracing the lady Nadia Itrivic with a sweeping gentleman's bow. "You see, my brothers and I are qvite interested in arranging a peace between ourselves and your Clan. However, your Clan numbers somevhere in ze tventies in number, ja?" Nadia Itrivic's smile turned slightly frosty, but she nodded to confirm his estimate. "Ve vould simply feel more comfortable having these capable gentlemen along vith us. You understand, yes?"

"Indeed I do, Richard Tiverski," she said. She turned and was ready to take flight into the night sky, when Akimaru cleared his throat rather loudly. When the white clad Ninja fellow spoke, Nadia seemed to hear the words spoken directly into her ear, as though he stood not twenty feet away, but only a few inches.

"Myself and my associate, Rage-san, cannot fly," he said.

Damn, Nadia thought, having hoped that by taking flight she could goad the three Tiverski brothers into either leaving their little hired helpers behind, or letting her range far ahead.

"Foot travel together would be best, Ms. Nadia," he added.

"Very well," she replied. "Gentlemen, if you would follow me this way, please." She headed into the darkening forest.

She did in fact wind up ranging ahead a little at first, but she passed it off as the five men falling behind because of the large green guloot. As she was passing it off, Richard Tiverski leaned in close to Akimaru, the two of them taking the forward position in the group. Trent and Simon took the middle, leaving Rage as a marching bulwark of a rearguard.

"Vell, vat do you think?" Richard whispered to the enigmatic Ninja.

"I do not trust her further than I could throw Rage-san," came the response.

Richard got a light chuckle out of that, which he kept mainly to himself. He didn't want to spook their guide, after all, or give her any indication that the Tiverski brothers were formulating their own plan on how to approach this evening's meeting.

"By the way, Richard, were you aware that there is a new village not far from here, set near the foothills north and east of us?"

"Nien, I did not know zat," the eldest Tiverski admitted. "Makeup?"

"Mostly Humans and Elves," Akimaru said. "Some Minotaur tribal families as well. I suspect that village is going to be the new source of blood they will reveal to you. I will tell you more when I have the chance." Akimaru clipped off his words as Richard looked up to see that Nadia Itrivic was waiting for the five men to catch up to her.

"Come along, gentlemen," she said, seemingly coquettish. "I won't bite." *No*, Richard thought, *no you von't, not ever again if you aren't careful, my lady.*

* * * *

North and east the company marched, first tromping over the slightly damp, moss-covered woodland floor, and then passing into the open flatlands between the Tiverski brothers' woods and the foothills fronting the northern mountains. Roiling clouds of gray and black floated overhead, often obscuring the moon in the sky above. "Hope it don't rain," Rage muttered mostly to himself. "I hate da rain," he added.

"Vhy vould zat be, my large green friend," Richard asked as he sauntered slightly ahead of the Orc and his brothers Simon and Trent.

"Da rain reminds me of my mudder," Rage said, looking up at the storm clouds, squinting his one good eye slightly. "Not sure why, but it does it every time. What about you? You like it at all?"

"Goodness no," Richard replied with a smile over his shoulder to the Greenskin warrior. "It ist terrible for my clothes, Mr. Rage! I cannot abide the odor of damp silk." The Vampire said picked a piece of lint from his flared shirt cuff.

The group continued behind the Itrivic woman in relative silence then, each member of the company quietly grateful that the swelling rain clouds seemed to be withholding their business until the band was inside the Itrivic Clan's home of operations.

The entire trip only took about three hours. After taking an easy, wide dirt road through the foothills, the company finally came upon a mountain range fronted by a large, stone structure in the style of a cathedral.

Nadia Itrivic stopped about five hundred yards away from the enormous double doors at the front of the building, and smiled at her guests. "Gentlemen, I present to you the Itrivic Clan home of this region, Jordesvein. This stronghold has been the central seat of power for the Itrivic family for generations." She looked north to the cathedral-like compound. "Recently, however, the primary core of the family moved to another location."

"So, Great Lord Itrivic is not within?" Trent looked his brother Richard in the eyes, trying to communicate his disappointment.

"No, he is not," Nadia said without looking back at her charges. She started to walk forward once more, leading them on their way. "The ancestral bloodline in command of the family Clan has secreted themselves away to another compound. Our resident Lord is the youngest brother of Great Lord Itrivic. Though younger, however," she said meaningfully, "he is no less capable a leader."

Nadia led them straight down the path two hundred yards or so, and then came to a sudden stop. "Wait here for a few minutes. I must go ahead and ask that the perimeter guards deactivate their locked defensive spells. Those who do not possess the blood of the Itrivic Clan or their servants will unleash magical traps that would likely destroy the lot of you," she said softly.

"Very well. We shall await your return or all-clear," Richard said without hesitation.

Nadia Itrivic sprinted ahead gracefully, leaving the three Tiverski brothers and the two Midnight Suns standing on the wide path leading to the compound. Richard spun on his heel to face the group, noting the way his brother Simon was staring past him, through him, at the flat fields before them. "Simon, your thoughts if you vould."

"The game has already begun," the smallest, palest of the Vampire brothers reported in his whispery voice. His eyes roamed over the pathway and the fields on either side, noting each point of magical concentration. "The defensive spells were only set a short while ago, for our benefit. This is their first move in the diplomatic game, brother. It is a move designed to gain our trust."

"Fat chance." Trent folded his arms over his chest. "Did they really expect this sort of ruse to escape our notice?"

Truth to be told, Richard thought, *I vouldn't have noticed. Only Simon could have seen this trick for vhat it is.*

"The magical traps are not their only deception here," Akimaru said suddenly, catching the three Vampires' attention. His eyes, barely visible in the slit in his facemask, seemed locked on something atop the cathedral's front wall. "There are snipers atop their stronghold, each one holding a mecha weapon of some sort." He pointed boldly right up at the rifle-toting guards.

As soon as his finger was pointed at each of them, Richard could just make out the silhouetted forms of the Itrivic snipers. However, as soon as Richard smiled upon sighting them, the snipers disappeared, most likely reacting to the fact that they had been spotted.

"Surely there ist a vay to ensure ve escape their weapons' range vhen ve leave," Richard said.

"Yeah, we crush them along with everyone else when we're done listening to their nonsense," Trent growled, cracking his knuckles.

Rage gave the brute of the Tiverski brothers a broad grin and nod of agreement, cracking his own huge, gnarled knuckles. "How long do you think they'll prattle on before we have to make our move, brother?"

"I'm not entirely certain, Trent," Richard said. He rubbed his chin thoughtfully, playing over several scenarios in his mind while waiting for Nadia Itrivic's return from within the compound. The first question to run through his mind was, *how greatly are we outnumbered? How many men and vomen inside? Vill they vait for some sort of signal from Lord Itrivic, and if so, how vill we know vhat sort of attack to expect?*

Similar inquiries played over Akimaru's mind at the same time.

While the Itrivic Clan had the advantage of numbers and home turf, however, the five visitors had the advantage of surprise. They already knew that the meeting would devolve into violent confrontation; Lord Itrivic only suspected that it *might* happen. The resident head of the Clan did not fully expect it to come to that, though. From what he had gleaned from holding and reading the letter written to Richard Tiverski, Akimaru had discovered that Lord Itrivic expected Richard to be reasonable and see that his position was not favorable in the conference. Lord Itrivic almost fully expected the Tiverski brothers to fold; he apparently didn't know them very well, Akimaru thought.

The giant double doors at the front of the compound swung slowly open and Nadia Itrivic stalked out into the dimly lit night just as the first drops of rain started to fall. Within minutes, she led the company to the open compound, making no further conversation with the group.

Akimaru, highly trained as a Ninja and sensitive to people's emotional state of mind through his strange lineage, saw that Nadia was not only tense, she was slightly embarrassed. Most likely, the white clad Ninja thought, she has been chastised for bringing myself and Rage-san along as well. *Her problem, not ours*, he thought.

The closer the group got to the open double doors, the higher up they appeared to loom over the company.

"I must say, I am impressed vith your family's taste in architecture," Richard Tiverski commented, walking along peaceably, hands clasped behind his back. "Third Age?"

"Actually, late Second Age," Nadia said with a wolfish smile. She was clearly proud to belong to one of the more noble Vampire family Clans, or if not noble precisely, then certainly one of the longest lasting.

"We have discovered the original floor plans in one of the basement chambers. It was dated 1224 2.A. Of course, it could have been a forgery." She stepped into the primary antechamber of the compound, her high heels clacking against the stone floor and echoing throughout the high-ceilinged chamber. "But we commissioned a Gnome Scholar to come and verify its authenticity. He was sufficiently impressed with his findings to confirm the date on the floor plans."

"So, how old vould zat make ze structure?" Richard asked, looking worriedly up and around the large, oblong chamber they had entered. The entire room was barren of furniture of any sort, and he could tell that the compound had been carved from the very mountain rock in which it was set. The interior of the antechamber was domed, with a ceiling that curved overhead and had an apex that stood about thirty yards up. He could just barely make out tiny cracks in the walls and ceiling, and he wondered for the first time, *if zey don't try to kill us, vill ze entire building just collapse on top of us? Zat vould be just my luck.*

"Well," Nadia said, guiding the group toward another set of double doors directly across from the main entrance. Doors also stood to their left and right, but these portals she gave nary a glance. "The Second Age lasted until the year 1300, if the historians are all in agreement. The Third Age lasted only until a little longer than that before being declared done and finished. The Fourth Age, the Age of Mecha, lasted much less, ending with the Fall of Mecha in 514, I believe it was. I'm certainly no Professor Swellskin, so I couldn't say with authority. And we are now in the year 876 A.F., or the Fifth Age, year 876. So, add that all up, my friend."

"Over twenty-four hundred years old," Simon replied without

hesitation.

Nadia turned from them and waved a hand at the armored Vampire guard blocking their passage through the doors before them.

"Madam, his Lordship is not prepared yet for his visitors," the Vampire in the black steel armor informed her. In his right hand he held a spear, with the blunt end resting on the stone floor. His long, silver hair flowed back over his head in waves, and he had a regal, handsome appearance, despite his air of servitude. He gestured toward the left-hand door of the antechamber with the head of his weapon. "He has instructed me to direct you to the primary library until the guests are sent for. You shall take them to the library and return to his Lordship at once, Lady Nadia," the guard said flatly.

"Very well. Thank you, Mensus." She turned to face the Tiverski brothers and their hired help. "Gentlemen, the library is right through that door over there. Please, make yourselves comfortable, and someone shall be by shortly to collect you. I apologize for the delay."

Without complaint, Richard turned and stalked toward the door leading to the Itrivic Clan's library, opening the door and rushing inside before he burst out laughing. As soon as Rage lumbered inside of the two-story library and shut the door behind himself, Richard loosed a volley of harsh laughter.

"I don't see what's so funny." Rage looked around at the rows and rows of books in the walls around him and in tall, stone shelving units placed around the interior of the in-house library.

Richard continued to guffaw for almost a full minute before he was able to sufficiently calm himself and regain his composure.

He didn't have to answer for himself, however--Akimaru explained.

"Rage-san, Mr. Tiverski finds it amusing that the Itrivic Clan is taking such heavy precautions with us. They are most likely plotting further to make up for the fact that you and I have been brought along for this meeting. Richard is merely amused by the apparent ease with which we have disrupted their plans." The Ninja cocked an eyebrow at Richard, and the Vampire nodded his acknowledgement. "Mr. Tiverski, what is our plan of action at this point in time?"

"For now, my friend," Richard said, moving toward one of the shelving units and selecting a fiction novel he had not as yet read. "Ve vait like the patient, polite guests ve are pretending to be."

* * * *

Nadia Itrivic's thoughts spanned the range between furious and intrigued as she followed Mensus Allahandro toward the stronghold's main dining room. Her uncle, Lord Itrivic of the Northern Itrivic Clan, had clearly been sent word of the Tiverski brothers' hired help as she had requested upon entry to the cathedral. He had deployed Mensus, one of his personal bodyguards and servants, to retrieve his niece so that they could discuss how to best deal with the Vampire brothers now that they had assistance.

She followed the rangy, stoic Vampire bodyguard through the gilded, richly decorated halls until he held open one of the side doors leading into the main dining hall.

Lord Itrivic was seated in a high-backed iron chair at the head of the twenty yard long oak dining table, his hands folded under his angular chin, deep in thought. His black silk tunics hung loosely on his gaunt frame, and for the first time in close to a century, Nadia truly worried about her uncle's health. Though her people could not die of age naturally, too much time between feedings could rob them of their eternal youthfulness. How long, she wondered, since Lord Itrivic had taken a feeding? Three weeks, maybe four? However long it had been, it wasn't healthy for him, and soon he would have to send someone from the family or the collection of bodyguards and grunts to go kidnap a Human for him to feast upon.

"Uncle, I am here," she announced as she approached the seat to Lord Itrivic's right.

He didn't look up from his musings, but indicated the seat with one hand.

She pulled out the elegant pine wood chair and seated herself, pulling it in close and bowing her head slightly to her uncle and local lordship. "You sent for me?"

"Indeed I did, Nadia," he said slowly, his voice like rough sandpaper scraping on her ears. "What is your impression of these hired men the Tiverskis brought with them? I am told that one is a Ninja in a white uniform, and the other is a one-eyed giant of an Orc. Have you any thoughts on dealing with them?"

"Well, your lordship, we may not have to deal with them if Richard Tiverski carries himself with any sort of reason. They will not be in any position to refuse our proposal," she said with a grin.

Lord Itrivic finally turned his eyes toward his niece, and the appearance of fatigue or weakness she saw in the rest of his body could not be seen at all in his yellow, gimlet eyes.

"They will refuse us, my lovely Nadia," he said quietly, his hands still propping his head up. "Regardless of our numbers and advantage, they will refuse us. Richard Tiverski is intelligent, and usually reasonable, but when it comes to such matters as these, he is immovable. When he refuses..." Lord Itrivic plucked a steak knife from the table and jammed it all the way to the hilt in the hard wooden table. As soon as he let it go, his hand returned under his chin. "We will be forced to destroy the lot of them. Now, tell me what you think of these strangers."

"Well," Nadia said, easing back in her chair and nodding to a servant as she poured her a wineglass full of fresh Elven blood. She took a light sip from the glass and smacked her lips. "Excellent, thank you. The Ninja worries me far more than the Orc, uncle Adrian. Something is very strange about him. I sense energy far beyond that of a normal mortal being in him."

"Is he one of our kind, do you think?" the elderly Vampire asked, accepting a glass of the same blood from the servant woman.

"Definitely not." Nadia crossed her left leg over her right. "But he isn't a normal mortal, that much is for sure. Also, just from observing the way he moves, I can say with utmost confidence that in the event of physical altercation, we shall need to focus most of our efforts on him and Trevor Tiverski. Which will need more attention, I am not sure."

"The Ninja," Lord Adrian Itrivic said bluntly, sipping his blood like wine. Some of the old flush of his cheeks returned as he imbibed the blood, and he actually managed a stern smile for a moment. "We have seen Trevor Tiverski in combat. Our soldiers know full well how to deal with his forthright style of fighting. He is a classical swordsman, Nadia. It really is a shame he will have to be destroyed. Now, the Orc?"

"A simple brute I'm sure, uncle," Nadia replied, swishing her drink around in its fine glass before draining it. "He seems more intelligent than most of his kind, though. He may actually have the ability to keep up with the negotiation process, though I doubt he will offer much input before the attack. Uncle, what if they do agree to our proposal," she asked suddenly, surprised that she would even consider it a possibility.

He raised one thin eyebrow at her, and finished his own drink.

"Then we will allow them to leave, and thank whatever Gods might listen to us for the opportunity to remain unscathed."

The servant woman poured them each another glass, and they enjoyed a leisurely drink before sending for their guests.

* * * *

Simon, Trevor, and Richard Tiverski all sat on one of the comfortably padded couches in the library, Simon and Richard both engaged in books, and Trevor sitting with his arms crossed over his chest, thinking through possible battle strategies for the incident to come. Surely nothing the Itrivic Vampires offered them in the way of a deal would be worthwhile, he assumed. Of all of the older remaining Vampire

Clans, the Itrivics were known the realm over as the most brutal and sadistic. They would be merciless with their dealings tonight, and combat was inevitable. But how would he and his brothers deal with the overwhelming numbers that Lord Itrivic could summon to engage them?

He trusted that Akimaru would be more than capable of helping them deal with the grunts and bodyguards of the Clan. And although he had never met with or seen Rage in combat, he felt confident that the Orc could take out a few Vampires on his own. The enormous axe he wielded wasn't silver or magical in nature, but that wouldn't matter so long as he hit his foes in the head or the chest. The Orc Berserker could probably rip their heads right off of their shoulders in any event, weapon or no.

The problem was that, as skilled a swordsman as he was himself, the Itrivic Clan of Vampires knew precisely how he would fight. They were, after all, his original family Clan. Trevor had left the Itrivic family after disagreements over their brutal method of securing their food sources--abducting defenseless men and women off of the streets of towns and cities. Since he had been trained in their fighting style, their opponents here would almost certainly know how to combat him.

Simon had magic at his disposal that would render melee combat unnecessary for him, and hopefully put the Itrivics at a disadvantage. The most diminutive of the three Tiverski brothers could hurl vastly destructive spells at large numbers of opponents. So long as someone stayed close to defend him, the small band of rebel Vampires and their hired helpers might make it out of this cathedral compound intact.

Akimaru, seated across from the Vampire brothers in a shell-shaped yellow recliner, also thought over his battle strategy. Leaned back in the chair, his hands behind his masked head, the white-clad Ninja wondered if any of the Vampires, either in the trio or the larger Clan, had detected his true nature. If they hadn't, he would bring that immediately to bear in a combat situation, thus buying his group time from the initial shock. As soon as he revealed himself, Rage-san would fall into the ranks of their foes like a force of nature, his axe or bare fists working to deal out death.

Rage himself was the only member of the group unseated, doing one-armed pushups to pump himself up for the coming fight. Though not the sharpest tool in the shed, the Orc Berserker knew full well that no diplomatic solution would be found here this night. Only battle, pure and bloody, would solve anything in the cathedral home of the northern branch of the Itrivic Vampire Clan. When it came, he would be ready.

Each member of the company remained locked in his own ruminations, until at last the door to the library opened with a creak, and the Vampire bodyguard who had led them to the library earlier, Mensus Allahandro, stood in the doorway. "The conference will now be held," he announced to the rising Vampire trio and their companions. "Please, follow me."

Without waiting to see if they would comply, the armored guard turned on his heel and started to stalk slowly down the decorative hallway.

The group moved in single-file behind the bodyguard, Richard in the front, Trevor next, then Simon, Akimaru next, with Rage bringing up the rear. The massive Greenskin warrior almost had to duck his head in the hallway, and more than once had to move sideways to keep from knocking over priceless pieces of artwork.

Before they had made half of the trek through the halls to the dining hall, Mensus Allahandro turned his head slightly to speak over his shoulder. "How long has it been, Trevor? Two hundred, three hundred years?"

For a moment, Trevor Tiverski was too taken off guard to realize that he had recognized the bodyguard from the very beginning. Mensus had served as the vice chief of bodyguards to High Lord Iosef Itrivic in the days when Trevor had been among the Clan's elite branch of warriors. The two had crossed paths several times, and apparently Trevor had left quite an impression with the local chief of bodyguards. Trevor cleared his throat and replied, "Two hundred and thirty years, Mensus," he said. "Time has treated you well, I see."

"Likewise," was the only response before the bodyguard opened a wide oak door to permit the group entry into the dining hall. "You are expected within. Please, seat yourselves accordingly across from the master."

Richard Tiverski headed inside at the head of the group, with his brothers directly behind and Akimaru and Rage following close after.

The meeting hall they had entered held an air of ancestry and greatness, with ornate tapestries and other works of art hung here and there around the walls. A long, smoothly varnished oak table dominated the center of the chamber, most likely a holdover from whomever had owned the structure before the Itrivic Vampire Clan. Multiple candelabras sat on pedestals and circular end tables around the chamber, combining with a candle-laden chandelier to offer ambient illumination to the room.

Seated at one end of the table in a high-backed, black wood throne, Lord Itrivic exuded an aura of commanding presence that brooked no argument. Clad mostly in black, he appeared to be the sort of patrician fellow who would speak partly through his nose, which would be aimed slightly skyward. While most preferred not to jump to such quick conclusions, Richard Tiverski felt comfortable enough making a few assumptions about this Vampire Lord, since he was notoriously 'old world' in his dealings.

As all five travelers approached the table, Lord Itrivic and his niece, the delightful Nadia, rose to greet them, each bowing gracefully but cautiously, keeping their heads up with their eyes locked on their targets.

"Ah, it is a fine thing to finally meet face to face, Richard Tiverski," Lord Adrian Itrivic said with a broad, fang-filled smile. He extended one clammy white hand, which Richard took only momentarily, enough for one shake.

"Would you like to take a seat, gentlemen? And to the Tiverskis, may I offer you a glass of fine Human spirit?"

"No, thank you," Richard said with a fake smile plastered to his face. "Ve prefer to get to know ze people who are villing to donate zere life blood to us. I assume zat your stocks vere not attained through volunteer donations of blood."

Richard took a seat on Lord Itrivic's immediate right. Akimaru walked around the table to sit next to Nadia Itrivic, with Rage next to him, so that there were three people occupying the closest seats on each side of the table to Lord Itrivic. As he seated himself next to his brother, Trevor could only think, *ah, and so the politics begin.*

"Your assumption is accurate, Richard Tiverski," Lord Itrivic said. "We take what we are due, when we wish, from the foolish mortal masses. It is natural that it be that way--we are Vampires, after all. We are superior to the fools whose blood we feast upon."

Itrivic took a slow gulp of his wine, thoroughly enjoying the taste and feel of it as all three of the Tiverski brothers seemed to bore their gazes into his skull. "What, you disagree?"

"In part, yes," said Simon Tiverski, much to everyone's general surprise. Neither side of the negotiations had expected him to speak much, but here he was, already interjecting something into the flow of conversation. Certainly Lord Itrivic hadn't expected any such talk from him, but he remembered quickly that the seal of silence would only take hold of Simon Tiverski if hostilities arose.

The lithe, pale, bald Tiverski brother straightened his back slightly, and proceeded to explain. "There are several prominent scientists throughout the lands of Tamalaria who have hypothesized that vampirism is actually a disease, a product of a sentient bacteria or virus that flows in the afflicted individual's bloodstream. But," he said, his voice becoming soft and demure once more, hunching his shoulders up as he usually did when trying to be unobtrusive. "It is only theory. If the theory holds true, then we are not superior, but merely diseased."

Stunned silence met this overall statement, with an occasional cleared throat from the other two Tiverski brothers and several as yet unseen individuals.

Akimaru, his senses trained to pick out would-be sneak attacks, might not have known the locations of several of those hidden assailants in the chamber and up on the upper walkways of the room had Simon not created such silence. Beneath his mask, the white clad Ninja smiled.

Lord Adrian Itrivic seemed to regain his senses first, and smiled politely at Simon Tiverski. "I trust that the theory you speak of is mere conjecture, and has no actual proof behind it. Besides, what do scientists know of destiny and the true order of things?" Lord Itrivic swished his blood around in its wineglass. "After all, they cannot even explain the arts and forces of magic, let alone the wonder that is the Vampire Race! Now, enough of this idle chit-chat." He leaned forward and planting his elbows on the long conference table, a subtle grin slithering across his lips. "Let us discuss the terms of our future arrangement and peace."

"Ve are villing to listen to vhatever offer or gesture you are villing to make," Richard Tiverski said politely.

"But that does not mean we will necessarily accept the offer or gesture." Trevor Tiverski crossed his arms over his chest in a defiant position.

"Nor does it mean that we won't have an idea or plan of our own design," Simon Tiverski finished a routine that the trio of Vampire brothers cycled through whenever these sort of diplomatic situations arose. They had done this exact routine approximately six times, but this time, they themselves were taken aback by the next speaker, who actually added to their own overall message.

"And rest assured, if you do not remove the snipers with the wrist crossbows from the chamber's upper walkways, the talking will end very abruptly, and the bloodshed shall begin," Akimaru's stressed neck was just visible under the mask and above the tunic top.

Lord Adrian Itrivic's only response to the accusation in Akimaru's statement was to bring his right hand up slightly in a fist, which he then opened and drew across his forehead. Shuffling footsteps could be heard faintly on the upper walkways surrounding the walls of the chamber high above them, the snipers with their wrist crossbows exiting the room.

"How very perceptive of you to have noticed them, my fine guest," Lord Adrian Itrivic schmoozed, pursing his lips out just slightly. "Is there anything else that any of the five of you would like to add before I proceed?"

Rage, who had remained completely silent the entire time thus far, cleared his throat with one fist to his mouth.

"You have something to add, mister, ah," he said, fumbling for the Greenskin's name. With one hand over his mouth, Lord Itrivic asked his niece 'what the hell is the foul green thing's name', and then proceeded. "Mr. Rage, something to add?"

"Um, just one question," said the Orc Berserker.

"And that is?"

"Um, where's da can in dis joint?" Rage's abrupt question shattered the tension that had been noticeably building up in the room.

Richard and Trevor Tiverski, Lord Adrian and Nadia Itrivic, and even the two guards who remained near the door where the company had entered from shared a good light chuckle at Rage's expense. Only Simon and Akimaru remained totally unaffected, both for good cause. Simon Tiverski was too busy trying to read all of the magic that Nadia Itrivic and a few unseen guards had. Akimaru knew that this was a social tactic that Rage had learned to use over the last few months in order to help such delicate negotiations proceed without getting too nasty too quick. The Orc probably didn't really need the bathroom; it was just a convenient show of Greenskin stupidity that folks like these would find amusing, light-hearted.

As a guard led Rage out of the chamber, the Orc Berserker couldn't help but smile a little at himself. *Well*, he thought, *dat worked pretty well ta ease t'ings.*

As the guard opened a restroom door, the Orc barely contained his mirth long enough to slip inside and muffle his laughter with his thick, meaty, callused hands. In the Orc language, a 'joynte' is a bed shared by a brother and sister. In essence, he'd gotten away with calling the Itrivic Vampire Clan a lot of incestuous whores!

Back in the meeting hall, Lord Itrivic, not wanting to proceed without all of his guests present (because that would just be poor etiquette, and if nothing else, the elder Vampire Clans prided themselves on being proper noblemen and women), offered each of his other guests something to drink or something to perhaps dine on. While Richard declined, as did Simon, Trevor and Akimaru both asked for some water and perhaps something small to eat. As Rage returned to the room, Lord Itrivic contained his previous mirth long enough to ask if he wanted something to eat as well, regretting his question the moment it was out of his mouth.

It should be noted now that sometimes, when someone is plotting something foul or wicked, it isn't always the noble, the good, or the square-jawed hero who mucks up their plans. Sometimes, the whole works are brought down by a simpleton, or by a badly timed question. Rage smiled like an idiot, and rubbed his belly. "You know, now dat yous ask, I am kinda famished. Akimaru, sir?"

The white clad Ninja didn't take his eyes off of the Vampire Lord of the house as he gave a small, brief nod.

"Okay, first I'll need da biggest samitch yous can make fer a fella. Ham, turkey, the works." He put one finger up to indicate that he had only just begun to order.

It would be almost two hours later, at three-thirty in the morning, when deliberations continued.

* * * *

As Rage-san proceeded onto his second course, Akimaru excused himself to use the restroom. A guard led the way out of the meeting hall, and escorted him toward the northern corridor from the chamber. When they had walked approximately seventy yards away from the meeting hall, the guard took up post by one side of the inward-swinging door wordlessly, gesturing curtly with his head to the bathroom.

Akimaru slipped inside quickly, stopping just on the other side of the door to survey his surroundings.

Turning around, Akimaru engaged the deadbolt on the small water closet and removed his left glove, touching one steaming hand to the knob. Slivers of ice jammed into the keyhole for the deadbolt, giving him some more time. As a half-breed ice elemental, the white clad Ninja had access to powers that would be useful in combat. As the son of a mother whose inborn talents had been those of a Psychic, he had powers that would be useful in non-combat situations like this.

Though he had little in the way of actual Psychic powers, one he used routinely was his ability to shift and transfer noises and sounds. Akimaru pressed his palms against the cloth around his forehead, and concentrated, pulling in the sounds of far away tavern restroom stalls to fill the air. When he heard the strains of a fellow in Desanadron in the bathroom, he ceased his pull, and started looking around for a way to secret himself out of the room for just a few minutes' time.

Looking up at the wall above the cylindrical porcelain commode, Akimaru spotted a ventilation grate. The duct behind the grate would be a little bit of a squeeze, even for him, but Akimaru didn't need to go very far.

Putting his left glove back on, the white clad Ninja pulled the grate down, setting it next to the toilet, and clambered up inside the duct. Wriggling along inside like a snake on its belly, Akimaru took three minutes to find the uppermost porthole where the ventilation ducts exited.

There appeared to be a central duct shaft with a high amount of Aeromancy locked into the stone floor, blowing all of the collected odors and air up out of a stack situated in the center of the building.

Dozens of other ducts emptied into this central shaft, and as Akimaru turned himself around just inside of the central duct, his face bore a smile beneath the mask. By using the proper amount of his elemental powers in that bathroom he was presently returning to, he could launch spear shards of ice to almost any chamber in the entire compound.

Had the Itrivic Vampire clan known about the ventilation system in the building that they used as their local quarters, they might have taken the time to disrupt the Aeromancy spell in the central ventilation chute, making Akimaru's gamble impossible.

But that, Akimaru mused, is the problem with nigh-immortal creatures. They don't take the time to look for the subtle little details that might be responsible for the removal of their immortal status.

* * * *

When Akimaru returned a few minutes later, Rage had only reached the one hour and ten minute mark of the two hours of his feasting. Lord Adrian Itrivic had excused his niece Nadia when she had asked to be summoned after their 'big guest's meal' was over, and now he was regretting that he hadn't passed the buck on to her to stay behind. The Tiverski brothers appeared to be infinitely patient, none of them offering conversation with him or the guards, or even much talk amongst themselves.

What sort of Vampires am I dealing with, Lord Itrivic wondered, sipping his glass of blood as he tried to discern the Tiverskis' thoughts.

Trevor Tiverski alone was well known to him. Born into the Vampire Race as Trevor Allishev, he had served as Commander of the Itrivic clan's Elite Guard. Having been won over by Richard Tiverski's promises of a victimless existence, he had gone to ground and joined the strange, semi-aristocratic Vampire at his home in those woods to the southwest.

Ah, yes, Adrian Itrivic thought, Richard Tiverski. Of the three Tiverski brothers, he was both the best known and the least known about. As undeclared leader of the Tiverski brother trio, all peoples involved in Vampire society and many involved in the various religious outfits across the lands of Tamalaria knew of Richard Tiverski. They knew he was a Vampire who took only offered mortal blood, and that only in containers, never from the source. But few knew of his origins, his clan, his heritage. Not even the Itrivic family, arguably one of the eldest of all of the existing Vampire clans, knew where Richard had come from.

And now, Lord Adrian Itrivic thought, *here he sits in my home, speaking nary a word to me, smiling like an idiot. I am superior to him in every way, and yet something about him seems to say otherwise. What am I missing?* The Vampire Lord cast these thoughts aside after a while, pleased to see that the enormous Orc had finally finished eating.

Lord Itrivic looked at the great black walnut grandfather clock on his left side of the table, and twitched a little when he was how late the hour had become. Three-thirty in the morning meant, in the northwestern climbs of Tamalaria, that he had only about two hours to deal with the Tiverski brothers in either a diplomatic or openly hostile fashion. After that, the sun would rise, and they would all be trapped inside of the compound. At least, his family would. The brother known as Simon had apparently taught himself and his two brothers a spell that would cast protective shadows over them even in direct sunlight, but the Itrivic Vampire family had no such talents. The sun would rise, and they would be left to do some considerable damage.

As a guard cleared away the last of Rage's plates with a grunt of disgust, Lord Itrivic sent for his niece Nadia to return to the meeting.

"Is there something about the ceiling that fascinates you, master Akimaru," the Vampire Lord asked as he observed the white clad Ninja staring almost straight up.

"Not particularly," was the Ninja's only reply. He had already pulled Richard close to tell him about the ventilation system and how he intended to use it, should things get ugly. One of the grated panels sat in the ceiling of the meeting hall almost directly above him. He wouldn't even have to leave the room to execute his fatal plan.

"Very well," said Lord Itrivic as his niece entered the room and reclaimed her seat at his right side. "Now my friends, let us discuss why I have summoned you here. As you may be aware, there is a newly founded village a little way to the south and east of our home here. Over the last four years, the village has been constructed, and these last few months have been spent populating the homes and business buildings. The populace is largely Human and Minotaur." Lord Itrivic made a small hand motion to one of his guards, who rushed to the table with several maps, giving one to each person seated at the long table. "We have circled the exact location of the village in reference to our home, and we have even labeled this location and your home. As you can see, the village is at a distance slightly closer to here than is your beloved Desanadron." Lord Itrivic eased back into his seat a little.

"Then may ve assume zat your intention is to make this new village your new feeding ground?" Richard looked at the map he'd been handed.

"That is our intention exactly," Lord Itrivic said. "You may be aware as well that my branch of the Itrivic family is getting low on guards and servants. We wish to secure some from the village, as well as some lambs. The guards will be made into those of our Race, but the servants will be made over into Ghouls."

"That is very cruel," Trevor said gruffly. "Ghouls have no more rights in the eyes of Vampires like you than would the chair I'm sitting in. They're no better than furniture to you."

"You would want us to turn every person we take into Vampires, Trevor Tiverski?" Nadia asked with a fox's grin. "That would be foolish, especially considering the types of servants we require."

"These lambs you wish to procure," Akimaru said. "I assume that you do not mean livestock animals."

"No, he doesn't." Simon looked up from his map and glared blankly up the table at Nadia and Adrian Itrivic. "In Vampire society, lambs are mortals who willingly offer their blood to a Vampire, straight from the source. All they ask in return is either favors from the Vampire who feeds on them, or the protection of the lamb's family. Sometimes they offer their services as lambs in exchange for the promise of being turned into a Vampire themselves."

"Who'd want to be a Vampire on purpose," asked Rage before he could think better of the question. As all three of the Tiverski brothers turned their heads slowly to look down the table at him, the Orc flushed a deep red-green, and muttered an apology.

"Anyvay," said Richard, turning his eyes on Lord Itrivic once more, trying to read his true intentions. "You vish for us to simply allow zis? Zat village is still fairly close to our voods, and thus, ve vould be obligated to protect its citizenry from outside threats such as you. Vhat makes you think ve'll just allow you to take vhat you vant from them?"

At this question, Lord Itrivic's eyebrows raised slightly, and he leaned forward, planting his elbows on the hardwood table and propping his chin on his hands.

"In exchange for your non-interference in this matter, we are prepared to invoke the Rite of Sworn Blood and swear never to attack Desanadron again," Lord Itrivic said, his eyes steel and inscrutable. The Rite of Sworn Blood would bind every member of Lord Adrian Itrivic's branch of the clan to the oath he offered, and that would mean an awful lot fewer Vampire attacks on the metropolis of Desanadron. The offer was initially tempting, but Richard had decided before ever having arrived at the Itrivic home that he would not agree to any sort of deal. He had to keep his composure for the moment however, and simply appear to be thinking the idea over.

Rage, never the quickest wit in the room, had nonetheless followed the conversation effortlessly. Everything seemed to be in order, though he didn't care much for the deal at all. If the populace of this new target village consisted predominantly of Humans, then the townsfolk would be almost defenseless against this Vampire Clan. Rage didn't understand the undead quite as well as his friend and Guild ally Lain McNealy, but he had a pretty good idea that Vampires, being of strong will and with many strange powers, would pose an enormous threat to a small burb. He hoped that Richard Tiverski would spit in Adrian Itrivic's face.

Trevor, meanwhile, analyzed the benefits and negatives of accepting such a deal. The Tiverskis were mostly sworn to the protection of mortals against such threats as the Itrivic, Bonava, and Tepes Vampire Clans. However, they being Vampires themselves, and only a trio, Richard could be pressed to accept the proposal out of sheer threat of total annihilation of the three of them. Sure, Trevor was a skilled warrior, Simon an incredibly talented mage, and Richard a nice, diplomatic mix of the two. All three together, however, could not stand against all of the old Vampire Clans. The only Clan that would publicly acknowledge that they wished to ally themselves with the Vampire trio from the woods north of Desanadron was the Norem Clan, one of the younger branches of the old Tepes Vampire family.

But Trevor then came to the same conclusion that Rage had come to a minute before him. *If we leave them unguarded*, Trevor thought, *then within a year the entire village will swear allegiance to the Itrivic Clan. That can't be allowed to happen! And why not? If the village swore allegiance to the Itrivic Clan, then the city of Desanadron would be declared the next available feeding source for the Clan again. This entire 'treaty' would then be for naught, for Lord Adrian Itrivic would simply use the additional forces to overrun we Tiverski brothers and do away with the one major roadblock stopping him from feeding his family on Desanadron every night!*

"You say you vould use the Rite of Svorn Blood?" Richard raised an eyebrow, his mouth twitching into a cynical grin. His black cloak ruffled slightly as he shifted position in his chair, the better to look into Lord Itrivic's face flatly. His royal purple vest, made of pure leather, creaked slightly as he stretched his arms behind his head, the ruffled cuffs of his white dress shirt peeking out. His feet he propped up on the table, a complete show of disrespect toward someone like Adrian Itrivic and his Vampire Clan.

Richard twirled his snow-white goatee between his right thumb and forefinger for a moment before returning his hand to its spot behind his head, webbing the fingers together and smiling discourteously. "I say you vould do anythink in your powers to deceive us und take vhat you vant."

Ever the player of whatever part was needed, Nadia Itrivic feigned shock and alarm at this, her hand flying to her ample bosom as she gasped rather loudly. "Why, Richard Tiverski! I cannot believe that you would insinuate such a thing, much less say it aloud!"

"I'm usually villing to play der game of politics," said Richard, bringing his feet down slowly from the table's surface, drawing himself up to a straight-backed posture of serious deliberation. "But ve have dealt vith you and yours for far too long to not see vhere this is heading. You vish us to stand aside and give vay to the Clans of old, the bloodmongers, the varlords. Ve vill not, und you know zis."

Lord Adrian Itrivic took the last sip of his blood from his goblet, letting it hang on the rim of the ceramic dish for just a moment before slurping it up himself. He brought the goblet down on the table hard enough to send a minor shock wave throughout the room, his patience clearly already at an end. "You won't even parlay with us about this, Richard Tiverski?" Adrian Itrivic's eyes narrowed as he tried to size up the average-looking Vampire before him. Richard Tiverski didn't appear much different from the older Vampire Clans, which was to say he was pale, elegantly dressed, aristocratic and well-read and spoken. But he broke with the old ways for unknown reasons, and had recruited two other Vampires into his cause. They called themselves brothers now, which Adrian supposed was fine, because he knew that Trevor and Simon had both come from other Clans and adopted the name Tiverski upon Richard's suggestion.

This left only one question for Adrian, which he would ask now, before giving the order to attack. The air in the room had already become so filled with tension that Akimaru and Simon were both silently preparing their powers, Simon muttering into his cloak, unraveling the seal of silence he'd detected under his seat, the white clad Ninja taking off his white silk gloves. "Richard Tiverski, I must know something about you."

Lord Adrian Itrivic rose to his feet and pushed in his chair, motioning Richard to follow closely behind him.

Richard shrugged, stood, and followed Adrian Itrivic toward the north end of the room, about thirty yards away from the table.

Adrian leaned against a section of the wall that, when tapped twice in rapid succession, would flip over, providing him an exit from harm when he ordered the slaughter of his 'guests'.

Richard, arms folded over his chest, gave Itrivic a sly grin, already expecting the coming question.

"I believe I know vhat you qvestion is, Adrian Itrivic," Richard said in a low whisper. "But it vould be rude of me to try to answer before it is asked, so go ahead."

Adrian Itrivic cleared his throat, looked toward the table, where his eyes met those of his lovely niece, and he gave her the slightest nod before turning his eyes back to those of Richard Tiverski.

"What is your real last name," said the local Vampire Lord of the Clan Itrivic. "From what family are you descended? I must know!"

Richard chuckled low in his stomach a moment before shuffling next to Adrian, putting one arm amiably over the Vampire Lord's shoulder.

"My family name is Tepes." Richard Tiverski watched with delight as he revealed this to Adrian Itrivic, whose family lineage was linked to the Tepes family only by four generation gaps and marriage.

Richard clutched tighter with his arm, bringing his mouth right next to Adrian's ear as he rasped, "Mine grandpater vas Vlad Tepes Dracula."

His words sent instant waves of fear and dread down into the Vampire Lord's blackened heart. "And now that you know this, your family must perish," Richard said as Adrian tapped the wall and disappeared, the panel shifting him onto the other side of the thick stone wall.

Nadia Itrivic rose and made a single sweep of her left arm, calling forth magical force, and summoning guards and mages to the meeting hall before Rage crushed her skull with a heavy cross punch to the face.

"Man, I've wanted to do that all night," Trevor Tiverski bellowed as the first wave of guards burst into the lower chamber, weapons raised and shields at the ready.

Trevor drew his long sword, Simon hurled a wall of magical spikes into the first wave of attackers, and Akimaru started streaming his ice power into the ventilation duct above.

Seeing what the white clad Ninja intended to do, Richard and Rage both moved to cover either side of him and defend him against attack.

Dozens of guards launched small arrows and crossbow bolts from the upper balcony level of the chamber, and more than a couple found their marks in Richard, Trevor and Rage.

Simon levitated to the center of the balcony level, his body suspended in air as he thrust his head back and his hands out to his sides, releasing forks of lightning into the assembled sharpshooters.

As the second wave of archers came into the room from the west entrance, Simon spun in mid-air and released a Holy Cannon spell upon them, bringing his hands together wrist-to-wrist and spreading his hands wide.

A single beam of white light, a foot and a half in diameter, erupted toward the new archers, barreling into them without sound.

The chamber trembled, however, from the sudden release of holy magic in such high concentration, and for a moment, Akimaru's concentration wavered.

"I do say, good brother, perhaps you could, oh I don't know, tone it down a bit," Richard Tiverski called up to the youngest Tiverski brother as he parried and dodged several swipes of a short sword by a guard. His rapier flashed and danced in his hand, carving the flesh of his kinsmen, some of whom could very well be his descendents. He had, after all, told Adrian Itrivic the undiminished truth about his lineage. Dracula, the lauded Vampire said to have been the progenitor of their proud and deadly Race, was indeed his grandfather. What few knew, however, was how common that claim had once been. Dracula had after all gone through several wives, many of whom he had turned into Vampires himself. Two of his wives had been Humans as well, leading to the birth of the Vampries, or half-breeds, and Vempores, those of three-quarters Vampire blood. Being a grandson wasn't much of a boast, once upon a time.

Now, of course, Richard stood as one of the last, a fact of which he was very secretly and immensely proud. If his brother Simon didn't control his magic more closely, however, or if Akimaru's ploy backfired, he might not be alive any longer to enjoy his private pride. Also he noted, as a spear stabbed shallowly into the left side of his abdomen, he needed to fight well to stay alive.

Richard backed away toward the white clad Ninja, and felt the air around him turn deathly cold. Even for a Vampire, he didn't enjoy the sudden chill in the environment.

Still, he thought, *at least nobody's taken a grave wound.* Richard Tiverski felt the shallow wound in his belly seal itself shut already, and the guard who had stabbed him turned away, wild-eyed, and ran screaming that he was not a Vampire, he was a monster.

* * * *

"Impossible," was the only word that Adrian Itrivic could say as he fled through the hidden hallways and corridors within the compound, seeking the secret exit he'd had installed in the event of just such an emergency. "It's just not possible! He cannot be so directly related to our great progenitor! For the Gods' sakes, he doesn't even hunt down mortal blood."

Twisting and turning, running headlong down the tunnels in a state of mental and physical panic, Lord Itrivic was suddenly very grateful for the blood he had imbibed in the meeting hall. Without its vitality, he wouldn't have been able to make such a swift escape. If only I could turn into a bat, he thought bitterly as he descended a set of stone steps toward his secret exit.

His escape route terminated in a narrow tunnel that lead up into the foothills slightly north and east of the compound. Approximately a mile long, he would be able to cover the distance in less than four minutes at a full-out sprint, which at this point he felt more than capable of. Charging down the corridor, Adrian Itrivic sped toward his safe escape.

* * * *

Vampires both of the Clan Itrivic and the various lesser families that provided guards for the Clan stood throughout the compound, encased in magical blocks of ice that robbed them of warmth, oxygen, and eventually, of life. As soon as they fell victim to Akimaru's encasing ice mist, needles of ice ruptured their vital organs from the casing itself, slaying them and turning most of the victims into crimson ice sculptures.

In the meeting hall, Trevor, Simon and Rage compared numbers mockingly as more guards clambered into the chamber, many of them hesitating since they could plainly see their dead and dying comrades. Above the din of their exhalations and destructive efforts, Richard could be heard giving them directions. "Finish them qvickly, then get out of the compound! Akimaru, you have done well, but the frost has most likely damaged ze strength of ze building! Everybody get out vhile you can!"

Though his brothers heard and began to obey immediately, cutting and blasting a swath of guards as they made their escape, Rage and Akimaru both noticed a strange phenomenon. Though they could clearly hear Richard Tiverski, when they looked around the meeting hall and the hallway they exited into, they could not find him anywhere.

* * * *

Just another hundred yards, Adrian Itrivic thought, and I'm free! He had remained untouched by Akimaru's frost powers, as the escape tunnel had its own system of vents and ducts through which fresh air could come from the outside. However, as he saw the end of the tunnel during the last fifty or so yards, he also saw a dark silhouette fill a large portion of the end of the tunnel. "Vhere exactly do you think you're going," the silhouette asked, the voice seemingly directed straight into his panicked mind.

Adrian Itrivic skidded to a halt perhaps ten yards away from Richard Tiverski, though the creature before him looked much larger and more powerful than the aristocratic and well-spoken individual he'd left behind in the meeting hall. His shoulder-length white hair appeared to have grown in the few minutes since their last exchange of words, flowing and flapping about his waist. In his right hand he held an estoc, a sword normally wielded with two hands by Knights or Paladins of enormous strength. Around his left hand, white smoke plumed up out of the cuff of his white undershirt, and he smiled so wickedly that for a moment Adrian Itrivic's blackened heart skipped a beat.

"I, uh, I'm getting the hells out of here," Adrian offered weakly. As he watched, dumbfounded, the white smoke roiling out of Richard Tiverski's cuff turned a slight blue color, and its course seemed to direct itself down to the floor of the tunnel. As it hit the floor, the smoke started to solidify into a vaguely recognizable shape; a large, blue metal boot of armor. "What, what are you doing?"

"It is a power passed down from generation to generation by my branch of the family Tepes." Richard Tiverski still smiled angelically.

Armored legs and an armored lower torso had formed in a few moments, along with what appeared to be a white sash around the creature's waist. "It is most useful vhen I don't vish to get my hands dirty. I believe you vill appreciate it." His smile vanished as he concentrated on forming his servant.

A minute passed, a minute during which Adrian Itrivic struggled to get himself moving, yet he found he could not. Every time he tried to surge forward, his eyes fell on those of Richard Tiverski, and his entire body lost its will to resist. One last time he made to lunge forward, to clear the danger before him, but could not. Now, as he looked to the left side of the tunnel, he saw standing in his path a large blue suit of armor, spikes on its elbows and shoulders, darkness in the helmet's visor, and its right hand clamped around a savage stone axe.

"What is it," Adrian whispered in awe as the suit of armor reared its weapon back behind its head.

"It is the end of you, Adrian Itrivic." Richard turned and stalked away as the axe-wielding armor let its weapon fly, cleaving the other Vampire's head cleanly in half.

Adrian Itrivic fell dead to the floor of the tunnel, and shortly after turned into a pile of dust.

As Richard withdrew his powers and aura, he cracked his neck and his fingers. "Remain here, in case somevone else tries to escape zis vay,"

Richard said over his shoulder to the armor, which had drawn another axe out of thin air.

It said nothing in reply, merely turning slightly toward its creator and giving a brief nod of its helmet.

In a whirl of smoke, the eldest Tiverski brother had disappeared.

* * * *

Hours later, walking back toward the cottage belonging to the Tiverski trio, Akimaru and Rage remained at the rear of the procession, while Trevor and Simon walked side by side in the middle, with Richard ranging ahead a good two hundred yards. Sunrise would be coming soon. Simon's magical abilities to block the sun's effects on himself and his brothers was most useful after high noon, when the sun was on it's way out of the waking world. The protection provided in the mornings was not adequate to shield them entirely until they got home if they didn't maintain their current pace, and the three Vampire brothers would suffer permanent sun damage despite the shielding.

As they followed behind, Akimaru asked Rage a couple of questions regarding the Tiverskis. The Orc Berserker agreed that they seemed an okay lot, for Vampires, and he indicated to the white clad Ninja that yes, he would work with them again if the event arose.

Trevor and Simon compared kills from the Itrivic compound, Trevor bragging and boasting about his masterful use of his long sword, Simon taunting him with his effortless use of magic against their own kinsmen. Neither of them could guess what was going through their elder brother's mind, and neither hazarded a guess.

So long it has been, Richard thought. *So long since I have been forced to take up arms against our own kind. And yet, it will not be the last time. And it won't be the worst situation we come across in the years to come, either.*

The two members of the Midnight Suns bid them farewell at their cottage door, and the three Tiverski brothers headed indoors. All three headed to their respective rooms, and two of them were swiftly asleep.

Richard Tiverski lay awake for a while, staring up at the ceiling of his room, and wondered if he would ever see his grandfather again.

* * * *

"Hmm," said a tall, regal fellow with powder white hair and an exquisite black cloak. As he rubbed his chin in appreciation, the soulless armor creature in the Itrivic compound's escape tunnel looked him over. It noted the crimson shade of the cloak's lining, the strong facial features of the man in the cloak itself, as well as the expensive-looking gentleman's clothes briefly revealed while the man rubbed his chin. "Not bad, if I must say," the man commented.

The armor creature only had a short while left to exist, and it was well aware that nothing moved inside of the compound it had been set to guard by its creator, Richard Tiverski Tepes. Normally, after twenty-four hours of guarding a place or person, this animated, conjured suit of armor would simply disappear. However, as the appointed hour approached, it felt itself becoming more and more self-aware, and with self-awareness came a realization; it was going to outlive its expected time.

The armor creature wondered if perhaps the man before it had anything to do with that. When the man had appeared, the armor had hefted up one of its axes, and prepared to do battle with him. However, the stranger had made a single low noise, and the armor had somehow known to stop.

"You are wondering how I was able to stop you from attacking me?"

The armor nodded its helmet of a head.

"Don't worry about it. Come with me." The stranger walked next to the armor and draped an arm around its shoulders. "I'll not waste a fine specimen such as yourself. My grandson might not appreciate it, but I need a few extra guards around my home...."

Tale Ten From Whence He Came

Dressed in his sailor's pants and flowing white shirt, a dark blue denim vest over top, the man known to the Midnight Suns as Mr. Striker lay on his cot in his private quarters on the condemned building's fourth floor, his arms resting on the pillows under his head, his hands rubbing at the back of his head. He wondered, not for the first time, how much longer he could keep himself under control, how long he could remain free to roam the realms of Tamalaria.

Not long, I suspect, he thought dismally. *Especially if the McNealy woman doesn't keep her wits about her when she goes on these little trips of hers.* But he could not begrudge Lain her trip to the Temple of Unaki. He had no room to begrudge her at all. Without her, he would still be stuck at Lake Prekka's shores, as he had been for far too long before her arrival there.

Striker sat up on the edge of his cot and drew a cigarette from the crumpled pack on his night table, lit it, and took a deep drag on it. *So long ago, this cycle started,* he thought. *And not since Asterion have I truly unleashed myself on the world. I have managed control since then. But how long will I last this time out? How long will she, for that matter?*

Though he suspected Lain McNealy would live a decent lifespan if she were careful, the man known as Striker had very much to worry about external factors of danger to the woman. And he had nobody but himself to blame for that condition. He finished his cigarette and lay back down, closing his eyes and thinking back to when his peculiar cycle had begun, and specifically, about the part he played in the destruction of an entire city, many years before.

* * * *

In the realms of Tamalaria, there are several places where one does not travel alone or even in small numbers--not if one wishes to see their next birthday. That takes a while according to the Tamalarian calendar, with thirteen months to the year and thirty days to each of those months. Still, you couldn't toss a stone without finding somebody who would do anything to see the next birthday coming along.

Among those places, the most well-known was without a doubt Mount Toane, a grand mountain in the eastern provinces known to be the habitat and breeding grounds of demons since the middle of the Third Age. Several city-states and townships had risen and fallen with Mount Toane in their politically accepted territories, but these had always tried to deny that the mountain was any of their responsibility. The only pseudo-political organization that ever tried to actually do anything about the creatures living and reproducing inside the guts of that darkened demesne was the Order of Oun.

But there were other dangerous places scattered throughout the realms of Tamalaria, make no mistake. Ancient ruins left abandoned, forgotten to the ravages of time. Castles and manors standing ramshackle and unkempt in tall grasslands and small woodlands. Spectral, haunted towns given wide berths by travelers, and to which the newest roads did not connect. Most of these places had residents of a sort, but seldom were they normal, sentient people. Rashum, the monsters of the realms of Tamalaria, usually lurked in these places, waiting for an unsuspecting adventurer or two to bumble along for dinner. Well, the Rashum's dinner, because the adventurers *are* the dinner.

One such place in the Fifth Age was the town of Asterion, a city of ruins that, to the casual eye, appeared to be the remains of a burned out township. One could almost assume that fire had been the cause of the state of the town, but records from the end of the Fourth Age, also known as the Age of Mecha, would tell a different tale. In the center of the township, during the year 233, 4A, a revolutionary Gnome Engineer by the name of Simon Tilburn designed and created a weapon so advanced and destructive that the ramifications of creating such a weapon were astounding. His scientific curiosity getting the better of him, he had a bunker constructed deep beneath the laboratory he owned and operated in the center of town in which to house the weapon. He just had to create it, since he had figured out how to do so.

Gnomes' racial curiosity often dominated their lives and actions. The only safeguard Tilburn made with regard to the weapon itself, aside from creating the bunker, was to create the weapon on a one-fourth scale, hopefully minimizing the devastation, should the weapon somehow be absconded either by the government of the city-state or thieves looking to turn a quick buck by selling off stolen weaponry.

Unfortunately for Tilburn, the weapon he designed worked, and all too well. The only fault he committed in its creation was neglecting to add in a power feed cutoff protocol. When the laboratory's underground bunker suffered a power failure, the weapon, drawing power from the main switchboard, ignited. The last thing that Tilburn saw in his relatively well-lived life was a flash of white light.

What had once been a laboratory building above ground was a crater in the aftermath. The pressure of the explosion flung several tons of concrete, steel blast walls and tempered, heat-resistant glass in a circumference of death throughout the city. Only a handful of residents were spared, most of them living or working in the outlying regions of the city. Thirty-thousand plus civilians, security forces and officials were slain by the debris flung by the explosion. One-hundred and fourteen survivors, nearly half of them burned by the sheer heat wave that ripped through the city from the weapon's detonation, started making their way to the next nearest known city, Sho-gre, of the Fiefdom of Lemago.

Of the survivors, forty-three died along the way during the twelve-day forced march, victims of the various rashum inhabiting the wilderness of the plains. A forty-fourth person, a slender young man whom none of the other survivors could claim to have known more than a very little at any time, disappeared from the group. Apparently taken victim by a group of monstrous fire beetles the survivors contended with during the twilight hours of their tenth day marching. The young man was forgotten entirely by the time the survivors reached the shelter of Sho-gre.

Unbeknownst to them, said young man had used the appearance of the rashum that evening to break away from their group. Off to the south he spirited himself, laughing merrily all the while. None of them suspected him of anything, and that, he supposed, was as it should be. He only found it sad that he would have to return to the place from whence he came soon, if only until he found another to attach himself to.

Dressed in the dark leathers and v-necked vest typical of a pirate, a black bandana tied back over his head, the eternally young man whistled between shining, metallic teeth as he made his way back towards his home haunt. He still had several days before he would be forcefully dragged by unseen hands to that place, so he resolved to be as joyful about the trip as he could afford to be.

In truth, this young man with the appearance of a human pirate was in point of fact an abomination, a hybrid of science and magic given human shape. Originally a demon spawned from the seventh ring of Hell and given the body of its summoner as a permanent host (thanks to some demonic trickery in the wording of his agreement with the human who summoned him), the creature had not been aware at first of the odd alterations which had already been made to the physical body of the man it now inhabited.

But those oddities quickly became apparent. Thinking back on it as he whistled, the young man started to skip a little along the benighted path. Only once did anything approach him out of a sense of predatory hostility, a pair of dire wolves with violence and dinner on their minds.

One look from the crazed eyes of the human-thing they blocked from the road ahead however, and they yelped and took flight as fast as their four legs each would carry them.

Lake Prekka, thought the young man who was, in fact, a demon.

That's where it all began. Stupid mortal. He really should have let himself just die. But faced with either death or incarceration at the hands of the Desanadron military forces back in the year 114, 4A, the bandit known as Theodore Remantose stumbled below decks as his crew fought with the boarding militia, several arrows piercing through his stomach and chest.

Drawing out an old tome pillaged from a seafront village along the northern coast of the continent, Remantose had turned through the pages until he found the incantation he had been seeking, and summoned forth a minor demon to bargain with in his quarters.

The demon, however, clever as any other, had tricked the man in the bargaining process. In exchange for getting him clear of his current circumstances, the human agreed to let the demon take his body for its own uses 'for a time'. The demon took control then, the arrows flying from its host's body as it healed over. Using a hatchet from the first mate's cabin, the demon tore a hole in the bottom of the boat, releasing itself from the battle and possible death or imprisonment by swimming down and out into the lake, away from the sinking ship.

When the demon got its host body to the shore several hours later, the human's soul rose up in an attempt to retake control. 'You have had your time, and got me out. Now return to me my body,' the voice of Remantose said within his own head.

'Ah, I think not,' the demon had replied. As the young man remembered this, he smiled broadly, once more displaying the shining metal teeth to the moonlight. 'You agreed that I could have your body for a time, and that time, I have decided, is forever.'

Screaming protestations, the demon stuffed Remantose's soul into the deepest, darkest place the demon could find. From then on, it had been enjoying itself.

However, there was one hitch to the demon's plans, and it was this. As a minor demon of the seventh ring of Hell, it could only remain away from the place it was first summoned if it was bound to another mortal through service. Otherwise, the demon had to remain on the shores of Lake Prekka, specifically within only a few hundred yards of a piece of the old bulkhead of the sunken pirate's ship. It had since then drifted up onto the shore, but the demon still found this restriction disturbing. Too heavy to carry and too vague to toy with, the demon had to satisfy itself with taking odd jobs for travelers who happened across his path.

But being demonic lent itself to the trouble of always wanting to cause wanton and rampant destruction among the mortals, and the worse the destruction, the more he enjoyed it. Hence his cutting the power to his employer's bunker, causing the detonation of the weapon the Gnome had designed. "Too bad he slimmed it down," the creature said to the darkness and the wind. "It would have been nice to see a bigger boom."

The demon had been in the lab when it blew apart, but being of the strange nature that he was, he survived the blast. That is where the scientific alterations the pirate already had fashioned for himself came into play. Early in the Fourth Age, it was not uncommon for Alchemists to experiment with replacing portions of the body with machinery and other non-native elements. Remantose had several of these replacements when the demon was first contacted by him, many of them made for combat purposes.

The first and most obvious were the metal teeth, set in a complicated series of gears implanted in the jaws and a set of rubber gums. The second alteration was a layer of flesh which was actually entirely hairless, just under the outer epidermis. This flesh was placed using the ancient Alchemy art of Focus, and came from the bodies of several Rendermen, a particularly vicious type of man-like rashum whose bodies were entirely impervious to any kind of fire or wind. Furthermore, the Rendermen's skins were extraordinarily tough, often likened unto a sort of bronze chain mail in terms of durability.

Third and most important to the demon's concerns, however, was the inclusion of a hollow alcove implanted where the left calf should have been. In order to make up for this absence, whomever had made the alterations for Remantose had used pistons and steel mesh to replace and support the missing muscle tissue. The hollow, made of wood, was kept closed on a latch and could be sprung open by the pirate whenever he needed it to be. Useful for stashing hidden weapons and emergency funds, it was also waterproof, and aided in his swimming ability by giving him an extra buoyancy.

The demon used these little advantages whenever he could.

* * * *

"Well, here we are again, old friend," the demon said to the bulkhead once again. This was not the end of the march he had been making when he parted from the survivors of the tragedy of Asterion, no. This was the end of yet another long forced march, one he'd made after getting yet another binding master killed. Once again no master, once again left to his own devices along the shore of Lake Prekka.

He had gone through a large number of such employers and masters in the time since the incident at Asterion. Always the story was essentially the same--he would be discovered by someone vacationing or passing through the region around the lake, and some idle small talk would be initiated. He would ingratiate himself with the man or woman, regardless of Race, and go with them back to their hometown to perform whatever labors were available to him. During these times, he would try to find work with somebody else, and sometimes he did, but the end result was always the same. The moment the first boss or master died, he would be forced to start heading back to the lake. If he did not, he would be dragged along the ground by an unseen force until he crashed headlong into the bulkhead.

The pain of the experience was excruciating, and he'd had to suffer through it three times. Healing took days, and he always felt a little less potent afterwards. At times, the mortal soul of Remantose would seem to surface, but the demon knew better. Some kind god had removed that man's soul many years ago now, not long after the War of Vandross. The demon was entirely on his own in the altered body he'd stolen by trickery.

"Good thing I'm demonic," he muttered aloud, laying back on the sand, eyes closed against the sunlight. "Otherwise this body would have rotted a long time ago." But once again he was speaking to the wind, for no other company did he have. After the long trek back from Trapperstown, having barely returned in time to the beach to avoid a painful dragging, he had nothing on his hands but time to relax and think about the many wondrous ways he could ruin the lives of those around him, should another opportunity come along.

He would be given an opportunity sooner than he expected.

* * * *

The next morning, as the demon sat lazily on the beach, a fishing rod in hand, the line extended far out into the lake, he sensed eyes upon him. At first, he did nothing about it, but after a few minutes, his shoulders began to hunch up in apprehension. He could sense deep magic in the stare he was receiving, and he didn't care for it in the least.

Setting the rod deep in the sand as not to lose it, he rose to his feet and cast his eyes about for the source of his disquiet.

Those same eyes quickly fell upon a pale but beautiful woman, dressed in a flowing black evening dress. To either side behind her stood a rotting, shambling corpse, each brandishing a rusted battle axe. Honey-brown hair flowed all the way down to her waist in the back, braided in a severe style the demon had not seen in several centuries. He had thought the style out of date, but here was a woman who wore it not only well, but with an almost regal air.

"Can I be of some help, miss," he said to the woman, who was clearly the mistress of the undead creatures behind her.

"Perhaps," she said. "I am late in getting back to the city of

Desanadron, to my Headmaster. I note you have a boat." She pointed to the small skiff that the demon had constructed several years earlier and never gotten around to actually using on the lake. "I am hoping you might be willing to row me across Lake Prekka, saving me the time of going around the lake."

"What about them," he asked, pointing to the zombies.

"They will make their way to me in due time, and if they do not, they can be easily replaced," said the Necromancer woman.

The demon considered the offer. He was being asked to do a single task, which would not by his nature allow him to go with her farther than the other side of the lake before he had to return to the bulkhead. She'd mentioned a Headmaster, though. *Is this woman in a guild of some sort?* he wondered. *If so, perhaps I can gain some more permanent employ.*

"Well, miss, I would be more than happy to help, if in return you can help me." The demon smiled aggressively.

"I'll not bed you, if that's what you're after." She raised her head slightly as if in indignation.

He waved his hands, dismissing the notion, though he would not have been averse to it. The woman was a looker, after all.

"I would not deign to suggest something so villainous, Miss, though I am a villain in truth and in nature," he said. "No, I was going to make note that you mentioned a Headmaster. What guild, may I ask, do you pledge yourself to, and is there room for someone to join up in the ranks?"

The woman lowered her head a little, and even offered him a cold smile. She shook her head slightly, but kept smiling as she looked him square in the eyes.

"I will not mention the name of my guild, sir, but I would be happy to introduce you to my Headmaster and ask if you may be admitted into our ranks. We don't exactly do a lot of publicity in our organization, due to its nature and circumstances. I trust you'll understand."

"I do, my lady." The demon gave a mocking bow. If he could, he would dance with glee, for the woman's offer was just what he needed to get away from the bulkhead, the wording just vague enough to allow him to go all the way to Desanadron. Should he get admitted into this guild of hers, though, he would still be bound to her, for she was his initial contact. He would have to take care to keep her alive and well. "Before we set off, for I assure you the skiff will carry the two of us well enough, I would know your name, Miss."

The woman took a few steps toward the demon, and offered her hand in the dainty fashion of a lady of the court. "My name is Lain

McNealy, sir. I am, as you have probably guessed, a Necromancer. And what, good sir, is your name?"

On this the demon had to think, because he had not as yet established for himself a new title by which to travel and work, but he had to be quick about it. Sometimes, he thought, it's best to go with an old name, one that suits you forever. So, without a moment's hesitation, he opted to give the woman his true name, the one that the pirate had invoked back in the early years of the Fourth Age.

"Striker, miss," he said. "My name is Mr. Striker, and I am humbly at your service." He gave her another sweeping bow, and made the skiff ready for launch.

When it was prepared, he helped the Necromancer on board, and together they began making their way across Lake Prekka. *What sort of chaos awaits me*, Striker thought as they glided along. *What sort of mischief can I get up to with this woman's guild, and will it be worth it?*

Only time would tell.

Afterword

Thus closes this particular chapter on the ongoing experiment that is Tamalaria. Some old stars and some new, and many that will be showing up again in later volumes of Tamalaria's tales. But before you go, friend, allow me to tell you a few things that I couldn't find an appropriate place for throughout the stories.

Firstly, Tamalaria is not the only continent in the world, but at this point in the history of Tamalaria, little is known of the lands to the far south of them, across the great blue ocean. A few Jaft or Minotaur sailors know of it, and they know that it is called Tallowmere. They also know that most of the Races and Classes present in Tamalaria are on Tallowmere as well.

The Fifth Age of Tamalaria, or the Age After the Fall of Mecha as it is commonly referred to by its denizens (A.F.), is quickly coming to a close. Portenda the Quiet, lead man in A Hunter and His Prey, will be having another grand assignment before the time comes, but rest assured, lots of folks will be making returns to center stage after his second tale.

And what awaits you, friend and reader, after the Fifth Age is ushered out? Well, let us just say that it would be beneficial for you to finally get a better idea of what Tamalaria's prior Ages were like. There will be a fiction/reference book forthcoming, a thorough account of what the realm was like back before the Fall of Mecha. Individual tales will also be told, and they will sync up (with any luck or talent on my end) with the history reference. However, like our own histories, the careful reader may find individual discrepancies in the history reference.

Well faithful reader, I bid you farewell, good luck, and Godspeed.